Version
and
Diversion

Version
and
Diversion

Judith Terry

William Morrow and Company, Inc.
New York

Library of Congress Cataloging-in-Publication Data

Terry, Judith.
Version and diversion.
Previously published as: Miss Abigail's part. 1986.
I. Title.
PR6070.E737M5   1987   823'.914   86-23637
ISBN 0-688-06961-4

Printed in the United States of America

2 3 4 5 6 7 8 9 10

BOOK DESIGN BY BETH TONDREAU

In memory of my mother, Kay
To my father, Leslie

Version
and
Diversion

I

The war is ended! At last there can be no doubt. We first hung out laurel and bay a hundred days ago, but the rejoicing was short-lived, for Boney rose again. This time the Duke has done for him. This time the French army is crushed beyond recovery, the mighty emperor forever fallen. I know some who will reflect sadly upon France's brave ideals, but none who cannot be stirred by a throb of pride. All England is brimful of loyalty. What is not named for the Duke or his battle is not worth naming. Two infants, one of either sex, if you please, were here christened "Waterloo" as the penalty for arriving in the world on the eighteenth of June. (The boy has the best of it as "Wat," I fancy.) There can be no more auspicious time to embark upon a new venture, or so I tell myself, for this victory heralds the beginning of a new age, and the martial trumpets sound success in my ears for encouragement.

Yesterday the bells rang out the whole day through, and Nature smiled from dawn till eve upon our triumph with a perfect summer's day. The sun played king to the revels, blazing in such red-hot splendor that I was obliged to retreat for an hour at noon, but indeed he was scarce less fiery at setting, and swung upon the horizon a vast distended globe, no whit shrunken by his outpourings. It was, I made sure, an occasion to be remembered. We held a great feast in the lower meadow, and roasted an ox, the biggest to be had for miles around (for which we paid handsomely). It took all day to cook, and the fire consumed nine small alders that had blown down in the spring gales. Despite the heat there were plenty to take turns at the spit, although the sweat dripped as fast as the fat off the beast over the fire. The steward set a succession of volunteers to carry pails of water from the river and keep the fire from spreading into the dry grass, and most of the turnspits, at their own request, got a dousing too. So irresistible was the cool water, indeed, that a number of young fellows and one or two of the bolder girls fell into the river on purpose. The wet cotton of their gowns clung to the girls' forms most revealingly; I am sure they were enticed at dusk into the woods for their pains, as they had all along intended. There will be one or two hasty weddings when the leaves turn.

I judged it the best sort of rural entertainment, with beef and ale in plenty, and pleasant diversions got up by the tenants and villagers, morris dancing, a game of cricket, and wrestling, for which we awarded a purse of one guinea and a leather hat. I understand that John Ruckle, who won the bouts, lost his guinea wagering on the outcome of the cockfight (which I did not see for we retired at three o'clock), so I trust that the hat fitted him. A rope dancer, not one of our people, who had heard of the festivity, arrived when it was almost dark, by design I suspect, for clever though his performance was, it gained much from the curious shadows thrown by the bonfire as he performed his tricks. The merrymaking continued until morning and they were throwing serpents and squibs and roaring at the moon until first light, when the remaining meats were consumed at a hearty breakfast, the number affected by qualmish feelings of the head and stomach being wonderfully small.

There were no mishaps either, though that was not for want of effort by the tenor bell ringer, a stout young fellow by the name of Sam Jephson. He insisted that nobody could sound old Jonah's throat as well as he, and swore he would not surrender his place to any but the Duke himself. That, mind you, was after cracking ten pots of ale carried a half-mile to the church tower by a succession of well-wishers, of whom Parson Chelme was first. (He it was who raised no objection to the naming of the infants. I fear he is a man of limited judgment, although by all accounts devoted to his flock.) It was October ale, well-aged and full of hops—none of your small beer for so great an occasion—and Jephson is six and a half feet high and with all the strength of smithying, so there was none bold enough to gainsay him. He rang the peals nonstop from noon till seven, and then went up on the rope and fell twelve feet to the ground. He was covered with bruises but never broke a bone. I tell you, nothing can go wrong now that Boney is defeated; or that is how the village tells it, and no doubt how Sam Jephson will tell it to his grandchildren. There will be plenty of those too, judging by the flock of maids who butterfluttered round him after the mishap. He drank another ten pots to recover himself, I heard. There will be no horses shod this day.

When an old dame asked me if I did not think the bells a wondrous thing, my thoughts flew instantly to London and how it would be there, not one peal ringing alone but a hundred, in a clamor of triumphant exultation; fog, dirt, stench and all, London is still the mighty heart of England, and I love the life beating there. That is one reason I was doubtful about retiring to the country, but I find ruralizing has its pleasures, among which must be counted my new role as lady, to which I hope I shall bring better understanding than many who play it. We shall never see the like again, said everyone yesterday. There is only one Napoleon to defeat, for sure, but another cause for celebration is already to be looked for, God willing, and I shall devise more. For that sort of generosity one may be justly loved, although I have heard many who should know better condemn such occasions as indulgence, commending instead charity. Now there is a word to freeze the marrow, a word by which the rich do often gratify their vanity and then have the gall to complain of their responsibilities. God forbid that what I do should ever be construed as charity! A feast warms the heart and lifts the spirit. It is the very thing of all to keep the need for charity at bay. But I shall have few wrongs here to right. Yesterday I saw no gaunt faces, nor nothing that was not respectable dress. There are no starving poor hidden away here, despite the hardship of the times. I should have been mistaken in my choice of a husband if it were otherwise.

I was the object of much curiosity at yesterday's gathering, as what new wife to the squire is not? All crowded round to bid me good day, and whatever I said was preserved, sweet or sour, to be made much of later. Necks craned, elbows nudged and I caught, as was intended, snatches of good-natured ribaldry. I smiled and spoke, shook hands and smiled again. If there be any difficulties attaching to my new station it will not be with the common folk but with their betters. I have already visited Lady Frame, and endured such silly gossip with her and her three plain daughters for two hours together that I could have screamed. She is somewhat forgetful, as well as deaf and hideously gap-toothed, so I could not tell whether her complaints about servants were the result of spite or ignorance. I held my tongue, but if all our neighbors prove so tiresome there will be little company to be had during our time in the country. I am determined not to shock anyone by my outspokenness, out of consideration for my husband, but it goes hard when a clutch of pampered females, sitting in the shadowy cool of a pleasant room, finds nothing to talk of but the shortcomings of those servants whose efforts have provided them with every bodily comfort, from the clean-swept floor to the row of buttons on their backs. What presumptuous vanity! They speak of those who wait upon them as if they were beasts of the field, that never understood more than ten words nor ever knew the misery of an aching head or an aching heart.

It is only natural that I should feel strongly on the subject. Indeed, that is one reason I determined to set down the following account: on paper at least I can relieve my feelings. Moreover, such an activity will provide regular daily employment which otherwise I shall sorely miss. Idleness is dull and unnatural, though it daily grows more ladylike. These are, however, but small considerations beside the obligation I feel to correct certain false notions that may be entertained by those who have heard, as it were, only one half of the story I am about to relate. I know full well I shall be accused of scandalmongering, but that is a common hazard of being in the public eye. I have been accused of worse and never minded. There is some part of the truth which can only be seen by she who turns her head to look behind; I have always thought Lot's wife prodigiously hard done by. Besides I itch to try my hand at this new task, even though the vulgar phrases I am apt to use will reveal all too soon the limitations of my talent. As to the truth of this account, you must judge it for yourself; I assure you that the other is more than half fiction.

So ends the war, and so, after a fashion, I see I have begun my tale, not in the right place perhaps, but then what is that? I have learned during my life to be wary of right places, although I was brought up to respect them. My own right place, as I was used to perceive it, was not near as comfortable as this. I sit here at the table on which rests my neat walnut writing desk, inlaid with green leather (a loving gift which arrived two days ago from town, and is the exact match to my husband's—but that his leather is red), and look out upon the peaceful landscape. Its gravel walk and yew hedges, the sheep grazing beyond, which, framed by the window, now lie before me, shall be my beginning and, after the circuit of a life which though short in years has been long in incident, my end. The full inkwell, the quire of paper, a fine new silver nib, tempt me to begin my task, which I do with both excitement and trepidation, struck at once by the distance I have traveled in so short a time from all those things which first I knew.

I was born to Robert and Eliza Hartwell, of the parish of Sotherton, in the county of Northampton, in the year 1795, my given name being Jane. Of my earlier ancestry I am ignorant, beyond what the tombstones in St. Sepulchre's churchyard tell of my father's family, and they go back only two generations. But I come of solid yeoman stock, the lifeblood of the country as they say, and nothing to be ashamed of beyond one or two born outside the blanket and an uncle transported for sheep stealing. My grandfather always told me that my mother and father were an affectionate couple, but I had no chance of observing this for myself, since my mother, bearing me late in life and being of a weakly disposition, died only a few months after I was born, in the terrible winter of that year. You might suppose that my father would have shown me the more affection in memory of her whom I was said to resemble closely, but it was not so. Perhaps he blamed me for her death; I know I was a lusty child and may have drawn my mother's strength from her.

However that may be, it was my grandfather, my mother's father, to whom I was closest in my infant days. He loved me dearly for his daughter's sake and, from the time when I could barely walk, would take me with him to the greenhouses at Sotherton. These were exceptionally spacious and well laid out, part of the estate which belonged to the Rushworth family, Sotherton Court, one of the finest properties in the county (where, I should like to point out, my grandfather was head gardener and not the village laborer some have lately insinuated). I wandered happily with him in the greenhouses amidst the warmth and greenery, which seemed to me then as vast and bushy as an Indian jungle. I played make-believe, or helped him check the leaves for blight and greenfly, or root geranium cuttings in the autumn. He always removed his wig for the heat, and hung it over a flowerpot left inside the door for the purpose. Later he would place it over the ball on top of the pump in the yard while he sluiced himself with water, and he made me do the same, holding that, in addition to promoting cleanliness, a dose of cold water, even when frost whitens the cobbles, is a tonic to body and spirit. I was not allowed to make a sound. Sometimes when he picked me up I would run my hand over the stubble of his hair and he would shake his head under my touch to tickle my hand and make me laugh. He wore a brown wig on weekdays and a powdered one on Sundays, right up to the time he died, which is only a year ago. He was very proud of the Sunday wig. I combed the other while he told me stories, but I was never allowed to touch the Sunday wig, which had belonged to his late master, Mr. Rushworth, to whom he had been very much attached—much more so, indeed, than to his son, the present master, James Rushworth. "Pineries and vineries, pah!" grandfather would say. "Young master don't know what's an apple and what's an orange!"

Grandfather told me many tales of witches, ghosts and fairies, of the kind thought proper for children, and sang rousing ballads (not quite so proper), and hymns too, for he was a stalwart of the church choir, although he sometimes fell asleep and snored in the sermons, for which he had been taken to task by the parson. "Never mind, my duck," he would say to me, for I was mortified. "The Bible, that's right enough. You read it yourself, you'll see. But what the parsons make of it, that's summat else. I'll get to heaven sooner than they will, you mark my words."

My grandfather lived comfortably in three rooms of the garden house at Sotherton Court, the remainder of which was occupied by other male members of the inside staff, and ate in the house with the upper servants, as he had done ever since being widowed. His acquaintance with the housekeeper, Mrs. Whitaker, had ripened into close friendship over the years, and thus I also came to know her well. I recall remarks, which I did not understand at the time, about intentions my grandfather was supposed to have had toward her, but whether he proposed marriage or not, I cannot tell. Mrs. Whitaker early took a fancy to me and (perhaps as a result) held a low opinion of my father, who was a gamekeeper on the Sotherton estate and, she considered, did not sufficiently mind my interests, my stepmother being inclined to put upon me. My grandfather was not overfond of my father either, considering that his daughter had been seduced by his robust good looks and should have done better for herself, so he was quite prepared to listen; and then, of course, I overheard, as children will. I also heard the housekeeper say that my father was not fit for much more than scaring birds, citing the prevalence of poachers and predators over pheasant and partridge. In this she was unjust, I am sure. It was generally allowed that the poachers had decreased in numbers and the Sotherton game increased a year or two after my father's second marriage, when he had discovered the advantages of being on the outside rather than the inside of his home. Indeed, he was promoted to head gamekeeper shortly after, which brought with it a house with six rooms, although the greater space did not encourage him to remain within doors. I do not say that he did not occasionally trade a hare or two to a wagoner and make a few shillings on the side in the season, but what gamekeeper is innocent of that? And he never did kill anybody in the exercise of his duty, which is more than may be said of some.

For all her sharpness about my father, I soon learned to love Mrs. Whitaker, for in her I saw tender maternal feeling for the first time and experienced the delight of being its object. I displayed my affection openly, running about after her and bestowing a hug or a kiss, those innocent childish tokens of attachment that are so endearing. It was natural that she should begin to take me about with her and, finding a ready pupil, teach me what she knew. At first it was merely ladylike deportment and refined manners: she stuck a sprig of holly in my bosom to make me hold up my head; presented me with a toothbrush, which she dipped in Spence's powder and taught me the use of; and when I ate fast or noisily would restrain me with the instruction which I shall in my turn no doubt pass on, since I shall certainly never forget it: "masticate, denticate, chump, grind and swallow." As time progressed I learned not only the household arts but my letters and what Mrs. Whitaker had herself of a modest education: geography, some history, even a little French. As my fondness for reading increased, she would slip me a volume from the library with many adjurations as to carefulness, although, had I lost one, it would scarcely have been missed, since no one but ourselves, the housemaids and the occasional party of visitors ever entered the library at Sotherton.

Neither Mrs. Rushworth nor her son James were in the least bookish (in that respect, as in so may others, my grandfather ruefully said, quite unlike his late master). All James Rushworth knew of literature was the Stud Book and the Racing Calendar (which, it was generally allowed, he knew from cover to cover); all his mother knew was the latest novel. As soon as ever the books arrived from the circulating library, Mrs. Rushworth and her maid, Anne Flower, retired to the privacy of her dressing room, where Mrs. R. lay on the French bed and Anne sat beside her to read aloud, a small table between them on which stood a triple sconce, a box of comfits and a dish of tea. It was a sacred hour, not infrequently extended to two or three, during which they were on no account to be disturbed, except for the delivery of more hot water.

Anne was uppish and inclined to condescend, even to Mrs. Whitaker, which was certainly improper, largely because Mrs. Rushworth, who had ruled the house while her son was young, remained all but nominally in charge, since even after he attained his majority James Rushworth showed no sign of cracking the whip. Anne, being her mistress's trusted confidante, was therefore, as I said, inclined to give herself airs. She discovered me one day sitting in a windowseat in the long gallery, tucked behind a curtain which had been drawn to protect the paintings. I had dozed off in the warm sun, and one of the ivory bobbins with which I was supposed to be making lace, but which I had adopted as the various members of a large doll family, dropped on the floor and startled Anne as she was passing. She gave me a tongue-lashing, as well as a box on the ear, for laziness, spying and other faults I was too young to know the meaning of. So severe was she with me that I made, to my shame and disgust, a puddle on the floor, thus incurring even greater wrath. For this I spent an infinity of time on my knees with sand, brush, beeswax and hot, salt tears. Anne's harshness imprinted the scene so vividly upon my senses that even now I smell the soap she held in her hand, Mrs. Rushworth's own deliciously scented sort that came from London. (It has occurred to me since that I surprised her filching, for we used an excellent green crown soap, made under Mrs. Whitaker's direction, all through the house, but it had no perfume.) From that time forward, Anne took against me. I was Mrs. Whitaker's pet, willful and indulged, and she insinuated whatever ill she might against me to her mistress, as a result of which Mrs. Rushworth frowned whenever she chanced to catch sight of me.

I had long been aware of the laughter which the name of Mr. James Rushworth occasioned, and the village girls (with whom I associated despite Mrs. Whitaker's disapproval) had explained it in whispers as far as they were able. Some of the pretty ones professed no interest in going into service at the house as a consequence: it would be the most tedious thing, Mr. James being the way he was. They looked at me slyly, wondering, I suppose, whether I knew anything about James Rushworth that they did not, but my innocence was answer enough. I understood not above half what they hinted at. I did understand, however, that Mr. Rushworth was a poor horseman. It was common knowledge that although he hunted with the Pytchley he contrived to ride over the hounds at every meet and was only tolerated because he could be relied upon to provide nine dozen bottles of the finest sherry at a hunt breakfast. Practice has not improved him. The latest rumor is that he jumped on the Master and broke his leg, but I do not yet know the truth of that.

James Rushworth was by no means an ill-looking young man. He stood half a head taller than most, had strawy hair that shone bewitchingly in the sun and eyes blue as borage. He was vain of his profile, which possessed a Grecian outline, for the recording of which his mother had employed two artists to paint his silhouette on glass, though she professed herself satisfied with neither. The line of his forehead did run unusually straight into his nose, to be sure, but that was because his forehead receded. As for his chin, like a baby's bottom, it was round, divided by a cleft and possessed of a tendency to wobble; indeed, it gave his countenance a similar air of innocence in need of protection. His lips were well-shaped but protuberant. They had, however, enabled him to perfect a piercing whistle, with which he could recall his dogs from more than a mile away. It was his most remarkable attribute.

Whenever he met me, James was kind, patting me on the head when I was small, and always taking time to ask me how my father did, in an effort, I suppose, to increase his information about his game, although his talk of poachers and preserves meant nothing to me and I stood there tongue-tied. As I grew older I was better able to parry the questions, which, I recollect, changed not a whit in form or content.

The library at Sotherton was my most beloved place, a large room, lofty and oak-lined, smelling of wood and leather and containing curious furniture, which I touched when no one saw, bookstands that swung out on metal brackets, and sconces with paper bells for reading by candlelight. Motes of dust flew in the bars of sunshine that came through the long windows and touched the glass-fronted cases of leather-bound treasure. In those days I felt the room to be half mine and made free with the books in a way that Mrs. Whitaker, for all her indulgence, would not have approved. By this means, I discovered *Robinson Crusoe*, the poetry of Thomas Gray, *Joseph Andrews* and *Evelina*.

One summer's day, I recall, I slipped away with Young's *Night Thoughts* to the kitchen garden, where I found shelter from the heat in my own little arbor of scarlet runner beans, devouring the contents of the book no less eagerly than the bowl of cherry curds which was the cream to my contentment. Sometimes I came across a newspaper, and read of disasters and domestic tragedies, or strange and spirit-stirring narrations of battles and distant countries which took me far beyond the confines of Sotherton. I even ventured occasionally upon the leading articles, until, for my station, I must have been a prodigiously well-informed child.

My grandfather delighted in this, you may be sure. He was a

rational, inquiring sort of man, with a streak of democratical independence and a great belief in reading as the way to betterment. When I was confirmed, I remember, he patiently heard me through my catechism many times, but after the service, in our favorite retreat, tamping the soil down vigorously around a tomato seedling with his thumbs, he repeated one of the questions. "What is thy duty toward thy neighbor?"

I duly recited the answer.

"That's the bit. That's it. Ordering yourself lowly and reverently to your betters. I'm not agin it, not at all, my duck, but who are they, these betters? A king's a king, and a duke's a duke, but that don't make them *better*, does it? It's not logical, that isn't. Duty's duty, but we must live according to what's right. Don't you swallow everything your 'betters' tell you; because they aren't, you see." I did see.

Owing to these circumstances, I had grown up somewhat superior to my own father's second family, even though I dwelled with him, my stepmother and the ten children she had borne. For one thing, my grandfather disapproved of my stepmother's superstitious ways and I had quite naturally adopted his attitude. Horseshoes nailed over the door, rowan berries and red thread to ward off witches and all the other paraphernalia of a credulous mind I had learned to despise. I hid it as best I could, but such things will out, and it was a constant source of aggravation to my stepmother, Martha Mary. I acknowledge she was not altogether unreasonable in this. My mother being grandfather's only child and myself her only issue, he did indulge me dreadfully. In the garden house, I had toys he had bought from the pedlar and kept there for my use alone: a set of colored bricks, a battledore and shuttlecock; even a tiny guillotine carved out of mutton bone by one of the "Mounseers." To add fuel to the flames, I was often absent when Martha Mary required my services. As a consequence, when the time came for me to go into service at Sotherton Court, as most girls of our village naturally did, she would have none of it. I was patient with the little ones, clever with a needle, and strong, and she wanted me by her with no further excuses. Had she not borne with my absences long enough? Was it not her right to expect some benefit from all the learning I was supposed to possess? The benefit, I knew, would consist in her obtaining an unpaid maid-of-all-work, back and forth to the well from dawn to dusk when there was nothing more immediate. I had grown more dainty, I admit. Though many females of my station had nothing better to look forward to, I dreaded it. The worst of it would be, as I was well aware, that she would allow me no minute to myself between rising and sleeping.

Martha Mary's good nature, such as it was, had been worn into shrewishness by incessant child-bearing and her nagging was a trial to the spirit, quite apart from the bruises that her beatings raised upon the body. Not that she treated her own children any better than she treated me; she had no fondling ways with any of us. The beatings were not regular, but we lived under constant threat of punishment, and she had a vile temper for which I was the most convenient whetstone. She cut off my hair in a fit of rage one day and that finally decided my grandfather against her. He never took to the notion of short hair even when it was the fashion, and it was a great grief to him to see the dark head that so resembled my mother's shorn of its curls. But I bear no scars, as many do, and the curls generously renewed themselves; indeed, they grew thicker and more lustrous than before. No doubt, in the way of these odd reverses, Martha Mary by this means contributed something to my rising in the world. Her unkind action deprived her of her maid-of-all-work, at least, for my grandfather would not countenance such ill usage of his darling and, once he and Mrs. Whitaker put their heads together, Martha Mary was no match for them.

A distant cousin of Mrs. Whitaker, William Wilcox, had but recently written to say that a housemaid was required in the family to whom he was coachman, the Bertrams of Mansfield Park. Sir Thomas and Lady Bertram were among the first people in the county, their house modern and comfortable; moreover, they had two daughters, the younger of whom was soon to come out, and required a housemaid who could undertake as part of her duties some of those usually performed by a lady's maid. Nothing could have fitted me better, for under Mrs. Whitaker's instruction I had learned much that would equip me for such a situation. She and my grandfather decided that Mansfield Park was, next to Sotherton, the very place they would have chosen for me, and consoled themselves further by reflecting that my reputation at Sotherton for being the housekeeper's pet might have made a position there uncomfortable both for her and myself. Rant though she did, my stepmother could make no difference, and my father's remonstrances on her behalf were only halfhearted. "You'll be snug as a mouse in a malt heap," said my grandfather, beaming with satisfaction, as he gave me, finger to his lips, a pretty netted purse he had bought to hold the two guineas he gave me at parting. "In case of need," he said. "Only in case of need, mind."

Mansfield Park was no more than ten miles distant from Sotherton, but at the age of fifteen, it might have been ten times ten miles away and I should not have cared, so excited was I by the prospect of change and adventure. But I did suffer some pangs when I bade farewell to my little stepbrothers and sisters. I had stood between them and their mother's wrath many a time, and knew that their comfort must be lessened by my removal. I was happy to know, some time later, that my dear Grandfather Pearce and my youngest stepbrother, little Timothy, who was a sickly child, with dark eyes and lashes like a sweep's brush to make his wan face beguiling, had discovered a mutual and consoling affection.

For my own part I was like any other youthful creature setting out upon the highroad of life. The tears I shed at parting I put aside without much ado, seeing the future beckon generously and trusting in its promise with innocent assurance. I looked forward eagerly to being mistress of my fate, certain that my winsome face would captivate all hearts and my little stock of learning see me safely through the world. To be sure, the confidence of youth is misplaced, but what joy it is! I wish all may feel as cheerful upon the threshold of life as I did.

# II

I knew very well that Mansfield Park was not to be compared with Sotherton Court in point of size or antiquity or interest, for Sotherton Court was known to be one of the finest places, as well as one of the largest estates, in the county. The two great houses, though both of regular handsome design, were, indeed, very different, without and within. Whereas Sotherton was of red brick, square-built round a courtyard, Mansfield had a high center wing flanked on either side by lower extensions, and was built of cream-colored ashlar stone. Whether it was the effect of the great banks of windows at Sotherton, each tiny pane of which reflected the light like so many dewdrops, or its turrets, whose domes broke the line of its roof, it seemed more pieced, more various, more interesting than Mansfield, whose elegance was of a plainer sort. But I was prejudiced and no doubt overvalued those things at Sotherton which pertained to earlier times: the great hall upstairs with its frieze and its royal coat of arms; the stewponds where dwelled a carp so old he had won, along with the name Methuselah, the right not to grace the table, and was so tame he could be hand fed. There was even a knot garden, Grandfather Pearce's especial pride, although not generally boasted of to visitors since it was so old-fashioned.

Mansfield Park had other attractions, however. It was set high (Sotherton was set low) and thus commanded a pleasing prospect of the surrounding countryside. Its grounds contained a grotto and a bridge, and a pretty, rustic boat house beside the lake to enliven the walks about the grounds. But it was withindoors that the merits of a modern house were most apparent. White-painted plaster instead of dark paneling made it light and airy where Sotherton seemed dark; the disposition of the rooms was more convenient and their size more comfortable. As to dust, Sotherton made as much in a week as Mansfield in a month. The principal staircase at Sotherton was oak, with solid panels so intricately carved that it took an hour to clean, although no doubt I slowed when I discovered strange goblin faces, and scenes depicting men and women entwined in lewd embraces. Great square newels stood at each turn, decorated with twining stems and swags of fruit and surmounted by an eagle, a lion and a gryphon. At Mansfield the staircase had wrought-iron balusters and fluted columns and rose from two sides of the hall in a great curve like a pair of angel's wings. Grecian statuary stood in niches in the walls, and above the well a glass dome set in the roof fragmented light upon the black and white tiles of the hall three floors below.

Sir Thomas Bertram, the master of Mansfield, had an eye for the latest inventions: there was a range in the kitchen with a boiler; the washhouse had a copper; the shrubbery masked an ice house. There were no less than three pumps, one in the yard, one in the washhouse and one in the scullery, and in the family's apartments three baths into which cold water might be run by the turning of a stopcock. All these conveniences were matters of wonder to me, none more than the ingenious system of bells, which sounded on a board outside the servants' hall from their positions all over the house. They saved a tedious amount of toil in carrying water and running to and fro in order to find one servant to send to fetch another. Not all the servants were of my mind, however. As in every company, there were those who were stubbornly attached to the old ways. A few Jeremiahs complained that the ringing made them jump out of their skins and gave them a headache. Needless to say these were the same as believed preservation in ice to be unhealthy and iron pipes to taint the water.

The servants' hall at Mansfield Park would have ticked as comfortably as the great clock were it not for Mrs. Norris, sister to

Lady Bertram and widow of the former rector of the parish, whose gratefulness to Sir Thomas for providing him with an income in the living of Mansfield can in no measure have compensated for the union with his benefactor's wife's sister through which he had deserved it. The wags had it that, from being a hale and handsome man, Mr. Norris had gradually shrunk until he appeared no bigger than his wife and that, by the time she had bullied him into an early grave, he was so small that she had argued the undertaker into reducing the price of the coffin. She was a most redoubtable female, small in stature and fine-boned, sharp-featured and, although prematurely wrinkled and possessed of a double chin, lithe as one half her age, tireless, devoted to economy and suspicious of all.

At the time of my arrival, Sir Thomas, together with his elder son, Tom, was away on an extended visit to the West Indies, where he had property, and Mrs. Norris was in full cry. She considered herself obliged to undertake Sir Thomas's responsibilities during his absence, which she did as naturally as she had over the years taken upon herself many of the duties of her sister, for Lady Bertram was good-natured but indolent, her energies fully absorbed by her pet dog and her carpet work. Her brother-in-law's absence increased Mrs. Norris's influence and our discomfort one hundredfold. It provided the perfect excuse on every occasion for bustling up to the Park at first light—when she had not found it necessary to stay the night—and busybodying herself about the place.

No new servant arrived without Mrs. Norris's welcome if she could so arrange it, and I was no exception. She took after me in her customary fashion, complaining in a most perforating voice (it was generally allowed to carry across the Park and through the village) about the carrier's cart in which I had made the journey from Sotherton. "I see you arrived in style, Hartwell. Could you not have carried your box up from the village? I hope you are not one of these weakly girls, for you will certainly have to be fetching and carrying here." She looked me up and down like a piece of cloth, inch by inch and end to end. "I hope that hobbledehoy was not a follower?"

"No, ma'am. He's the carrier's boy from Sotherton."

"We do not encourage followers here, you understand. A girl cannot attend properly to her work if she is mooning over some fellow and sneaking out to see him whenever she can. We have had enough of that kind of thing. The last housemaid brought shame and disgrace upon herself. You come highly recommended. I hope you prove worthy of such confidence. If you conduct yourself well, you will be given every consideration, but if you are idle or ill-mannered you will be turned away immediately. There is no humming and hawing and second-chancing here. Lady Bertram cannot abide idleness and neither can I. As for loose behavior, consorting with young men and such, that is quite out of the question."

She looked at me long once more. I should not have been surprised had she pinched my arm to test the strength of it, and I knew she noted the curls not altogether hidden by my cap. With a world of disapproval she said at last: "What a pity I did not see you first!"

I spoke up for myself, in some confusion. "How have I displeased you, ma'am?"

Pursing her lips, she shook her head vehemently, thoroughly disapproving me and my question. "That is not for you to ask. That is for me to tell you." She continued to stare at me as she spoke. "Take off your cap."

I did so. My hair was not yet grown again from my stepmother's cut, but it was short and thick and not unbecoming. She clicked her tongue. "You will wear that cap at all times, Hartwell. Mrs. Glover, I shall look to you to see to it. This is most unfortunate."

I still had not quite understood her drift, and thought she referred to the shortness of my hair. "My stepmother cut it off for a punishment."

"I have no interest in your stepmother or her punishment, although I am sure it was well-deserved. You will keep that cap on at all times, and no ribbons, do you understand?"

I grew hot with injustice and was about to speak, but Mrs. Glover forestalled me.

"Wilcox was very positive in Hartwell's favor."

"He was, indeed. I am afraid I allowed myself to be prevailed upon against my better judgment. It is the fault of my good nature. We should have tried to find someone from the village."

"You wished to hire a housemaid and obtain a lady's maid, ma'am. There was no one suitable."

"When Sir Thomas is absent, Mrs. Glover, it is the duty of us all to seek out economies wherever they may be found."

"I hope Hartwell will do very well, ma'am."

"She had better do so, indeed. It is a very great chance for her. I hope you appreciate your good fortune, Hartwell. There is no finer place in all England, I dare say, for learning the habits of industry and thrift that should be every servant's prime object. I hope you take note of this, Hartwell. I have your measure and so has Mrs. Glover."

Mrs. Norris's habitual style you may deduce from this exchange. Servants were to be universally distrusted, and if there were no immediate cause for complaint one must be invented. In return she was thoroughly detested by us all. Whatever disagreements might exist, we were as one against Mrs. Norris. She was always snuffing the air for something to pounce on and make a meal of, but she had no allies, and we fudged wherever we could. Some were never fast enough, but the housekeeper, Mrs. Glover, who was respected for her discretion, could take her for a round or two and still contrive not to be impertinent. She was not averse to it either, and often put a stone under Mrs. Norris's wheel, for which the servants were grateful, since in this way she protected them from many petty tyrannies.

It did not take me long to recognize the source of Mrs. Norris's dissatisfaction: she thought me too pretty. She has greater occasion now to regret hiring me, but I have no doubt she contrives, as she always did, to blame everyone but herself. It was, of course, most unusual for a girl to be brought in from outside the village, and it set me apart, as did the curious mixture of duties I was to perform, for both of which Mrs. Norris was responsible.

Sir Thomas and Lady Bertram had four children, two sons and two daughters, and I was to be part housemaid, part lady's maid to Miss Julia Bertram, the younger of the daughters. Mrs. Norris, who had devised the position, perceived it as an economical solution to a disagreement that had festered in the household since Sir Thomas's departure. At his elder daughter's coming out, Sir Thomas had been prevailed upon to hire for her a lady's maid, part French, and Julia was wild with envy at Maria's good fortune. Their father's intention had been that Amelia Ellis, the maid who had waited upon them since they were children, should become lady's maid to Julia. Since Amelia, good-natured though she was and wonderfully patient with little ones, had nothing to recommend her as a fashionable lady's maid, Julia did not intend to be inferior to her sister by so much. Sir Thomas being away and a position as upper housemaid vacant, Mrs. Norris had proposed the remedy: I was gradually to be sidled into the position of lady's maid, and Amelia was gradually to be sidled out. It was like Mrs. N. to come up with such a solution; quite apart from its other merits, her scheme had the advantage that neither Amelia nor I would quite know what we were about and she could have more of a hand in telling us.

Amelia Ellis told me much of this at our first encounter, though it took some unraveling. It was just like her to come out with it all at once, open and frank as she was. Amelia was without a shred of malice but also quite without restraint; for all she knew I might have made things worse for her. Her eyes filled with tears as she rushed headlong into an account of her woes: how Miss Julia no longer wanted her and would like to turn her away even though she had nursed her all through the whooping cough; how she loved them both and now had been forsaken. Poor Amelia. As a child of three she had been sold away to the lacemaking in Northampton, but her eyesight had begun to fail and she would have ended up in the workhouse had not Sir Thomas, touched perhaps by the contrast between that poor mite and his own first son, then newly born, taken pity on her. Arriving at Mansfield with nothing but a prayerbook, tongue-tied and short sighted, young, awkward and goodnatured, she was easy prey for the old tabby.

Amelia admitted she was no good with a needle, despite the spectacles she resolutely set upon her nose. When I saw the piece of muslin on which she was working, more gray than white and crimped at the edges with overtight stitches, I understood Julia's objections. There was Amelia, not far off thirty and sewing worse than my little sister. If anyone had been born under a threepennyhalfpenny planet it was she. Even her appearance was against her. Sophie Boucher, Maria's French maid, was trim and neat, and I was too, but Amelia was large and, like a bolster with thin ticking, always had bits sticking out here and there.

Mrs. Norris was concerned to establish me firmly in the inferior part of my place from the start, no doubt that I might be more grateful for the privileges of being half a lady's maid once they were mine, but one advantage I had immediately: the largest attic room, which had two windows (whereas the rest had only one), all to myself. My very own room! A tester bed, its canopy angled to fit the eaves wash-hand stand, a chair, a scrubbed deal floor, a feather mattress; I am used to a grander setting nowadays, but it means no more to me, I assure you. The disadvantage was that the attic was situated directly above the great clock of Mansfield Park, which announced the quarter hours with lengthy chimes. The whir-rings and chirrings with which it began its toil kept me awake all night for a week, but I quickly grew accustomed to it. I have always said that the noise of London is nothing to a maid who has learned to sleep on top of the engine of a great clock! It stopped only once while I was at Mansfield, and by that time I knew it so well that I predicted trouble from the whistles and wheezes and rumbles the previous night.

For the better part of a month I was not presented to Julia, although I sewed for her. I mostly worked at housemaid's tasks alongside Amelia, to whom I often spoke impatiently, as I now recall with shame. She rarely bridled, accepting my unkindness with humility. Our worst drudgery was lighting the fires. The footmen carried the coals and emptied the cinder pails, but we had to set and light the fires, and I swear it is worse than emptying the slops, so unexpectedly will a fire not catch, or only smolder, or smoke, and put you behind. I filled the breakfast room, which was my charge, with smoke more than once, for its draft was altogether unpredictable no matter which way the weathercock turned. Even then I managed better than Amelia, who had ten times the practice. I swear she filled her rooms with smoke twice as often as I, although she regularly laid the poker across the grate in the hope of luck being with her where skill was not. Mrs. Norris was in the habit of standing by so that poor Amelia might be spit and roasted as soon as the first gray cloud billowed out of the fireplace, the like-lihood of which was, you may believe, ten times increased by her baleful presence.

A housemaid's work is certainly not such as anyone is apt to miss, and I am heartily glad that I am no longer obliged to do it.

One task in which I still find pleasure, however, is the final rubbing, with a piece of old silk, that brings up the brightest shine on fine wood, satin or cherry or walnut (my favorite). There is something, perhaps, in the warm texture of what was once alive and of the earth, and the gentle repetitive labor is soothing to the spirit.

It was in many respects due to the presence of Mr. Wilcox, the old coachman and cousin to Mrs. Whitaker, that the servants' hall at Mansfield Park remained such a cheerful place. He knew Mrs. Norris and her ways, and the regular cure for a leathering from that quarter was to sit on the stool at his side while he read aloud, ostensibly for the benefit of the whole room, the latest news from the *Mercury*, his spectacles sliding down his nose meanwhile. "It takes your mind off it," he would say soothingly, "when you see how much better off you are than some." I shall always remember toasting my toes before the fire and listening to dear Wilcox's halting account of a visitation of God upon some poor unfortunate. Being afflicted with the rheumatics, he had a special place by the fire, which was alight for his benefit through all but the hottest months of the year. It was the sort of extravagance which Mrs. Norris frowned upon, but since Sir Thomas had ordered it, she praised his generosity at every opportunity and thus appropriated some of it herself. Mr. Wilcox's sweet temper worked its spell even upon her, however. Large and slow as an ox, with wattles as red as a turkey's and skin burned by hard weather, he sat in his old leather-seated chair, inherited from Sir Thomas and made softer by cushions fashioned for him by maids long gone, benevolent of countenance even when dozing, and scenting the room with his liniment.

Many a joke was cracked about that liniment, daily applied for his rheumatics, for the smell of it was overpowering. Wilcox himself took a harmless delight in remarking the effect upon newcomers as the sharp odor first stung their nostrils. "It's the sal volatile as does it," he would explain, shaking with laughter until he wheezed as he saw them catch their breath. "Lord bless me if it doesn't near choke you, but it clears the passages. It clears the passages wonderful."

He who concocted the liniment was Stephen Turnbull, the under-

coachman and most remarkable man at Mansfield (not counting
only the servants), although neither by reason of his appearance,
which was of a sandy, freckled, undistinguished sort, nor his conversation: a man less given to speech I never met. If questioned,
he would reply as briefly as was consonant with politeness and common sense, but it was a rare occasion indeed on which he himself
volunteered a remark. For all that, no one was long in discovering
his superior talents. He had a skill in dealing with dumb beasts,
especially horses, that seemed like kinship. Octavian, the great bay
horse owned by Tom, the elder son, which had been left in Stephen's care during Tom's absence with his father in the West Indies,
was highly strung and skittish as a kitten. Something disturbed the
animal one evening, and it was whinnying and stamping in great
perturbation. I myself saw Stephen climb over the end of the stall
and, holding on to the bridle and putting his face close, blow gently
into its nostrils. I was amazed to witness the beast go quiet, and
its terrified whinnying subside into a contented snicker of pleasure,
Stephen said it was an old trick he had learned from his father,
and that Octavian sometimes pretended agitation to get attention
and then frightened himself with it; by which you may judge the
precise understanding of the horse's disposition Stephen possessed.
Gentlemen would send for him from thirty miles distant, so well
were his skills known. In physicking, training, the judgment of
wind, stamina and speed he was thought by some to be without
equal. This netted him some extra income, which he further en-
larged by turning his knowledge to use in laying wagers on races
and matches and, since he was generous in sharing his opinions,
we all benefited.

What he could do for horses, it seemed he could also do for men.
He could set a bone to make it good and straight or ease Wilcox's
rheumatics as readily as he could cure a horse of the putrid fever.
He had once been summoned by Lady Bertram to relieve the pain
in her ankle, when she slipped off the footstool as she was climbing
into bed. So successful was he in this endeavor that the pain was
quite gone by the time the surgeon arrived. The latter was recom-
pensed for his trouble by several glasses of Madeira, while Stephen
was the recipient of a handsome pair of Hessian boots.

As was not to be wondered at in such circumstances, Stephen

was regarded with some affection and even more respect by the servants. Indeed, some of the more superstitious thought his skill smacked of witchcraft, and one of the village women who used to come up on washday confided in me that his skill with animals was entirely owing to his having been raised for three months by a badger when he was an infant.

III

Once Mrs. Norris judged me sufficiently humbled by washing windows and emptying slops, I was introduced to the ladies of the house, including she who was to be my mistress, Julia Bertram. So much stir and flutter there was about my being summoned to the drawing room for inspection, you would think it a presentation at court. I had Mrs. Norris's measure by this time, however, and, as everyone else did, said "Yes, ma'am" and "No, ma'am" whenever it appeared to be required and shut my ears to the rest of it.

As evidence of my stitchery, I remember, I took my Sunday gown, a pretty thing of spotted muslin softened with blue ribbon. The stuff had been a gift from Mrs. Whitaker and she had overseen the doing of it. I had spent several contented hours cutting and stitching it under her patient direction and knew I had done it well. It is curious how these unimportant items bear the impress of people or times. That gown, I fancy, is yet at the bottom of one of my chests. I never could bear to part with it.

I did not begin too well in the drawing room. At my entrance, the pug dog which lay on a cushion beside Lady Bertram set up a prodigious commotion, barking and snapping so that we were all fit to be deafened. Lady Bertram attempted to calm it without effect and Maria Bertram, who was making a paper mosaic at the desk, covered her ears. Julia ignored the noise and continued to read.

Mrs. Norris finally made herself heard: "My goodness, Hartwell, can you not help quieten a dog? Come over here and perhaps it will stop barking." She looked round. "Where is Fanny? She should be here to assist Lady Bertram."

Fanny Price was never far away. She was a daughter of Lady Bertram's younger sister, who had run off and done ill for herself by marrying a sailor. In order to fulfill family obligations and relieve her mother of the care of one child of a numerous family, Fanny had been brought up at Mansfield without ever being allowed to forget she was the poor relation. Although her face was not ill-made, it lacked that vivacity which makes less regular features appear more beautiful, and among the servants it was generally allowed that she was pale, mild, somewhat insipid and much put upon.

"There, there, Pug." I could not but admire the way Fanny soothed the dog, which though small was of a nature to terrify the boldest heart, and maintained a grip despite all its wriggling. Fanny could be decided with dogs as she never was with people.

"You must forgive Pug," explained Lady Bertram. "She is only fierce with strangers. On all other occasions she is the most angelic creature, aren't you, Pug dear?"

To Pug, a little prick-eared creature which snored rather than breathed and had gray coat like a rat's, Lady Bertram was unaccountably devoted. It had bitten three servants, one of them quite badly. Mrs. Glover, who could not abide it, regularly steeped primrose roots in white wine: "Just in case," she said. But it was no mad dog despite appearances.

"Where had you got to, Fanny?" demanded Mrs. Norris. "Here we are, trying to settle a matter of importance for your cousin and you are nowhere to be found."

"You have a pretty little curtsy," remarked Lady Bertram to me. "Someone has taught you well. Did you tell me that she can sew too, sister?"

"I hope so," said Julia, "since she is to attend me. I must have Ellis still, though she is the stupidest creature in the world. Two housemaids are a poor sort of substitute for a lady's maid, but I am to make the best of it as always."

"You have been complaining for weeks," said Maria. "I am in hopes this will put an end to it."

"Two maids instead of one." Mrs. Norris was brisk. "That is the way to look at it."

"Providing I do not find each as bad as the other."

"Come, come, niece. Consider your good fortune. Lady Bertram and I were content with much less, were we not, sister?"

"Your position was a little different, aunt," said Julia.

"It was, indeed, but we never complained."

"I am sure I do not complain," Maria said complacently.

"There is no need for you to complain," replied Julia indignantly. "You have Boucher."

"Dear me," said Lady Bertram. "This is all rather disagreeable. I am sure Hartwell curtsies prettily enough. I do not think Ellis ever manages it properly."

"If my father had not had to go away so suddenly, I should have had a French maid too."

"I doubt it," said Maria. "Sir Thomas was quite decided that nothing should remove Ellis."

"Your father's wish must be everything to us," said Mrs. Norris.

"Ellis is a most horrible fright," complained Julia. "I should like to see you putting up with her."

"I do wish Sir Thomas were here," said Lady Bertram. "Then we should not have all this anxiety. I am sure I wish you could both be as content as I am with Chapman."

"Everyone has a French maid," continued Julia. "Even Helena Palethorpe. We are the first people in the county and I am to make do with housemaids!"

"Only be a little patient, niece, and you shall find everything most satisfactory," said Mrs. Norris. "Come and look at this gown. Hartwell may yet prove a treasure. This is excellently sewn."

"Sir Thomas sets much store by quietness," said Lady Bertram. "I do myself. Ellis drops things. I hope you do not drop things?"

"It is very well stitched," Julia admitted, a trifle less querulous as she saw what I could do. "See here, sister."

Maria consented to inspect the gown, "That should content you," being the measure of her approval.

"There!" Mrs. Norris was triumphant. "What did I tell you? It will be an amazingly convenient arrangement. It is a pity the gown is too fine. That ribbon is unnecessary, Hartwell. Everything is done properly here, you know."

"I should think, if she is to be my maid, she may be allowed a ribbon," said Julia. "Can you dress hair?"

"I love to do it," I answered, "but I have had little chance to try."

"Any girl who is quick with her fingers is bound to dress hair well," said Mrs. Norris.

"But how long does it take to learn?" pouted Julia. "I am to go to six balls this month at least, and I cannot rely on Ellis even to put the pins in so that my cap will stay in place."

Mrs. Norris was not easily gainsaid. She turned to Maria. "Suppose Hartwell was to stand by while Boucher does your hair a time or two? That would answer."

Maria was reluctant. "Boucher cannot bear to do things slowly. She will certainly complain, and I cannot blame her. She is not here to teach country girls how to wind a curlpaper."

"Could she not watch Chapman, sister?" Lady Bertram interposed. "Chapman is so very obliging, I am sure she would not object. I certainly should not."

With this promise of help from her mother's maid, Julia had to be content, although when the matter was mentioned in the servants' hall, Maria's maid was perfectly accommodating. But then, Maria did not care to be generous. On the whole, even in those early days, I preferred Julia, whose peremptory and disagreeable moods often seemed merely a reflection of Maria's. If Julia were pleased she could change face in a moment, and when Maria was not by, her natural response was more often kindly than not. Julia, being younger and having no well-formed notions about herself, was apt to take her color from the company.

Since what Julia wanted was to be entirely equal to her sister, there could be no better arrangement than that I should learn the finer points of a lady's toilette from Maria's own maid, Sophie Boucher, who was much more willing than her mistress that I should do so. I embraced the opportunity gladly, without realizing that it would also be the means of providing me with my dearest friend at Mansfield Park.

Sophie was not generally liked among the servants, her Frenchness being suspect. Even Mr. Wilcox found himself unable to excuse Sir Thomas's yielding to his daughter on this point: English gentlemen were best not to tangle with any such nonsense as French ladies' maids, although Miss Boucher was as delightful a young woman as you might find anywhere. It was generally considered that Maria had got the better of her father in the matter, as was not uncommon, she knowing full well what an appearance of quiet reasonableness mixed with persistence would be most likely to win him. In fact, Sophie was only half French, but that was scarcely of consequence since she spoke a fractured English. She also possessed a certain directness of speech which had not recommended her to those already inclined to distrust her, but she was lively and decided, and her charms were not entirely lost on the company.

For my part, I liked her instantly. She discovered that I could speak a little French, which none other of her own station in the house could do, and when the two of us were alone she would talk to me, delighted to be speaking a tongue she loved even if I comprehended not above half what she said. My own fluency improved as a consequence. Indeed, only last year when I was in Paris, the Commissaire Royal commented upon the naturalness of my accent. Though I am not such a goose as to suppose his remarks less than half flattery, I recalled with conscious pleasure the hours I had spent with Sophie.

There is nothing so consoling to the spirit as a trusted friend with whom to share one's confidences. Although some of the other servants were a little less warm to me as a consequence of my friendship with Sophie, there was no one with whom I did not regularly exchange a cheerful word. As for waiting upon Julia, once she discovered the superiority of my services to those of Amelia Ellis, her confidence in me increased and she would often leave me to select the color of ribbon or the jewelry she would wear. She possessed a large gold pin set with diamonds and amethyst which had belonged to her paternal grandmother and had lain in her box since she had chosen it as a remembrance. I used it to fasten a dyed ostrich feather to a quilted satin turban, which she wore to great effect, as I knew when she could not forbear telling me that Maria had expressed a passing regret at not choosing the pin for herself.

Maria's more demanding manner never bothered Sophie, who was confident and sharp-tongued and did not suffer criticism quietly. Curiously enough, Maria seemed to value her more on that account. Maria was really only a country girl, Sophie would say, and expected some signs of spirit in a French maid. Sophie disliked Maria cordially, but she did not care whom she worked for; she said it was all one. Yet she knew exactly when to be civil, and when a pert reply would go unchallenged, and I am sure Maria never had an inkling how low she stood in Sophie's esteem. It was a wonder to me that Sophie could so conceal her feelings, but I never thought the worse of her for it; indeed, I admired her cleverness. A servant neglects the art of dissimulation at her peril.

I was particularly successful with Julia's hair, mastering the technique of winding ringlets evenly and smoothing the back hair (hers was fine and flew up in damp weather) so that it appeared glossy and thick. Her front hair, which was short, had, after Amelia's efforts, lain upon her forehead like a row of dumplings. I tried a softer and more feathery curl to frame her face, after a picture I had seen in *Ackermann's Repository*, and wound the remainder into a loose knot on the top of her head. Since this was *très à la mode* and became her exceedingly well, she received many compliments, in consequence of which she gave me a saffron-colored gown that she had tired of. I appreciated the mark of favor; poor Amelia had never received so much as a petticoat. If it had not been for Amelia, indeed, I might have responded to Julia's generosity by liking her more, as is often the case where we feel ourselves to be valued, but when I saw Amelia in tears over some harsh criticism, I could not help but ask why it should be so. Amelia had done Julia many kindnesses and deserved better.

Sophie taught me much that was useful: the sewing of rosettes and delicate embroidery; twisting and folding tricks in making artificial flowers; curious ingredients for perfumes; the use of vermilion and rice powder; the making of pomades and bandoline. With a copy of a magazine from London before us, on the long evening of a ball, Mrs. N. being well out of the way chaperoning her nieces, we would even practice dressing each other's hair in the latest fashion. Sophie, being customarily more daring than I, in addition once brought out a gown of silk and silver tissue belonging to Maria and persuaded me to put it on. I sat before the looking glass beneath the domed ceiling in Maria's elegant dressing room with its Chinese wallpaper, the Java sparrows twittering sweetly in their cage, while Sophie wound a silver fillet around my head and clasped it with a glittering pin and a satin rose. It was my first experience of acting the lady, the first occasion on which I recall a positive pleasure in being waited upon. When she had finished, we considered our reflections, my face below hers, her hands upon my shoulders, our images softened in the candlelight.

"*Alors, que vois-tu là-dedans?* Two fine ladies. Like the Bertrams, but more handsome and more agreeable, *n'est-ce pas?*" She lifted the puffs of sleeve with her fingers to improve the line. "I fetch a necklace." I demurred, but she would have none of it. "We do no harm. Who will know?" She placed a double row of seed pearls from which depended a crystal teardrop around my neck. "Ah! *Que tu es belle!* We should go to the ball."

"We need nothing but a pumpkin, six mice and a lizard."

"We are as good as them. Better. It is chance, that is all. What do they do to deserve it? Nothing. They know nothing, they do nothing."

"That is true. They are horribly ignorant of anything useful."

"They can do nothing for themselves. I am ashamed if anyone does for me what I do for them. *C'est insupportable!* Making their pads and cleaning their nails and digging out their corns. Do you know that Maria has a terrible corn? She wears too small a shoe."

"How can you bear to wait upon her? She is worse than Julia. I could not do it."

"*Tout au contraire.* It is not difficult. I am older than you, do not forget, and I come from France. Paris during the Terror, that was a place to escape. There was no food. When there is no food, all else is nothing. I do not wish to be hungry again. I live for myself. I can endure Miss Maria. What I think I do not say."

"You must long to be free."

"*Naturellement.* What servant does not? But what is freedom? I ask you that. What one wants, it is not always possible. Always I think of France, but I cannot return."

"Your mother was English."

"She speak French always. She live most of her life in France. My poor father's heart it break when we leave Paris. They accuse him of betraying the Revolution. He dies soon after. *Qu'est-ce qu'on peut faire?* We cannot live. We must go to England. I do not regret it. If we stay, we starve. Perhaps we die. But still, England is England. I cannot love it as I love France."

"We heard terrible tales," I ventured.

"Do not believe it. The Revolution is splendid at the beginning. My poor father, he believe in it. Even I remember *les journées révolutionnaires*. The singing! I hear it now. A great crowd, huge, everybody singing, full hearts. Such hope, such joy! We all feel it. *Même les petits*. That is the real Revolution. My brother had to learn by heart the Declaration. I learn it with him. What noble sentiments! What vision! The world will be transformed." She sighed.

"But the weeds come up with the seeds."

"What?"

"My grandfather says that the weeds come up with the seeds."

"*Justement*. That is it." Sophie laughed. "The weeds come up with the seeds. I have an uncle in Normandy. He has an apple orchard. Just the same. Such wisdom. Why is it that the Revolution had not such wisdom, tell me? It is too young, that is it. Like a grandfather, it must be old. Then it will be wise, *n'est-ce pas?*" I did not instantly reply, and she continued: "I know. You English, you detest the Revolution. But it is possible to happen here also."

"Oh, no." I was shocked that she might think so.

"Why not? Why not? There are wrongs here." I was more certain then than later of the impossibility of such a thing and I shook my head again. "You are like Maria," said Sophie scornfully. " 'Do not speak of it, Boucher. It is impossible.' "

"Maria discusses the Revolution? That is even more impossible!"

"Ah! A few words only. It is nothing. She is not interested."

"It is strange, is it not? They have so little to do, yet are interested in nothing."

"What life! They flirt, cut out paper, dance, play cards. They ride on horseback if it does not rain. But I forget! Maria carried jelly to the almshouse on Wednesday. It is the most useful thing she does all year."

"She did not go in the end. Neither would Julia. Fanny went in their place."

"*Bien sûr!* Fanny Price. Of course it is Fanny."

"Poor Fanny. She is worse treated than us."

"It is her own fault. She must face them."

"She could never do it. She is altogether submissive."

"She is silly. She is a goose. I could shake her."

"She is much nicer than her cousins."

"That is to say nothing at all. They are idle and selfish. Fanny is born to suffer. She never say no, only yes. She has no friend here but Edmund and that one, he is a dull nothing."

Edmund Bertram, who was presently at home and managing the estate in his father's absence, was the younger son who made up the quartet of Sir Thomas's children.

"She is uncommonly fond of Edmund."

"*C'est évident.* He is always kind to her. Kindness is very proper for one who goes into the church. Fanny adore him. *Naturellement.* No one else is kind. But there can be nothing in it. Two mice together. It will not do. Now Tom, his brother, Tom is different. You have heard of Tom! *Que veux-tu?* That one, he is handsome, more interesting than his brother. Gaming, horse racing, ratcatching, always naughty. Tom is a complete flirt. That is why his father take him away. Tom cannot resist a pretty face. Pretty faces cannot resist him. That is why Mrs. Norris does not like you. She does not hire you if she see you first.

"Here is the little mystery. Tom goes to Antigua, then Kitty Huckle, the maid before you, begins the morning sickness. Now, Stephen Turnbull is *amoureux de* Kitty, we all know that, it is impossible not to know that. So, she will marry Stephen, *n'est-ce pas?* So we think, but she does not. What a surprise! Why not? Only because it must not be Stephen. Me, even if it was not, I would marry Stephen. Such a man! He will be a good husband, she will be her own mistress. *Quelle chance!* Why does she not marry him? *C'était tout à fait étrange.* You know Stephen. He is good with horses, better than any. He places one shilling for me and wins ten, and I am not the only one. We all benefit of Stephen, especially Tom Bertram. When Stephen say a horse win, it win. Look at Octavian. Sir Thomas wishes it sold before the departure, but Tom absolutely will not. Anything except to sell Octavian. So Stephen cares for it. What a beast! *Magnifique!* But it has a white eye. Everyone is afraid of it, but not Stephen. He love it. He says Octavian win. For him, I think so. Then it is not horses only. A German duke give him five guineas for curing his leg. Five guineas! They say he save enough to buy a livery stable. I believe it. If he ask me to marry him, I say yes before he finish!"

"What happened to Kitty Huckle?"

"Who knows? She left and we never knew. She was pretty, like you. Stephen, I have much pity for him. But such a thing, it is not uncommon. Always in a house someone is put to the door for it. Poor Stephen. All the same, Mansfield Park has no interest without Tom, I assure you. For myself, I am glad when Maria marries. Then we travel. But it is better to be independent."

"Perhaps you will get married."

"*Peu de chance!* Oh, I do not despair, but I am too French, too old."

"What about Stephen?"

"*Qu'est-ce qu'on peut faire?* Give him a potion? He does not see me. He burns for Kitty."

"She is gone."

Sophie sighed. "Perhaps. I do not think so. I am still a stranger here. But I like very much to marry. What female does not? Look at Maria. She is wild for it."

"Julia no less. They think of nothing else."

"Maria shout at me yesterday because she has a spot on the chin."

"Julia has exercises for the mouth." I began to imitate them. It was as fair a selection of grimaces and mirror tricks as you might see at a freak show, and not, I swear, exaggerated.

Sophie laughed. "What is this? Even Maria does not this."

"Exercises for the mouth. Julia thinks her mouth too big. She is terrified of having a double chin like her Aunt Norris."

"Now I try," said Sophie. She sat down beside me.

"No. Like this. One must purse the lips, so."

Sophie made kissing noises. "This is not for a small mouth. This is for lovemaking."

"Exercises for kissing. Of course."

"When she has a lover, wait! Then she is sweet as honey!"

"She is much more agreeable already."

"This is nothing. This is because you make her pretty. But what is a good waiting maid beside a lover?"

IV

Sir Thomas and his elder son were expected home about a
twelvemonth after my arrival at Mansfield. In the event,
however, since sugar, slaves and whatever other business had
demanded Sir Thomas's presence in the West Indies, was not completed as he had hoped, he was obliged to remain longer in Antigua,
and Tom Bertram returned alone.

There was quite a to-do at the arrival of Master Tom, whose
lively disposition had endeared him to more servants than his strait-
laced younger brother, Edmund, despite the idle, spendthrift habits
which gave his father so much anxiety. The cook, Mrs. Alsop,
with whom he was a particular favorite, baked for two days ahead
of his arrival, hot September days at that, filling the larder with
those dishes on which she said he was wont to sup at any hour of
the day or night: a black and white hog's pudding (made to a most
lavish receipt, now in my possession, of a score of eggs, a quart
of cream and a pint of best sherry) and an everlasting syllabub, as
well as more homely fare, tripe and onions and apple pie. For his
part, Tom brought her a great blue and yellow macaw, as big as
a hawk, its wings clipped and its leg attached by a chain to the gilt
perch up and down which it prowled. He had taught it to say
"More tea!," which it did infinitely often, in addition to several
other less polite phrases it had learned from the sailor from whom
Tom had purchased it, following them with a raucous shriek that

could be heard all over the house. Mrs. Alsop became most un-accountably fond of the curious creature. One might well suppose Tom as fond of the cook as of his mother, seeing that the hour he spent at his mother's side upon his arrival was instantly followed by two in the kitchen. Moreover Lady B. received a strange, heath-enish carving, which was not to her taste and nothing beside the parrot. Tom was certainly the sort who finds the servants' quarters as congenial as those upstairs.

The house was scarce large enough for Tom. He leaped the stairs two at a time, wood creaked, doors slammed, glass rattled; wher-ever he was it seemed a stage had just arrived with a new comple-ment of friends, come for a day, a week, a fortnight, shooting with him, hunting, depleting his father's cellar despite the best efforts of the butler, Mr. Baddeley, who was devoted to Sir Thomas and did not approve of Tom's racketing and carousing. Sometimes he would bring his friends to sit round the scrubbed deal table where Mrs. Alsop rolled pastry, and they would yarn and flirt with her, criticizing Baddeley's beer while consuming great quantities of it, as a means of getting their own back. As you may believe, Tom was a devil-may-care sort of fellow, whose bad habits, instead of being, as Sir Thomas had hoped, amended by the visit to Antigua, were rather increased.

My first encounter with Tom followed the night he and two friends had spent rat-catching in the stables and outhouses in mem-ory of their schooldays at Eton. It was a Friday morning (otherwise they would not have chosen the bakehouse), and I had gone to fetch a loaf fresh from the oven, that Julia might indulge herself, as she liked to do, in a warm slice of bread spread with butter and gooseberry jam. As I pushed open the door and stepped inside, something unpleasant, stiff, furry, cold, with a wretched smell, bumped most unwelcomely against my face: the carcasses of some score of rats had been hung up by their tails in a sort of curtain across the inner entrance.

At my exclamation of disgust, there were roars of delight from where Tom and his friends sat in the half-dark awaiting their next victim, two of them upon a wooden table beside the vast iron trivet on which a batch of new bread cooled, the other on what appeared to be one of the best Chippendale chairs from the drawing room.

The chair was balanced on two legs, its back against the hot bricks of the oven, on which a jug of claret stood warming. The smell of scorched varnish mixed with that of new bread and dead rat. Evidently none of them had been to bed.

One of the friends, Charles Maddox of Stoke, as I later discovered, came forward to see what it was they had caught. I was brushing my face and shaking my head to rid myself of the horrid touch of the rats. I never cared for such pranks, although they are all the go, and was a little put about.

"One for me," said Maddox. "I told you not all the maids were timid."

"That makes four for you, three for Tom." The other friend, he upon the chair, was keeping a tally.

"She screamed," said Tom. "It's one for me."

"I challenge that," said Maddox.

"Wasn't that a scream, Oliver?" Tom demanded of his other friend. "She screamed. It's one for me."

"I did not scream," I said indignantly.

"Oh-ho," said Tom, peering at me through the half-light. "But I say you did!"

"There!" said Maddox. "She drew in her breath, but you could not call it a scream."

Tom continued to peer at me. "Who have we here? Do I know you?" I said nothing. "Who are you?"

"Never mind who she is," said Oliver. "First we must decide whether she screamed."

"I did not scream," I repeated angrily.

"Oh, damn it," said Tom. "I suppose we may agree she did not. Now, tell us who you are."

Oliver noted the score. "You're still on for a hundred, Bertram."

"Monstrously pretty, Bertram," said Maddox. "I'm surprised you can't put a name to her."

"I am come for the new bread," I said. "Where is Mrs. Alsop?"

"Mrs. Alsop is in the kitchen. We are distributing the bread this morning."

"Then, if you please, I will have a loaf."

"Deuce take it, there's no hurry."

"There is indeed. Miss Julia likes the bread warm. That is why I am come."

"Ah! My sister's maid!" exclaimed Tom. "I see. What might your name be?"

"Hartwell, sir. If you please, I will have the bread."

Tom picked up a loaf. "You shall, you shall. It is the least we can do, is it not, gentlemen? The first batch of the morning!"

As I approached, he held the loaf just out of my reach. "Hartwell. It's a good name. What goes before it?"

I reached up and he moved the bread higher. I stepped back, answering unwillingly, "Jane."

Tom, smiling, lowered the loaf but still held on to it. "Jane Hartwell. Now there's a name to conjure with. The most courageous maid at Mansfield. She did not scream. Let us toast Jane Hartwell." They raised their mugs and drank. I moved forward to take what I had come for, thinking their little game was over, but as I did so Tom started. "Your cap. It's crawling! They must be off the rats!"

I had my cap off in a minute, you may believe, shaking it vigorously. When I had done and dropped it into my pocket, I looked up and understood that I had revealed my hair, as Tom had intended (although I doubt that he invented the vermin). He put the loaf behind his back then. "One last payment for a loaf: a single kiss. Here." He touched his cheek. "Cheap at the price."

I did as I was bid from as great a distance as I could contrive, and Tom gave me the loaf with a most speaking look. Then they bid me a teasing good-bye.

As you may collect, Master Tom had notched me on the tally stick, and was not likely to pass me by in the hallway or on the landings without acknowledgment in future. Indeed the very next day, when I was preparing Julia a bath, he came in at a gallop with two pails of hot water he had taken off the footman, and tipped them into the tub with fine carelessness, paying more attention to me than to what he was doing and thereby splashing me with near-boiling water. Whereupon I stepped back involuntarily, and he took my wrist and pulled me back, saying, with no truth: "You will fall in." That was all, and of course it was nothing, and then again it was a vast deal. It was the first time he had laid his hand upon me, and he knew it, and intended that I should register it also. Skin to skin, his hand said as the fingers closed about my wrist, skin to skin, yours to mine and nothing between. Moreover, as he pulled

45

me toward him his grip was strong and peremptory. All uninten-
tionally I was close to him. And then, although I was perfectly
decent, my arms and neck were bare in preparation for my task.
How could I not know what he wanted me to know? What he did
was not improper, not precisely, but he imparted so much by his
touch that although he held my wrist for only a second, it seemed
infinite.

I made up my mind to have no dealings with Tom. But that was
next to impossible, as those who blame the servant in these irregular
liaisons do not properly appreciate. Master and servant, living in
the same house, albeit a large one, walking on the same paths, using
the same corridors, having dealings with the same people, how is
it possible that they should not encounter one another? And that
is without being intent upon it, which Tom was. And then, although I refused his blandishments as well as I could, there comes
a time when one must become less polite if rejection is not to sound
half like acceptance.

"I shall saddle Miss Price's little chestnut mare for you. She has
an angelic temper. Come this evening."

"I cannot."

"Why not?"

"I must not."

"Come."

I beg you to consider the many variations there may be to such
a conversation, the many ways in which a young man like Tom
may make himself obliging and agreeable, and how very tiresome
it becomes to say no. The worst of it is to control one's tongue
and not answer up with spirit. For that is the danger, although I
think it is not well understood. If I spoke out to Tom as freely as
I would to those in my own station, instead of saying no like a
mouse, I should be making us as equals, taking the first step toward
familiarity, the very thing I desired most to avoid. But of course
I took it nevertheless. I was no mouse and did not want to be
thought one.

I shall not say that I dreaded the regular encounters with Tom.
Life was not so diverting that I did not relish the spice that such a
flirtation offered. There is much in a servant's life of the "Yes,

ma'am," "No, ma'am," "Thank you, ma'am" variety, and something more natural in the way of repartee is to be welcomed as a pleasant exercise of one's wits. These are all matters to which no thought is given when blame is apportioned. It is not my intention, however, to lay all the fault at Tom's door (the very thing I would not have others do to the servant). It would have been quite against nature for a pretty sixteen-year-old to be unresponsive to the attentions of a personable young man of superior station. Tom was tall and broad, strong as a bull, had the curliest hair imaginable and was at ease with the world and everyone in it; if he had seduced a maid or two, then it was no more than was to be expected. Besides, Tom knew very well how to insinuate himself with the gift of an orange or a ribbon or a trinket. He often had something in his pocket for me, keeping such things about him much as he carried sugar lumps for the horses. I remember he gave me a tiny looking glass on one occasion, enameled in blue and green with a peacock. The speech he made about what I should see when I looked into it was so neatly turned I was half sure he had made it before, but I was accustomed to more clumsy phrases and charmed even so.

I was walking back to the Park from the village late one wintry afternoon carrying a bolt of muslin for a gown which was to be made all in a hurry for Julia. It was getting dark and began to rain. I have always enjoyed walking, but this was not a day to choose for it: the weather had promised fair and turned foul within the hour, the ground underfoot was full as a sponge, I had only just turned into the Park gates, and the steady downpour threatened to turn the way into a regular quagmire. My shoes and stockings were getting damp and, what was worse, the paper wrapped about the bolt of cloth began to spoil and I was afraid for its contents. At such a moment Tom Bertram chose to arrive out of the dusk at my side.

A man on horseback offering assistance at such a time might wear horns and a tail before one would willingly refuse it. Tom put me up behind him, with the bolt of muslin somewhat awkwardly set between us, and we trotted down the road. I had my hood up and was sheltering against his back, so I did not immediately notice that he had turned the horse aside and across the grassy verge into the trees. When I remarked on it, he answered merely, "You shall see what it is like to travel behind a good rider on a fast horse."

"I shall be quite content to go straight back and slowly."

"What? And miss a bit of excitement? You disappoint me. Have you noticed the mount? Can you not feel the pace?"

Indeed, I began to, for even with two of us up the stride and speed were prodigious. It was, although I had failed to remark it, Tom's pride and joy, the lord of the stable, Octavian.

The great horse had been bought on Stephen's advice when it was but a yearling with a suspect temper, the very uncertainty of which had enabled Tom to buy it for one third of what such an animal would otherwise have been worth. Tom fancied himself as a gentleman jockey, but he had not Stephen's touch with the animal, and probably never would have, although he put down his difficulty to Octavian's lack of acquaintance with him over a long absence. Whatever its faults of temper, the horse was, according to Stephen, a magnificent runner, unbeatable in heavy going and courageous. Now that Tom was home it was to be matched and raced whenever possible, with Stephen up. Octavian being so notoriously difficult to handle, Tom rarely rode him and I was surprised that he took the risk. It was most unwise. Yet it was just like him to take the horse out on a whim and collect me on another.

"Should you ride him so?"

"Why not? He's my horse, the best ever. There wasn't a mount to equal him in Antigua. I wished I had him there, you may be sure. He would have shown the locals a thing or two. He must accustom himself to me again. He knows his master's touch on the bit, I swear, although it's been more than a twelvemonth. What's the matter? Are you afraid?"

As we came to clear ground again, Tom urged the horse to a gallop, so that if I were indeed frightened I should be more so, and I clung to him tightly, as he had no doubt intended (although the bolt of cloth was something of an encumbrance in that regard). We galloped across the Park in the owl-light for a half-mile and then turned aside toward a break in the fence overgrown by a low quickset hedge. The horse scarcely seemed to alter his pace as we cleared it, although the jolt when we landed near threw me and my bundle off. Tom was obliged to slow to a trot as we were now on rough ground and the horse had to find its way along an ill-defined path through trees, underbrush and bracken. Tom bent his head to avoid the branches and I followed suit. Tall ferns brushed their moisture against my ankles and water dripped onto my cloak; I began to feel damp about the shoulders.

"Did you miss me?"

"Miss you?"

"I have been in Ramsgate."

"I did not know."

"Hey ho! I thought I should return and find you wild for me."

"I did not even know you were gone."

"I imagined you searching in vain for me, hideously miserable."

"I saw you but ten days since."

"Ten days! Ten days is an eternity when someone has made an impression upon your heart. It is too long for me."

"Am I to believe that you spent your time in Ramsgate pining for a lady's maid at Mansfield?"

"I ate and drank and swam, to be sure. The sea is very fine for swimming, especially after champagne at two o'clock in the morning. Then I fell asleep and dreamed of you. Did you not dream of me?"

"Never once. But I do not dream."

"Not even with your eyes open?"

"I never thought of you at all. Is not that strange?"

This put him out of humor. "What a cold little piece you are! Have you no heart? You are devilish hard on a fellow." There was silence for a few minutes and then he resumed. "It's a gray sea at Ramsgate, and most of the time it is infernally cold. You should see the color of the sea in Antigua. Sink me if I don't sometimes long to be back there! The water is turquoise and jade when it is not sapphire, and swimming in the torrid zone is perfect bliss, warm as a bath. The women there are not so hard-hearted either. Sporting in the sea, skin out, with a dusky female not overburdened with false modesty is a pleasure, I can tell you."

"You have been spoiled for our cold northern ways."

"For *your* cold northern ways," he replied feelingly. "By God, a smile, a look, a touch on the arm. They were as hot to the matter as I. You might have whatever you wanted for the asking."

"I am sure you were not slow to ask."

"I was not slow to be appreciated."

Again there was a pause. "You must regret the necessity of returning," I said at last.

Tom did not reply instantly but when he did it was with better grace. "My staying out there wasn't part of the old man's intention. He's still trying to reconcile me to my duties. But I daresay, if I persist in being the prodigal, he may send me back."

"Then you have good reason not to reform."

"Oh, one has some feeling for the old place after all, don't you know. But the beauty of it! Antigua is a paradise. The black women are magnificent. Of course, they flog 'em, out there, so a bit of kindness in a gentleman is welcomed. None of *your* sort of silly games."

"Flogging!"

"Are you shocked? The slaves need it, you know. I hardly ever saw anyone flogged worse than I was at Eton. My father didn't like it overmuch, but you can't run a plantation without having discipline. They're uncivilized. They won't work without it, and the climate weakens them."

"I do not believe in slavery."

Tom laughed with some scorn. "I might have known *you* would have an opinion on something about which you are altogether ignorant."

"Why should you suppose so? It is a matter of much debate," I replied indignantly. "No man has the right to own another."

"It has existed since the earliest times. It is a condition of mankind."

"I do not believe it."

"You are a contrary wench and I should not expect you to. Nevertheless, it is so. Abolish slavery and the colonies will be ruined."

"Are the slaves flogged on Sir Thomas's plantation?"

"No more than is necessary. Mind you, we had had some trouble. That's why the governor went out there in the first place: sugar yield falling, profits reduced, all that sort of thing. The manager had got slack. It is a fault of the heat. The slaves were, not starving exactly, but riven with disease. Since they eat nothing but a mess of strange vegetables and a bit of salt cod, I think it scarcely to be wondered at, but the old man got into a pother about it, as usual, and blamed Keating, the manager. I thought he was a bit hard on him. I got along with the fellow quite well, though of course I couldn't let the governor see that. Keating was living with two or three of the women. He showed me a thing or two."

When we reached Aston's Lane Tom turned down it, in quite the opposite direction from Mansfield, and began to gallop once more.

"Where are we going?"

"Only a short stop on the way. No one will miss you yet. I must see Maddox. He wants a try on the box and doesn't know Sturmey. Besides, he goes to London and will renew my bills, otherwise that damned old Jew will be after me." He patted Octavian's neck. "No matter, I'm sitting on my fortune."

It was a question of money, as you may devise. Tom was always short of money. His father held him by a promise to abstain from gaming, but he had circumvented that restriction without difficulty, and could no more resist the invitation to double or nothing than a wasp a honey trap. Wealth was always round the next corner. Several of his friends, indeed, including Oliver, had no money but what they made on gaming, and everyone knew the story (which Tom never tired of telling) of how Oliver had come home addled with drink one night and stuffed a thousand pounds into the chamberpot, which he then mistakenly pissed upon. Tom was not quick enough to calculate the odds at hazard as finely as Oliver, who was accounted something of a mathematician, but when it came to laying wagers on the outcome of a match between horses or men, if he had Stephen at his side he was generally allowed to be a man of judgment, and he turned a hundred guineas often enough to consider betting a fine occupation for a gentleman.

Tom jumped Octavian no more, much to my relief, although we pushed through a hedge so that he might hold to his principle of never paying a toll and my leg was badly scratched on a maythorn thereby. The rain came down harder than ever and I was glad that the bolt of fabric at least was well protected, for when we were on the London road beyond the toll bar, Tom posted along for about three miles, as far as the Rose and Crown, which he approached with a caution so uncharacteristic that I could only suppose the bills of which he had spoken must be for very large sums indeed.

In this regard, the choice of Octavian as a mount was foolish, for he was not the sort of horse to go unremarked. Tom was lucky that the stagecoach was not yet due or, rain notwithstanding, the yard would have been all a-bustle. As it was there was no one about and he led the horse along the grassy edge of the yard, where the hoofs would make no sound, to the large and commodious stables which were furthest from the inn itself. There he dismounted and lifted down first my bundle and then me, Octavian behaving all the while with the utmost decorum, as though he were nothing but a quiet old pony. When Tom went to lead him into an empty stall, however, where he might be both unseen and out of the weather, the horse's mood changed. He took exception to the unfamiliar surroundings and began to fidget and pull back. He even whinnied a little.

"That will do you no good," I said. "Someone will hear."

"Damned beast, I should not have brought him. He is infernally jumpy."

Do what we might, we could not get Octavian through the door and into the shelter of the stable and Tom was at last obliged to tether him outside.

"You stay here," he said to me with his customary consideration. "Five minutes should see this business done," and he ran across the yard and into the back door of the inn.

Having secured a dry place for my bundle, I sat down on an upturned pail within the stable door to wait out Tom's five minutes, which extended, as I had guessed they would, into three times as many more. I was cold and damp and regretting my escapade, you may be sure; I should have done better to get my feet thoroughly soaked on the way back to Mansfield than to sit here getting chilled to the marrow. The rain came down more heavily still. I watched the lights of the inn and listened to Octavian blowing down his nostrils and champing on the bit. He was becoming, I thought, as impatient as I.

I think I must have shut my eyes and dozed, for the next thing I heard was the coach horn. The Rose and Crown being the first stage on the journey from Northampton to London, the coach was regularly to be expected at this hour. As soon as it arrived the inn would spill out light and noise and people into the now deserted yard. I started up, intending to go and warn Tom, but I was the day after the fair for that. The steady drumming of the sixteen hoofs upon the road, the clinking of harness, the creaking of wood and the rattling of metal, the coachman's bellowed instructions, were upon me before I had gone two paces. I ran instead to Octavian, taking hold of the bridle in anxious anticipation, for the vehicle, its moons beaming like monstrous eyes, resembled nothing so much as an apparition from the underworld. Ostlers and boys were out, pegs and blankets at the ready, bringing half a dozen more lanterns to brighten the scene.

Octavian was terrified. Despite all that I could do, he jerked so violently that the ring to which he was tethered threatened to come out of the wall. Had Tom not emerged from the inn at that moment and sprinted across the yard to assist me, the horse would have been off. Tom's superior strength prevented that calamity, but he was quite unable to calm Octavian. Eyes rolling and ears laid back, the horse was all a-twitch with fright at the sudden din and clamor.

By this time the ostler had the steps down for the inside passengers, who in such weather preferred to hurry into the warm travelers' room, where hot spiced rum awaited them, rather than take a turn around the yard and stay to observe our antics as they might otherwise have done. None but those who could not afford to await an improvement in the weather traveled outside, and they numbered only two, a shabby young man who climbed down agilely and made for the shelter of the eaves, and an old woman, layered in an assortment of rusty clothes that must have seen more years than she, who lowered herself with such difficulty from her elevated perch that it seemed doubtful she would ever ascend again. Taking cover from the rain seemed a useless precaution, since they must both already have been wet through, but the young man shook the drops from his hat, looked at us and prepared for a little diversion. The old woman, by contrast, stood hunched like a milepost, with no appetite for any of the activity around her, of which there was plenty. The horsekeepers were intent upon the change, and four boys led out the fresh team while four others stood by ready to lead away those animals which still stood in the traces, mud-

spattered and smoking from their exertions. All those occupied
with the change were experts in horseflesh by virtue of their calling
and kept a sideways eye upon us, instantly intrigued by Octavian.

For its part, the great horse continued to whinny and prance, to
Tom's mortification in that horsy company. Indeed, when he could
by no means soothe the animal's temper, Tom began to lose his
own. To mount and be away before the coach departed with more
fanfaroo that would further agitate Octavian was his chief object,
and since it was clear that he could not achieve that without more
assistance than mine alone he summoned the shabby young outside
traveler, who came willingly enough when he was offered a shilling
for his services. Even with one of us on either side of his head,
however, Octavian continued to back and skitter and pull away.
We were by this time well off the stones and into churned dirt.
What a sorry sight we all were by this time, you may devise. We
slipped and slid, the rain dripped into our eyes and the horse threw
mud over us every time it moved.

When Tom at last contrived to mount, Octavian instantly reared
and he fell off into the mud. I let go of the bridle, and if it had not
been for the young man, who with admirable presence of mind
maintained a loose hold upon his end of the rein, Octavian must
have bolted. The horse swung round and Tom scrambled out of
the way, cursing under his breath. We had by chance drawn nearer
to the old woman, who was thus unable to avoid noticing the
commotion, although no one gave her a second glance until she
moved out into the rain, perilously close to the horse, and spoke
to Tom. "It's you, Mr. Bertram. It is you. Why, I cannot believe it."

Tom was in no mood for polite exchanges. "Out of the way,
old dame," he said impatiently, as he began moving around the
horse for a second try. She, however, merely stepped after him,
oblivious to all else. "Mr. Bertram, you must hear me. Will you
not hear me?"

She had placed herself in alarming proximity to Octavian. Tom
spoke to me. "For God's sake, get her out of the way."

I was obliged to relinquish my hold upon the horse to attend to
her, although one of the horse boys, his task by this time completed,
took my place.

The old woman would not readily suffer herself to be led away, however. "I will speak with him," she insisted. "He shall hear me."

I soothed her as best I could; whatever she had to say, this was no time for it. "Only wait a little. Wait until he has quieted the horse." From her mazed look, I concluded that she was ill, or wandering, or a little weak in the head. "Only look at me." I pointed at my soaked and muddied garment. "You can see the trouble we are in."

As I spoke, she began to peer intently into my face. "I look, my dear, and I see, and I am sorry for it."

She spoke in riddles, and I sought to calm her. "You are wet through. We must get you nourishment and dry clothes. How far do you travel this night?"

"It isn't the weather I'm thinking of, my dear. 'Tis you and that one there."

I looked where she nodded. "Mr. Bertram?"

"The very same." She looked toward him and then spoke more to herself than me. "The good Lord has seen fit to bring him and me together. It is a sign."

I was sure she was distracted. As she made to step forward again I anticipated the movement and caught her elbow. She had, however, more strength than I had supposed and was very determined besides. She twisted free of me, stepped out toward the spot where Tom and Octavian still pranced around one another and spoke again to Tom, her voice loud and firm although she did not shout: "You did my Kitty a great wrong."

I heard the quaver which told of the emotion she barely suppressed. Octavian felt it also; her presence and the tone of her voice together undid the progress that had by now been made in calming the great horse. "God damn it, woman," said Tom to me as Octavian plunged once more, "can you not keep the old fool quiet?"

I urged her out of the way but she took no notice. "Old fool I may be, Mr. Bertram, but I am Kitty's mother and I will speak with you."

Tom did glance at her then, and the bay, sensing perhaps that Tom's attention was now divided, chose that moment to swing his hindquarters round and lash out with his hoofs; one caught the old woman a glancing blow to the hip and she fell to the ground.

I ran forward instantly, took her beneath the arms and began to drag her clear. The other outsider came to assist me and between us we picked her up easily. She was slight beneath the many layers of cloth, to which she owed her preservation from greater hurt. Indeed, despite the considerable blow, she was sufficiently in her right senses to recognize that she had not achieved her prime object, and summoned up wind enough to sob pitifully. It was a gasping, doleful sound. Setting her down upon some sacking, I ran back and endeavored to prevail upon Tom to grant her request.

"I have more to do than listen to the prattlings of a Bedlamite. Did you see what she did to the horse? Here I am laboring to calm a highly bred animal, worth a thousand guineas at least, and all is set at nought by a stupid old woman!"

"For pity's sake, it will take but a minute. Let her have her way. She is old and ill and quite beside herself."

"I cannot. The stage will be off and we shall be in a worse state than before. You listen to her."

"It is not me she wants. Did you not hear the name she used? I saw you. You knew it. You must hear her."

Arms akimbo, with ill grace he stood over her, looking back all the while toward his horse, but the old woman was not to be discouraged. "Do you remember my Kitty?"

"I have been away. It is a long time ago."

"Kitty Huckle it is. I am her mother. Do you remember Kitty?" Tom barely nodded. Whether he remembered her or not, I did: Kitty Huckle was the maid whose place I had taken, she whom Stephen Turnbull was supposed to have loved. "She's gone now, and I am all alone, quite alone. The others are dead and there is only her left, and where she is I don't know." Mrs. Huckle began quietly to weep.

"What is all this to me?" Tom demanded.

"Your child," said the old woman through her tears. "It is your child."

Tom frowned but he began to attend. "What child?"

"Kitty's child. Her child and your child. 'Tis a half-year since I had word, and what am I to do? She was dear to me, my Kitty, very dear. There is no one else now."

"There is a child, then?" I queried Tom in a whisper. I glimpsed a world of suffering, casually inflicted.

He shrugged angrily. "Perhaps."

"It is yours?"

"Who shall say? It may just as soon not be." He cursed quietly. "If it is money she wants I have nought but three guineas on me." My heart went out to the old woman. She had neither begged nor bullied, and all her loneliness and grief were belittled by Tom's remark.

Mrs. Huckle, scarcely aware of us, continued. "What could I have done? Jem at home on account of his back, not a penny coming in and me with two little ones still in petticoats. There was only Kitty to help. And now, bless me, the two little ones are in the churchyard and even Kitty's been taken from me."

"I cannot stay for this," said Tom impatiently. "Here." He emptied his pockets and gave me what he had.

"I see you, Master Tom," said Mrs. Huckle, no longer wandering but all attention. "I see you giving her money. Be careful, my dear, or it will happen to you, what happened to my Kitty."

Tom ignored her. "See to her. Then hire yourself a quiet nag. Octavian will not suffer us both again, that is certain. Attend to her first."

"You will not leave?"

He looked toward Octavian. "I must see to the horse."

"But what am I to do?"

"Whatever you think necessary. There is no knowing how this cursed affair will set back his temper. It is devilish ill luck! And he just beginning to get used to me. I must get him away from here. There's no time to lose. Make sure she does not come begging again."

He ran back to the horse, which he mounted this time without mishap, although Octavian took off like a cannonball as soon as he felt Tom upon him and bore him away into the dark.

Mrs. Huckle was in no state to pursue her journey that night and, having seen her carried to a small room with a good fire, I sought to make some arrangement that she might travel a few days hence. The driver of the mail coach to whom I applied was none other than the renowned Bob Sturmey. Every young blade on the ground between London and Northampton vied for the privilege of paying to sit next to him on the box and taking a turn at the reins. Tom had done so more than once, and swore that Sturmey was the best coachman in the country. I approached him apprehensively, quite expecting a curt reply from such an elevated personage to the draggletail I appeared at that moment. I was encouraged to see no swell dragsman, however, but a man of a comfortable ordinary appearance in an old-fashioned mulberry-colored many-caped benjamin and a beaver hat. Bob Sturmey had few pretensions, as I was later to discover, and even now, when he boasts of his friends Sir This and the Duke of That, he has never affected a more dashing getup, his only concession to fashionable daftness, as he calls it, being to wear a geranium in his buttonhole during every month of the year.

"Hey day!" he said, before I had a chance to speak. "The master's left you behind, has he? Well, I don't know what's afoot, but it looks like mischief to me. He's a scallywag and sometimes worse, like all the others."

By which, you may believe, the dramatic scene enacted in the yard had been observed with considerable interest and some shrewd guesses as to what had passed. Sturmey was full of sympathy for the old woman's plight and instantly agreed to my request. "Mr. Bertram's money, is it?" he inquired as he dropped the guinea into one of his capacious pockets. "Ah, well, that's all right then. I doubt it's enough for the trouble he's caused. I'll look after her, never you fear. As for Mr. Bertram, you can tell him Maddox will be taking a turn with me next week." He was about to step away, but then turned back. "I mustn't forget my commission. If Mr. Bertram hadn't been in such a hurry I would have given it to him." He rummaged in his pocket and produced a small oilskin-wrapped package. "You may take it for me instead, if you will. It is for Stephen Turnbull, something from town for his potions. I don't usually act postboy, but Stephen's done me a good turn more than once. You tell him that if he needs anything, he's only got to send word. And you might tell him, if you remember, that Telfer's horse has come on wonderfully." He looked toward the coach, into which the last passenger had now climbed, and acknowledged the guard's salute; then he paused a moment, thoughtfully. "Stephen Turnbull's wasted at Mansfield, that's the truth. Mr. Bertram's no better than he should be and no good to a man like that. Stephen's a healer, no doubt of it. Tell him to recollect the story of Dick Whittington: he's not the only one to find the streets of London paved with gold. Remind him of that. Dick Whittington. And tell him to look me up if ever he comes to town. The Cross Keys in Gracechurch Street, that's my snuggery, the Cross Keys in Gracechurch Street."

After the coach had left, I procured hot water, a change of linen, and the services of a chambermaid with an ample white apron to provide for Mrs. Huckle's comfort. By the time she had partaken of hot spiced rum and a bowl of good mutton broth sopped up with bread her spirits had greatly improved, even though she could not move her leg without pain, and she had adopted me as a friend. "I must go to my cousin first, that's plain, but then I'm going to find her, my dear, that's what I'm going to do. I never heard of Willishall, but then it's only a village. I've heard of Ely and the fen country. Flat it is, and the wind cuts like a knife. I think of her there, cold and lonely. I do blame myself, that I do. I knew what kind of a lad he was. Even a child shall be known by its doings. 'Twas a pity the master were away. Mrs. Norris, that's My Lady's sister, she had the doing of it. There's an old witch for you. All smiles one minute and mouth set like a trap the next. Turned her off, she would have, without a quiver of conscience. 'Tis a heart of stone and no mistake. My Kitty stood up for herself, she did; told her it was Master Tom and not one of the village lads. That foxed her. She promised money and a place, but Kitty had to go, right away, with no word to anybody. I didn't like it, not at all. I was for her staying with me, where she was born and bred, but she wouldn't listen. She said Mrs. Norris spoke fair. The devil's always at his worst with a smile on his face."

After confiding so much of her story, the old woman fell into a doze, and I made the most of the lukewarm bath and a change of linen to restore my own well-being, thinking meanwhile upon what I had heard. It was a commonplace tale, nothing but a confirmation of earlier nods and hints. Yet for all that I felt it deeply. Such an event dresses rumor in glaring colors and puts it center stage so that one is face to face with all its ugliness. I had never greatly taken to Tom, for all his sheep's eyes and trinkets. I contemplated the old woman and her daughter, the few paltry crowns with which Tom thought to pay off his obligation, and I was full of indignation and ashamed of my own thoughtless acceptance of his flirting ways.

The old woman slept peacefully, and I knew I must be on my way. I brushed the haystalks off my bolt of cloth, put the remainder of Tom's money and what little I had of my own into Mrs. Huckle's pocket and left the inn quietly, on a tired old post-horse. During the five-mile jog in a mizzling rain, I invented an excuse to explain my tardiness, but it did not prosper. The old beldame found me out, as I should have foreseen. She went to the draper and questioned him about the length of time I had been occupied in the shop, and whether he had advised (as I had intimated) that for the safety of the cloth I should wait out the storm. I cursed the mealy-mouthed draper and stuck to my story although she tried to catch me out for a month after. She marked me for a mischief-maker and a drab, although she knew nothing for certain. I think she never did discover exactly what I had been doing with my time, but her suspicions weighed scarcely lighter than certainties, so highly did she value her own judgment.

V

Immediately upon rising the day after a ball, Maria and Julia Bertram would meet for a comfortable chat, in order to rehearse the previous night's doings in infinite detail, while Sophie and I went quietly about our customary tasks, airing stockings, brushing hair and fetching chocolate. We always enjoyed these occasions. Although nothing of significance to the great world outside was said, the gossip was diverting: why Mr. This had danced with Miss That; the quiz of a hat their friend Miss So-and-so had worn; the horrid behavior of the ugly Mr. Thorogood. They spoke, you may believe, with perfect indifference to our presence, as though we had neither ears to hear nor tongues to prattle. It was therefore most unexpected when Julia one morning urged Maria: "Ask her. Go on, ask her. It can do no harm. If you wish to hear the truth, ask a servant. Servants know more of their masters and mistresses than anyone." She and Maria tittered.

"Tell us about Sotherton, Hartwell," said Maria.

"Sotherton?" I wondered what was to come. "What do you wish to know?"

"Tell us all," said Maria. "What Sotherton Court is like, how many drawing rooms it has, how many bedrooms, how many servants are employed, the size of the park, what the servants think of Mr. Rushworth, what tea Mrs. Rushworth drinks." They tittered again. "What sort of temper Mr. Rushworth has in the morning."

I thought I began to see the way the wind blew, but I could scarcely believe it. Maria could surely have no interest in Mr. Rushworth of Sotherton, the Mr. Rushworth I knew, Mr. James Rushworth who was considered a dunce by all his acquaintance. "I could talk of Sotherton all day, but I am a partial observer and sure to overpraise everything."

"We shall not mind," said Julia. "At least, my sister will not. She will drink up every word you say."

As I told of Sotherton's seven hundred acres, the fine woods and water meadows, the greenhouses and trout ponds, the large, rambling Elizabethan mansion with its lofty rooms, shining floors, solid walnut and rich damask, they listened attentively, Maria interjecting now and then with a question.

"Well, sister," said Julia with a tinge of envy when I paused, "I think you will be mistress of a very fine estate."

Maria did not deny it. "Sotherton," she said, lingering over the word. "I think it is a fine-sounding name, do not you? It seems to have a greater air of consequence than Mansfield. I suppose that is something to do with its antiquity."

"If we are to talk of names, how shall you like being Rushworth instead of Bertram?"

"I think there is nothing much to choose between them. Both have two syllables. Either a B or an R enables one to make a grand flourish."

"You should practice your signature. It is a pity there is not also a title."

"An ancient name counts for more than a title, and Mr. Rushworth's goes back—oh, ever so far."

"To Henry the Eighth," I said. "The earliest portrait is dated 1541."

"You are very well informed, Hartwell," said Maria, not without a shade of disapproval that I should be so.

"Still, I think it is a pity there is no title," Julia persisted.

"Titles are vastly overdone nowadays."

"You would not say so if he were an earl. Perhaps he is cousin to an aged bachelor with a title."

"I never heard it. There are no titles that I know of," I said.

"One cannot expect everything," said Maria.

"You have made a fine catch, sister."

"It is not landed yet."

"Only imagine, you will be married and your own mistress. Then it will be my turn. I hope I may have as much luck."

"Mr. Thorogood was very attentive," said Maria.

"Mr. Thorobad! Do not mention him if you please! I would rather be hanged."

"Perhaps someone new will come to the neighborhood. It is a singular disadvantage that there are so few unmarried gentlemen of property hereabouts."

"Well, if you may do it, I suppose I may also." To this Maria made no reply. Julia, a trifle put out, turned again to me. "Come, we have not heard above half what there is to hear about the eligible Mr. Rushworth."

"He is good-natured and kind," I ventured, endeavoring to speak some praise which did not stretch the truth. "He has improved the roads considerably since he inherited the estate."

Julia laughed. "Now that is a great mark in his favor."

Maria frowned. "That is something the villagers would naturally find important. It is not to be discounted."

"You must know something more," said Julia. "What else is there to gossip about but the master of the estate?"

"What do you know of his mother?" asked Maria.

"Mrs. Rushworth was once kind enough to show me some relics of the family."

"Was there any jewelry?" inquired Maria.

"I saw none, though I have heard that there is an emerald pendant of great beauty."

"A pendant," said Maria; "I might like that."

"You would have to have it reset, I suppose," commented Julia.

"I was shown other things: a gown with slit sleeves and a baby's christening cap, two hundred years old; the great seal of the family."

"How interesting," said Maria, without the least feeling that they could be so. "I have always been told that emeralds suit me very well."

"Mrs. Rushworth has made quite a study of the history of the family."

"La, Maria, and Miss Lee always said you were no good at history."

"It is not history Mr. Rushworth is interested in." Both sisters

63

tittered again, little knowing by how much their innuendo over-estimated James Rushworth's interest in anything else. "Many find him handsome," Maria continued. "I do not know that he is handsome exactly, but handsome men are always prodigiously vain. His eyes are very blue."

"He is tall," added Julia. "Do you like him to be tall? But he is clumsy. Anne Temple said that he was quite out of step in the dance last night."

"Anne Temple! She was fortunate to be engaged at all; I am sure her card was more empty than full. I do not greatly care what Anne Temple said. I was quite surprised at Mr. Rushworth. Who could admire her with teeth like that? Her complexion is well enough, though she has to make shift to cover up a few pimples, but those teeth! I never dare look at her for fear I shall stare at those three black teeth."

"Poor her! They are certainly a horrid misfortune." Julia opened her mouth to reassure herself of her own white ones by contemplation of them in the mirror. "All the same, I am sure Mr. Rushworth is no dancer."

"How should you know? I am the one who danced with him all evening. I am sure I have been led by many worse."

"Tell me what he said to you."

"Oh, it was no more than chitchat. We debated the weather and the number of pheasants taken this season. He told me the name of his favorite pointer."

"Is that all?"

"The words were nothing, but he looked a vast deal."

"Love me, love my dog," said Julia. "He sounds a trifle tedious."

"I hope you may light upon a gentleman who is all perfection. They are not easy to come by."

Mrs. Norris was ecstatic at Maria's netting Mr. Rushworth. "Your father will be most gratified, my dear niece. Only think what a splendid match it is! Caroline Dudley did not make a better and she was out five seasons."

"We are not yet married, ma'am. Mr. Rushworth has not yet proposed."

"It can be only a matter of time. Your modesty does you credit, but Mr. Rushworth's admiration was obvious to everyone. Mrs. Temple remarked how fine you were looking last night. He had eyes for no one else. Even Mrs. Smith-Barton remarked upon that, and she scarcely ever approves anything. Your cap was particularly becoming. Miss Windlesham was quite put out that hers, which she had paid four pounds and eight shillings for, was not half so much praised as yours, which Boucher made for three pounds. She was overcharged, that's for certain, but then she is such a sorry-looking little thing, just the sort tradespeople always take advantage of. That blue bombazine she wore was altogether unsuitable. Can you believe that she entertained hopes of Mr. Rushworth? Her mother turned quite green when he passed her without so much as a glance. It is amazing how interloping people like that can have such an opinion of themselves. Her mother's father was in wool!"

"Does Mr. Rushworth have a house in town, Hartwell?" asked Maria.

"I once heard Mrs. Rushworth's maid speak of it. She said she preferred it to Sotherton. It has fireplaces in all but the attics and is very comfortable."

Mrs. N. sniffed. "These modern houses are monstrously wasteful."

"Do you know the address?"

"Wimpole Street, I believe."

"You could hardly do better than that," said Julia.

"My dear niece, I should say not! It is the heart of fashionable London. I believe I remember driving along it when I accompanied Lady Bertram on the occasion of her fourth confinement—bless me, it seems only a year or two ago."

Julia spoke with longing: "Only think, sister, you will be at Vauxhall and the opera and Almack's every week."

"That is the advantage of marrying well," said Mrs. N., "but I have no doubt, my dear Julia, that we shall make a good match for you. One sister marries and the other will soon follow suit."

"Like you and my mother do you mean, Aunt?" said Julia spitefully. It was not until some half-dozen years after her younger sister's marriage that Miss Ward (as she then was) had, as the alternative to no husband at all, been obliged to settle for the Reverend Mr. Norris.

"It was very different in our day," said Mrs. Norris, conscious of no offense. "Young ladies were excessively modest. I was so concerned not to appear forward that I believe poor Mr. Norris must have proposed six times before I plucked up courage to accept him. I have always thanked my good fortune that I did. A clergyman needs an able wife. I struggle on without him as best I may."

"You will be able to spend the season with me," said Maria.

"There you are! I declare it is a pleasure to behold such affection between two sisters. It was always the way between your mother and myself. When we were very young she would cry if she had to part from me. Even now I am happier doing something for Lady Bertram than for myself. I think I may say without exaggeration, my dear niece, that I have never done a better thing than introduce you to Mr. Rushworth."

In possession of £12,000 a year and the ancient manor of Sotherton with all its rights of court-leet and court-baron, James Rushworth was, indeed, in the eyes of the world, a most desirable suitor. Maria basked in her triumph.

What Sophie and I made of it, however, was something quite different. When she knew Maria's choice had fallen upon James Rushworth, Sophie expressed herself forthrightly. *"Mon dieu! C'est affreux! Qu'est-ce que je vais faire?"* At first I was quite in the dark as to what she meant, and then, when I understood her to refer to the most intimate connection of man and wife, I took it lightly, as an example of her Frenchness, for who of our nation would make so much of that aspect of marriage? Yet I am bound to say that later events proved Sophie's misgivings more than justified. She considered Maria excessively passionate, and, if her proposed husband were only half as incompetent as I described, nothing could be looked for but a most unhappy union, productive of every kind of misery, most of which would be visited upon her who waited on the dissatisfied partner. Instead of looking forward to Maria's marriage, Sophie now thoroughly dreaded it.

She first reasoned that she must instantly seek another situation, then, at my suggestion and later with my connivance, she resolved upon a different stratagem. It was not much more than the kind of game girls often play, although its intent was more precise: to secure the affections of Stephen Turnbull and thereby a marriage and independence. He was only the undercoachman, and she therefore above him, but why not, after all? She had often expressed to me her admiration of him, and if opposites in marriage are, as is so often said, happily complementary, there could be no better pairing than voluble, quick Sophie, with taciturn, slow Stephen. Several others had set their caps at him, but it was generally allowed he had loved no one but Kitty Huckle. I did not see why he should not be ripe for the plucking. Sophie was older than Stephen by some years, but she was neat and elegant, *une jolie laide*, with a complexion like enamel which compensated for her somewhat irregular features. I did not see how Stephen could fail to be flattered.

It was the most complete thing. Sophie developed a pain in her shoulder that spread to her neck, and inconvenienced her mistress so mightily that Maria herself suggested Stephen's services be called upon. Sophie acted the part vastly well, and then, of course, Stephen must touch her; when and where, how and what, became matters of such moment that in the space of a month the servants' hall was set on its ear by the wooing. Stephen was retiring where females were concerned (and indeed he must have been caught sooner if he were not), but Sophie's attentions set him on fire. Those who disapproved of Sophie clicked their tongues warningly over seductive French ways, but Stephen was not one to be swayed by their prejudice. The three hours he spent with Sophie in Maria's dressing room, when most of the family were gone out a-Rushworthing, were the very *coup de foudre*. Instead of letting the fire low, we heaped on the coals (that Sophie might do likewise) and left a half-bottle of Madeira wine that Maria was accustomed to take with water conveniently on the dressing table. The wine proved unnecessary in the event. The connection was made, Sophie bloomed and Stephen was happily committed. Neither of us could imagine why she had not resorted to such a ruse long before. They were to marry, that was sure, but the details were not easily decided, for Sophie's desire for independence Stephen would not agree to: Octavian, Master Tom, a hundred and one reasons he dreamed up. But the truth was he was disinclined to change, a stay-at-home for all his talents. He would not leave Mansfield and set up for himself

67

and she would not marry him unless he did. No garden house at Mansfield for her, be it ever so pretty. Despite this disagreement, however, they had sufficient pleasure in each other to believe that the difficulty would be overcome, and it was hard to doubt it; there were times when, bells or no bells, I was obliged to go hunting them up.

Maria's impending union with Mr. Rushworth thus benefited her maid in a way she never knew. Indeed, the connection Sophie had been pressed into establishing with Stephen promised more contentment than ever might be expected from that which had given rise to it.

The proposed engagement also had advantages for me. Mrs. N. was determined that Lady Bertram should pay a morning call on Mrs. Rushworth to set the seal of approval on the match and bent all her energies to that end. The weather was so bitterly cold that winter that the coaches were often delayed and the letter bags had to be taken on horseback. It was therefore a triumph of her persistence that she persuaded her sister, who rarely ventured beyond the church, and never in bad weather, to make the journey. Even then, it was generally allowed that Lady Bertram would never have consented had she known that two poor women, traveling as outside passengers on the Carlisle coach, had frozen to death only a few weeks before. But she only heard what was read to her by Fanny Price or Edmund, and Mrs. Norris so arranged it that the account of this tragedy, the sort of tale to which her ladyship, with many expressions of concern, customarily paid full attention, should be omitted in favor of topics less prejudicial to her scheme.

I was bidden to attend Lady B. in order that her own maid, Ellen Chapman, might take a half-holiday without inconveniencing her mistress, and a vastly complicated undertaking the whole outing proved to be. The amount of trouble would have been enough to see most people off to Italy. Once Lady Bertram was persuaded I was capable of attending properly to her needs, the carriage leather had to be polished, all drafts stopped, new carpet fitted, refreshments for the journey provided, a new coat made for Pug, and two stone bottles of enormous size purchased from Northampton so that her ladyship might not take cold. To cap it all, Ellen Chapman discovered at the last moment that moths had got into the lining of Lady B.'s best muff, which was not often in demand, and we had to turn it inside out and stitch in new merino, she and I together, to get it done in time. For an hour's stay, it was a prodigious amount of work, but since winter visits to Sotherton were not generally to be thought of, I was well satisfied and spent a pleasant half-hour with Mrs. Whitaker and my grandfather.

VI

The excitement attaching to such a momentous event as the engagement of Sir Thomas's elder daughter was of short duration. At first the affair proceeded with the requisite appearance of haste for, if neither of the two chief parties was greatly active, Mrs. N. had zeal enough for three. But Maria's initial enthusiasm for James Rushworth waned as the winter drew on. It could hardly be otherwise. Neither his blue eyes nor his fortune could for long disguise the fact that her lover's best lines were consumed in a half-hour's conversation, and his wooing was the result of a desire to do the proper thing rather than the improper. Indeed, during the evening of the very day on which the engagement received its official frank in a letter of consent from Sir Thomas, when Maria might have been expected to be re-animated by a pleasurable excitement, she was more than uncommonly snappish with James when he made his usual mistakes in a game of backgammon.

In such circumstances, it was not, therefore, unexpected, however much it was to be regretted, that in the summer, three months after the public announcement of her engagement to Mr. Rushworth, Maria Bertram fell well and truly in love with someone else. The gentleman in the case was Henry Crawford, a newcomer to the district, who had recently come to Mansfield with his sister Mary. They were staying at the Parsonage with their sister, Mrs.

Grant, whose husband had held the Mansfield living since the death of the Reverend Mr. Norris, and the lively manners and engaging disposition of both brother and sister speedily made inroads upon the sensibilities of the Bertram family. Henry Crawford was, indeed, adored on the instant not only by Maria but by Julia.

He was, there is no doubt, a most agreeable gentleman. His open, easy ways, animated conversation and diverse and amusing talents were of the sort to make his presence welcome in any company, and he quickly became the bellwether of the small flock. He could fashion rabbits out of handkerchiefs, recite Shakespeare or the latest plays by heart (with such feeling he seemed born an actor), make, mend and invent as circumstance required. He it was who suggested a match in hopscotch between ladies and gentlemen, and a picnic to visit Becket's well and sample the medicinal spring. On one occasion he spent two hours in the kitchen demonstrating the making of an orange sauce for roast duck which, he insisted, was the receipt of the Prince of Wales's own chef. Maria and Julia in borrowed aprons, faces shining from the heat, stirred the sauce and hung upon his every word. In short, he attached their affections in much the same way as (according to his menservants) he did those of most young women within his reach, playing Maria and Julia like hooked fish, with silken lines of glance and expression so delicate that they blew on the air like cobwebs, and always in both directions, so that which of them he preferred no one could make out. Julia thought him hers by right, but he was not readily appropriated. He might have favored either Maria or Julia or neither. The servants watched it all and were hugely diverted. "What price now your free rides to Sotherton?" Stephen Turnbull said to me; we did not give a pin for James Rushworth's chances now, engagement or not; Henry Crawford had quite put him into the shade. Henry was not as handsome as James, and quite opposite in appearance, being black and plain and not particularly tall, but his intelligence, spirit and wit made one glance from his dark eyes seem infinitely more desirable.

Henry's affairs with Maria and Julia were not the only amours under way. Edmund Bertram, old sobersides, was infatuated with Mary Crawford in scarcely more time than it had taken his sisters to fall for her brother. The house was in a turmoil. Sophie maintained that the whole silly business was the result of living in the country and having too little to do. However that may be, latent passions flared up like dry straw under glass, and all the daily episodes of an easy, uneventful life suddenly acquired a novel significance.

There were as many possible variations on the partnerships as you would find in the most elaborate figure of a country dance: James Rushworth loved Maria Bertram; Maria Bertram loved Henry Crawford; Julia Bertram loved Henry Crawford; no one loved James Rushworth, and Tom Bertram loved no one, or rather he made one of the dancers but with no great interest in the dance, to the disappointment of Mary Crawford. For she made, as it were, the opposite figure to her brother, with a possible choice of two brothers as he of two sisters, but Tom (whom as heir she favored) proved impervious to her attractions, preferring, as I was in a position to know, housemaids. I must not omit mention of little Mistress Mouse, Fanny Price. She permanently sat out the measure, faithfully loving her cousin Edmund, her jealousy evident only in her refusal to be as pleased with Mary Crawford as was everyone else.

I am not sure why it should have been that those below stairs were so much more quickly aware of what was afoot than those above. It seemed unnatural that such goings-on should pass without remark in the family; Fanny Price observed them but no one else did. Mrs. Norris, triumphant arranger of one engagement, saw only the possibility of another. Maria was to marry James Rushworth; now Julia must marry Henry Crawford. By the time Sir Thomas returned she would be able to take to herself credit for the betrothal of both his daughters. She was so carried away with the exceeding satisfactoriness of it all as to be quite blind to the changed direction of Maria's affections.

It was a battle royal between Maria and Julia over Henry. Sophie and I witnessed them spit at one another like cats, whereas they had always been, so far as easy circumstance and pleasant living had ever tried them, good friends. I am afraid the servants laid wagers on the outcome. The odds were on Maria, though Sophie and I bet low on Julia, hoping she would win but not really giving much for her chances. Maria was, according to us, behaving ill. We knew she cared not a fig for James, but many unsuitable matches are made and hobble along after a fashion. He was rich, she had made her choice, she was officially engaged and should have been restrained by some sense of propriety, even if she could not bring herself to be generous to her sister. If anything, the imminence of being Mrs. Rushworth seemed to spur her away from the post in the Crawford stakes.

Upon James, who might be thought the most deserving, I am afraid we did not spend much sympathy. He did not improve upon acquaintance; indeed, at close quarters, he was, in my opinion, worse than even the Sotherton villagers had allowed. Whinny Prinny we called him, for a little princeling he most truly was, with the unquenchable assurance of his ignorance and a most hideous high-pitched laugh, like the neighing of a horse. Maria and Henry might have been mousing beneath his very nose and he would never have noticed.

The necessity of the Crawfords' company was the occasion of much to-ing and fro-ing between Mansfield Parsonage and house, and what with the Crawfords and their relations, the parson and his wife, and James Rushworth tagging along, the place was livelier that summer than I had ever seen it. Invitations to dine were frequently exchanged and the dinner parties themselves became the cause of harmless rivalry between the cooks at the Parsonage and at the Park. Our Mrs. Alsop considered her at the Parsonage to be a bit above herself, and set out to meet the challenge. She was a prodigious good cook, but apt to be as irritable in the dressing of her meat as Julia could be in the dressing of her hair, and she was never more so than on these occasions, especially since the weather was hot and the kitchen like a Turkish bath, for all that Sir Thomas's range was a great improvement on its predecessor.

She excelled herself one evening: salmon with lobster sauce, lamb cutlets, a haunch of venison and, to finish, her incomparable strawberry iced pudding. After the ladies had retired to the drawing room, the gentlemen passed the port with greater frequency than usual, exchanging anecdotes which the footmen took great delight in relating to us, especially when they verged on the indecent. Tom Bertram was a four-bottle man when opportunity allowed, and Mr. Crawford could hold his own, but by the time the bottles were well into double figures, we knew they must be three sheets in the wind. The ladies meanwhile were cooling their heels, wild for company while pretending nothing was amiss.

By this time many of the servants were off duty. All but one of the footmen had gone down to the village to play skittles, Mrs. Alsop sat outside on a chair in the cool, overseeing the scouring of the cooking pots, and there was a clatter of dishes from the scullery where the plate was being cleaned. I sat alone in the kitchen with a final choice titbit from the feast: a portion of Mrs. Alsop's strawberry iced pudding. I was eating very slowly with an elegant long-handled silver spoon—it was far too delicious to eat fast, though almost melted—when John May, the remaining footman, came from the dining room.

"Oh, lord," he said. "It's that bloody animal. It's lost again. Lady B. is about to be in a taking. We've all to be up and looking for it."

Pug had gone missing, as she sometimes did. Usually the little beast was to be found stinking from a wallow in a newly turned dungheap. Nothing caused greater stir in the house, for, since the mislaying of her favorite was inclined to agitate Lady Bertram—on all other occasions the epitome of serenity—Mrs. Norris always made the most of the upset, swelling like a bullfrog with indignant temper: whoever was not responsible for losing the animal was to be held guilty of not finding it. Angry reproaches were heaped on every head. Tonight, as we well knew, Mrs. N. had additional cause for aggravation in her nieces' long and impatient wait for the gentlemen, and would undoubtedly find more when she discovered that some of the servants had gone a-skittling to the village without exactly having permission. I gobbled the remainder of my strawberry pudding and the kitchenmaids left their scouring. Only Mrs. Alsop stayed where she was. "If it gets into my kitchen," she said grimly, "I'll catch it all right, but then it'll catch something too, from the sole of my shoe, I promise you that. Spoiled little monster."

Searching for Pug was not, after all, an unpleasant task on so beautiful an evening. Dusk approached, but it was warm, and the day's legacy was a radiance of light and air that is one of the joys of high summer. I watched the swallows which nested in great numbers beneath the eaves of the stable as they swooped and chirred after insects. The air was perfumed by a white philadelphus which bloomed in the shrubbery and I hunted there first, without urgency I admit but, hearing voices raised in the distance, the necessity of finding the animal impressed itself upon me. I bethought me of the ice house.

The ice house, which lay beyond the dairy and likewise faced northeast, was cut into the side of a slope and had an inner and outer door to keep the atmosphere as cold as possible. Sir Thomas had introduced this modern convenience but, since even the best of these buildings is not decorative, had taken care to have it masked by the shrubbery. He had had some difficulty in persuading the servants of its usefulness. Mrs. Alsop, despite her infinite regard for the master, could not quite see the point of it, and had lapsed during his absence, so that you would often find a brace of pheasants hanging where they had always hung, in the cool pantry, though she did say that the ice house kept fish better than anything. At that time of the year, the stock of ice was depleted, and not only from the effects of a hot summer: in Sir Thomas's absence no one had remembered to give instructions to flood the lower fields near the river the previous winter, so the ice had been collected from the ponds and was of inferior quality.

When I reached the ice house, I stopped in the porch to light the lantern that hung there, for the ice house was, of course, window-less. Within, it was like a cave, lined with great slabs of stone that glistened damply in the shadowy light, airless and full of the odors of ripening meat and sour water, a perfect paradise for a dog, as Pug had discovered on one of her previous jaunts. Indeed, since, on one memorable occasion, a fox had got in, and we had had pack and riders milling around in the rhododendrons, Pug, not lacking doggy instincts despite being so pampered, had no doubt made use of the same entry, which gardeners and gamekeepers had sought in vain. Sheets and blocks of ice were packed in straw and stacked against the walls, and from them the water flowed in runnels to a drain in the center of the angled floor and kept up a constant soft purling. In the ceiling were large hooks from which hung carcasses of venison and lamb; the fish were kept in an old stone horse trough packed with ice and covered with a slab of slate. Slate made other shelves on which stood those items less subject to vermin, among which I saw the ice pail in which sat a lidded pewter basin containing what remained of Mrs. Alsop's strawberry pudding.

As the inner door swung to behind me, I listened for sounds of the dog's presence. The animal was, of course, perfectly aware that the ice house was out of bounds and I did not expect it to come rushing up wagging its stump because I called its name enticingly, but I did hear some scuffling which might have been it or some even less pleasant creature. I began to search the room from corner to corner, peering close where the light of the lantern fell, expecting something to run out squeaking. I continued to call, hearing, as I thought, amid the sound of running water, Pug's labored breathing. But if it were indeed she, she kept cunningly quiet, and I called repeatedly without success. I began to think the animal must be elsewhere when another noise intruded upon my senses. I straightened up and looked back toward the entrance from whence it came. Nothing was visible beyond the light of the lantern. "Hello?" I ventured.

There was no immediate reply but I felt the presence of someone else besides myself in the ice house and inquired again.

"Well," said Tom Bertram's voice at last, "it is Jane, so it is, indeed, by God. What do you do here?"

"The same as you I daresay."

"That cursed animal!"

"They rousted you out as well, did they?"

"Did *she*, you mean. That old bat, my aunt. 'Tis a pity that dog does not get lost for good. It ought to be fed to the hounds. Is it here?"

"I cannot be sure. I thought I heard it a while since."

"It is after the meat, of course. Two pair of eyes are better than one, at least." He walked over to me. "Thank heaven I need not go to the drawing room. What a bit of luck you are here. I'm infernally sick of Mary Crawford making eyes at me."

"You take this lantern. I shall go and fetch another."

He clasped my arm to prevent me. "Why so? We shall do very well with one."

"There!" Hearing a rustle in the straw behind me in a corner where a carcass dripped, I made the most of it. "That must be Pug." I turned and moved toward the sound. As I was about to bend down to investigate, Tom, who followed close behind, put his arms about my waist and his lips to my neck. "How long shall it take us to find Pug?"

I did not reply to that, but twisted out of his grasp. "You go that side, then she cannot escape. I shall watch this side."

Such attempts at distraction were futile. Tom took no notice, but came after me. "Let it be. There are more immediate matters than finding my mother's wretched lapdog."

"She would not wish to hear you say so."

"She never shall hear it. The drawing room is miles away."

"Let me go."

"Why are you in such a hurry?" He took the lantern from me and set it down.

"Let me go."

For answer he pressed me close. I smelled his sweat, the wine on his breath and the clean linen of his stock as he forced another kiss upon my mouth. By no means did I like Tom well enough to take pleasure in this sort of amorous game, and yet I knew that he was incapable of believing his attentions unwelcome. So far I had been yielding. Now, as I felt his hands moving over me, I pushed him as hard as I could. He was sufficiently taken by surprise to lose his balance momentarily, although he did not fall. Then a pretty game we had of it, playing catch-as-catch-can round the hanging carcasses, the stone chests and the horse trough. He grew more determined to catch me, and more angry as the minutes passed and he could not, the wine playing its part in working him up into a fine passion of righteous indignation and frustrated lust, until what had begun as a game was one no longer. He started and feinted and pursued me round the room, calling me a number of names which I shall not repeat and always contriving to keep me away from the door. I began to be frightened as I perceived he meant me real harm. I had so far evaded him, but fright is a sure way to lose advantage: keeping too close an eye on him, I paid not enough attention to the way I was going and ran smack into one of the carcasses hanging from the ceiling. I fell down in a heap and Tom threw himself on top of me. I fought him off as best I could, kicking and biting, but he was strong and determined. He threatened to inflict on me every indignity when I should be subdued, and I had begun to think that I had been unwise to resist, when we heard someone call: "Bertram? Are you in there?"

Tom stopped and listened. The question was repeated, and this time, realizing that Henry Crawford was come after him, Tom scrambled to his feet.

"Bertram?"

I sat up as Henry Crawford entered. I was sadly awry, my dress wet and indecently torn, bloodied with the meat, my cap off and my hair loose. He could see in an instant what was afoot. What does a gentleman do in such circumstances? Henry Crawford stepped forward with calm assurance and offered me his hand. "Why, Bertram, you certainly choose strange places for your lovemaking. It is ten times warmer outside and a deal more comfortable."

He helped me rise, taking in my bedraggled appearance which could not be disguised even in the fitful light of the lantern. Upon this sudden rescue and kind consideration, I burst into tears. Henry glanced at Tom. "You have made quite an evening's work of it."

"She's a teasing wagtail."

Henry frowned. "Who is she?"

"I can answer for myself," I said, my outburst over, trying to cover my bosom with what was left of my neckerchief and sniffing meanwhile, "though it is no thanks to Mr. Bertram that I have any breath left to speak with."

"You are not obliged to answer for anything," said Henry gently, offering me his handkerchief.

"You won that bout," said Tom to me, "but I claim a return."

"I think the game should be over for good. The match is over and your pretty maid unwilling."

"Do not be deceived," said Tom. "She is not so put upon as she would have you believe."

At that I lost my temper. "No, indeed. No maid is put upon by you. You think yourself so desirable that you may take a flyer with any girl you choose and she will up and thank you for it." I choked and spluttered and shed a few more tears. "Well, I do not choose and I never shall. It is a hateful liberty you assume."

"Well," said Henry, "I see you are in no need of a champion."

"Only listen to her!" Tom said. "You shall not speak to me like that. No servant speaks to me so. You had better remember your place."

"If you forget yours, what need have I to remember mine?"

Henry intervened. "Talking of places, let us make shift to get out of this one. It is infernally damp and cold. Save your quarrel. Your maid must put herself to rights and you need some straightening. We have to show ourselves, Bertram, or they'll be sending the beaters out after us."

At that moment the appalling Pug chose to appear from wherever she had secreted herself. She made not a sound, but stood there, far enough away to be out of reach, her mouth full of something that had once been alive and now rotted. It was I who espied her, and I pointed wordlessly. Greater concerns were instantly consumed in lesser ones. Tom and Henry both dived for the little beast, but it danced neatly out of the way, its mouth too full for it to yap, thank heaven, but devilment for the game in every mincing step.

I was myself in no state for the pursuit, and took the opportunity of quitting the ice house as quickly as I could while Tom and Henry were thus occupied, not unrelieved to be removed from the center of attention in my painfully improper state of undress, and concerned chiefly to gain the shelter of the Clock attic without being further observed. There, I burst into tears afresh, the shameful ordeal to which Tom had subjected me, the indignity of my appearance, anger with myself for not soon enough perceiving his intent, nor contriving escape, quite overcoming my senses. Tom judged women fit to be snared like rabbits. The threat of violence and ravishment as I lay upon the slimy floor of the ice house with him on top of me was palpable. I had known a moment of cold terror. He who will inflict that upon another, man or woman, servant or peer, is truly to be despised.

VII

I doubt not that I should have gone for Tom like a spitfire at our next encounter, but that he took off almost immediately for Bansted Down and the races. This was to be Octavian's first important trial. Stephen had already gone ahead with another groom, riding Octavian to the meet slowly (and carrying with him a pocketful of wagers on behalf of the servants). Now Tom, with another pair of grooms, followed, their mounts three lesser nags that were also to be tried. What would arise at Epsom was a matter of no little debate in the household, you may believe, but in truth the other race, that going on at Mansfield beneath our very noses, occupied our interest even more. The two Bertram sisters were running neck and neck in the Crawford stakes, both still full of stamina and spirit, although Sophie and I were among those hard ridden as a result. Standards of dress were exacting as never before; it was no small matter to appear handsomer than one's sister and get a nose in front. I had the worst of it, I fancy, since Julia was always more uncertain. As I was stitching some velvet leaves round the hem of a gown she had insisted on having altered at the last minute, she rapped me hard over the head with her fan for being slow. It was no lashing and I should have been grateful she did not carry a riding crop, but I had been laboring all day in the heat to finish the gown and was mortified.

Julia was not above contrition, however. I fancy that was why, when a visit to Sotherton was proposed, she said that I might have the day to myself, might also go to Sotherton if I chose. The expedition blew up as the consequence of a sudden interest in landscaping. It was Henry, of course, who started it, and where he led the others followed, including old Whinny Prinny, who took a principal role for once by deciding that landscaping was of all others the very thing to improve Sotherton. His anxiety in the matter provided the perfect excuse for an outing, especially since the weather continued fine, and everyone declared themselves delighted with the notion. Maria, indeed, might have been supposed to be a little hesitant, for the occasion could not but remind Henry Crawford forcibly of her situation as James Rushworth's intended bride, but she was not; perhaps she thought that the favorable impression Sotherton must make would give her a consequence in Henry's eyes that an acquaintance with the owner of it alone could never bestow. It set a price upon her higher than Henry could afford. James Rushworth had £12,000 a year, Henry but £4,000. It might encourage the man she loved to see whether he could propose for a bargain. Mrs. Norris, understanding nothing of such delicate calculations, delighted in the opportunity of accompanying the young people and congratulating herself further on her promotion of the Bertram-Rushworth match as she contemplated afresh the glories of Sotherton.

My intention was to ride horseback ahead of the party. When so few of the family would be left to notice, it was not at all impossible to obtain the use of a horse for the day, although it was necessary to be a little circumspect. Soon before dawn, therefore, on the day planned for the expedition, I left for Sotherton on Fanny Price's quiet little mare. I was glad to ride in the cool of the morning, the shadows long on the ground, the dew rising in a mist as the sun reached it, and all nature brisk about its business. I was riding sidesaddle, as became a lady's maid. It is an elegant but awkward seat, since one can neither mount readily without assistance, nor, worse, apply pressure to the right side of the horse, whereby the use of a whip, which I have always thoroughly detested, becomes unavoidable. However, that I could do it at all was a measure of my advancement in the world and I was in high good humor with myself. (I do not ride sidesaddle now.) Tittupping along, I reached the village before eight o'clock, and it was still only ten when I made my way up to Sotherton Court, well before the hour when Henry Crawford's barouche was due to leave Mansfield bearing the visitors; I should have plenty of time to stable the mare and pay my respects to Mrs. Whitaker. All was bustle and preparation for the occasion. The horses, their hoofs carefully wrapped in woolen mufflers, were still drawing the great rollers across the lawn, and James himself was to be seen issuing orders for a final raking of the gravel drive before the principal entrance. No stone should be left unturned in his efforts to have Sotherton appear at its most neat and pleasant, his instinct to be jealous of Henry Crawford, deep-buried though it was, showing itself in this small vanity.

From the window of her apartments, Mrs. Whitaker and I observed the arrival of the Mansfield party which included, besides those who might have been expected to make up its number, little Fanny Price, all a-tremor with anticipation since she never customarily participated in these entertainments. Maria had never looked handsomer, nor, indeed, appeared fonder of James, as she moved graciously up the stone steps, slightly in advance of the others as befitted her interesting situation, and greeted her betrothed affectionately. The almostness of being mistress of such a fine estate was evidently much to her taste, however much the finality of marriage with James Rushworth was not. Certainly her position afforded her sufficient pleasure to compensate for a disappointment at the beginning of the journey, when Julia rather than herself had secured the most desirable seat in the barouche, that on the box next to Henry Crawford. Julia's satisfaction was writ clearly upon her countenance and even Mrs. Norris appeared agreeable, from a distance and in that sanguine state induced by a warm summer's day with the prospect of nothing but pleasure ahead. It looked a most happy family party and Mrs. Whitaker was delighted. It fulfilled all she could have wished for me of belonging to an orderly and harmonious establishment, in the contemplation of which I had no desire to disillusion her.

Grandfather Pearce was not so content; indeed he was positively vexed. He began with the heat and its effect upon the bowling green, the state of whose turf he displayed to me with great irritation. Wearing woolen oversocks, we considered the brown patches that disfigured the surface on which we stood. "Will you look at that now! The buckets of water I've had the boys bring up, and all to no good! Something's amiss, and it's not just drought. There's always something spoils it. I wish I had done with gardening, that I do. All my labor gone for nought. What is the point of it, eh? Nothing's done right. Unless I stand and count, you may be sure they cheat on the number of buckets. It wasn't like that in my day, let me tell you. There's a few things have changed and none for the better." My grandfather did not often lose his temper, but once something started brewing in his mind it fermented till he was fit to burst. As I had devised, the turf of the bowling green was not the principal cause of his dissatisfaction; it was the proposed landscaping. "Have you heard Mr. James's latest scheme? He wants to have the grand avenue cut down. The grand avenue! Did you ever hear the like? What would his father have said? I'll wager the old master's turning in his grave. Cut down the oaks, he says, open up the prospect, he says. I'd like to cut him down and open up his prospects. There'd be an empty peapod and no mistake. The trouble with that young gentleman is that he's got straw between the ears. No sense of what's proper. Do you know how long those oaks have stood? Two hundred years. Good Queen Bess were a lass when they were saplings. Two hundred years, and now some whippersnapper wants to chop 'em down! I shouldn't mind so much but he's got all these others egging him on. 'Smith at Compton does this,' he tells me, and 'Crawford at Everingham does that.' How his grand old father came to sire that paper-skull I shall never know. He minces outside to me and starts laying down the law with a lot of long words. All gammon, that's what it is. Have you heard him? Utility, he says, beauty, he says, picturesqueness! I tell you, my lass, he doesn't know the meaning of half of 'em. I've known this place since before he was thought of. And that was a pity, that was." He paused for a moment, feeling better for venting his anger. "Mind you, he's good-natured enough. He gets in such a stew with these enthusiasms. If you go along with them for a week or two, they blow away. But now there's this fellow Crawford on the doorstep. I don't know how to get him to see sense."

As it fell out, my grandfather had a chance of speaking with the arch-promoter of James's schemes there and then. It had generally been supposed that the visitors, having partaken of an elegant lunch, would be occupied for at least an hour upon a tour of the house, in which they were to be conducted by Mrs. Rushworth, but instead the party emerged on the lawn in no time at all. (They could not have viewed one quarter of what Mrs. Rushworth was prepared to show.) Most of them were soon occupied in admiring the pheasants Mrs. Whitaker was feeding, but Henry Crawford strolled across to join us on the bowling green. "Good afternoon, Hartwell. I am glad to see you looking so trim and neat, so altogether recovered"—he glanced at my grandfather and changed what he was about to say—"from this sweltering heat." He paused. "I scarcely expected to see you here." I explained the connection, and he greeted my grandfather civilly with some compliments on the condition of the park and gardens. I cannot say these were met with Grandfather Pearce's best graciousness, but they were followed by some knowledgeable remarks on the rising of roots with underwatering as a possible reason for the brown patches, and then the exact naming of a dahlia which bloomed abundantly in the planted area between the lawn and bowling green.

It is curious, is it not, how a chance remark, spoken with genuine feeling, can effect such a difference? The dahlia was a magnificent red flower, of the variety Countess of Liverpool, I remember. My grandfather, from being disposed to dislike Henry Crawford on sight, was quite won over, for a dahlia then was still unusual, and this was a specimen obtained with difficulty and nurtured with loving care, to which few visitors could put a name although many exclaimed over its beauty. Such friendly relations were established, indeed, that a tuber was promised for Mr. Crawford's own garden, and my grandfather sufficiently at ease to raise the subject of his most immediate concern.

"Shall you be looking at the avenue Mr. Rushworth proposes to cut down, sir?"

"Cut down! I think he does not propose to go as far as that."

"As any gentleman who knows his garden will appreciate, those are grand old trees. To my mind, you couldn't do better than leave them as they are."

"You lobby on behalf of the oaks, eh, Mr. Pearce? The final

word is not mine, but I shall certainly advise carefully. For my part, I am a great lover of trees. In Norfolk, where my own estate is, the forest trees do not generally grow well. The oaks are mere scrub. So a massive oak has at once my respect and affection. Believe me, I should not lightly prescribe the removal of a single one."

"Mr. Rushworth thinks you about to do so," I interposed.

"It is no more than his enthusiasm for the new scheme."

"Then you will restrain him, will you not?"

"Must I be held to that? I do not think I can altogether promise."

"It's all very well," said my grandfather, "but you can't tell me it's right to chop down those trees."

"You must consider the replanting, Mr. Pearce, the appearance in years to come."

"How can you suppose anything should improve upon those trees?" I said. "What can be more satisfying than to watch them leaf in spring and turn color in the autumn?"

"Nothing. In that we are at one. But here there are many trees. If the luxuriant growth of one obscures the prospect, surely nothing is lost and much is gained by removing it to reveal the view."

"I should never think a distant prospect compensation for a barren foreground."

"It is a debate of some interest," said Henry warmly. "The foreground would not, of course, be barren. In any case, it is extremely rare for a whole avenue to be felled; the most common practice is for the line to be broken. One thing has to be weighed against another. The genius of the place is of prime importance."

Grandfather snorted. "You can take an oak down in a day and not put it back for fifty years."

"We shall not be hasty. Of that I assure you. I promise you we shall not be hasty. But we have to plant for the future. If you did not till the soil in the autumn, Mr. Pearce, how should you sow the seed next spring? We improve upon the scene so that it will be more beautiful a hundred years hence."

"It is even more important not to be swayed by passing fashions, then," I said. "How can you be sure that what you propose will be considered an improvement by posterity?"

"Well, now," he said teasingly, "try as we may, no one can be sure of *that*. I have no doubt posterity will try to improve upon us." Seeing that my grandfather no longer paid close attention he spoke more quietly to me alone. "I am sorry beyond measure for the other evening's misadventure. You vanished before I could convey it to you. I did not like to see you disappear without apology."

"Apology! I think that was unlikely. You were kind and I am most grateful. I know what the world thinks of such things."

"That the female is generally to blame, do you mean? I did not think it. Bertram behaved exceedingly ill and I told him so."

"I do not imagine he cared much for that."

"No. I fear we are not such friends as we were."

"He is not to be changed."

"Perhaps he will grow old and good like the rest of us."

"He is vain, empty and coldblooded; altogether without principle. Such things do not change."

"You are bitter, indeed. Has he done worse to you?"

The hesitant inflection of the "No" I gave him for reply provoked Henry to inquire, "What, then?"

"He was cruel and heartless to the maid whose place I took."

"How is that?"

"There was a child, while Tom was in Antigua."

"A child!"

My indignation and bitterness came forth in a rush. "Tom cares not a fig. His own child, its mother are nothing to him. Mrs. Norris sent Kitty miles away, to a village near Ely. Ely! How should anyone get to Ely! Kitty's own mother is sick and without means. Tom does nothing, no more does his aunt. Out of sight, out of mind."

"Ely, do you say? Perhaps something yet may be done. My own estate is not far from Ely."

I told him what little I knew. As I finished, he interrupted, raising his voice and returning to the former subject. "Have no fear for your oaks, Mr. Pearce." By which I concluded, although I had my back to the remainder of the Mansfield party, that we were no longer to be alone. "We are Solomons in judgment, are we not, Rushworth?" Henry called cheerily to the two who approached. Mr. Rushworth and Maria joined us, the latter, I thought, well satisfied to discover that Mr. Crawford's conversation was so exactly concerned with the matter in hand that she could have no doubt where his interests lay. Like many an insecure lover, she was prey to passing suspicion, as I knew from the merest glance she gave me.

The small groups into which the party was now divided began to make their way across to the terrace, which adjoined the bowling green and overlooked on the other side a small and pretty wood of about two acres. On such a day, with the sun at its height, the cool shade beckoned invitingly, and after a while, by common consent, almost everyone turned off through the gate and down the steps into the trees. Julia, to her disappointment and annoyance, was the only one of the young people to remain. She was obliged not only to keep the tedious Mrs. Rushworth company since her aunt was still engaged with Mrs. Whitaker, but also to witness her sister, full of animation and high spirits, disappearing into the infinitely desirable wilderness in the company of Henry Crawford and James Rushworth.

Grandfather Pearce and I moved off toward the greenhouses where, to our surprise, some little while later we were interrupted by the reappearance of old Whinny Prinny, all in a lather.

"I need the key, Pearce, the key," he said with exasperation. "Miss Bertram wishes to go out into the park and the gate across the ha-ha is locked. I was on the point of taking the key with me. I shall do so next time, I assure you. There is a great deal to do on these occasions, and one cannot be expected to remember such trifling details. I have been thinking that all this is most inconvenient. The gate should have been left unlocked and then one would not have to be forever thinking about keys. This hurrying about is a devilish thing."

He went himself to fetch the vital key from within an outhouse and puffed off again. Imagine our concern, therefore, when my grandfather discovered, some minutes later, on looking at the board upon which the key customarily hung, that James had taken the wrong key. There was excuse for his mistake, since the correct key was off its hook (for which my grandfather blamed himself), but each key was carefully labeled nonetheless. We shook our heads at his slow wits before I took after him while my grandfather hunted up a spare key.

James did not take the news well. "I am quite out of breath as it is," he said. "I do not see why I should run about any more. I am distinctly hot and the sauce on the cutlet we had for lunch rises in my gullet. I do believe I shall be quite ill if I am obliged to run further."

As a result, he decided, complicating a simple matter as only he was capable, that I should run ahead to the gate and tell Miss Bertram and Mr. Crawford that the key was on its way while he returned more slowly to fetch the correct one. I did as I was bid, but to save time took a short cut through the trees, through gaps in the shrubs and hedges that I knew unerringly from childhood, across a fallen beech that lay half-buried in weeds and made a bridge across the ha-ha, to emerge in the park, not far from the gate. To my surprise, who should I see in the distance but Maria and Henry, the locked gate having proved no great obstacle after all, and they making such good speed across the ground that, far from waiting for poor Mr. Rushworth, it seemed they made haste to get away from him. I ran after them but they were some way ahead of me and too much engrossed in each other's company to observe my approach, and before I could reach them they were lost to sight among the saplings of a small thicket that topped a rise. I followed them, slowing my pace as the ground inclined upward. They were behaving most improperly, and I began to think that abandoning James was only the start of it. Nothing could have prepared me, however, for the sight that met my eyes when, having at last achieved the top of the rise and scanned the opposite slope, where I judged them to be, I glanced below me into a grassy dell. Maria Bertram and Henry Crawford were close bound in the most passionate embrace.

In view of what had already passed between them, it was not, I suppose, entirely to be wondered at. But, however wide and straight the path to the cliff edge, it is a different matter to jump. I own I had not guessed the extent of Maria's passionate nature as Sophie undoubtedly had. I did not turn my eyes away as decorous behavior demanded, nor did I feel obliged to interrupt them to deliver my message (which was, in any case, superfluous). They moved against one another like tinder and flint, and the kindling took fire quickly. There was a flurry of petticoats and limbs indistinguishable and they slid to the ground. Maria's favorite gown, a spotted cambric with a low neck, thin and fine for the weather, was no obstacle to her activities. It was around her waist in no time, and her white silk stockings picking up green from the grass.

On a hot day, it was lovemaking fit to be envied. I began to wonder what I should say to Whinny Prinny. It was no surprise that he was long in coming: not finding Maria and Henry where he expected would confuse him entirely. I myself was caught in the dilemma which all too often afflicts servants: possessed of knowledge I should prefer to be without, and wondering what would make life least unpleasant, truth, lies or evasions. Maria and Henry might not be obliged to say anything of substance to Mr. Rushworth, but *I* should. Maria still lay on the ground and Henry sat upon the grass beside her, his hands clasped round his knees. She seemed in the mood for more playful lovemaking, but I thought I discerned in him some thoughts of time and discovery. I decided upon discretion, and quietly retraced my steps through the shrubs and bracken of the thicket and down the slope. Then I set out for the gate across the ha-ha. Before I could reach it, however, I met Julia, out of breath and out of countenance.

"What are you doing here, Hartwell? Great heavens, you seem midmost to everything this afternoon. First you are talking with Mr. Crawford on the bowling green, for all the world like a lady, and now I find you here. You are having a fine time, indeed. I only wish I were. Have you seen my sister and Mr. Crawford?"

Here at once the dilemma posed itself acutely. I had as yet given no thought to Julia in all this. If I told her where they were, the whole simmering caldron of love, jealousy and passion which presently animated Mansfield Park would at once be overturned. Like most in a similar situation I preferred to avoid the consequences of being the one responsible for the upset. I temporized. "I was come to find them by Mr. Rushworth's instruction, when we were searching for the key, but they did not wait."

"Was there ever such a fuss about a key? There has been nothing but disappointments today. Wherever I go it is my fortune to be last. Even Fanny is having more amusement. I have been stuck for an hour with that old fussock, Mrs. Rushworth, until I could scream with boredom, and when I at last escape, everyone is disappeared.

Are they playing hide-and-seek or what? It is too bad, indeed it is."

"They were supposed to be at the gate, waiting for the key."

"I know that well enough," said Julia, gloomily. "A curse upon the key! It is easy enough to climb around the gate if you choose to do so, as I found out. *They* got round easily enough once Mr. Rushworth was out of the way."

"Perhaps they made for the knoll," I suggested, pointing to one at a little distance and in the opposite direction from that which I had climbed. "That is where the best views of the avenue are to be had."

With this Julia had to be content, and we set off in our two directions, Whinny Prinny being next to appear, wiping his face with a handkerchief, the key in his possession at last.

"This is a very ill-managed business, Hartwell. First of all I have the wrong key, then Pearce cannot find the right key and I am kept waiting for fully a quarter hour. Now, upon my word, I am more out of breath than ever and all about the finding of this key. And it is quite useless, for Miss Bertram has climbed around the gate. It is most vexing."

He was so fretful that I touched his arm momentarily to comfort him, thinking all the while, I admit, what a ninny he was. "Why, Mr. Rushworth, I declare you have had a hard time of it. Such things are sent to try us, I do believe."

He was somewhat mollified, flattered as even a squire may be by the sympathy of a pretty maid. "It was to be such a splendid afternoon, but everything has gone wrong. How am I to decide what to do if Crawford cannot even be found to give me his opinion? I am beginning to think this fuss about landscaping is not worth a candle. I should not be surprised to find that everything is best left as it is."

"Who could say you were wrong? Sotherton is your home. A feeling for it is bred into you. I know that, for I grew up here and love it. Your own opinion must be more valuable than any."

"What a sensible girl you are! I may very well do nothing. Yes, indeed, that will surprise them all."

Having thus dealt with James, I returned to the house by my own short cut, without further encounters, although I saw at a distance Edmund Bertram and Mary Crawford, sitting together beneath the trees of the avenue, another loving couple, if more decorously behaved. Midsummer madness had so taken hold that I began to wonder whom I should find gazing lovingly into Fanny Price's eyes, but she was the only one I saw nothing of at all. Passion was abroad but poor Fanny might as well have been at home.

At the house, however, somewhat to my relief, things continued with a reassuring regularity and tedium. Mrs. Norris was still with my grandfather and Mrs. Whitaker, in a discussion of aches and pains, fevers and frets, which she interrupted only to greet me with a most unaccustomed warmth, assumed entirely for their benefit. "Why, here she is! I have been telling your grandfather and Mrs. Whitaker how admirably you are suited to Mansfield. My niece sings her praises constantly. She bore so patiently with Ellis for years, and Ellis was only a housemaid brought in to help with the children. She is good for nothing else, I am afraid. But Sir Thomas is the kindest master and never will turn anyone away. There cannot be too much care in the selection of a servant. I never allow myself to be content with the first girl I see, but then I am not one to rest when there is a task to be done.

"Lord bless me, but it is hot!" She fanned herself. "I doctored your cousin's rheumatics all last winter but, as I told him, this warm weather is just the thing. If Wilcox would only pay attention to his diet, I could cure him. These rheumatics are the result of a bad diet, don't doubt it. Barley gruel and whey, as I have told him a hundred times. But there, I swear the cook slips him a mutton chop when I am not looking and all my care is gone for naught. I insisted that he rest today and benefit from the sun."

"My grandson Timothy, now, Jane's half brother that is, the heat does him no good," said my grandfather. "Three weeks he's been poorly, and I swear it's on account of this weather. Things breed in the heat. I've never seen such a plague of greenfly as we've had this year."

"What are his symptoms?" Mrs. Norris inquired.

"It seemed as though he'd just taken cold, but then he was in pain. In a sweat and sick and then up again. We've hardly known what to do with him."

"That is an ague. I know the signs. Depend upon it, that is an ague. I have treated more people for ague than I can count. I shall send him the groundsel bag, Mr. Pearce. I had the receipt years ago from a good old woman in Chapel Brampton. She insisted upon giving it to me after I had done some little kindness for her son. It is an excellent good remedy. You must tie the bag around so that he wears it on the pit of his stomach, not too high up, and be sure that the side I mark is next to his skin. The groundsel bag has never failed yet. He should have plenty of exercise and a light diet with plenty to drink. A teaspoon of hartshorn in water would not do any harm in the meanwhile. I shall send the groundsel bag."

There she was, advocating slops and roots again, as she always did. For my part, I believe in port and mutton chops. But then, we all advise according to our bias. There was an immediate economy in eating less that profoundly satisfied Mrs. N. My sympathies were with little Timothy. What I had observed of Mrs. Norris's remedies had not persuaded me of their efficacy. Mr. Wilcox put up with her nostrums like a lamb, but what relief he had for his rheumatics was provided by Stephen Turnbull. One evening I swear I saw the old coachman pouring Mrs. Norris's bottle of "ammoniated gum," as he called it gloomily, over the stones in a corner of the stable yard.

As you may devise, Mrs. N.'s opinion of the day at Sotherton was that it had all been exceedingly satisfactory. While her niece, in a frenzy of desire, had been giving herself to Henry Crawford in the park, her aunt, the chaperone, had spent her time talking of cream cheeses and pheasants, gratifying her inquisitive and acquisitive instincts in the company of my grandfather and Mrs. Whitaker, with whom she curried favor by some judicious praise of me. They, knowing nothing of what a two-faced puppy's mamma she was, were entirely deceived. Mrs. Norris thereby obtained for herself not only one of Mrs. W.'s famous cream cheeses, but also the receipt (which was closely guarded), and some pheasants' eggs to hatch. My grandfather, moreover, conducted her around his greenhouses, an honor by no means regularly accorded the visitor, and gave her a beautiful little heath, one of his own hybrids. There was, I considered, a measure of justice in that the plant later died.

One might have supposed that the outing to Sotherton had produced all its surprises, but the journey home provided one more, as I later discovered. To my astonishment, in view of what I had witnessed earlier in the day, when the moment came for choosing who should occupy the position on the barouche box beside him on the return, Henry spoke once more for Julia's company. Maria, who thought she had won the game for certain, was mortified to be thus ignored, particularly since she had, as you are aware, played her highest trump. She was downcast as Julia was jubilant, up and down, the pair of them, like a seesaw, with a nasty jolt at every rise and fall. Julia savored her triumph, and Maria, who might otherwise have been inclined to intimate to her sister why she thought she had had the better part of Henry Crawford at Sotherton, felt sufficient doubt to keep mum, while being obliged to hear Julia's delighted account of her tête-à-tête with Henry.

"I do think the present fashion for riding on the barouche box is sensible," said Julia. "The air is so much better, and there is no harm to be taken on a warm evening. I took the reins, you know. Mr. Crawford insisted I should, but he held his hands over mine to be sure that I did it correctly." She laughed. "La, what a sly fox he is! He is up to everything. He was so close to me! I never thought I should like a small, dark man, but he has charmed me into it. You should hear his stories. He told me such a quaint tale about two dogs in love. He said it was told him by his Irish groom. I swear I didn't know whether to stop him or not."

"Dogs in love?" said Maria scornfully. "I never heard of such a thing. I fear you must have been a trifle bored."

"By no means, I assure you. Mr. Crawford is such a clever raconteur, you know. It was the most diverting thing. Of course it is near a two-hour journey, and one must say something to pass the time."

"I can think of more interesting subjects," said Maria.

"Ah, if you had heard the story, you would not say so. *She* was an elegant high-blooded setter bitch; *he* was an ugly little cur. The gentleman who owned the bitch was so vexed with the attentions of the amorous cur that he drew one of his pistols and shot it dead. But from that day forward, his setter pined. She wouldn't eat, she wouldn't sleep, she lost her nose. And—which is strangest of all —when she was later coupled to another fine setter at great trouble and expense, what should her litter be but the very picture and

93

color of the cur, and not setters at all. What do you think of that?"

"I think her master could not have been watching her very closely."

"Is it not a copy of true devotion? Such as any lady might be proud to show a gentleman, and any gentleman to receive?"

In such fond exchanges did the two sisters pass the week following the visit to Sotherton.

VIII

Henry Crawford knew how to be well in the way and well out of it. It would have been no easy thing, even for him, to remain at Mansfield and keep Maria at bay after the incident in the dell; her high-strung temper would have forced him at last either to a declaration or a bitter division. But the opening of the shooting season provided him with the perfect opportunity and excuse to leave the district, the two weeks of absence on his own estate serving to cool Maria's heat and set things back much where they had formerly been.

As to what I thought of Henry's behavior, it was neither more nor less than I had always thought. He had taken what was given freely and I did not blame him in the least. Indeed, a gentleman who would refuse a gift so pressingly offered might well be suspected of lacking necessary spirit; moreover, I admired the bold adroitness with which he contrived not to be bound by it. Like many such gifts, this one carried an obligation, and Maria was not easily thwarted. It is often assumed that the advantages in making a match are altogether with the male, *his* right to speak and *her* obligation to be silent, giving the gentleman all the power of choice. Yet there are subtle pressures that operate wordlessly, and a clever woman may so manipulate matters that the man in the case feels obliged to do the expected thing, even though it may not be very much to his taste. Henry was not one. By his clever ruse of setting

Julia beside him on the barouche box on the return from Sotherton he had quite outwitted Maria.

Henry thus quit Mansfield with calm assurance, having handled his love affairs, it was generally allowed, as the best coachmen handle their teams, keeping to his time without unduly distressing his horses, whose endurance he knew to a hairbreadth. Indeed, no more than two days after he left, Maria and Julia were moping after him, each with a wonderful conviction that he loved her and her alone. As for me, I had, as it were, seen him go down a hill steep as Sandcroft without a chain on the wheel. It was no mean feat that he could now coolly draw on his gloves and, looking immaculate as ever, tip his hat to us as he took off for Everingham. There were not a few who would have reveled in my account of how I had seen him make the going down Sandcroft hill, but I told no one except Sophie, and she was the soul of discretion.

The shooting season was also the cause of Tom Bertram's return to Mansfield, announced first in a letter to the gamekeeper which accompanied a Newfoundland retriever bitch, of the real St. John's breed and black as soot. The keeper, who was to have charge of training Juno, whom Tom had won in a bet, said she was a most promising animal in the field. In the field she may have been, but not in the house, which is where she was the rest of the time, as Tom's favorite. She slobbered over the floor and lay in doorways so that we all tripped over her. We became rather fond of the silly, affectionate young beast, the worst inconvenience being that Lady Bertram's Pug was instantly jealous of her.

Tom Bertram made a triumphant return with a retinue of friends and servants. Octavian had won two races at Bansted Down, and they came in the full glory of victory. Tom had, indeed, already celebrated in roaring style during a visit to Weymouth immediately following the races, which must have divested him of a considerable portion of his winnings, but by thus delaying he contrived to match his arrival to that of his horse. He and Octavian together made a grand progress from the village; the great horse, a man at the bridle on either side his head, decked out in a garland of flowers, a royal blanket across his back in blue and red with golden tassels and his name embroidered upon it in gold thread. Tom himself wore flowers and a paper crown, stuck round with the tail feathers of a cock pheasant. Half the village followed, wearing cockades and bent on tomfoolery and horseplay, and bringing up the rear (so as not to upset the horse) was a hand organ, its noise augmented by two fiddles and a trumpet. Punch and cake were provided in the kitchen yard, and there was dancing to the improvised band. John May turned seven of his famous somersaults.

As you may believe, what had been won in the way of wagers (and it amounted to near two hundred guineas among all the servants) inclined everyone to drink Octavian's health three times over, and the celebrations later moved to the village, along with many participants from Mansfield Park. The alehouse was patronized as if it were Whitsuntide, and there was more dancing, and singlestick, for which Tom awarded a handsome purse. Edmund Bertram, thinking the proceedings a trifle boisterous, went on horseback to oversee the revels and remonstrate with his brother, but on the way he encountered a crowd, who, being in a jolly temper and bold by virtue of the beer they had consumed, linked arms to form a line across the road, and prevent his passing until he should dismount and kiss the prettiest girl. It was a forfeit he paid with considerable embarrassment, and it appeared to convince him that whatever passed in the village it was too late to stop it, because he afterward turned tail and rode for home.

Stephen Turnbull had seemed, unlike everyone else, in sober spirits upon his return. Considering the horse's success and the heavy lining to his pockets, this was unexpected, but we were used to seeing him solemn, and it was not until Sophie had had him to herself that we discovered the truth of the matter: it was not Stephen who had ridden Octavian to victory. While Tom stopped in London on his way to the races, he had taken a fancy to someone he had met by chance in a fashionable coffeehouse in Fetter Lane, and when Stephen had been taken with a low fever a day or two before the race, this in-between gentleman, Alexander Belzoni by name, had temporarily taken his place. But Belzoni did so well with the horse in the trials that on the day of the race Tom put him up instead of Stephen, on the grounds that Stephen was ten pounds heavier. It was a sad blow to Stephen, and no better for Tom's reasoning that since Belzoni had won the first race on Octavian, he had better ride him in the second, which he did, and won again.

Alexander Belzoni had found so much favor with Tom, indeed,

that we now had him permanently at Mansfield, where, being as ill-provided with income as most of Tom's associates, he was hired as some kind of footman. This did not sit well with most of us, you may believe. Stephen regarded him with cordial loathing, as was only to be expected, and the irregularity of his appointment, the imprecise nature of his origins and his general assumption of superiority irked most others, although we grudgingly admitted that he must know something of horses in order to have managed Octavian. He was of Italian extraction, his father being a native of Mantua, and since he had a fine tenor voice, black eyes and played the violin, we had no reason to disbelieve him, although everything else about him was open to doubt. He spoke like a gentleman and shot like one too, as we knew when he bagged fifteen brace the first morning Tom took him out. He also told us he could put ten shots on the ace of diamonds at thirty feet with a dueling pistol, but that smacked of high living we knew nothing of. He referred grandly to his connections, and was quick to inform us that he had come to Mansfield by way of Paris and London. This may have been mere pretense, but he was a·footloose fellow, the sort who never stays long in one place. He did not enlighten us as to the reasons for his straitened circumstances, but there were some shrewd and not always complimentary guesses. He had contrived to acquire a string of credentials from the Duke of This and the Earl of That, one or two of which he flourished for Mrs. N.'s benefit. She being customarily inclined to indulge her nephew, and Belzoni no stranger to the art of flattery, his hiring met with little opposition.

Tom was, you may believe, supremely indifferent to Stephen's mortification, and made no attempt to make amends, quite unmindful of the obligation he owed him for loyalty, as well as more practical benefits he had frequently derived from his superior judgment and advice. Stephen was quite displaced. Belzoni was the one; Belzoni was to be consulted on all matters; nothing could be done without Belzoni, whose facility for talk and grand schemes was of a sort to appeal instantly to Tom, whereas Stephen's silent and measured ways often irritated him.

To swell the number of Tom's cronies, the Honorable John Yates arrived but two days after Octavian and his master. The latest of Tom's intimate friends, Mr. Yates had commended himself by the abandon with which he had entered into the ten days of riotous celebrations in Weymouth and had swiftly taken up Tom's subsequent invitation to visit Mansfield. He was the younger son of a lord, with a tolerable independence and thus tolerably impecunious, as were most of Tom's friends, and no less susceptible to having his head turned by notions of glory and an infinite income. Mr. Yates, Tom and Belzoni yarned for hours in the stable. The pleasurable contemplation of what Octavian should do next scarcely seemed to include Stephen, even though the great horse was once more almost entirely in the undercoachman's charge. Such wealth and success were proposed as would have demanded the ownership of ten Octavians. Alexander Belzoni was to ride him here, there and everywhere; John Yates was to renew his fortunes by some judicious wagering; Tom himself was to have a stable equal to the Duke of Beaufort's, his own hounds and a meet to outdo Melton. It was all very fine, and came to nothing, though rather more quickly than could have been foreseen.

The dogs began it, curiously enough (Pug having, when I consider it, a role in the action far greater than that of her mistress, Lady Bertram). Tom was out shooting regularly, and we would often see him and his companions, of whom Belzoni not infrequently made one, coming back around breakfast time after an early start, guns bent over their arms, bags bulging, and black Juno prancing around in puppyish enthusiasm like a bear. In the first of a series of misfortunes, Fanny Price happened to be in the vicinity one morning, exercising Pug.

Juno had a soft disposition, but at the sight of Lady Bertram's Pug the fur rose along her back and she set up a bark that must have outdone Cerberus. She rushed forward to the attack. Pug stood her ground stoutly and snapped viciously. Then the little beast bounced like a ball, attempting to sink its teeth into Juno's neck. Pug caught hair only, but the great black dog backed off, surprised. Juno was deterred only for a moment, however. Deciding she was not to be put upon, she launched herself upon Pug again, more eager for a game than for a contest, and quite misjudging the temper of her opponent. Pug was not in a playful mood; she was for battle, and proceeded to exercise her teeth upon Juno in earnest. Juno squealed, rolled over, got up, ran away, was chased, and found herself obliged to be warlike if she was to survive. Tom, by no means displeased that his soft-tempered beast should learn to defend herself, roared with laughter. Fanny Price, anticipating such damage to Lady Bertram's darling as was not to be thought of, clapped her hands to her face in dismay and ran toward the pair, who were so inextricably wound up together that it was well nigh impossible to effect a separation. Only Belzoni had presence of mind enough to go into the fray. There was the second misfortune: Juno was without a collar. Being unable to hold her, he went instead after Pug, but the little snapper retreated to the nearest cover. What should the direction of her retreat be but the stables in which Octavian was kept? And there was the third mischance: the door was open.

When Tom saw that, he stopped laughing, but he had recognized the danger too late. Pug rushed into the stable, Juno after her, Belzoni close behind, Tom and the other rag, tag and bobtail who had come out to gape at the scene following on. The commotion thenceforward was indescribable. Pug ran under the gate into Octavian's stall and stood there, snapping and barking while Juno, too large to follow, threw herself at the obstacle separating her from her mortal enemy again and again. What Octavian made of all this, you may devise. He instantly began to whinny and rear and roll his eyes in fright.

This might not have been of such great consequence had Octavian been in a regular stall, but he was not. He was in a "loose box," such as are still uncommon. It was one of Stephen's notions, he considering it more healthful for a horse than the regular stall; indeed, until this incident the horse appeared to have taken no harm from the innovation.

Now, however, Octavian began to throw himself about the stall in a panic, kicking and rearing with increasing violence. How Pug escaped a mangling it was hard to fathom, but, although she seemed to pay no attention to the horse, yapping at Juno in a frenzy, she nevertheless contrived to keep out of the way of its murderous hoofs. Juno, wild at Pug's inaccessibility, threw herself at the planks which made up the gate to the box, equally unmindful of the crazed horse, which rocketed around the stall from side to side as though it recognized no such restraint as a wall. The gate rattled on its hinges and threatened to give way under the sustained battering. Juno's deep-throated bark mixed with Pug's yapping and the horse's terrified whinny. The noise was deafening.

Alexander Belzoni at last discovered a leather strap with a buckle, part of an old harness which hung on the tack-room door. Tom threw himself upon Juno's hindquarters and, grabbing her round the belly, restrained her as best he could while Alexander contrived to get the strap around her neck and pull it through the buckle. Then, the dog half-throttled, with Mr. Yates shoving from behind and Belzoni pulling from in front, between them they contrived at last to get her through the stable door and slam it shut behind them. The abominable Pug was still within the loose box, but now that Juno was out of sight she seemed to take fright at her own temerity and cowered under Octavian's manger, the volume of her barks beginning to subside.

Octavian was, however, in a worse state than ever, the continuing presence of the small dog seeming only to increase his madness. Tom and Alexander Belzoni, leaving Mr. Yates outside holding Juno, had instantly rushed back into the stable, their prime concern being to quieten the horse. Fanny Price, who had followed them in and shut the door, stood quietly by it, her countenance a mirror of fright and anxiety. In the minute they took to leave and re-enter the stable, Octavian lowered himself to the floor of his box. Whether by intent or accident, whether by some desire to roll on the wretched little dog to which he had taken such a dislike, or simply because one of his uncontrolled movements finally forced him into it, was not to be known, but there he lay, at first thrashing back and forth, but then, as Alexander climbed upon the partition with a halter, ceasing to move altogether, his hoofs against the outside wall of the stable, himself seemingly wedged firm between one wall and another, lying still, breathing quietly, at peace it seemed, but immovable.

The horse must, as they both knew, be got upon its feet without delay. Pug still cowered beneath the manger. "Get that cursed animal out of here," Tom shouted at Fanny, "or I'll shoot it!" But Pug would not come. Octavian's plight was such that Alexander decided to ignore the dog and began to climb down into the stall for the purpose of affixing a halter, but as he did so Pug bit his ankle. Alexander retreated, cursing, Tom rushed outside, and the little beast, with some sixth sense of what Tom intended, decided to make a run for it, followed in quick succession by Fanny.

Then the business of raising the horse to its feet began in earnest. Alexander once more climbed down into the box, minimizing the chance of being kicked by avoiding the gate, entry through which would have meant that he must climb across Octavian's hindquarters. Indeed, climbing in at all, considering the horse's unpredictable temper, required some courage and, even as he descended, Octavian lashed out with his near hind leg from his prostrate position. Alexander contrived to put on the halter, however, but no matter what tricks he and Tom employed, they could by no means rouse Octavian. They pulled on his head, they moved his legs to free him as far as they could and then they tried a quick shout or kick to shock him into setting up his forefeet and making the effort. But Octavian, he who would start at his own shadow, for once responded not at all. Tom at last, in foolhardy desperation, entered the gate, took hold of Octavian's tail and pulled, while Alexander, on the ground at the beast's head, pushed hard on the halter from in front. For a moment it looked as if they would succeed, but as Octavian scrambled to get a purchase on the floor with his right forefoot, he slipped and went down again, lashing out with his hind legs in agitated fear as he did so and catching Tom a blow in the chest which knocked him backward out of the door. Tom was winded, but he did not appear to have any ribs broken and, after swallowing a glass of brandy, he and Alexander continued their efforts. They even tried to turn Octavian over, by means of a rope Alexander attached to the two legs, one fore and one hind, which lay against the ground. Alexander narrowly missed being kicked during this exercise, and after that they repeated the simpler, less dangerous stratagems, once, twice, ten times. At the end of two hours they were both sick, angry and irritable. Alexander let go of the halter, and Octavian laid back his head upon the straw and sighed with weary resignation. At the horse's uttering of that deep breath Tom Bertram suddenly lost his temper.

Tom turned everyone in the place inside out, beginning with Alexander for dropping the halter rope. He cursed the one careless enough to leave the stable door open (the culprit was never identified), then the carpenter's son, little Dick Jackson, who had been responsible for the placing of the planks on the gate; he blamed the gamekeeper for not seeing that Juno's collar was on, and he berated Fanny Price for not sufficiently minding her aunt's pet. It was the completest exhibition of a master's high hand and uncontrolled temper, and Stephen Turnbull arrived just as Tom had warmed to his task, to catch the brunt of it: "Where the devil have you been? Look what has happened! That horse is ruined, quite ruined. He will be good for nothing. I daresay he will have to be shot. I'd rather shoot you and that's the truth. That horse is worth more to me than any useless servant. You lazy blackguard! I'll give you a shirt full of sore bones for this! Where were you when you were needed? Feet up in front of the fire dosing some maid with your potions, I've no doubt."

Stephen flushed to the roots of his hair under Tom's unwarranted attack, but he said only: "Get the wall down."

The loose box being something of an experiment, the wall dividing it from the remainder of the stable was not the stone-built solid structure it would otherwise have been. The sense of Stephen's suggestion was instantly plain. With mauls, picks, hammers, axes, anything that lay to hand, several of them went at the wall, Tom among them, while Stephen took his place at the horse's head, Tom acknowledging by his silence the undercoachman's right to be there. It did not seem likely that Octavian would take further fright from the noise, although that was considerable. He lay quietly, his flanks beginning to show sweat, his breathing shallow and quick. His head lay toward the inner wall, to the advantage of those who knocked it down, since they were not obliged to mind his hoofs, but even so it took the better part of an hour for the wall to be leveled and the rubble cleared. Then the attempt to get the horse to its feet began again. First Stephen tried the halter and, when that did not work, two blankets were folded and slid beneath Octavian's chest and belly. Then, with ropes affixed to the blankets making a sort of sling, four men were employed to drag the eleven hundredweight of great bay horse away from the wall. By now, nearly four hours after Octavian had first lain down, the lapse of time gave less reason to hope that he would rise, but the efforts were repeated.

No further words were exchanged between Tom and Stephen, nor between either of them and Belzoni, except such as were needed for the work at hand. They were covered with dust, sweating, worn and dispirited. The day drew on and much of the household held its breath over the fate of Octavian, although to those upstairs it was really no more than another sick horse in the stable. Mrs. N. came bustling out twice to remind her nephew of the ball which was to take place that very evening at Mansfield. It was no grand affair, to be sure, since it had been got up only that morning, on the heels of the discovery that Belzoni could play the violin, but it had been promoted with zeal by Tom himself and, however much he now regretted it, the raising of five couple obliged him to attend, as it also obliged the Honorable John Yates and Alexander Belzoni.

We could all have done without the distraction of that silly entertainment, I assure you, except perhaps Fanny Price for, small though it was, this was her first ball. She had not returned to the stable after catching Pug, no doubt because what went on in the stables was quite outside her customary realm of activity, and the nervous excitement of such a disaster provoked a headache. It was unlikely to have been because of a lengthy toilette for the ball: apart from being too meek for such vanity, she was ill-provided with finery. For the rest of us, at least, the ball was a penance. Every last thing that could go wrong did so. The cook had a cold and was thus somewhat put about by the requirements for supper, even though it was not a large gathering. She determined on making apple snow, a favorite dish to be done in a hurry since it looked handsome and the ingredients were usually to hand. In the absence of the kitchen maid (from whom Mrs. Alsop had caught the cold), Amelia Ellis was set to whip the egg whites. Amelia, as a result of her poor sight, misread the stiffness and added the apple pulp too soon. It was a sorry mess, the whites running to liquid and the apple pulp, to which she had omitted to add lemon juice, turning brown beneath her gaze. Mrs. Alsop fairly screamed at Amelia that she couldn't so much as turn away to blow her nose without something going wrong, and the housekeeper sailed in like a three-master a few minutes later. Mrs. Alsop took umbrage at the interference, and there was the whole kitchen in a hugmug, Amelia in tears and everyone about to be at each other's throats, until the timely arrival of two carriages brought us to our senses. We were all out of sorts over the horse, and what with turning the apple snow into a pie, and running in and out to the stables with hot cloths, gruel and port, we did not know whether we should be in pattens in the drawing room or slippers in the stable.

To no one was the ball a greater source of vexation than Tom. As you may devise, looming larger than Tom's fondness for the animal was the threat to that which was to be his way out of debt and into wealth. With such weighty matters on his mind, he cursed the necessity of dancing and chitchat and, dismissing nicer habits, washed himself under the pump in the yard and changed his clothes in the space of fifteen minutes. Only his mother thought to remark upon his wet hair when he appeared in the drawing room, Mrs. Norris averting the trouble which did not threaten by instantly praising Tom's devotion to his stable, and reminding the company of how he never picked the wings off flies when he was little, so tender was his heart.

As musicmaker-in-chief, Alexander Belzoni was obliged to be more particular in his appearance (indeed, he absented himself from the stable long enough to incur Tom's disapproval). His black hair, lathered in macassar oil, shone like a raven's wing, and he sported a blue silk stock above his dove-colored coat. He looked handsomer than ever, and one or two of the young ladies who were partnered by the duller gentlemen of the neighborhood fell prey to his charms. He played the violin so capably indeed that, after a more than usually lively *écossaise*, he was requested to perform some piece of his own choice, while the ladies rested and fanned themselves. He chose with such admirable taste that the audience demanded an encore, and then he sang, to a piano accompaniment offered by Helena Palethorpe, a haunting, melancholy love song from his own Italian countryside. Miss Palethorpe looked, we were told, as though she would have eloped with him there and then.

During Tom and Alexander's absence at the ball, later in the evening, not long before the lamps were lit for what would plainly be an all-night vigil, Stephen contrived to get the great horse to its feet. I was there at the time, and saw him do it, entirely on his own, with no use of strength at all. He had been murmuring to the animal, noises of encouragement which clearly soothed it, blowing down its nose as I had seen him do before, his remarkable affinity with animalkind never more plainly to be observed. He pulled on the halter, the same device the three of them had tried so many times before, but this time Octavian planted his forefeet firm, pushed his forelegs up and, wonder of wonders, his hind legs followed after. Sweating, trembling, head dropped low, he was sick, but he stood; he most certainly stood. There were not a few of us in the stable at the time and a ripple of delight ran round the company. Octavian had done what was required, and he had done it for Stephen. The horse's unpredictable temper was matched by the greatness of its heart. Stephen's delight was to be heard in his quiet words of praise. He rubbed the horse's neck with his hand, and then laid his cheek against its soft hide. Tom was instantly summoned from the drawing room, as he had instructed, while, with further soft words of encouragement, Stephen began to walk Octavian slowly in circles.

Tom was cock-a-hoop. "What price his chances now, Turnbull?" he inquired cheerfully.

Stephen was grim. "He's no better, not at all. He has a terrible colic and has passed nothing, not even water, since I have been with him."

Tom changed on the instant, his disappointment that everything could not yet be said to be progressing as well as it should clearly writ in the irritable gloom that overcast his features.

It was to be a long night. The smell of leather, wax, straw, the smell of the good beasts themselves comes back to me as I think of it. The lanterns were lit, and some extra ones brought, so that the glow reached to the far end of the long stable. It was a handsome building, with a pitched roof, two rows of stalls and a floor angling to a drain which ran down the center. Brass railings ran along the top of the wooden partitions and, like the brass plate engraved with the occupant's name which was attached to every stall, gleamed softly in the light. Octavian's royal blanket had been nailed up on the wall; it hung there as a sad reminder of his recent glory. Mr. Wilcox sat upon his chair, carried out from the servants' hall, and smoked his pipe. Each time before refilling it he checked the other horses (for they all grew restive, sensing Octavian's pain), giving particular attention to the four matched roans, Flicker, Firebrand, Flame and Reveller, who drew the carriage and were his pride and joy. His presence as much as his occasional word was encouragement to Stephen, who continued to walk the horse through the duration of the ball and long afterward. There were many who had no sleep that night: Tom, Alexander and a goodly complement of servants, including Sophie, whose anxiety was for Stephen as well as the horse. Weary though he was, he refused to give the task of walking Octavian to anyone else. In the dark hours before dawn, however, he handed the halter rope to Tom, that he might go outside to relieve himself. He might have chosen not to do so; none there was so proper as to have been shocked. Tom might have refused to take the rope but, after a moment's uncharacteristic hesitation, he accepted it. In the time that Stephen was gone, Octavian, whose recurrent desire to lie down and roll Stephen had so far successfully thwarted, pulled again. Alexander rushed forward, and he and Tom contrived to keep the animal upright until Stephen was back inside, half-buttoned. It was a desperate moment, and none was unaffected. Mr. Wilcox, who had dozed off, stood up and dropped his pipe, scattering ashes over the floor, which he was then obliged to stamp upon; Sophie wrung her hands in misery. For all their efforts, Octavian once more went down. We all knew what that meant. Mr. Wilcox sat down again, trumpeted noisily into his handkerchief, and then began another slow check along the stalls.

During the next few moments no one spoke. Stephen was occupied in running his hands over the animal's flanks, toward which Octavian continually turned his head, attempting to reach that part of his body which racked him with pain; Alexander looked on; Tom, unable to stand still, began to pace the floor. When Stephen stood up, he said nothing, but continued to gaze down at the horse, his stance one of weary resignation.

"Well?" said Tom, his impatience palpable. "Well?"

Stephen at last looked up. "There's nothing more to be done."

The finality of the statement was more than Tom could stomach. "What do you mean? Of course there's more to be done! We can bleed him. We can feed him. He hasn't eaten for twelve hours. I don't expect you to give up yet, damn it, Turnbull. That horse means everything to me."

"We must bleed him," Alexander reiterated.

"It will do no good," said Stephen quietly. "It is a waste of time."

"I know what you think about bleeding," said Tom, "but just because you do not approve of it, that's no reason not to try. Many better men than you would have bled him hours ago."

"It will simply weaken him and hasten his end."

"His end!" Now that the word was mentioned, Tom's temper took off. "I'm not letting that horse die in front of my eyes without some effort to save him. We are not finished yet."

"I'll go and get the leeches," said Belzoni.

"You'll put no leeches on him while I am here to stop it," said Stephen calmly.

"What the devil!" said Tom. "You upstart son of a bitch! I'll show you who's master here. Get the leeches!"

"He's dying," repeated Stephen. "Neither leeches nor nothing can save him."

"If you had not left him, he would not have gone down."

"You took him."

"You left that horse for some female propriety about piddling in company. It's your damned fault he's down, and now you'll do nothing about it."

"You bring those leeches over here and I'll put them on you," Stephen warned Alexander, who was returned with the jar.

"By God," said Alexander in reply, "I'll not take that from you. You think no one but you knows anything about horses. Well, I do, and so does your master. That's two of us who think you a crackbrain."

"Belzoni rode this horse to victory, I might remind you," said Tom. "You didn't much care for that. You thought this horse your own property, didn't you? To be managed by you alone. Even now you think it."

Stephen's color had risen again. "If you put leeches to this horse, that will make an end of it."

"It is a remedy everyone of sense believes in but you. You are a contrary wretch who does nothing by the book."

"That animal should have been fed. That's the truth of it," said Alexander Belzoni. "How can he retain his strength otherwise? You should have used the drenching horn."

"What is the use of forcing food in one end when nothing comes out the other?"

"I say what goes here," said Tom. "And I say you're a pigheaded, stubborn fool."

Slow as ever to catch fire, Stephen did so at last. "If you had taken more care, Octavian would not be where he is now, you and that bloody great bear of a dog!"

"Get out!" said Tom. "Get out!"

Stephen paused. "It's the last you'll see of me."

"Out! Out! Do you think I care for your threats! If you think so highly of yourself, you may try elsewhere. We can do without you at Mansfield."

Stephen looked at Octavian with anguished tenderness. He could not refrain from bending down and bidding the great beast farewell. Then he stood irresolute for a moment, but Tom did not speak. With a determined step and no backward glance, Stephen left. Sophie ran after him.

As for Octavian, it was as Stephen had predicted. Tom and Alexander could not save him. The great horse died one hour after sunrise.

The undercoachman quit Mansfield not much later, to the dismay of most of the servants, particularly Mr. Wilcox, who expressed his concern by a constant invocation of the absent master of the house: "If only Sir Thomas was here!" and "What would Sir Thomas say?" accompanied by a most sorrowful shake of the head. Sorrow, indeed, was everyone's response to Stephen's departure, even Sophie's, for although she had herself urged him to do exactly what he now did, the manner of it was much to be regretted, and Stephen himself in a state of angry agitation that was not to be controlled. He who never lost his temper had now done so in earnest. Tom Bertram was no gentleman; he would go to London, by God, he would; Sturmey would help him to it; he would show them all. He would write to Sophie; she was to come with him; they should be married once he had established himself; the promises were warm but Stephen unable to speak them anything but coldly. Sophie was left to reflect upon the possibility that the very thing she had most urged upon him, which had come about with such disastrous suddenness, might be that which would irrevocably divide them.

109

IX

When I offered some small help caring for the plants in the conservatory at Mansfield, it was for my own pleasure. What I knew of gardening from my gandfather, and what the head gardener knew of him recommended me, and I spent an hour or two there once a week, watering and snipping and dusting leaves. Sotherton had a greenhouse and a pinery, and we grew fine oranges, but there was no conservatory. I loved the conservatory at Mansfield. It was designed to please the eye, and its plants had been chosen for beauty and scent rather than rarity. Stone steps and balustrades led down to a stone-flagged walk with several nooks and unexpected vistas, which revealed palm trees, or a tall heliotrope with great purple flowers, a vine, or spiny cactus with flowers of unusual brilliancy. The damp heat and strange plants gave to the place a characteristic smell quite unlike that of a garden in the cool outdoors. In the center of the conservatory was a small ornamental fountain, made of marble and lined with blue and yellow majolica tile, surmounted by a nymph with a pitcher from which the water trickled by degrees into the bowl beneath. I could hear the pleasant sound as I stood at dusk on a small stepladder, reaching to test with my fingers the dampness of a hanging basket of fern. It was there that Henry Crawford found me on the first evening of his return from Norfolk, which occurred promptly after two weeks. He swung a string net in which he carried a small, round, cloth-wrapped bundle.

"I am in constant danger carrying this," he said. "Quick, take it, or I shall be asked what it is I have stepped in as I crossed the pasture."

I had descended the stepladder by this time and put down my watering can. He threw me the bundle, and I caught and sniffed it. The smell was indeed exceedingly strong. "What is it?"

"That is a Stilton cheese. You must be very circumspect or I shall have all the maids asking for presents, but you may give it to the cook and recommend it as an aid to the digestion. I assure you it is delicious. This one is made on my own estate, to the original receipt, no less." I sniffed the bundle again and must have looked doubtful. "That is the best cheese in the world. You may rely upon it."

I laughed. "I shall do my best to enjoy it."

"I shall expect an opinion when you have tried it, remember. Do not disappoint me."

"And if I do not like it?"

"There is not the least chance. I have complete faith in your good judgment."

There was a slight pause. He showed no sign of leaving. I bent down to pick up the stepladder, but he was quicker. "Let me."

"Will they not miss you in the drawing room?"

"I shall be there soon enough."

"But they may come looking for you, surely?"

"They think me gone to the Parsonage to fetch my sister's music. So I am, but I saw you through the glass and sprinted both ways, so they do not expect me yet. What do you here? I thought you to be a lady's maid."

"So I am, indeed. But I pleaded to water the plants, as I always love to do with my grandfather. I do it most carefully, under supervision, I assure you."

Henry looked about him. "The sound of water, and a most delicious perfume; I did not realize what a pleasant place it is."

"You smell the gardenia. Three blooms today."

"Do I indeed? Where is that?"

When he had admired the bushy shrub, he continued: "I must tell you: I went to look for Kitty Huckle."

"Kitty Huckle? So you did not forget? You went to find Kitty? I never thought—"

"Why should you? No one thinks a gentleman concerns himself with such matters, but I would not have you believe all gentlemen unprincipled."

"I am greatly obliged to you."

"It was no trouble. Ely lies on my path. What I have to tell is some news and no news, I fear. Kitty has quit Willishall for London."

"For London?" I was startled.

"I saw the child," Henry continued. "She remains in the village, and is well cared for. The Baillies have none of their own and treat Betsey kindly. She is a winsome little thing. She patted the hunter's nose without the least fear, but turned away for shyness when told to bid me good day."

"Why should Kitty leave?" I was puzzled.

"She needed money."

"But Mrs. Norris was to send money. There was to be an allowance."

"Then it must have ceased. It was certainly for lack of money that Kitty left. Farmers do not make mistakes about such things."

"But what should she do in London? How should her mother find her? What a sad muddle it is."

"There is money to be had in London. Kitty will fend for herself better than if the child were with her."

"You heard nothing of her mother?" Henry shook his head. "That good old woman. She had no one left but Kitty. What is to be done?"

"Nothing more, I fear, at present. I asked that Baillie let me know as soon as ever he has news. Kitty is bound to write, for the child's sake."

"I am grateful to you for taking such trouble."

Henry shrugged. "I do it as much for you as for her. General philanthropy is not to my taste. It is a sad business; one may be swallowed up in the great maw of London easily enough. But you may rest assured Baillie will be true to his word. If he hears, so shall we. I promised him an invitation to Holkham and an introduction to Coke as inducement."

"Was he kind, do you think?"

"Baillie? I doubt Kitty starved, not if the child is anything to go by. Oh no, Baillie is a taciturn fellow, shrewd but not unkind. I enjoyed talking with him. Once we started to debate the merits of Southdown sheep over Merino and the coombs of wheat he has taken off his fields this harvest, he came on wonderfully and we were fast friends."

"You begin to sound like a farmer yourself."

"Does that surprise you?"

"I never imagined you to enjoy ruralizing."

"I hope not. I am at pains to hide it. It does not sit too well with most of my acquaintance. If I began to talk of Coke's clippings in certain company, that would make an end of the conversation. They would think I meant *horses*, perhaps, but *sheep*, never."

"You amaze me. I thought you enjoyed the fashionable world."

"So I do. I should not wish to wear a smock all the days of my life. But it is the perfect counterpoise to the existence of an idle young man which I enjoy the rest of my time."

"I fear we have misjudged you."

"Others may; I hope *you* will not."

"I shall speak up for you."

"Do not, I beg you. I prefer to keep my eccentricities to myself. If I were to be known as a farmer I should be rusticated for vulgarity from polite company. What do you suppose Mansfield would think if I began upon a speech about good husbandry as the foundation of comfort and wealth for all?"

"You would be suspected of leveling tendencies and other heretical notions."

"Just so, and I am far too comfortable for any such thing. Yet I admit to you that I do advocate revolution."

"You tease me. Mr. Crawford a Jacobin!"

"Oh, every word is true, upon my honor. Only my revolution shall be agrarian rather than political. We have our meetings, and lay our plans. The revolution across the water shall be nothing to ours."

"I believe you mean to frighten me."

He laid his hand upon my arm to assure me how impossible that was. "Revolution! Ah, revolution! Why are we so afraid of it? Why, if a gentleman fell in love with a lady's maid, some might call that revolution. What do you think?"

I moved away. "That is no revolution: it happens every day.

Such gentlemen are foolish, and the maids even more so."

"You have no taste for it?"

"How should I, with Kitty for my example?"

He was quiet for a moment. "I cannot fault you there."

I regretted my sharpness. "Tell me about your agrarian revolution. That is much more unusual."

He answered thoughtfully. "So it is, more's the pity. What we propose is no more than common sense and benefit to all, but there are always those too thick-headed to see it."

"What is it you propose?" I asked curiously.

"Nothing less than a change in method. Nothing more. No bloodshed, no guillotine, no barbarism, but a steady rise in the yields of the harvests, a lowering of the price of wheat, an end to poverty and starvation."

"It cannot be done."

"But it can. The poor starve, the rich blame God and the weather. Yet if the landlords were not so thoroughly ignorant of their proper business, they would see that improvements are possible and make efforts to change. It will be slow not sudden change, but it is the only way. Give us another twenty years and no one shall starve. There will be food to fill every belly."

"How?"

"Do not start me on that, or I shall not finish before the sun goes down. Besides, it is all dull stuff, about Swedish turnips and mangel-wurzels and cropping and the like. You could not possibly be interested."

"My grandfather is a gardener."

"So he is, indeed. I forget myself. I am not in company now, where the necessaries of life are not fit subjects for discussion. Well then, it is nothing more than the application of science to farming, quite simple tricks once you have thought of them: digging deep so that rich soil is turned up instead of flints and sand; breeding choice animals to improve stock. Mr. Coke of Holkham is the prime mover in these schemes. He treats his tenants with great generosity, and rewards them with long leases and gentlemen's residences for their improvements instead of raising the rents. I tell you, with the best tenants clamoring for a lease on his estate, it behooves the rest of us to look to our practices. But that is no hardship. Coke has increased his revenues tenfold and shown us how to do so too."

"You make it seem as if no man is the loser."

"It is so, I assure you. It is a pleasure to see the difference it makes to the farmers. They learn a new pride in themselves. I would have them all like Baillie. He offers me a glass of port wine. I see a clock on his mantelpiece and a set of handsome dishes on his dresser. He himself tells me he keeps several milch cows— something his father would not have dreamed of."

"How convincingly you speak!"

"Speaking is nothing to the pleasure of observing the proof of our success. Norfolk shall soon be called the granary of England. I have seen a rich harvest where before there was nothing but a meager sheep walk and a patch or two of rye and oats. There is no greater satisfaction. A wind always blows across the fields in Norfolk, and at harvest time the corn rustles so that the grain rattles in the ears. There is not a weed in sight, neither cornflower, cockle nor poppy and the wheat grows so close it looks like gold. It *is* gold, indeed, for it is better than money in the pocket."

"I hope that it may soon reach the pockets of the poor, then. Food has never been so dear."

"Those golden fields are the key. I look over them and feel cheered."

"I wonder you can stay away from Everingham as long as you do."

"Ah, you suspect me. I sometimes suspect myself. I should not call myself a true enthusiast. I enjoy the common pleasures; too many of them perhaps. For all its joys a country life can grow tedious."

"That is why you hasten back from Norfolk to Northampton-shire?"

"I shall not deny the attractions of Mansfield. One in particular."

"Only *one?*" I inquired teasingly.

He laughed. "Here, as everywhere, the servants observe more than their masters and mistresses ever do."

"Do not be too sure. They are slow, perhaps, but even Mr. Rushworth will come to it in time."

"Mr. Rushworth? What has Mr. Rushworth to do with this? I suspect that I have been under scrutiny."

"You take large risks."

"Caution is not one of my virtues. What fun would there be in playing the game if there were no risk?"

"It is a game then?"

"I beg leave not to answer that. With all the insight I attribute to you, I shall allow you the privilege of discovering that for yorself."

"I should not have asked."

"No, you should not. My own two sisters do not quite dare, and you certainly should not. What difference could it make? You are not, I trust, concerned that I may be the occasion of a little heartache to the Misses Bertram? They have confidence enough to survive that, I assure you."

"I am surprised you do not regard them more fondly."

He looked at me closely. "Why should I do so?"

"I thought Maria at least had captured your affections."

"What is this? What have you heard? I see you have heard something."

"Not heard. Seen."

"Seen, then. Out with it."

"Mr. Rushworth sent me after you that day at Sotherton. I saw you in the dell with Maria."

Henry laughed, not a whit out of countenance. "There! My remarks come home to roost. My sins are discovered! Did you watch us then? I hope our little amorous play did not disappoint you."

"It was not my intent to spy."

"But what a chance! To catch your mistress in such a dereliction! What maid could ask for more! We seem to become involved in one another's little escapades willy-nilly, Jane. There is some fate at work. I find I am not sorry for it."

"Then you should be. I must counsel you strongly against a third flirtation in the same house. Two in the drawing room, one in the conservatory. However shall you keep us all apart? It demands too much, even of your talents."

"I never refuse a challenge. But you are right. I am afraid you are beginning to know me too well for my own comfort. It would be next to impossible to deceive you."

"I should not forgive you for flirting with two others at the same time."

"Not even though I should prefer you to either of them?"

"So you might tell me, but I should be as foolish as they are if I believed you."

"But they would not know about *you*, whereas you know about *them*. Does that not give you the advantage?"

"Only to be better armed against disappointment."

"I should not disappoint you."

He kissed me then, and a very sweet, slow kiss it was.

"Only imagine what Maria and Julia would do if they were to discover themselves challenged for your affection by a maid!"

Henry laughed. "That would be the greatest joke in the world!"

"For you, perhaps, but not for me."

He took one of my hands between his own. "I would not willingly harm you, Jane."

I began very much to wish to believe him.

X

Of all the events I have so far recorded, none was of such import to me or to the Bertram family as that which came next. Although it was got up simply as a diversion for the family, to while away a few dull, wet autumn days, it assumed, both then and later, a significance for most of its participants, including myself, which at its chance beginning no one could ever have imagined. I speak, naturally, of the play.

It all began with the Honorable John Yates, the particular friend whom Tom had met at Weymouth after the races. John Yates had thin, rather curly hair, which stood out from his head so that you could see the scalp beneath, and it receded from his brow, which was pale and prominent, giving him the appearance of intelligence. This was misleading: he was only a very middling sort of man, even in stature, although the high spirits and loudness with which he conducted himself suggested otherwise. Having recently participated in private theatricals at the seat of the Right Honorable Lord Ravenshaw in Cornwall, he was passionate in praise of such a diversion, and the idea took hold, first with Tom, then with the family, and gradually with the servants, until at last everyone was theater-wild, if not by inclination, then because every spare moment was directed toward the theater, the acting, the lighting, the scenery, the costumes, and every last small detail that concerned the putting on of a play.

First of all was the setting-up of a theater. The billiard room answered the case perfectly, since it adjoined Sir Thomas's room, which might, without more changes than a redisposition of the furniture to free the communicating door, be adapted into a green room. The mahogany billiard table had to be moved out, great heavy thing that it was (and Alexander Belzoni took a chip out of it, too, when he caught it on the door jamb. The housekeeper went to work with walnut juice and beeswax, but it had spoiled the carving and she was never so sympathetic to the play after that). Then in no time at all Christopher Jackson, Sir Thomas's carpenter, was building a platform and hammering away at some flats, and Mrs. Norris, who was as enthusiastic for the project as her two nieces could wish, had sent away to Northampton for a roll of green baize to make a curtain. The whole house was in thrall to the play.

There were those who doubted the wisdom of this enterprise, among them Edmund Bertram, Fanny Price, the butler, the house-keeper and Mr. Wilcox. Their conclusions, though separately arrived at, were much the same: that Sir Thomas would take strong exception to private theatricals at Mansfield. Edmund voiced his disapproval, but it was as a straw before the flood, overruled by his brother and sisters in a moment. Tom, Maria and Julia, Henry Crawford and his sister, were all vastly pleased with the notion, and by number and temper they were bound to win the day. Edmund, indeed, could hardly be unwilling to be argued down, since his views put him at odds with Mary Crawford, the woman he loved. At last, despite his misgivings, he even persuaded himself that he was obliged to undertake a part to avoid the further impropriety—as he saw it—of importing an outsider for the purpose (Charles Maddox of Stoke being canvassed by Tom as a likely candidate). Since Edmund was to play opposite Mary Crawford, this hardship had many compensations, and he rather enjoyed it after all. Even Fanny, though steadfastly refusing a role, enjoyed the excitement and activity, the merriment and bustle consequent upon the production of a play.

Since I can hardly be supposed indifferent, my opinion of the propriety of theatricals, private or public, is not likely to be taken seriously, but I stood quite outside it all at first, I assure you, and even then had little sympathy for the nice moral scruples of those who were opposed to the venture. I respected the loyalty of the older servants to Sir Thomas, but I should have preferred them to sustain their argument with other reasons. That, however, they could not do, and I dismissed their objections as petty refinements of moral sensibility acquired from Sir Thomas and only to be comprehended in an idle, wealthy family. In that I have not changed. I still say that I care not a jot for such theoretical morality. But, as far as the practical side of it went, I thought it excessively indiscreet that Maria, engaged to James Rushworth, should act opposite Henry Crawford, the man she loved. For that is how it was to be.

After a deal of debate, the play settled upon had been the very one in which Mr. Yates had so recently been a participant, *Lovers' Vows*, by the prolific Mr. Kotzebue, a writer of no little talent whose works (providing they have been trimmed by Mrs. Inchbald) are amply suited for entertaining the public. The assignation of the principal roles among the men was made without difficulty: Mr. Yates, at whose suggestion the scheme had been adopted, was rewarded by that of the Baron (which on the former occasion he had coveted and been denied). It was a good ranting part, in which his loudness promised to become deafening. Tom pleased himself with taking on several minor comic roles. The plum part, the hero, Frederick, went to Henry Crawford, whose low-pitched and well-modulated voice, together with his ability to deliver lines feelingly, made his unquestionably the prime talent of the company. The great question then remained of who should play the women's parts, Agatha and Amelia. Agatha, like the seat on the barouche box, was the position to which Maria and Julia both aspired, since Agatha was mother to Henry's Frederick and there were plentiful opportunities for fond maternal embraces. Which of them should win Agatha? It was a matter of crucial importance, and we all wondered, myself as much as any, how Mr. Crawford would this time contrive to please both sisters. He might have left it to others to decide; he might have encouraged the toss of a coin; he might have shrugged his shoulders and sworn them equally well suited to the role. But he did not. He spoke for Maria in the part. It seemed once more that Maria must be first past the post after all. Were the Crawford stakes finished before the play was even begun?

Maria thought so, and was accordingly triumphant; Julia thought so, and was accordingly heartbroken. Julia, indeed, retired altogether, refusing to play Amelia since Agatha was denied her. It was generally allowed among the servants that upon Sir Thomas's return Maria's engagement to James Rushworth would be broken and another made. What did I make of it? I voiced no opinion, you may be sure, but, although I did not entirely agree with the other servants (had I not witnessed Henry slip out of the net before?), I shared some of Julia's disappointment at the turn of events. I had built not a few dreamy spires and pinnacles upon the insubstantial foundation of that kiss. I consoled myself, however, by recollecting Henry's reputation as a flirt, and determined to think no more of the matter, which I managed very well. Indeed, the advent of the play itself was a great antidote to foolish daydreams, providing such real-life excitement as it did.

For, to my great delight and satisfaction, I was assigned a role. My services were at first in demand for sewing both costumes and curtain, but later, when it proved impossible to fill all the roles from within the family, a number of the servants were recruited to play the sort of minor parts to which they were accustomed in life. I was to be the country girl, a part in the opening scene so insignificant that it would have been an insult to propose it to anyone else. Indeed, earlier it had been decided that the character might be omitted from the performance altogether but, as enthusiasm for the scheme grew and those who had originally disapproved were reconciled or silenced, the country girl was put back in, the argument being (as eloquently stated by Henry) that she emphasized the misery of Agatha's plight and would excite the audience's sympathy on the heroine's behalf. Since Agatha was a poor, seduced woman with a son, blameless but for that one lapse, who could see in the country girl traces of the young woman she herself had once been, there was something to this. For my part, however, I thought Henry's plea not entirely disinterested, especially when he winked at me privately when the thing was decided. Julia was much put out that I should participate when she did not, and for a while quite determined that someone else must be found, but since the whole company was ranged against her she at last yielded, in particular to the arguments of Mr. Yates, with whom, in default of Henry Crawford, she was dallying, attracted by the splash and swagger conferred upon him by his role as Baron. At any rate I was to have my chance; and although Julia was inclined to give me ten unnecessary things to do as penance, I was no whit deterred. I had exactly thirty-seven words to say, but I was so excited you would think I had been offered the role of Lady Macbeth at the very least. As some excuse for this vanity, I must explain that it was the chief role assigned among the servants, whose parts were otherwise the nonspeaking sort in which they played themselves. Only Alexander Belzoni took a role that had more than four words, and that was scarcely to be counted since he only nominally made one of us.

It was in keeping with the continual enlargement of the proceedings that Matthew Quinney arrived. Matthew was a scene painter, imported by Tom from town by way of Gold Street, Northampton. The upper servants were quite horrified, for Matthew Quinney proved not only a scene painter of extraordinary ability, but also a regular up-ender of the ordinary; he delighted all the younger sprigs with his stories, which were, said Mr. Wilcox ominously, calculated to fill a few heads with nonsense. Even those who had been abroad in the world, like Sophie, found him unusual, and those who had not, of whom I made one, passed from tittering at his appearance to gaping in wonder at his opinions. He was exceedingly tall and thin, a maypole of a man, with a narrow, not ill-shaped face and a brown skin. His striking figure was emphasized by his dress, which was outlandish in cut and color. He wore leather breeches and shoes and, instead of a shirt, a loose overblouse like a rustic smock, belted at the waist and made, if you please, of striped red calico. For warmth, he put on a long coat of rabbit skins, and when he was at work a pair of baggy seaman's trousers to protect his stockings from the splashes of distemper, not entirely successfully. John May said he must have picked his clothes out of the burlesque box without looking, and there was some truth in that.

I wish you could have seen Mrs. Norris's face when she first beheld Matthew. She drew herself up like a cat arching its back at a dog and preparing to spit in its eye. When Tom introduced him she inclined her head but did not speak; if ever she had doubts about the wisdom of the Mansfield theatricals it must have been at that moment, and woe betide the servant she caught listening to the scene painter's stories. The scouring was long enough and loud enough to overwhelm him too. But he was impervious. I never knew anyone so slow to take offense at personal slight.

Tom was triumphant at having secured Matthew's services, for here was a genuine man of the theater. Although he was at first engaged to paint only one backcloth and some side wings, Matthew's presence was a considerable inducement to a greater number of scene changes. After all, what use in having him if his talents were not to be fully employed? Christopher Jackson, the carpenter and our stage manager, was soon building wooden frames and stretching canvas over them at Matthew's direction, and the first time the scene painter laid color on canvas it was quite remarkable how many members of the household contrived to come and go so that they might observe him at work. Matthew's profession was such as to make him a universal object of curiosity, and I was more fortunate than most, since the sewing of costumes provided sufficient reason for my being present to wonder at all the ingenious tricks of his craft. He sketched the scene in charcoal, and then used a sponge to apply the color, with that rapidity and confidence which are the surest signs of skill.

"I wonder you can do it so fast," I said, when he stood back to view the effect.

Matthew was quite willing to indulge his audience's curiosity. "It would not be much good otherwise. In a theater large, bold effects are best. Drury Lane and Covent Garden are so vast that none but those will suffice. If I painted slowly, I should paint small and fine, and that would not do. I shall add detail when the background color is on."

"This must be very small compared with what you are used to," said Alexander Belzoni.

"It is better to change about. If you become too used to any one size or style of theater, the eye becomes so accustomed to a certain perspective that it cannot see things freshly."

"I haven't ever seen a play," volunteered Amelia Ellis.

"Then you will make a good audience for this," Matthew said. "The first time is like no other."

"Be sure to bring the sal volatile," said Alexander. "People who have never seen a play before are sometimes so affected that they scream and faint."

This caused a murmur among those present. "I saw one last St. Andrew's day. I didn't faint."

"Is it like mumming then?"

"You didn't need to faint. You were drunk as a lord."

"What is this? What is this gathering?" Mrs. Norris entered. "Get about your business at once! You never want an excuse for idling, do you, John May? You have forgotten there's the silver to be cleaned, I suppose. Off with you! And you, Ellis, what are you doing? You had better be making yourself useful, or I shall want to know the reason why." She took the garment Amelia was sewing and inspected it. "Look at that! This is for Mr. Rushworth! The stitching is a disgrace. It is all to do again!"

"If you please, Mr. Crawford was quite certain that she was to do it with large stitches." I defended Amelia.

Mrs. Norris took no notice. "I have undertaken Mr. Rushworth's pink satin cloak myself, and it was not so that you should spoil his blue dress."

Matthew Quinney intervened. "It is not like regular sewing, ma'am. What a man on a galloping horse will not see, no one will. It is an effect of the lights."

Amelia took courage at this show of support. "Post along, that's what Mr. Crawford said. Post along!"

"What you know about the theater, Quinney, may be a great deal, but we do not skimp things at Mansfield. They are done in a thorough fashion. Post along, indeed! You need not think to excuse your lazy work by some appeal to Mr. Crawford. It is our dear Mr. Rushworth for whom you have cobbled up this disgrace, he who will soon be a member of the family. This will not do at all. Indeed, it will not."

Having thus broken up the company to her satisfaction, Mrs. Norris swept away upon her broom. Despite all the years Amelia had suffered Mrs. N.'s tongue-lashings, she was no more inured to them and quite crestfallen.

"She does not send you to make a fire," said Sophie comfortingly. "Be content! You sit here still and watch the painting."

Four of us had, indeed, escaped banishment, since besides those who sewed, Alexander Belzoni remained. He had appointed himself unofficial assistant to the scene painter, and was handy enough with hammer, brush and instant opinion to carry it off.

"Have I seen Mr. Rushworth?" inquired Matthew. "He appears to be of great consequence."

"He is the fellow who cannot remember his lines," said Alexander.

"He plays Count Cassel," I explained. "At least, we think he does. It is not certain whether Mr. Rushworth is playing Count Cassel or Count Cassel is playing Mr. Rushworth. One coxcomb is playing another, that is for certain. No part was ever so well-suited. Old Whinny Prinny does not need to act. He would outdo them all if he could but remember his lines."

"He is to marry Miss Maria," added Amelia.

"Or so he thinks," said Alexander.

"The question," said Sophie, "it is who has her at last, Rushworth or Crawford."

"Surely it is rather who will have Mr. Crawford," I said, "the one sister or the other."

Matthew was amused. "I thought I had come to a quiet well-regulated country house, and here I find myself in a hotbed of amorous intrigue."

"The amorous intrigues," said Alexander, "being the result of Mr. Rushworth's lack of ideas about hot beds."

Amelia tittered and Sophie clucked disapprovingly. "La! What will Mr. Quinney think!"

"By the sound of it," said Matthew, "Mr. Rushworth is a prime candidate for the Celestial Bed."

"The Celestial Bed? What is that?"

"You mean to tell me that you have never heard of the Celestial Bed?"

"Listen to him! Celestial Bed! Bizarre! Every man thinks his presence in one makes it so. *Allez raconter.*"

"I disclaim any personal knowledge of this invention," Matthew began. "My maternal uncle, who taught me the art of scene painting, told me the tale. He got in to view the bed somehow. None but the wealthy could afford to use it. It cost fifty pounds for the privilege even then, and that was forty years ago.

"Dr. Graham invented this rig—not that he knew anything of medicine, you understand. He set himself up in a handsome house in the Adelphi Terrace, stood a pair of finelooking fellows in livery outside, learned a few Latin tags and lectured on health—well, that's what he called it. He illustrated his lectures with poses and musical interludes performed by nymphs of fifteen or so draped in a little silk.

"I tell you, he had full houses every time, and hundreds who couldn't afford to get in came to gape outside. It was all a ruse to sell the use of the bed, of course. The Celestial Bed was twice as big as any other in existence. It had a domed canopy supported by forty glass pillars and was lined with looking glass. Perfumes and spices filled the air, sweet music played and a pair of live turtle doves murmured on a bed of roses. It is said to have cost ten thousand pounds. At the head of the bed, sparkling with electric fire, was the message 'Be fruitful, multiply and replenish the earth.' For the purposes of which the mattresses were stuffed with hair from the tails of English stallions."

"I like the detail," said Sophie. "I like the panes of looking glass."

"I have heard something of this," said Alexander. "It was quackery or genius."

"Oh, laws!" said Amelia. "If Mr. Baddeley should hear you! He calls London the great Babylon. Electric fire! Oh, my!"

"I fear even the Celestial Bed would not bring Mr. Rushworth to the point," Alexander said.

"I admire Mr. Graham," said Sophie. "It is a harmless deception. Only fools lose money."

"The bed did not survive long," said Matthew. "At the most two or three years. After that Mr. Graham slowly descended into poverty and madness."

"He must have been rolling in money," said Alexander. "Only imagine! Fifty pounds a night!"

"What happened to it?"

"No one knows for certain. A prince was supposed to have bought it entire."

"Nymphs also?" inquired Sophie.

"If there were any left by then. The nymphs regularly eloped with aged members of the aristocracy seeking to prolong their life, improve their performance and beget strong sons. Children conceived in the bed were supposed to be the healthiest, most rational and beautiful offspring. That was the justification for the whole racket."

"Surely no one could believe it was anything but an excuse for a little lechery," I said.

"That is the whole cleverness of it," said Alexander.

"I'll wager some of the nobility hoped it was more," said Matthew. "Think of your Mr. Rushworth. He is the very mirror of his class. It was in order to avoid begetting sons like him that they laid out their fifty pounds."

"Mr. Rushworth is no aristocrat," said Sophie.

"The principle applies."

"He is very kind to me," said Amelia.

"That is certainly in his favor," Matthew allowed.

"You have some interesting principles, it seems," said Alexander.

"It is true I wish those who rule us bred a little more wisdom."

"You do not think much of them."

"Not when they sit in Parliament and make the laws that govern us. Parliament is full of fools like your Rushworth."

"You are eager for change, then?" said Alexander.

"If we are to improve the lot of the poor, there must be change. A laborer gets three shillings for twelve hours at the plow, while some are given one thousand pounds a year by the government for doing nothing. And some are given twenty thousand! The government hands out sinecures and pensions to its friends and never gives a thought to the poor."

"God watches over us." Amelia was quite agitated. "It is His will. As we serve so shall we be rewarded in heaven."

"It is an agricultural revolution we need, not a political," I said. "We need richer harvests to bring more wheat."

"Pray to the Lord for good weather, then," said Alexander.

"Even now there is more food than they would have us believe, enough to keep thousands from starving if it were more equitably distributed," said Matthew.

"There are such changes afoot that in twenty years there will be food for all," I continued.

"Twenty years!" Sophie commented. "How many starve in twenty years?"

"Mr. Jackson's oldest brother fell ill in the winter of eighteen hundred and could not feed his family," Amelia reflected. "A quartern loaf cost one and tenpence then, and he had seven children to raise. Three of them died in the spring, one after the other. His poor wife has never been right since."

"Any hardworking man may fall sick," said Matthew. "At the very time he most needs his income, he loses it. He cannot procure the common necessaries of life when he most desperately requires them."

"It seems you are as much at home on the platform of a meeting as a play," said Alexander.

Sophie frowned and shook her head. "It is enough. It is dangerous."

"Every man has a right to his opinions," Alexander said.

"Some he keep to himself," Sophie returned.

"If every man were too fearful to speak, then nothing would ever be done," said Matthew.

"So you do speak?" Matthew only shrugged in reply to Alexander's question. "Have you addressed meetings?"

"What if I have?"

"Oh, it's nothing to me, but there's been a lot of trouble lately, one way and another, round here."

"How do you know?" queried Sophie sharply. "You are here only one month."

"It is in all the papers. Riots in Nottingham. They say it will spread to the shoemakers."

"Oh dear, oh dear!" Amelia lamented. "It's bad and I do believe it's getting worse. Whatever shall we do?"

"They are an unruly mob," Alexander said. "Didn't you hear about it, Quinney? They ran all over the course at the races last spring. A few whippers-in charged them, just to clear the way, one or two got a crack on the head and then the whole crowd went mad. It was a regular battle."

"The ringleader was transported," added Sophie.

"There were more than a few cracked on the head as I understand it," said Matthew. "They were defending themselves only. I should if I were cracked on the head."

"A scene painter with radical leanings. What an uncommon man you are." Alexander spoke lightly.

"Where do you stand?"

"Anywhere and nowhere." Alexander laughed. "I take only a passing interest in politics. I prefer to travel and keep my pockets well lined."

"That's the trouble with half the population. They are too busy looking after themselves to give a thought to anyone else."

"What do you propose, a bloody revolution?"

"Nothing of the kind. Justice through reform, that's all."

"That's all! No one I know who heard you talk would believe so."

"Who *do* you know?" Matthew inquired.

"As many interesting characters as you, I'll warrant."

"He's been with a lot of really grand folk," said Amelia. "You should hear him!"

"Oh, I can match your Celestial Bed any day, Quinney." Alexander had quite recovered his bantering tone. "I worked for the Earl of Yarmouth lately. There's a strange one. Thin as a lath and with a wayward taste in women. He used to collect up half a dozen in Covent Garden and take them into the country for six months. They lived like princesses but had to travel in closed carriages. He would never let them be seen. Not that it stopped the gossip. He had such a collection of whips and things as you never saw."

Amelia covered her mouth and rocked with laughter at Alexander's daring. Matthew merely observed quietly: "This must have been a comedown for you, leaving the Earl of Yarmouth for Mr. Bertram."

"Oh, he didn't do that, did you, Alexander?" said Amelia. "What about the Duke of Tiptree?"

Alexander laughed. "You see? Amelia remembers all my best stories. The Duke of Tiptree was even more eccentric in his tastes."

"Perhaps it was he who bought the Celestial Bed," I said.

"And when were you with the Duke of Tiptree?" Matthew inquired.

"On and off during last summer. I come and go much as you do yourself."

"Then you are as uncommon a footman as I am a scene painter."

"What is life without a little change? That's what I say."

"I suppose you have worked in many London theaters?" I asked.

"Most of them," Matthew replied, "if you count the time I was a stripling of ten and only allowed to carry the pots and grind the colors under my master's direction."

"Where else have you been?" asked Alexander.

"Wherever there was work. With a trade such as mine one may travel and find employment in all sorts of places."

" 'An epitome of the world!' " I recited.

"That play!" exclaimed Sophie. "You are mad for the play! Are there any lines you do not know?"

"Who cannot know Mr. Rushworth's lines?" I answered.

"Oh, I know them! Do I not know them!" responded Sophie. " 'In the wilds of America I learned love,' he says. I wish he had. A little of the art of love and he satisfy Maria. *Voilà*. Everyone is happy."

"He could not do it. He would never be able to memorize the order of procedure. You would have to stand by with a prompt book," said Alexander.

"I do not blame her for tiring of him," I said. "Is it any wonder she prefers Mr. Crawford?"

"Everyone prefer Mr. Crawford," teased Sophie, casting a significant look at me.

"What's this?" demanded Alexander instantly, his nose for scandal hot on the scent. "What's this? I thought your favorite was Mr. Bertram. It is Mr. Crawford now, is it? Mr. Bertram is to be cast off." He began to laugh. "He *will* be in a pet. What a lark! You know your way about, don't you?"

I blazed up at the careless insults. "Tom Bertram is odious. I detest him. I despise him. I always have. Now I find he is a liar."

Alexander put up his hands in mock discomfiture. "No offense, no offense. I withdraw. I shall never refer to the subject again. No word of it shall pass my lips."

"Tom Bertram try to ravish her," said Sophie angrily.

Alexander shrugged. "My apologies, I'm sure. That is not how he tells it."

"Would you expect him to tell the truth?" I asked bitterly.

Matthew shook his head. "How can you bear to remain here?"

"It is a regular occurrence," said Sophie.

"A condition of your hiring? You are too acquiescent."

"What should we do, up and leave on the instant?" I demanded. "It is all very well to talk."

"Why should you not?"

"It is different for you. You can leave when you please."

"So can you."

"We are servants, and must carry more references than a paintbrush. And women too. What can a woman do, alone?"

"More than you think," said Matthew. "It is difficult for you—more difficult for you than for me—but not impossible. As for my paintbrush, is that so much better than your needle? Besides, you do not have to rely on that. You should think of becoming an actress."

Alexander laughed. "A practical suggestion from a scene painter!"

Sophie was horrified. "What are you saying? It is madness."

"What is wrong with becoming an actress?" Matthew inquired.

"An actress! It is a life of misery and poverty."

"The players I have seen can barely keep body and soul together," added Alexander.

"Most of them take to the road hardly knowing how to read. They have not Jane's talent."

"How many, that is what I want to know. How many succeed? One in a thousand."

"I do not customarily recommend it. I prefer people to read, to think. There are too many enthusiasts for the stage. I discourage them. But I speak as I find: Jane has beauty and a natural talent."

"How much promise can there be in thirty-seven words?" Alexander asked.

Sophie supported him: "Thirty-seven words! One says 'Good day' and 'How are you?' It is ridiculous."

Matthew smiled and shrugged. "There is an air, a certain presence, when a superior talent sets foot upon the boards. It scarcely needs words. I cannot believe you have not noted it in Jane."

"But what a risk!"

"Stephen took it," I said at last, not without knowing it was unkind to use his example against her. "He left. He thought the chance worth it."

131

"Ah-h-h-h!" Sophie spread her hands and answered sadly, thinking of him as well as of me. "This, it is different. This, it is the theater."

"There are compensations for being a servant, I acknowledge," Matthew said. "You sit with your feet beneath someone else's table, even though it be Tom Bertram's. You will not go short. You may continue all your life in such a fashion. Perhaps Henry Crawford will offer to make you his mistress, and then you may have pretty gowns and a carriage to travel in."

"I had not thought of such a thing," I replied indignantly. But I had. Although the situation he described was not unusual, he made it a paltry prospect. My cheeks burned.

"It is not always bad to be the mistress of such a man," said Sophie.

"You may make a good thing out of it," said Alexander. "The Duke's mistress had a pearl the size of a pigeon's egg. I daresay Mr. Crawford would be generous too, in his way."

Matthew shrugged. "He will patronize her until he is tired of her and then pension her off, if he can afford it. She will occupy that inferior position to which she is already well accustomed. If that is what you would look forward to, Jane, then by all means do so."

"You take too much for granted," I said.

"I am glad to hear it."

"I shall do as I please and think for myself. Nothing has happened between us, nothing at all. He is set to marry one of the sisters. Everyone thinks so, and I believe it. My existence is pleasant enough. It is no great hardship to serve Julia."

"I should have thought you would find it irksome to obey such empty-headed, ill-tempered mistresses."

"Perhaps *you* do not care to obey anyone," said Sophie.

"I obey those whom I respect. Do you respect Maria and Julia? They have no superiority of sense and understanding to make obedience tolerable."

"A not uncommon thing between servant and mistress—or master," said Alexander. "I have often turned it to advantage."

"I find it a sorry condition." Matthew responded with heartfelt conviction, and I could not disagree. "What gives them dominion over you?" he continued. "Only the possession of a large income, which they have done nothing to deserve. And for that they expect to govern every aspect of your life. They set rules for you which they themselves would not think of obeying. Nothing matters to them but their own gratification."

"Mercy on us!" To Amelia this speech, but half-comprehended, was heresy. "We are all given the places and duties best fitted for us."

"The Church is a great comfort to you, I see," said Matthew, gently. "But some of us feel we must take action."

"And some of us might think you an infidel of the true Paine school," Alexander commented.

"I am not ashamed to be so," answered Matthew quietly. "It is better than having no principle but money."

"There speaks an idealist!" Alexander was scornful.

"What of your friend, Tom Bertram, whose approval you depend on for your living? What if he were in charge here? What would he do, do you suppose, after he'd lost another wager? Put up the rents and turn a blind eye. Wait until he's master."

"I'm sure I know Master Tom," said Amelia. "I've grown up with him, so to speak. He has his faults, but there's no need to drag him down. He's a bit of a scamp, but all young gentlemen are wild. He'll settle down."

"And what if he doesn't?"

"It is unjust," said Sophie, "but life is unjust. This is foolish talk."

"The hereditary principle insures that only the first born inherit the wealth, title and privilege. What happens to the rest? Think of the younger brothers who are thus impoverished."

"Only think of Mr. Edmund!" I said. "Isn't he a prime case? Nothing but a paltry few hundred a year for a living, while his brother wastes the inheritance in gaming and racing."

"Sir Thomas will see Mr. Edmund properly set up," said Amelia.

"If there were any justice, Mr. Edmund would be master," asserted Matthew.

"Do I hear aright?" Alexander was indignant. "By law, Tom Bertram will be master. By law. That should be enough for you."

"Why shouldn't the inheritance be divided?"

"Divided! That would be a fine thing! Then there would be nothing for anybody."

"But that would be terrible!" exclaimed Amelia.

"Let him rant on," said Alexander. "Such men are their own worst enemies."

"I am not afraid of speaking out," said Matthew. "The truth must be heard."

"The truth!" Alexander was contemptuous.

"Whether it is truth or not, they can surely arrest you for saying such things," I observed.

"He speaks like a man who has lived with the threat for some time," said Alexander.

"I am not ashamed of that. Many live with worse. They can hang a child for picking a pocket of a shilling handkerchief. If I am to suffer for trying to alter such things then so it must be."

"But that is stealing!" Amelia was horrified. "That is breaking one of God's commandments!"

"Yes, stealing. And who is the thief? A poor, ignorant, half-starved child, who needs food and education, not the gallows. Justice! I fear justice more than the rope!"

"Ah!" said Sophie. "You are like my father. He speak so before the Revolution. It is very fine, but it bring sorrow, it bring death. I do not wish to hear it."

"You're nothing but a damned Jacobin," said Alexander.

"By no means."

"Then one of us does not know the meaning of the word."

"We do not need a revolution." Matthew spoke without heat. "There was a time when England was a nation to be proud of. All men were fed, all men worked, all men prospered. They were treated with simple justice. We need a return to our great heritage."

"You'll have me piping my eye yet," said Alexander. "Such impossible dreams! Do you suppose those with money and power will lightly give them up? They will fight to keep what they have."

"You English, you sit, you argue, you admire," said Sophie. "You wish the change without the battle. You are in the clouds. I have seen it and I know."

"You are wrong. It can be done. The working men suffer, but they will not suffer in silence for ever. If we work to relieve their distress before it is too late then we can achieve change without revolution."

"You dare say that while the Luddites loot and burn and destroy!" Alexander shook his head unbelievingly.

"They are not criminals. There is no food on the table for their wives, their babes, themselves. No food and no hope of any."

"We hear," said Sophie. "They murder innocent people. It is a mob. Not many persons, just one. Not even a person. An animal."

"Hunger turns them into animals."

"I go hungry. I was not an animal. If you are a child where I am a child, you know. But you do not. Not here." Sophie tapped her stomach. "We eat what we find. It is a rat once, a large, gray rat, thin. I know hunger."

"Then you must feel for them more than anyone."

"It is no good," said Sophie. "It is an animal. It is too late."

"It is never too late," replied Matthew. "I shall never believe it is too late."

XI

The first full rehearsal of the three opening acts of *Lovers' Vows* promised to make an agreeable evening's entertainment. Chairs were set up as for an audience, and Lady Bertram had been invited to attend (although it seemed unlikely that she would do so). There were, of course, one or two snags. Matthew had not altogether finished the scenery, and Mrs. Norris, earlier in no doubt as to the curtain (her especial charge) having too many rings, had now decided that it had too few; consequently Amelia Ellis was busy stitching on the rings she had recently been employed in snipping off. The second, which threatened to be a much greater setback, was that the parson's wife, Henry Crawford's elder sister, was unable to be present to play her role. Fanny Price was at last prevailed upon, much against her will, to stand by to read it in her place. She had sat through the play until she knew everyone's lines by heart, so it was really no great hardship, but she trembled like a leaf. Although she considered playacting improper, she was quite unable to stand up to the arguments of her four cousins. I should not wish to cast aspersions upon such an inoffensive creature, but in such circumstances one is bound to reflect upon the uselessness of a moral conviction that will not stand the test of action.

"I hope you are finished Maria's ragged gown for the first act, Hartwell," said Mrs. Norris, in the last-minute bustle before the rehearsal should begin. She called to Maria: "The hem should be torn a little, I think, do not you, niece? But neatly, as becomes the poverty of a gentlewoman."

"I think perhaps I shall wear a black fichu," said Maria. "More black will compound the tragic effect."

Henry Crawford inspected the scene which Matthew had just completed, of a country road with an inn upon one side. "Look here, Miss Bertram. Do you not see something familiar?"

Maria reflected a moment. "It is the road into Northampton from Mansfield."

"There, we have found you out, Mr. Quinney. I congratulate you."

"The countryside here is beautiful. I could not resist copying it."

"I suppose that is your excuse for being exceeding slow," said Mrs. Norris. "I only hope my nephew has made it clear to you that this is not piece work. Your absence the other day did not go unnoticed, I assure you." But even Mrs. N. was gratified by Matthew's clever representation of a familiar scene. "Why, there is Northampton in the distance. That is the spire of St. Peter's. I have traveled over that piece of road enough times to recognize it. If I do not mistake, that is the very spot, three winters since, where Sir Thomas's carriage was near swallowed up in a slough by that idle farmer Harris's fault. He will drive cattle across it, no matter how many times he is told. He is a very stubborn, impertinent fellow. I shall advise Sir Thomas not to renew his lease."

"Yet here is not a mud puddle in sight," said Henry. "All is so elevated and perfected that it provides a most romantic scene. Even the Rose and Crown has a much needed coat of whitewash."

We laughed at that, but were, like Henry, full of admiration at the green hedges and trees, the rutted road, the distant prospect of the city.

"Are we not also to have another side piece, Quinney?" asked Henry.

"The cottage makes one, as you see, and thereby provides an entrance behind the wing. The other will be some trees, which will be profiled if Mr. Jackson can oblige. With the door into the Rose and Crown, here in the backcloth, the scene is complete."

"Bravo! A maximum effect with a minimum of pieces."

"If the profiled leg is made sufficiently large, it can slide across to mask the inn, and thus we shall have the empty road for Act Three. With cottage and castle interiors, and a gauze for the cell scene, we are all but complete."

"Capital. You will save us money in the end."

"I am glad to hear it," said Mrs. Norris. "People take the expense of these matters too much for granted. I myself have managed to economize a little here and there. I saved a full three-quarters of a yard on the curtain."

"Query: shall I like a gauze for my prison cell?" said Henry.

"It is a common device for it where there is no stock scenery," explained Matthew. "Darkness is all. Some lamps directing their light against a set of bars for the cell window; all shadowy within; you showing a dramatic profile in the half-light—"

"Excellent! I hope our acting will be up to it," said Henry. "That is my prime concern. I do not like to be outdone by the scenery."

"That is unlikely," said Maria. "You are a better actor than most of those whose profession it is."

"But yours is the part, niece," interrupted Mrs. Norris. "Yours is the part. I do not think you will be easily outdone. You always spoke up well, even as a child. I remember remarking on your talent."

Since Act One, Scene One called upon three of them to speak, as far as the servants were concerned, the opening scene was the best of the play. My own part and Alexander Belzoni's made two; the third belonged to John May. The footman, who was such a performer at the Christmas mumming that he had us holding our sides, proved unequal to this occasion. He had only to say "Good day" but I believe it gave him as much trouble as James Rushworth's two and forty speeches gave him. John could not get the inflection right: it was a squeaking or a bellowing, or an unhappy mixture of both, or an up and a down in tone, when it should have been a down and an up. I promise you, it was a revelation to hear the many ways of saying "Good day" and all of them wrong.

"A willing fellow, but no actor," said Henry to me. "Ah well, we must make do with the talent we have. If only we were all like you. If we were, we might take over Drury Lane. I never saw greater natural ability. It is you who should be playing Agatha."

"Agatha?" queried Maria. "What about Agatha?"

"I am trying to explain to Hartwell how she must respond to Agatha. There must be more pity and horror as she observes your condition."

"I do not know that she need do so much," said Maria. "These small parts are sometimes a distraction."

"I cannot agree. They throw the major tragedy into relief. By such means all attention is directed toward *you*. It must and should be so. There must be no distraction from Agatha."

Maria was not altogether reassured. Whatever advantages were to be had from the general insignificance of servanthood were fast being denied me. I saw that she kept an eye on us, and I doubted that she missed the small attentions Henry paid me, although he thought them unobserved. Nothing sharpens the sight like the uncertainties of love.

The rehearsal began promisingly. In the opening scene, Maria made an acceptable Agatha, as starving, sick and pitiable a figure as a healthy, blooming, rich young woman may contrive to appear, and Tom was suitably stony-hearted as the landlord who turns the penniless female out of his house. John May, Alexander Belzoni and myself stood behind the backdrop in company with Henry, awaiting our catchwords, for we were on in succession, John first, then Alexander, to be followed by me and then Henry. Henry and I were thus left alone. We watched Maria as she began her long monologue.

"She wants your naturalness," whispered Henry into my ear.

"She never wants feeling when she speaks of her Frederick."

"I wish you might speak of me so."

I said nothing and he kissed my ear. "She will see." I nodded toward Maria, who was at that moment on her knees, her hands upraised to Providence, begging that her life might be spared long enough to see once more her only son, Frederick.

"Not she. She is too much occupied with the appearance of expiring." I felt his lips brush my neck.

"How can you do so? We shall be seen."

He replied with a line from the play. " 'Love comes just as it pleases, without being asked.' "

"You must not!" I was more urgent. "Only imagine if they should discover us! She suspects already, I am certain of it."

Henry was contrite. "Upon my life, you are right. Forgive me."

"We must be careful."

"I shall make amends. I shall pay Maria such particular attention that not a shadow of suspicion shall cloud her vanity."

Meanwhile he stepped back from me, but as he did so, he rested his fingers upon my neck. He was behind me and it was a secret touch. So gently did he place his fingertips upon the bare skin of my neck, it was as though he laid them upon porcelain. They were cool, yet through them electric fire ran into me. I was aware of nothing at that moment but the imprint of those five fingers. The scene before me continued, yet seemed suddenly to recede, as if it were no more than what passes on a magic lantern. Where Henry's fingers touched, lightning ran into me, out of me, making the two of us one. We were the pulse of the universe, beating with such intensity that I could not believe anyone present not instantly drawn, as by the operation of a spotlight, to the presence of Henry's fingers upon my neck. And when he began to draw them delicately back and forth across my skin, I could hardly breathe, could not hear Maria speak, although I saw her mouth moving.

My catchword came at that moment and I left him, feeling like a bird amongst limed twigs, but not without a taste for the game.

Having played my part as the country girl, I watched from the wing the enactment of Agatha and Frederick's touching reunion. Maria, describing the pitiful misery of her years alone, struck a graceful pose, the back of her hand to her forehead. She leaned on Henry for support, which he gave with fervent attention. She looked into his eyes and he took her hand and pressed it to his heart with every appearance of devotion. That Henry had instantly contrived to restore Maria's confidence was plain by the way she settled into his embrace. I could not but reflect upon the trifling actions which Henry charged with such significance that they became, for both Maria and myself, the bridge between passion and indifference.

Into the midst of these amorous byplays, at the very moment of that fond clasp between Henry and Maria, Julia burst into the theater with news that made us jump with the suddenness of a thunderclap. The great event, which was daily to be expected yet not to be thought of, was upon us: Sir Thomas Bertram had come home.

It would have shocked Sir Thomas to know what mixed emotions his arrival aroused in his children. The presence of a father who would curb their amusements in favor of a quiet life was not looked for with any great joy. Though it had been spoken of with exclamations of regret, his continuing absence had been more the cause of relief, and there had been a determined effort to secure as much enjoyment as possible before he was there to spoil it. Now he was to find them in the midst of putting on a play, an activity of which they knew he would disapprove. Their understanding of his views on theatricals, argued away easily enough in his absence, could no longer be ignored when he was upon the doorstep, in the hall, in the drawing room, about to enter the very billiard room and his own study which had been so unceremoniously adapted as a theater. He had caught them red-handed, as he might have caught them making ink pellets in the nursery years ago, and they were thrown into similar guilty confusion. Only Fanny Price had reason to be joyful—and more: she was quite overcome with relief. His timely arrival retrieved her from the brink of that horrible degradation from which she had been unable to save herself: taking part in a play.

"My father is come! He is in the hall at this moment," cried Julia.

"*Quel coup de théâtre!*" Sophie whispered. After a pause, like the indrawn breath of an audience when the specter appears all bloody upon the stage, a pause during which Henry carefully retained hold of Maria's hand, there was a sudden frenzy of activity. The lesser members of the cast, John May, Alexander Belzoni and myself, gave the lead in making exits as neat and speedy as anything we had ever managed for the play. Hotfooting it to the servants' quarters, we were still two steps ahead of the butler, Mr. Baddeley, who was coming from the main entrance at a most uncommon approximation to a run, his face alight with smiles, exclaiming for the benefit of all: "Sir Thomas is come! The master is home!"

The joy in the servants' hall at this news was more sincere than any above stairs. Within a minute all was in a regular train. Mrs. Glover, having instructed the maids to heat some water and John

May to carry it upstairs, was gone to fetch linen; Amelia took tinder and flint to light the fires in Sir Thomas's apartments; Mr. Baddeley vanished into the cellar to select a bottle of Madeira, Sir Thomas's favorite restorative; Mrs. Alsop, having chivied the kitchenmaid into stirring up the fire, lifted the lid of the stockpot and tried to decide what, from all she knew of the master's preferences, he would best like a bite of; and Mr. Wilcox, having dispatched a groom to see after the horses, sat in beaming state amidst the stir and bustle.

Sophie and I, feeling ourselves betwixt and between, at one neither with the gaiety downstairs nor the subdued welcome upstairs, retrieved the costumes from the erstwhile dressing rooms and hung them at the back of a dark closet, not so much out of the way that they could be said to be hidden, yet not where Sir Thomas might come upon them unexpectedly, as an unhappy reminder of the large scope of our proceedings. They were later whisked away by Mrs. Norris.

Matthew, who had of all least part to play in this, sat himself down before the fire with a tankard of ale, observing the hurry and scurry good-naturedly and disposed to laugh at the animated questions that buzzed around him, questions of the What will Sir Thomas say to? . . . Will the master notice? . . . and Whatever will he think of? . . . variety, many of which centered, naturally, upon the play.

"Surely he cannot be so nice as to object to playacting?" said Matthew. "I cannot believe, if he is as just and reasonable as you say, that he can possibly object to the performance of a play."

"You might not believe it, Mr. Quinney, the theater being your bread and butter, so to speak," said Mr. Wilcox, "but that's the way he will think, for all that. What is proper in a baronet's family is not always understood by those in the lower ranks of society."

"Ah, I see! Sir Thomas's rank confers upon him finer feelings than the rest of us! You will forgive me if I disagree. Only money separates us. We are all born equal. The Bertrams are merely more fortunate in being born rich."

"There never was a better master nor a kinder gentleman than Sir Thomas." Mr. Wilcox turned red with anxiety. "To hear you talk you'd think he lay abed till noon. He knows more about hard work than you ever will, I'll warrant."

"You mistake me, Mr. Wilcox," Matthew answered gently. "I do not attack Sir Thomas. By all accounts he is a very good sort of man. There are too few like him."

"Ah, that's all very well. You twist what you say like a braid. You've a fine collection of words, Mr. Quinney, but there's a lot more to it than you allow for, a lot more. I can see you are sincere in your beliefs, and I admire that in a man, but there's a lot more to it. Thank the good Lord the master's home at last. Thank heaven indeed. I've had enough playacting to last me a lifetime—and lent you my best sponges too, I'm sorry to say. Now the master's home things will be very different. He won't like all he sees, I can tell you that. If I were you, young man, I'd start packing my box."

XII

S ir Thomas was so full of joyful content at being once more amongst his family, once more at home, once more at his beloved Mansfield, that he did not utter one-half the reproaches he felt his children deserved. The full extent of his distaste for the theatricals was instead to be measured by the zeal with which he was out of bed at cockcrow the very morning after his arrival in order to rid his house of every speck and blemish of the play. Every unbound copy of *Lovers' Vows* was burned: consigned with relish to the flames of the dining-room fire and prodded until it was ashes and no black word of it remained entire. Matthew Quinney, similar evidence of unwholesomeness, was paid off and instructed to be on his way by noon. It would have been dawn, no doubt, but that Christopher Jackson would require the scene painter's assistance if the dismantling of stage and scenery were to proceed as speedily as Sir Thomas wished.

The great business of cleansing the house of the play overrode all else. Every servant was kept at it. Even Lady Bertram's maid was to be seen with a pail of water and a piece of chamois leather, quite out of her customary character. I made one of those assigned to the restoration of the anteroom floor, where various of Matthew's willing but inexperienced helpers had spilled paint, size, turpentine and gum. Six of us scrubbed away with sand, passing the time (though not within Sir Thomas's hearing) in recollections of the play. We effected a remarkable improvement to the floor, especially after retouching the inlay. It was sufficient, at any rate, to win Sir Thomas's praise, although some of the stains were not entirely to be removed, no matter what remedies Mrs. Glover suggested. They were as indelible, you might say, as the remembrance of the play which had given rise to them, fast in our heads forever, although hidden beneath a Chinese rug.

I contrived to see Matthew before he left. He was rolling up canvas, not a whit out of countenance at his summary dismissal. When we had said our farewells, he dived into his bag. "Here. For the most promising actress of my acquaintance." Despite my protestations he insisted that I take the little book of plays. "The bag is too heavy. You do me a favor."

"Do you go straight to London?" I asked, looking at the small, elegant volume in my hand, my yearning to be heard in my voice.

"I shall not go so far, not yet. I must get my shoes mended first." By which I knew he intended to visit the shoemakers in Northampton. "After that I shall be in the great metropolis, where I fully expect to encounter you some day."

I hastened away, full to overflowing with such a mix and stir of feelings that I hardly knew how to control them. With Matthew gone, I recognized more plainly than I had yet done the absolute nature of the change at Mansfield. It was not only that his going marked the utter ruin of the play. A violent transformation had taken place, so swift, so palpable, that in the space of a few hours the very air in the house seemed different. Thanks be, all now runs in its proper channel, I heard the older servants breathe at every turn; but to me, who had never lived under Sir Thomas's rule, it seemed that his return had acted upon the smooth motion of our existence like the sudden onset of a hurricane.

I shall not deny the large part that Henry Crawford played in my regrets. I did not doubt that our little affair must be utterly overwhelmed by the recent turn of events, and I wished heartily that it need not be so. My head was not, however, as full of him as that of another member of the household. Maria Bertram stationed Sophie by the window that she might be informed of the exact moment he was to be seen walking toward the house. For of course, that is what he was to do. She had it all pat. Now her father was returned, Henry was to declare himself. He would request an interview with Sir Thomas in which he would ask for her hand. This was the moment; there could be no other. As the day drew on and there was no sign of him, her excitement changed to anxiety. She began to be racked with the dreadful possibility that Henry would not come at all, with the attendant horrors of being obliged to reconsider marrying James Rushworth. She developed a sick headache as a result, consumed a bottle of Madeira and kept Sophie up all night. Henry did appear next day, but by then I was sure it would do her no good. For I knew in advance that he would come, knew it sooner than she: Henry, through one of his manservants, had made an assignation with me.

The boathouse was a pretty, two-story place all in the Gothic style, with arched doorways and a grinning imp for a waterspout. It was not greatly used for its prime purpose since rowing was an activity the Bertrams only occasionally enjoyed. In the single large room of the lower level, which gave on to the lake, there was but one boat, which had been recently brought in for the winter and now hung upside down from the rafters. Two sets of oars rested upon hooks in the wall, their varnish still bright. Apart from a coil of rope and some garden tools which had found a permanent home there, the room was clean and empty and mostly remained so. The upper level, however, was a favorite place for summer picnics. In contrast with the room below, to which it was connected by a staircase, it opened on to the path which ran around the lake and was, at this point, the height of a story above the water. The upper room made a perfect little summerhouse, with windowseats and leaded panes in keeping with the outside. There were even a fireplace and a handsome tall chimney, though nothing was to be found in those but starlings, since the family used the room only on fair-weather days. Dust lay upon the long table, and bits of straw and twigs in the hearth, but cushions still lay upon the seats, and the mild morning sun of October made it a pleasant enough trysting place.

I was there a full half-hour early, having carried with me my new book of plays, as a sort of talisman, I suppose, of my aspirations, although I did not quite know what those should be. It was a handsome volume, printed on India paper, bound in brown calf and gold-lettered on the spine. I had hidden it beneath the mattress in the Clock attic, anxious for its safety in the wake of Sir Thomas's book-burning, and this was the first chance I had had to examine it by daylight. It was the eighth volume of Mrs. Inchbald's *British Theatre*, and contained five comedies by George Farquhar, including *The Constant Couple* (a coincidence on which I have later reflected with pleasure). I sat upon a cushion in the sun and began to read with keen attention.

When I heard steps upon the gravel walk, however, I closed the book, stood up and watched the door open, in a flutter of delicious trepidation such as only lovers know. And lovers we were. A single exchange of glances confirmed what I had, through so long a short absence from Henry, been scarcely able to believe.

"Come with me, Jane," he urged, after an ecstasy of kisses. "I leave at once for Bath. I should be on my way already if it were not for you. Come with me. I shall find a handsome set of rooms and we shall live in great comfort and style. You shall be rich and fêted and amused beyond all your dreams. No more waiting upon the Bertrams."

"To Bath? Why do you go to Bath?"

"I promised my uncle. I keep my promise to him, and thus do *not* have to make any promise to Maria."

"You run off!"

He laughed. "After such a demonstration of false affection as you obliged me to, I am bound to run off."

"If you wished it, she would have you, for certain."

"But I do not wish it. And now she knows I do not. I have but just called at the house to pay my respects and say good-bye. I spoke polite nothings about the necessity of going to Bath; how I held myself absolutely obliged to return and resume the play at a moment's notice; how the play should never be lost through my fault, and so on and so forth. It was all a sham, of course. There will be no play at Mansfield this side of the Day of Judgment. As to marrying Maria, she could never please me. You know who does." He paused to kiss me again. "We can be away instantly. It must be done quietly. Do not even return to the house. You need bring nothing with you. I shall buy you a splendid new wardrobe in Bath." For all his lively enthusiasm, I was slow to reply. "What is it?"

"I cannot."

"Cannot? What shall prevent you?"

I shook my head.

"You will not come?" After a moment's reflection he thought me only waiting to be persuaded. "You think I do not love you enough?"

"Once I go with you, I never can return."

"Why should you wish to return? A life of wealth and ease awaits you."

"Must that decide me?"

He was perplexed. "How can you say so? You will come for love of me, that we may be together. Is not that enough?" I was silent and he continued. "Most women of your rank would welcome the prospect of such a comfortable life. I did not think you would be so nice as to despise it."

I was agitated. I did not know what I wanted, but he touched my pride. "To be slavishly dependent, to have to rely on you so entirely! I could not bear it. Love is best between those who are more equal."

He laughed. "It is I who shall be your slave."

"You speak in jest; I do not."

"Well then, if I may not jest, I shall say that it is prodigious strange for a lady's maid to talk of being slavishly dependent."

"Oh, but it is different! I am dependent, but then I do not *love* Julia Bertram. I am free to love or despise her as I choose. Only that part of me which labors to earn my bread is subject to her. I have only to please her and keep my thoughts to myself. But to love you and become your mistress! Almost better to become your mistress and *not* love you. What a clinging thing I must become! I should depend upon you entirely for the comfort of my heart as well as my body. You could not fail to despise me."

The tender caresses with which he demonstrated to me how impossible that was were irresistible. "Buried away here, you forget how common a thing it is for a man to take a mistress. Why, it is more common for a man to take a mistress than a wife. The great Nelson had a mistress."

"Oh, even in Northamptonshire we have heard of mistresses."

"My uncle's mistress lives as happily with him now as if they had been married twenty years."

"I have heard of *that*. Your sister was obliged to leave your uncle's house because of it. What happiness is that? I do not wish to be shunned."

"You make too much of it. Mrs. Holland has been there only since my aunt died, nearly a year ago. She has been his mistress for much longer than that."

"While your aunt was alive, you mean. What a scene for misery is there set out, in which the women mostly suffer."

"Not at all. My aunt could not abide the sight of my uncle, and she was as glad for him to be out of the way as he could be himself. She had her consolations. They were always army men. She would never have anything to do with the navy on account of my uncle being an admiral. She was quite content, believe me."

"I do not think it a very comfortable arrangement."

"What can it have to do with us? I am not married. I do not intend to be. I draw a picture of them, not of us. It would be different for us. My uncle's affection is but a pale shadow of mine. His devotion is at best a cold thing, born more of dislike of my aunt than love for Mrs. Holland, who is a kind, homely sort of woman."

"And what is your love born of?" I could not forbear asking. It was, I suppose, a sort of invitation which he was not slow to accept. For all my doubts I loved him hotly and did not wish to quarrel with him, nor think upon the morrow. He told me how beautiful I was, item by item, with gentle touchings and such a preparedness to delay the real business—which less courteous lovers lack—that I was almost persuaded to believe him. I listened with much pleasure. Truth as to fact is of no importance in such circumstances. Then he lay back upon the cushions. "There are much more solid reasons than your beauty, you must know. I am so free in being with you, so completely at ease. No polite affectations, no insincere compliments, no dull proprieties. I do not even have to pretend to an interest in marriage. Could there be a more rational regard? I count myself lucky to have discovered you. There can be no place for us to be but together." Since I did not speak, he continued. "I am so full of love for you that I must be sanguine, for when you love me in return, as I know you do, what else should you do but come with me to Bath?"

"The first months would be delight, but after that?"

"What an anxious little maid it is! What should follow but delight upon delight? Come here to me. Forget all this. Tell me how much you love me. *I* do not enter into this lightly, I assure you. I never loved a lady's maid before."

"No kitchenmaids, housemaids, laundry maids?"

"Only one. An underhousemaid when I was fourteen."

"How much did you love her?"

"Oh, mightily. She was my first lover (though I was not hers), a bran-faced, red-haired wench with a gentle temper. She was only a year or two older than I but full of tricks and willing to lie with me all day if she could."

"And how many mistresses?"

"It is a long list. I shall not bore you with it."

There was only one possible end to such pigeon murmurings and neither of us was averse to it. The windowseat was long and broad, the cushions soft; the sun shone benevolently in upon us. Lovemaking in such a place on such a day was no hardship, although in truth I think nothing but a tempest could have quenched our ardor. We raised dust from the cushions, threw them, flattened them, lay quiet, ran about, whispered, shouted, lay still again. I stood upon a flint and cried out, whereupon Henry sat me upon the table to examine the wound. It was all such silly games as lovers play, with what forfeits and conclusions you may devise. We were so keen about our business that we quite forgot all caution, or I suppose we might have heard the door open or the stair creak. But we did not. Someone came and caught us lying bread-and-butter fashion on the windowseat. I opened my eyes and looked over Henry's shoulder to see Tom Bertram, his hand on the newel post, having climbed the stairs from the lower room. He was, you may believe, the picture of astonishment.

"Good God!" said he, his temper gathering. "What sort of trick is this? Here is this particular friend who turns me over twice in the pot for trying to lay a pretty maid, the same friend who read me a lesson or two on obligation and responsibility, and lo and behold I find him pumping up and down in my own boathouse with the same pretty maid. And you so anxious to oblige your uncle and get to Bath! I should lay my stick across your backside now, Crawford." Henry rose hastily. "What a canting hypocrite! Worse than a bloody parson! At least he is obliged to put on a show of saintliness for his function. You have no such excuse."

"I need no excuse. Where there is mutual affection no excuse is necessary."

"I shall not be taken in again. You pretend to high principles, but give in to your appetites just like the rest of us. At least I am more honest."

"I am not a stick of wood to be used or not used by anyone," I said. "I have something to say in the matter."

"When do you not?"

"Is speaking not allowed, then? I must be dumb as well as willing, is that it? Well, I did not choose to lie with you, Mr. Bertram, for all that you are the son of the house, and I never would."

"What does he give you? A guinea or two for your services?"

"I am not to be bought."

"So you say. I am not such a Johnny-raw as to believe you. I wish you joy of her, Crawford. Banbury, I think you hoped to reach today. Well, ride-a-cock-horse, ride-a-cock-horse. Although this is no fine lady. She'll give you a high old time and a dose of the clap besides."

"Let us try to talk this business out sensibly," Henry interposed.

"You are accustomed to talking your way out of everything, Crawford, and perhaps you are admired for it, but not by me, nor by any man of honor. Only a coward turns off every insult with a smile. I might have my seconds out after you if this were not such a paltry affair. But no doubt you would have argued your way out of that, too. You are a hypocrite and a cheat."

"You couple with women as a dog with bitches, and leave your litter scattered over the countryside, yet you speak to me of hypocrisy!" said Henry, in a fine rage at last.

"What do you mean?" asked Tom, affronted.

"What do you know of honesty or responsibility?" Henry continued. "A dog is honest. He cocks his leg up where he will and runs after a bitch in heat as soon as he gets a whiff of her. That is honesty, oh yes, a dog's honesty, your sort of honesty."

"The man is mad," said Tom, "stark mad."

"He speaks of Kitty Huckle," I said.

"What is she to do with this?"

"The child. Had you forgotten the child?"

"I never heard of a child."

"Her mother told you."

"That old dame? She was only half in her right senses. Who could take the word of an old fool like that?"

"She happened to speak the truth," said Henry.

"You keep your nose out of this, Crawford."

"I despise your mean, secret dealings," said Henry. "I am only sorry for the poor female you treated so shamelessly."

"What about *your* mean, secret dealings?" continued Tom. "You flirted with my sisters, who doted on you, poor fools, and all the while were lying with their maid. That is honest, is it? At least I make love to only one at a time." Tom scored with me there. My heart leaped.

"I have never abandoned a child."

"I did not know there was a child."

"Oh, there is a child. I have seen her."

"You have seen her?" Tom was taken aback.

"She is a bonny infant, who so much takes after you that I believe even your father would acknowledge her parentage."

"My father! Do you threaten me, you blackguard? By what right do you sneak about behind my back, poking into my affairs?"

"Kitty was sent away by your aunt," I said. "No one knew where she was gone or what had become of her."

"You're a sharp, meddling puss, Hartwell."

"No one in this family but your aunt paid attention to the maid you debauched, or the child."

"Well, and isn't my aunt enough? It does not need an army of Lady Bountifuls to deal with one proliferous serving maid."

"Your aunt!" said Henry. "Do you know so little of your aunt that you leave such dealings to her?"

"You insult the whole family now, I see, Crawford. Considering the hospitality you have received and the way you have insinuated yourself—"

"You shall not distract me from your lack of responsibility by exclaiming over mine, Bertram."

"Your aunt sent Kitty away," I continued. "She cared not a fig for her. She did what she did only to protect your reputation and the reputation of Mansfield. She sent Kitty far from home, with promise of an allowance. And once she was out of sight, she stopped sending that."

"What a lather you are in over nothing. I might have known it would be money. That is always the way of it. If she had been handsomely paid, we should have heard no more of it."

"You are a cold fish, Bertram."

"You are a dupe. I am amazed at you, Crawford. Taking her part against me! She has bewitched you. What are you in for now, I wonder? What promises has she got out of you? Are you to set her up as a little cocotte, with a handsome drawing room and a diamond pin?" Tom had scored again. This was Henry's offer in the light in which it would generally be regarded. Tom shrugged. "I shall leave you to your sport. It seems that for all your posturing we are much the same, Crawford. I have lain in this same room with several willing maids. There's a coincidence for you. Mind you do not get caught in the same spring. You had better not leave Jane with a swelling belly."

"Jane is coming with me," Henry stated.

"There! I knew it. She has well and truly winged you. What an artful piece! Don't give in to her. She'll play you along for all you're worth."

"The offer was freely made. She comes with me to Bath."

"He is caught worst who does not see the trap," Tom commented. "I have done my best to warn you."

"I am not going to Bath," I said. "You asked me to go, but I did not say I would. I am not going to Bath."

Tom laughed. "There's a grateful wench for you! I must say, if I had made such an offer, I should not expect to be refused. Still, there's your chance. Take it and get out while you may. Better to be stood up by a housemaid than face six months of misery and expense." Tom turned to leave and, as he did so, caught sight of the volume I had brought with me. He picked it up. "What's this?"

"It belongs to me."

He opened it carelessly, and caught sight of the inscription on the flyleaf. He laughed. "There's a thing, Crawford. Do you know whose name is written here? Quinney's. How do you like that? It belongs to Quinney. How do you suppose she came by this? He must have been a very particular friend, that scene painter. I'll warrant she never told you how particular, did she?"

"You are hateful to insinuate such lies!" I said.

Tom shrugged and tossed the book onto the table. Henry did not take it up, but I saw his eyes directed toward it, and he hesitated momentarily before he spoke. "You will be sorry if you do not come to Bath. I do not make such offers every day."

He had been stung by Tom's remarks, and the manner in which he spoke was sufficient proof of what I had already suspected. If I did go with him, I should be no more than a petted lapdog, best loved when it is servile.

"The bid is unacceptable," I replied. "This piece of flesh is not for sale."

"You see?" observed Tom. "She is too wayward to be of use to anyone. Now you know why she refused me. You're not used to refusals, I daresay. No more am I. Don't let it trouble you. I'd lay you fifty to one you would have cause to regret your generosity. She would make your life wretched after a week. Leave her to her own devices. She will learn to repent what she's refused. You might have had either one of us, Hartwell, and made a good thing of it, too, but you are proud and stubborn and will end up with nothing."

Henry looked at Tom and then at me. "Is that all you have to say?"

"Like to like," I answered him. "Two spoiled young lords together. Go if you please and don't think I shall lament it. You may stand nose to tail and swat the flies off one another as long as you wish."

XIII

All my waking thoughts after Tom had come upon us in the boathouse were directed toward Henry. In the night's solitude I lay miserable and dry-eyed, tormented by the knowledge that I had refused him. He was so easy a man to love! I had lost him forever, and through my own fault. A hundred times I commended my good sense; a hundred times more the recollections of our tender lovemaking drowned my reason in a flood of longing.

I arose next morning, weary and low in spirits, to encounter one consequence of the previous day's doings I had never considered. When I entered Julia's apartment, my arms full of clean linen, a grim tribunal awaited me. Maria and Julia stood, two accusers full of malicious spite; their aunt sat, hands folded in her lap, a black-gowned, partial judge, verdict all but pronounced. I knew instantly what was to come, what I should have foreseen: Tom, smarting under his indignities, had told his sisters what he had discovered. It was a mortifying revelation to them both, but exceedingly so to Maria. Hourly expecting Henry's visit to Sir Thomas to ask for her hand, in a rage of frustrated passion when he did not come, she now found that he had been making up to her sister's maid, had, indeed, even while she was shedding bitter tears over him, been offering to set up that maid as his mistress in Bath.

"Close the door," Mrs. Norris commanded icily. She looked me up and down with all the savage disapproval of which she was capable, and nodded to Julia. Julia was my mistress, Julia was to begin.

"This is a most disagreeable task. I have never had to speak so to anyone before. I never thought I should be obliged to. I thought you knew how to conduct yourself properly. It is quite disgraceful. I wish you had never come here."

Maria could not contain herself. "It is odious, it is despicable! Such insolence, such ungratefulness! You have been treated with every consideration. How dare you!"

"You think yourself pretty, I suppose," said Julia, "though I cannot see it myself."

"No one could be captivated for more than a moment," Maria snapped. "It is only a sort of milkmaid look, after all. You make yourself a laughingstock. You need not think he will give you another thought."

"I should think not," Mrs. Norris said, so intent upon her own wished-for scheme that she did not yet perceive the true state of affairs. "It is Miss Julia he is fond of, Miss Julia, your mistress. Do you understand what you have done, you dreadful girl? You have driven Mr. Crawford away. How could he speak to my niece after this? He would be too ashamed. It is a wicked thing you have done."

Maria, unwilling to hear any more of how much Henry Crawford loved her sister, hastened to the attack: "You should be ashamed, creeping about trying to make much of yourself. Cunning little minx! After all my sister's kindness to you."

"The play was the worst mistake," said Julia. "It all began there. I do not think she was so bad before the play."

"Do not be deceived," said Mrs. Norris. "The signs were there from the beginning. I blame myself for trying to think the best of her. I should have known when I saw that ne'er-do-well she arrived with. I find it hard myself to believe such vile corruption, but I shall not weaken. We must be strong against the devil and all his works. Mark my words, you will come to a bad end, Hartwell. I see no repentance in you. What you have done is worse than stealing. You are nothing but a harlot. It grieves me to speak such a name in this house, in front of my nieces, but that is what you are and I shall not be afraid to name it. Such lewd behavior! I know my duty, and the good Lord knows that I do my best to follow it. You have offended against the commandments. You have offended against this family. A harlot is what you are. To write it large and pin it to you for all the world to see would not be too great a punishment. You have brought disgrace upon Mansfield."

"What am I to do?" demanded Julia. "You might have considered that. I go to all this trouble to get a maid—it was difficult enough, God knows—and now I am to be without again. No sooner are you able to dress my hair and sew a gown than I am to lose you. And my father just returned, too! He may very well insist upon my having Amelia. How shall I bear it?"

"Only think of all you have learned here," Mrs. Norris followed. "We have taught you everything. When I consider the chance that was given you! And the comforts you have enjoyed and the food you have eaten! You have a greedy appetite, I know it well. What thought did you give to those who provided for you so generously? Ungrateful hussy! You are a disgrace to your home and family. Why, even the fair name of Sotherton is blackened by your wickedness. I think of your poor old grandfather and Mrs. Whitaker and my heart bleeds for them. What have they done to deserve this? They bring you up at great trouble and expense and this is how you repay them. You do not deserve to cross their threshold again. If I had the misfortune to bear such a child as you, I should bolt the door against you, I should indeed. I should go down on my knees and pray God to forgive me for bringing such a monster into the world."

"I have given you my gowns and let you go off at your pleasure," said Julia.

"She has been thoroughly indulged," said Maria, "and this is the result."

"In the old days you would have been whipped," said Mrs. Norris. "It is a pity that such punishment has gone out of fashion. There is nothing that so imprints a knowledge of wrongdoing. I see you do not hang your head. It is just as well. We are not to be taken in by any false sign of penitence. I have watched you long enough. I know what you are like. The only way you will learn a lesson is to have it marked upon your back. You should be whipped."

I had withstood the lambasting more patiently than I might have done had they not taken me by surprise. Now I began to realize that no caution was necessary; I was free for once to speak the truth; I need not stand in a pillory of my own making.

"If I am to be whipped, then Miss Maria had better be whipped too."

"What?" Maria was outraged. "How dare you!"

"You will gain nothing by insolence," said Mrs. Norris calmly, not displeased at having provoked me into it.

"Ask her whether she has lifted her skirts for Henry Crawford."

"You vile creature!" Mrs. Norris stood up.

Julia's curiosity was aroused. "What do you mean?" She looked at Maria and then at me.

"Ask her what she did when she climbed around the gate at Sotherton and went off into the park with Henry Crawford. Ask her whether she broke the commandments."

Mrs. Norris's sticklike straightness hardened into iron. "I shall not stand by to listen to such treachery."

Julia was watching Maria. "Did you?"

Maria's look hardly wavered. "It is something to have one's own sister ask that. She is the one, not me. It is just what she would like, to sow discord between us. That would gratify her beyond everything."

"It is true," I said to Julia. "I saw them."

"True!" Mrs. Norris was outraged. "How could it possibly be true? Every word you speak is a lie. It is a cruel, vicious trick. I wonder you give it a moment's thought, niece. What other tricks have you deceived us with? No doubt you could tell me the whereabouts of that fine silver chain I mislaid. I well remember your sly look."

"You shall not make my sister and me disagree," said Maria. "We have bonds of love and affection you know nothing of. You shall not alter that. We are not to be taken in by monstrous lies you invent about us." She put her arm around Julia's shoulders. She was, like others I have known, a superlative actress offstage, though only indifferent on. Her timing and gesture were perfect.

"I saw you," I persisted, "what you did there in the dell beyond the ha-ha, the selfsame thing you would chastise me for."

"You did go off into the park," said Julia uncertainly.

"Of course I did. She knows that. Is it not the very thing to give substance to her invention? She is full of artful deceits."

Julia, reassured, decided against me. "You are worse than I would have believed."

"She is full of low cunning, like all her class," Mrs. Norris observed, "low cunning and carnal appetites. I never saw worse."

"What about Kitty Huckle?" I inquired, determined to score where I could. "I suppose you spoke more softly to Kitty, seeing that the child she was to bear was Tom's."

This was unexpected. Maria and Julia could not disguise their astonishment, and their aunt turned red with indignant righteousness. "That has nothing to do with the case."

"What happened to the money you promised to send her?"

"I treated her as she deserved."

"Do you suppose Sir Thomas would think so?"

"You shall not bring Sir Thomas into this!"

"Does he know about Kitty Huckle?"

"This is outrageous. I shall not listen to a word. I do believe you intend to threaten me. Do you hear her, niece? Do you hear her?"

"Did Kitty Huckle bear Tom's child?" asked Maria curiously. "I never heard that."

"I should hope not, indeed. It has been all my care to protect you from such unpleasantness during your father's absence. We do not want to set a lot of idle tongues wagging."

"Does Tom know?" asked Julia.

"Your concern does you credit, dear niece," her aunt answered somewhat testily, "but these sorts of matters are best forgotten. We must address ourselves to the matter in hand. We shall do no good by talking about something long over and done with. Hartwell merely tries to distract us."

"You shall send the money you promised," I said. "For the rest you may do as you please, but you shall send the money. The child is still to be cared for."

"I have done what was best and shall continue to do it. You will gain nothing by all this."

"You treated her abominably. You cared for nothing but preserving the family dignity. I despise your penny-pinching, and your crafty, spying ways."

Mrs. Norris's nostrils whitened and she delivered a stinging slap to my face. "Strumpet! Do you think it matters to me what a profligate twopenny servant thinks?"

"You belong on the streets," Maria snapped.

"I shall make my way. You think I cannot, but I shall."

"On the contrary, no one could doubt that you would do very well," Maria replied. "You may sell yourself quite profitably, for a few weeks at least. You have had plenty of experience it seems."

"Sell myself! Who are you to talk of selling? *You* sold yourself to Mr. Rushworth for his money and his estate. Enjoy it if you can. He is all you have now. There is nobody else but old Whinny Prinny. You will be obliged to marry him. You will never have Henry. He was the one you wanted."

This time Maria would have hit me but that I stepped aside. Mrs. Norris was enraged. "You will apologize to my nieces and myself for your scandalous behavior before you leave this house."

"Henry Crawford is nothing to me," said Maria in a low voice, "nothing. Whatever may have passed, he is nothing now, neither to my sister nor myself."

"If Mr. Crawford's taste is for maidservants then we have no more to say to him," said Julia.

"He was led on to it, my dear niece, be sure of it." Mrs. Norris was unwilling to admit the ruin of her matchmaking while a shred of hope remained. "Young men have quick passions. They cannot help themselves."

"He is not to be excused, aunt," said Julia.

"There! Only see what you have done!" Mrs. Norris turned on me once more. "The wicked mischief you have caused in this house. Have you no shame?"

"I shall quit Mansfield this very day," I answered. "You cannot be half so glad to be rid of me as I am to be rid of you."

This was not quite what they had intended. It would greatly inconvenience Julia if I left so soon, as I well knew. Mrs. Norris spoke for her. "You go when you are told, not a minute before and not a minute after. It is we who say when you shall leave. You go without leave and you break the law, remember that."

"I cannot do without a maid just now," complained Julia. "Where am I to find another inside a month? Why should it always be me? Whenever anything goes wrong, I am the one to suffer."

"You shall share Sophie," said Maria sweetly.

"Oh, it is all right for *you*." Julia was not to be mollified. "Why is it always my maid with whom there is trouble?"

"Boucher is worth ten of her," Maria comforted.

"You may finish the violet silk, I should think, Hartwell," Julia said plaintively to me. "It is almost done."

"She is best out of the house," said Maria. "We can do without her."

"I need the violet silk for the ball at Stoke. I must have a new gown. I am sure I do not have so many new gowns that I should be denied one for Stoke."

"Bring us the violet silk," commanded Mrs. Norris. "You shall sit here and finish it before you leave."

"You may fetch it yourself, and sew it too."

I turned upon my heel then, and left them there, the last insult mine as I snapped the door most decisively shut.

XIV

The momentous change is often made by a single throw of the dice. If afterward some pattern is discernible in the events which shape our fortune, what purpose do we spy? Is it a pattern of our own making? God's design? Or one we wishfully impose upon the random fall of the numbers? What smoldering desires lie within us awaiting a small breath to flame up? How many flicker and die for want of air? At that moment all that I had lately seen and heard caught fire and blazed up into a certainty that consumed my doubts and fears. I would quit Mansfield, go to London and seek my fortune. A mist of dreams lay over the metropolis, thick enough to mask the cold realities of which everyone spoke. Golden pavements stretched before me. I would leave Mansfield gladly, I would be an actress, I would . . . I knew not exactly what, but that it should confound them all and I was not to be dissuaded from pursuing it. My heart exulted as I shut the door upon the old black bat and her two nieces. I took my place at youth's eternal gaming table and joyfully wagered, as must everyone who sits at it, my past, present and future. Whatever vanity it is that urges the players on, I would not have it any other way. The stakes are high and the winners few, but without such daring one might as well live beneath a teacup.

I was not entirely romantic and impractical, I assure you. I did not intend to go to London alone; I proposed to seek out Matthew

Quinney. The possibility of the scene painter's help gave substance to my impetuous resolve. I began to see that an opportunity awaited me such as I had never dreamed of, perhaps would not have recognized as opportunity at all, had not a series of accidents—of which Matthew's presence made one—conspired to beat like birch twigs upon the customary dozy operation of my thoughts. I had been intrigued beyond measure at the world of which the scene painter had given me a glimpse, a world which recalled to me all that I had read and pondered as a child, bewildered, uncomprehending, but seeking enlightenment, in the library at Sotherton. There was so much to know beyond! My life enclosed me like a windowless room, old and quiet and comfortable, when suddenly a crack in the door shows the sun and sky outside. The division of rich and poor, servant and master, slave and owner, were matters that puzzled me as a child, but the child had laid such questions aside, trusting that age would bring understanding, as I innocently supposed it had to others, seeing all else they knew and did that I could not. Now I understood that such matters were not to be mastered like the baking of bread, that others merely became acquiescent, that I grew like them. I began again to consider those questions, to seek the answers with a measure of independence, to understand that the ways of the world were not all wise; some of them were as truly unfathomable as the child had thought. There is a tide in the affairs of men which, taken at the flood, leads on to fortune. The line is as familiar to me as my own name and yet it moves me no less than when I heard it first. I thrilled to a new sense of what might yet be, of what I might yet become.

I was deeply affected at leaving Sophie, but for her the parting was even harder to bear. It was but a short while since she had been deprived of Stephen; now she was to lose me also. She had not even the comfort of knowing how Stephen fared, for she had heard nothing since his departure. It was early to expect news, and a thousand good reasons might be adduced for his silence, but the possibility that she would never hear preyed upon her mind. Her single unshakable conviction—that Stephen would have great success in the world beyond Mansfield—contributed to her anxiety, for was his success not the very thing most to be feared as the easiest means of causing him to forget her? He sent no word; she would ask for none. Now, with almost equal suddenness, I was to leave. Yet she did not, beyond a few familiar warnings, try to dissuade me. When I brought out the box stowed beneath my bed, in which I proposed to pack my few necessaries, she said: "What is this?" It was a heavy wooden piece that my grandfather had made with a view to durability rather than convenience. "It is good to bury a dog, that. Leave it. I have something." She fetched a yellow carpetbag, very finely worked, that I knew she was fond of, and insisted that I take it. It was a particular token of her affection that I much valued. Our lives were on the change, and who knew when we should again see one another?

"You will not come with me?"

"Two of us on the road, what use is that? You go to London. Perhaps you see Stephen. Tell him I wait. Tell him. If you need help, you send to me." She pressed two guineas upon me.

"I have a guinea saved of my own, and there is what my grandfather gave me. There is no need."

"Not now, not now. But who knows?"

"What shall you do?"

"The same as now. Attend Maria. Wait for Stephen. I look after myself."

I left Mansfield quickly and quietly. For all her protestations, Mrs. Norris would not prevent me. It would no doubt have pleased her to pursue me for a forty-shilling fine (or even three months' imprisonment), but it was a positive convenience to her that I and my story of Kitty Huckle should disappear. Apart from Sophie, only two others knew of my going. I inquired of John May where in Northampton his cousin the shoemaker dwelled, and I told Mr. Wilcox, although I wondered at first whether that had been wise, so heartily did the coachman reproach himself for having been the means of bringing me to Mansfield, and so unhappily did he fret over what he should say to his cousin, Mrs. Whitaker, when my departure became known. But I was cheerful and determined in my reassurances and, although he continued to shake his head woefully, he began to make the best of it, like the good man he was. Indeed, he himself took me in the gig to Northampton, where he went on errands for Sir Thomas who, in all the busy enthusiasm for being newly at home, required numerous small purchases.

At the moment when the gig, with Reveller in the shafts, turned out through the handsome arch of the stable yard, I experienced those feelings of regret which must accompany the quitting of any place where one has not been entirely unhappy. I heard the great clock striking and thought of my own small room above, where the chiming of the bells on every quarter had marked the progress of my days and nights until it seemed as much a part of me as the beating of my own heart. I saw Christopher Jackson consulting with Sir Thomas by the sawmill, and knew when we passed the creaking timber wagon, two great draft horses straining in the shafts, that some large scheme for improving the estate was already commenced. I saw the chimney of the boathouse in the distance, the lake water glinting, and thought of Henry. I even caught sight of Fanny Price exercising Pug. It was a busy, new-wound little world that I felt myself, with a grand condescension, to be quitting for a larger.

In one of the poorer bystreets of Northampton, in a district where the acrid odors of curing leather were so strong they near choked me, John May's cousin brought me to a house outside which a bullfinch sang in a cage of rushes, and a child sat on a three-legged stool by the door, waxing hemp. The man within, who wore the brow band and black apron of his trade, sat at his block, stitching a pair of box calf boots. Gunnary Binns was a man of sullen and cloudy aspect, whom Noah May evidently held in awe. The footman's cousin had told me he knew nothing of Matthew Quinney but, at my urging, had at last reluctantly agreed to conduct me to someone who might. Gunnary Binns was plainly ill pleased to be so consulted; he stared out from beneath his brows with intimidating dislike, asking Noah, with more threat in the words than they usually convey, what he meant by it.

"Just trying to help a lady," squeaked Noah and scuttled away. Binns sat down and resumed his work.

Expecting him to attend to me when his stitching was done, I waited some minutes before I understood he meant entirely to ignore me. I repeated the inquiry about the scene painter.

"Never heard of him."

I explained further.

"You won't find anybody of that sort here."

The man's surliness did not dispose me to believe him. "But he told me most particularly that he would be among the shoe-makers."

"Then you must have misheard."

The ensuing silence was broken by the entry of Mrs. Binns, who suckled an infant and had two other wan-faced little ones clinging to her skirts. She was less forbidding, and I rephrased my question. She said not a word but looked for guidance toward her husband. I began at last to think they knew but would not tell. How should I persuade them? I bethought me of my book. Mrs. Inchbald's *British Theatre* should speak for me, although it was surely the strangest use to which it had ever been put. I showed Matthew's name upon the flyleaf to the shoemaker, then to his wife. Neither of them could read, but Binns was sufficiently impressed; he laid down his tools and, after turning over the volume in his hand, went out with it. Released from the constraint of her husband's presence, Mrs. Binns nodded, smiled and offered me a drink of small beer and a slice of bread and dripping. I accepted gratefully although I thought, looking at the thin faces of the two older children, she could ill afford such generosity.

Gunnary Binns was absent the better part of an hour, but when he returned he brought Matthew with him. Although the scene painter wore countryman's drab, its rough cloth and dull colors most unlike his usual outlandish garb, nothing could disguise his tall, thin form. He greeted me with his customary grave pleasure, and I chattered on, explaining the whys and wherefores of my unexpected coming, no little relieved to see him at last.

"You find me just in time," he said, when I stopped for breath. "I leave tonight."

"You have rough country to cross," said Gunnary Binns. "She'll not do in that." He evidently disapproved of what I wore.

"I travel by the Grand Junction Canal," Matthew explained.

"You'd best cover up," Binns interposed, nodding toward my gray pelisse. His wife acted upon his words and disappeared, he calling after her, "Bring sacking too!", saying to me, with a further contemptuous nod at my leather half boots, "They'll spoil in no time."

At that moment, I began to wonder what kind of an escapade I had embarked upon, and to have some doubts about my own part in it. In truth, all that I had so far seen bespoke a sort of secrecy and bold daring of which I knew nothing, of which I had anticipated nothing. Here was I, but a few steps on the way, and already found wanting: what other things awaited me for which I should be equally unprepared?

Matthew took all in his stride, as if we embarked upon nothing more than a healthful walk. "Have you never seen the canal? It is a pleasant way to view the country."

"Is it unsafe for you to travel by stage?" I could not forbear asking.

Matthew took no offense at my curiosity. "It is always better to take precautions where I can."

"What do you fear?"

"Nothing. I fear nothing. But I addressed a meeting here. These things become known."

"A meeting!" He only spoke what I had already guessed, yet the very utterance imprinted the fact upon me suddenly. At Mansfield, Matthew had been so open about his political views as to be indiscreet, but in those sheltered environs what he spoke of seemed remote.

"There is nothing wrong with a meeting, except if some spy confuses it with a Luddite mob. If you are alarmed, do not come with me."

"Have you ever been arrested?"

Gunnary Binns frowned at that but Matthew merely laughed. "By no means. And I certainly do not intend to be. But there are those, a few here and there, who would not be disappointed if I were."

The cloak Mrs. Binns brought me was threadbare, but I did not need it for warmth and, being dark and voluminous, it was admirably suited to the purpose; it even sufficed to cover the yellow carpetbag. I gave the kindly, silent woman, who had still not said a word, seven shillings, which I trusted would buy her a warm replacement.

The shoemaker was to take us as far as the canal. He started off at a brisk pace and never slackened, urging us forward in the necessity of reaching our destination before darkness fell. A made road covered part of the six miles between town and canal, and a well-worn track the rest, but it seemed we must travel even less obtrusively, and two miles outside Northampton we turned aside and began to walk across the fields. As I contemplated the miry way that lay ahead of us, I once more questioned the wisdom of the enterprise. It was a chill October afternoon, beautiful enough if one has a snug room and fire to look forward to, but with the cold, wide world open before me not altogether enticing. Unbidden there came into my mind the image of my servant's place at Mansfield: privileged, sheltered, protected, sharing some of the pastimes of the idle genteel whom I served. Now I stood in the middle of nowhere, my companions a Jacobinical scene painter and a gruff, silent son of Crispin, both liable to arrest as far as I could tell. I did not know where I should sleep that night nor yet the next. I did not know whether I might end in India or Africa, or murdered in a ditch for the paltry contents of Sophie's yellow carpetbag. If this were the way to fame and fortune it was treacherous indeed.

The best antidote to such cold thoughts is a brisk beginning, and I assure you I made it. We strode out over the fields and through the spinneys with a will, hugging the hedges so that we might remain inconspicuous, and hoping (correctly as it turned out) to encounter neither shepherd nor laborer. It was a misty day that drew in fast to dusk and Gunnary Binns's intention was to see us within reach of Blisworth Tunnel so that we might be up at dawn and board one of the boats that customarily tied up there for the night. Post along as we might, however, it seemed as though we would not get far enough before darkness fell. There was no straight way, and twice we were obliged to circle three sides of an enclosed field to find a passage through the willows and brambles. And then, of course, crossing a plowed field cannot be done with dispatch, although I prided myself on not hindering too greatly the speed of our progress. I had pulled up my skirts between my legs like a field girl and, although my boots took mud and wet despite the sacking, my dress was thus saved from the worst. Cold though it began to be, the walking stirred the blood and kept us warm.

A near-full moon had risen when, having made our way through

a thick expanse of plane trees, Mr. Binns, indicating that we had
no more than another mile ahead of us to Blisworth Tunnel, prepared to turn back. "Thank you, Quinney, thank you," he said,
shaking Matthew's hand with a warmth that surprised me. "It's
such as you that give us courage. I'm a plain man. I don't seek out
trouble; it's on the doorstep. There's some who think we had a
hand in the assassination. It was a bad day for us when the prime
minister was killed."

"He was not sympathetic to us, but few of them are. He had at
least secured a few government contracts for the bootmakers. We
shall do no better with the next one, I am afraid."

"Something worse, if you ask me," said Mr. Binns grimly. "But
we shall petition, you have my word on it."

With this exchange, by far the lengthiest the shoemaker had
indulged in, he nodded his farewell, which included me scarcely at
all, then turned on his heel and made back the way he had come.

The plane wood was relatively dry, and we considered bedding
down there for the night. In the event, however, we decided in
favor of moving on, tempted by a stand of trees, only a little to
the south of our intended direction, the outline of which was still
visible against the darkening sky. There we would be almost certain
to find equally suitable shelter. I was more anxious than Matthew
to be as close to our destination as possible before we rested. Indeed,
I spoke for reaching the canal itself, although Matthew pointed out
that it would be as well to be cautious since bad characters were
said to infest the neighborhood of the tunnels. (Of which by general
reckoning we made two, as I told him.)

As it turned out, either we had traveled further or it was much
closer than we had allowed, for after trudging the extra half mile
we found ourselves, quite suddenly, almost on top of the canal.
When I saw the moonlight reflected palely in its calm surface, my
spirits revived amazingly. It was a small achievement in which I
took inordinate pleasure. As more proof that luck was with us, we
espied, close at hand, a lambing hut, earlier hidden from view by
the sharp slope leading down to the canal, from which it was
effectively screened by three small thorn trees, and therefore less
likely to be already inhabited. Three-sided and roughly thatched,
it provided more comfort than we had dreamed of, especially since

there was a plentiful supply of dry straw within.

I fell almost immediately into a sound sleep, from which I awoke some three hours later as the chill entered into me. Matthew still slumbered, and after that I drowsed like a cat with half an ear open, partly because of the cold, partly because I knew that we must be up betimes, and in no small measure because I was excited about what lay ahead.

When Matthew awoke, at the lightening of the sky, we surveyed the canal from our vantage point high upon the eastern side of the enormous cut that had been made to accommodate it, the very stand of trees we had previously observed surmounting the entrance to the great tunnel of Blisworth. It was an awe-inspiring sight in the daylight: the entrance to the tunnel faced with brick and stone, the ground above it rugged and picturesque, the trees topping the whole in a miraculous fashion, as though their roots had never felt any disturbance from the great excavation that had gone on beneath. Truly it was a testimony to man's infinite capacity to master nature, and I thrilled to it, my doubts of the previous evening quite evaporated.

Smoke rose from the chimneys of two of the three narrow boats moored where the lilac and silver ribbon of the canal was snipped off by the dark entrance, and the horses, hobbled in a croft beyond, were even then being untied. It was clear that the boats would shortly be on their way. We made speed down the slope and bartered for our passage. As it turned out, only one of the narrow boats, which carried coal, went the distance.

The first part of our journey was the strangest. Matthew walked over the top with the horse and the lad who minded it, but the boatman motioned me to stay on board. Then he lighted the lantern and took the helm, while the two stout young fellows who had been hired to take the boat through the tunnel removed their upper garments and, applying themselves to the poles, began sturdily to move the boat into the dark.

"D'ye sing?" the boatman asked me abruptly, so that between the unexpectedness of the question and his curious dialect, I did not at first comprehend what was said. "It helps 'em," he explained. I willingly complied, though I did not at first see the purpose of such a request. I have not a powerful singing voice, but it is sweet and true, and I usually contrive to acquit myself creditably. In those days, you may imagine, it was nothing more than a jolly jig or rousing hymn that I had learned as a child. I have had a music master since, but I still take pleasure in the old songs.

Oh, but that is hard work, shifting seventy tons of coal with nothing but the power of two pair of hands! What with the rank air, and the dark, and the endless rhythm of the work, there was good need to sing: nearly three hours below ground, nearly three hours in the bowels of the earth. I sang, and they sang, and I sang again, while the tunnel gave to the songs a strange resonance I never shall forget. The voices, even my own, seemed to belong to phantoms, the walls throwing the sound back in a reverberation more mysterious than that of a ventriloquist. I felt a great wonder at the chill and eerie place. We left behind a red and gray dawn, to journey, it seemed, into the underworld, the lantern casting grotesque shadows on to the brick roof, slimed with damp, that arched over us. All we could see outside the lamp's uneven flicker was a point of light from the barge following; all we could hear, outside the mournful echo of the singing (however merry the song), was the splashing of water, which dripped from the roof or slapped against the wall as the movement of the boats imposed an unnatural swell upon its stillness. When we came out into the sunshine at Stoke Bruerne, it was as though I had crossed from one land into another, so far did I now feel from my previous existence. I came up from the darkness like a hedgehog in the spring, stretching to the warmth and sweet air as to the light of a new life.

Three shillings and a quart of ale apiece the two brothers Aylott, our polers, received, and well-earned too, I thought, seeing the sweat running off them. But they could do the same task thrice more that day if called upon, made a handsome living and were muscled like blacksmiths. Matthew and the boy awaited us, and we all drank together, my throat dry although my thirst was no match for the brothers'. The younger one directed at me some pert remarks and cream-pot looks, the older was soon deep in conversation with Matthew, with whom he clasped hands in farewell (an odd thing in itself), and I noted an uncommon sort of grip, such as I thought I had before observed when Matthew parted from Gunnary Binns. It struck me then that it was a sign of fraternity, such as might be passed along the way from one group of sympathizers to another.

"You discover acquaintance everywhere," I said to Matthew, as we waited for the first lock to empty.

"I had not met them before, but their elder brother is a shoemaker. He was at the meeting where I spoke."

"Word travels quickly."

"Sometimes too quickly." He glanced back at the boatman, but Mr. Harris's stolid face betrayed nothing.

As the boat continued to drop through a vast staircase of seven locks to the valley below, I watched the great gates open and close, the water run in like a flood. My wonderment at the scene outside was only equaled by my curiosity about Matthew. "How do you come to be one of them?"

Matthew took his time to reply. "By no one circumstance alone. My mother was widowed. I went hungry often enough to ponder the reason. I was hardy and survived, though I am but one of five who did so. That was due to my uncle, my mother's brother, a scene painter also, the same from whom I learned my trade. He taught me to read after my own father died. He was a fine sort of man, an inquirer after the truth, but a wanderer, as indeed in my work you needs must be. He was always generous to my mother, and he took me as his own at her request, though it nearly broke her heart to part with me. Good soul that she was! She died but a few months later, worn out with grief and hardship, and my two remaining sisters whom she had with her survived not long after.

"My uncle read Paine and others; some of the books I now carry belonged to him. He met with the small groups of working men in each town, those who read, who wanted to better themselves. They shared whatever they had in the way of books and newspapers, discussed the affairs of the nation. I take all my views from my uncle."

"What happened to him?"

"He died five years since, in America."

"America?"

"He was convicted of sedition in the nineties, and imprisoned. Later he was in the Corresponding Society, and escaped to America. Only just in time. All the others on the committee were seized a few days after he left Liverpool."

"What did the poleman want with you?"

"He was anxious for news of what happens in Northampton."

"And what does?"

"Much the same as elsewhere. The men wish to combine to press for improvements in their working conditions. The law is against it; the masters are against it."

"There are no calls for death or liberty, then?"

"Heaven forbid! There are some hotheads, of course, but we are no enemies to law and order."

"You break the law by meeting at all."

"The law is unjust. We petition to change it."

"What about the assassination?"

"We had nothing to do with that. Perceval was one of the members for Northampton, but that is the single connection. The prime minister's murder was the act of a madman. I much regret it. Such a thing is the very opportunity for those in power to stir up feeling against reform. Yet if we do not soon have reform, I fear we *shall* have revolution."

"Do you attend any more meetings?"

"I have friends living not far from London whom I propose to visit on the way, that is all."

"Shall I go with you?"

"It is probably wiser that you do not. I do not know personally all who will be there. Some are very restrained, some wild. Some are known to the authorities. Such gatherings are viewed with great suspicion. If I were to be taken, the chances are that it would be at a meeting. Someone turns King's evidence and we are all done for. Then where would your theatrical aspirations be?" He glanced again at Mr. Harris. "Enough of this. Our boatman must not think us anything but simple rustics."

It was then Matthew's turn to question me. There was little enough to tell about my life, so quiet and free of incident was it beside his own, but I warmed to the task when I described my grandfather, for were they not two of a kind? My grandfather would have shaken his head at Matthew's activities, but he was no less quick and keen to perceive injustice. The most curious coincidence then came to light: Matthew's uncle had known my grandfather. Not in a great way, to be sure, but as one of those whose views and intelligence accorded with his own.

"George Pearce," said Matthew, wonderingly. "George Pearce. I recall hearing about George Pearce. It was my uncle's mission to persuade people like your grandfather to join us. What a chance! George Pearce's granddaughter and Davey Archbold's nephew! What would they make of that, do you suppose?"

I had no doubt that my grandfather would most heartily have disapproved, but the discovery of such a connection was a welcome bond between us.

"Come," said Matthew, "we must improve upon our appearance of harmless foolishness. Let us begin your theatrical education, that will do it. An interest in the dramatic art is bound to persuade Mr. Harris we are halfway to Bedlam. Besides, although I can talk the manager at Covent Garden into hearing you, you must have some set pieces to prove yourself."

Matthew's books, the chiefest reason for the heavy weight of his large traveling bag, as I discovered, were an apt reflection of his interests: Tom Paine was there, and some yellowing copies of Cobbett's *Register*, unbound editions of various modern plays for which he had been painter, several volumes by poets whose names were then unfamiliar to me, and a much-thumbed edition of the works of Shakespeare. It was no wonder, as I told him, that he was so eager to be rid of Mrs. Inchbald. He set me to reading, and the learning and delivery of several speeches. How should I ever forget my first acquaintance with Juliet? For of course, I must learn to be Juliet. And, since I knew the part well already, I was to do Agatha also, despite Matthew's low opinion of *Lovers' Vows*.

The weather remaining clement, we walked along the towpath, as we were not obliged to keep out of sight. Although it was against the rules for the boats to carry passengers, providing the cargo arrived on time the company turned a blind eye. During the occasional rattling shower we took shelter in the little cuddy which Harris had made over to us, he and his boy making do with a tarpaulin. It was a pleasant sort of quiet life, with nothing much to do but look after ourselves, admire the variegated beauty of the scenery and read the best authors. The steady movement of the boat, the brisk exercise, corned beef and hot roast potatoes for supper, made a simple and healthful existence such as many greater folk would profit from. Harris also kept on board a sort of grayhound, a decided poaching dog, of whose excursions we were the beneficiaries.

I declaimed my speeches, so that I might learn them by heart and benefit from Matthew's comments upon the delivery, as we walked ahead of the boy who led the horse, a bright, cheerful lad in his tenth year, and a great one for chat, who observed our antics with interest. Matthew discovered that he could not read and would have begun to remedy the deficiency, but that Harris regarded this activity with such mistrust that he withdrew the lantern on some trumped-up pretext. Both lad and horse were well fed, I will say, for all that their master was a surly fellow. I was obliged to turn my eyes sometimes from the bags of bones I saw being whipped along the towpath, poor, wretched beasts.

Harris neither volunteered information about himself, nor asked a question of us. He even discouraged the boy's curiosity. But his reticence, so far as we could tell, was not the result of distrust. Indeed, by the time we reached Leighton Buzzard, where Matthew bought fresh eggs from a farmer's daughter hawking them on the wharf and two jugs of good ale from the inn and offered to share them, he was almost agreeable, and we had a merry evening, hearing of the marvels and disasters of the canal trade. Harris even told a most indecent story, about a navvy's theft of undergarments from a lock-keeper's wife, and Matthew countered with some stories of the theater, a trifle unguarded himself, I thought. We heard how Harris's wife had died, and he had been obliged to sell his own narrow boat because he could not afford to employ a helper. His ambition was to get out of the business of coal-carrying altogether and work for Mr. Spode, who had a reputation for treating his work people fairly, and whose great manufactory, with its eighteen furnaces and two steam engines, the usually taciturn Harris described for us with enthusiasm. I have not infrequently wondered, when visiting Mr. Spode's showrooms in Portugal Street (where I purchased my favorite dinner service), whether the boatman ever achieved his modest ambition; or whether, indeed, that promising lad ever learned to read.

XV

I prevailed upon Matthew to let me accompany him to the meeting of which he had spoken. Indeed, he needed little persuading, since Chandler's Cross was some twenty miles from the metropolis and, by quitting the narrow boat a few miles north of Watford, we should avoid the meandering curve by which the Grand Junction Canal reaches its terminus at Paddington Basin, and thus shorten our journey, which we should complete by a day's walk into the city.

At Chandler's Cross, which was nought but a hamlet, dwelled two old friends of Matthew's uncle, David Archbold, the scene painter. Many years before, in the first heady days of the French Revolution, the three had been drawn together by common interests, and the friendship had never waned. Matthew had thus known them since he was a child, when they had shown him great kindness. Their most daring assertion of their views had been, like my grandfather, to drink Napoleon's health behind closed doors in the privacy of their own homes, but they remained friends of liberty and as fond of Matthew as he of them. Consequently, whenever occasion allowed, he went to see them, and they, recapturing the days of their youth, drew together a few others of the same persuasion to meet the scene painter, of whom they were not a little proud.

Chandler's Cross was not much above two miles from the canal, and we made our way through the pleasant countryside of Buckinghamshire late in the afternoon, a short walk before us and the promise of a warm welcome and feather mattresses for the night ahead. What Matthew's friends might think of me, traveling alone with him, gave me pause, but when I touched upon this in a sidewise fashion, Matthew made nothing of it. He was expected to live outside the conventions, he reminded me, although he did so much less than was generally assumed. He showed himself, neither then nor later, I should mention, in no way disposed to take advantage of my position, although most of those we encountered evidently assumed that we traveled as man and wife.

On the main street at Chandler's Cross, opposite a respectable public house, stood several cottages of sturdy seemliness. To one of these we made our way. Two stories high, built of limestone and decently thatched, with massive stone chimney stacks and a neat garden, it bespoke comfort. The dame who opened the door greeted us as warmly as we could have wished, and her husband, Mr. Sefton, who came out but a minute later tying on his spectacles, was no less hospitable. The apothecary was of small, wiry build and had a habit of smiling widely in moments of enthusiasm, to reveal blackened gums which he then attempted to conceal behind his hand. We were conducted to a well-appointed parlor fronting the street, where two persons already warmed themselves at a good fire, and where we were soon joined by a few more. Heavy shutters insured our privacy and when all were present, introductions were made as necessary, with the exchange of the handshake I had already noted as a sign of fellowship. Mrs. Sefton did not make one of the gathering, disappearing into the back offices after providing us with a delicious game pie, but I was not the only female present: a sister to one of the men was evidently a regular member of the company. She was a large, ill-featured woman, most strangely dressed in a Barcelona petticoat of very old-fashioned cut, with enormous pockets which bulged on either side, from one of which she extracted a small pipe and some tobacco, which she proceeded to smoke. Her appearance was misleading, however. When she spoke it was in a striking, low-pitched voice of carrying tone and much to the point. She it was, I discovered, who made the other friend of David Archbold. The apothecary, taking pleasure in his duties as host, bustled round to collect what chairs he could that we might all be

at ease. "Ah, Matthew!" he said. "If I had but to set another chair
for Davey, it would do my heart good! We miss him more than
we can say, do we not, Sarah?"

"He would be proud of you, Matthew, indeed he would, carrying
on the good work as you do."

"We are all proud," said Mr. Sefton. "It is an honor as well as
a pleasure to have you here, is it not, friends?"

By the time the last invited guest, the landlord of the Three
Feathers, entered, carrying a jug of ale from his premises across
the road and inquiring whether Matthew and I wished to eat, there
were eleven of us in all, and I had seated myself inconspicuously
in the window.

"Eat all you can," advised one man, a cooper by the name of
William McTavish, as round as his wares but somewhat curmud-
geonly. "It's all you'll get by way of contributions."

"We have already eaten, thanks to my good friend, Mr. Sefton,"
Matthew replied. "I require no payment."

"I'm glad to hear it. Some make a regular business out of speech-
ifying and I don't approve of it."

"I don't myself," Matthew answered pleasantly. "But some have
given up a decent living for the cause and must have something to
keep body and soul together."

"We don't begrudge a few shillings," said Mr. Sefton.

"It all depends," growled McTavish. "I cannot abide speechi-
fying."

"I'm not sure I know what you mean, sir," said Matthew.

"Whipping up the mobs," explained Sarah Bell, "inciting them
to violence. That's what Mr. McTavish means, isn't it, William?
You would be surprised to know, Matthew, how many of the
missionaries like to work themselves and others up into a frenzy."

"I believe in reason," said Matthew.

"Of course you do. Aren't you Davey Archbold's nephew,
after all?"

"William is anxious, as I am myself, about being drawn into
violence. We do not want to break the law," said the publican,
Mr. Syrett.

"That's all very well," said another man who had not previously
spoken, "but it is the perfect excuse for doing nothing. I don't
know that I can go along with it."

"I've yet to hear you make a better suggestion, Elias," said the cooper belligerently.

"Things are moving a little," said Matthew. "I can say that for certain. There are those among the landowners and gentry who incline to our view. Some of them have come together and formed an association where these matters may be discussed and reforms sought. It is to be called the Hampden Club. They are in hopes that such groups will spring up all over the country. This is where our strongest chance lies."

"It doesn't seem much, Mr. Quinney, I'm bound to say," said Elias Low. "I am a weaver, born in Nottingham, that unlucky place. All my family are stockingers and I hear that they are in a terrible way now, worse than when I left. Last winter half the population was on relief, close to fifteen thousand people that is, fifteen thousand all but starving. And this year it is no better. No one in my family has work. They are dying by inches."

"There's nowhere worse than Nottingham," Matthew agreed. "There is such a garrison, it is like a siege."

"What did I tell you?" Elias Low turned to the others. "You think I exaggerate, but Mr. Quinney knows I speak true."

"Great crowds of them cheered at the assassination," said Mr. McTavish. "I can't abide that."

"What other way can they show their disaffection?" asked Matthew. "Parliament has legislated against frame-breaking. It is now a capital offense. And seventeen people have been hung already in the north this year. How else can they express their disapproval?"

"Only think on that, William," said the woman. "Poor Elias here, he's wondering which of his family and neighbors will be hung."

"Two years ago," said Elias, "when the troubles first began in Nottingham, we took the jack wires out of the frames, and that brought the hosiers into line. I'm all in favor of it. Action, that's what we want. We petition and plead and the government does nothing. What I want to know is how long we must sit around and talk before something is done. It costs nothing to talk."

"You've had a lot to bear, Elias," said Mr. Sefton, "but don't run down talk. It's slow but it's sure."

At that moment I heard the sound of hoofs upon the road. Sitting in the window, I glanced round at the shutters and then caught the eye of Mr. Syrett. He, like the good landlord he was, hearing the sound almost as soon as I, assumed it to be the arrival of a traveler or two upon horseback at his hostelry (which, as you will remember, was only the breadth of a road away). Mindful of his business, he evidently considered whether he should absent himself from the meeting in order to see to his guests.

"That sounds like a goodly few travelers you've got out there, Jack," said one man. "They'll keep you busy."

The landlord frowned. "I could have wished them on a different night."

There was something remarkable in such numbers. Nothing was said, but the company was silent while I unbolted one of the shutters and opened it a crack. The landlord, who peered over my shoulder, reassured himself by saying: "It is probably no more than some young bloods from town. It would be just like them to be out on some rampage and want my best supper."

What we observed from the window was indeed an unusually large number of horsemen, six in all, of whom two were dismounted and four remained in the saddle. At first glance they might have been taken for travelers, but there was an air about them which suggested otherwise. The single lantern which hung beside the door of the Three Feathers was enough to reveal that they looked around them with more than common interest. While we watched, two other horsemen came up at a fast canter, with surprisingly little noise. I whispered, "The hoofs are muffled!" Two others of the company came to look.

"Close the shutter," commanded Matthew, "or they will know they are observed." At that moment, by the fitful light of the lantern, I caught sight of the face of one of the last two men to arrive. There were whispers among the company:

"The harness was muffled."

"Didn't I see a musket?"

"Come, my friends," said Jack Syrett, "let us not be too hasty. We must not jump to conclusions."

"Matthew," I said, my voice quite strangled by fright, "one of the horsemen . . ."

"What is it?" said Matthew urgently. "What did you see, Jane, for God's sake?"

"I saw . . . It was . . . I am sure it was . . . I think I saw Alexander Belzoni!"

"Alexander Belzoni! In the name of heaven!"

"What can he have to do with this?" I whispered.

"Who can guess? But it is too far for the long arm of coincidence. If they are the King's men, we must escape. This meeting must never have happened."

The group stood transfixed in stunned amazement, like rabbits in the light of a lantern.

"We must move quickly or they will be upon us," said Matthew, taking charge. "Do you burn those papers, Mr. McTavish."

The cooper began to protest, "We've done nothing wrong!," though even as he did so someone whispered: "We shall never get away."

"If you do not burn them," said Matthew fiercely, "they will be used against you." The cooper ceased protesting and did as he was bid. "How many back ways out are there, Mr. Sefton?"

"None but the one," the apothecary stuttered. "It leads out into the garden which is walled. There is a gate into a side lane."

"How high is the wall?" asked Matthew. "And what lies beyond?"

"How high is it?" the apothecary repeated stupidly.

"Could we climb over it?"

"Perhaps. Yes. I think so, but you must be strong and agile."

"There is a five-acre field beyond," said Sarah Bell briskly. "And on the far side of that a small wood."

"Mr. Sefton," said Matthew, addressing the apothecary, "you must attempt as regular an appearance here as possible." He turned to the woman. "Miss Bell. You and your brother may quite readily remain here as if you were consulting Mr. Sefton, may you not?" She nodded. "John Armitage, where are the two horses?" He spoke to one of two brothers who had ridden in from the village of Sarratt.

"In a field behind the Bells'," was the reply.

"Well out of sight," Miss Bell added.

"That's good," said Matthew, "that's good. I may have need of them as much as you do. Lie up a bit, all night if need be. Take no risk of being seen. You, sir,"—this to the publican—"you have the jug of ale. Rustle up a dish or two, Sefton, and Jack here may

181

make shift to be fetching back the supper or some such. The rest of you leave by the side gate if it is not too late. They will be round the house as soon as they are sure they have discovered the right one. Before you leave, get rid of the pots, I beg you, and clear this room of the appearance of numbers."

The company made haste to do as Matthew had advised, so far as was possible with half of them in a state of fear and trembling. Mr. McTavish knocked a pot off the table, which fell with a dreadful clatter and, as they and Matthew, who had picked up his bag of books, closed the back door after themselves, the wind caught and slammed it with noise enough to raise the dead. The room now contained myself, Jack Syrett the publican, Sarah Bell and her brother and Mr. Sefton, whose wife joined us with the remains of the game pie. She stood holding it, with no notion of what to do until Miss Bell said sharply: "Mima! Give that to Jack!" The publican, equally unable to think for himself in this crisis, took it obediently. We had contrived to disperse only just in time, for almost immediately came a loud and peremptory knocking at the front door.

"He will recognize me!" I said suddenly, horribly alert to my own danger.

"Here!" Sarah Bell said to me. "Quick!" She produced from one of her ample pockets a long black woolen scarf and wound it around my head and neck so that it half covered my features. "You are sick with a quinsy. Mr. Sefton, do you hear?"

The apothecary, though visibly agitated, nodded his head and prepared himself to answer the front door, smoothing down the lappets of his coat and nervously adjusting the spectacles upon his nose. He gave a passable performance of amazement, though he was too mild a man for indignation, but he did not manage to keep the intruders outside for long. Three of them entered the room almost at once, one carrying a musket. I saw with relief that Alexander Belzoni was not among them.

"What's going on here?" asked he with the musket, who appeared to be in charge.

"Going on? What should be going on? Who are you?" Miss Bell was not lightly to be put upon.

"You'll find that out soon enough, old woman."

"It looks cozy," said another. "I'd sooner be warming my feet in this hearth than beating up the country, Lennox."

"So would we all, Batey," said Lennox, who carried the musket, "but we have a job to do and we're going to do it."

"And what are you beating up the country for?" asked Miss Bell, with asperity.

"You know well enough," said Lennox, "but since you're asking, I'll tell you. We have a warrant for the arrest of a certain well-known reformist, and our information is that he is hereabouts. In fact, we have reason to believe that he is in this house and that a private meeting has been taking place. That kind of thing is against the law, as I've no doubt you are aware. If you've any sense, you'll tell us what you know."

"All I know is that I've got a maid here with the quinsy," said Miss Bell.

"Where are you off to?" Lennox spoke sharply to the publican, who was proposing to leave.

To his credit, Jack Syrett answered up. "I'm landlord over there. This is nothing to do with me. I came over with supper, as you see. It's time I went back; I can't leave my customers any longer."

"You'll do as I tell you, and I tell you you can't leave." Lennox prodded him with the musket. "Sit down, man, and speak when you're spoken to. What's that you've got there?" He gestured at the dish in the landlord's hands.

"Search the rest of the house," he ordered the other two men, as he began to consume the remains of the game pie. "Now," he said to Miss Bell, "let's have a bit of straight talking. Have you seen him?"

"There's nobody here but my brother and me and poor Susan."

"Poor Susan, is it? She'll be a lot poorer by the time we've finished, if you don't stop playing games." Lennox turned to Sarah Bell's brother. "Speak up, man. Don't let the women do all the talking for you. Where is this fellow?"

George Bell was large and strong, but when he spoke (for the first time that I could recollect), his voice was as squeaky as a door wanting oil. In order to say even those few words, he was obliged to clear his throat. "What man is it you seek?"

"His name is Matthew Quinney."

"That name is unknown to me." George Bell shook his head. "Is it, indeed?" Lastly, the questioner turned to me. "What about you, poor Susan?"

Rather than answer him I put on the most terrible cough, and at that moment one of the other men came back into the room shaking his head. "Nothing to be seen, Mr. Lennox." This man regarded me with some solicitude. "That's a terrible cough she's got. Do you think we've got the right house?"

"Don't be a fool, Dick Batey! Of course we've got the right house. These are some of them. Go and try again. Check every place you can think of and a few more besides."

A further knock sounded upon the front door. The apothecary himself, fresh from following in the footsteps of Dick Batey, hurried toward the door, but Lennox reached it first. He opened it and to my dismay admitted Alexander Belzoni.

"What have you caught here?" he asked as he walked into the room and looked us over. Lennox's reply went almost unheard as Belzoni instantly came across to where I sat. Miss Bell's summary disguise had not survived his scrutiny. "You may unwind the scarf, Jane Hartwell. It is a pity to conceal that handsome countenance. Well, well." He turned to Lennox. "That makes it certain Quinney is here. Turn the place inside out; we cannot fail to have him.

"I wondered if we should find you with Quinney," he continued, throwing himself into a chair. "You have got yourself into a bit of a hobble, haven't you? Who are your friends?"

"They visit the apothecary," I said, uncertainly.

"To be sure. As you do. Now you will tell me it is a botanical meeting, or a benefit meeting or some such. Where is he? You could save us a deal of trouble."

"I can scarcely believe it. I know you try your hand at anything. But *this*!"

"I hope you're not going to waste my time. It's precious, my time. Do remember that."

"Why do you do it?"

"Chance is a fine thing; chance and Sir Thomas."

"Sir Thomas? What could he have to do with it?"

"He hears on all sides report of a trouble-making scene painter, rumors of meetings with the shoemakers at Northampton. When he speaks with the local magistrate, he discovers that Quinney is considered a dangerous agitator. Naturally he perceives it as his duty to apprehend him."

"You lend yourself to this?"

"Why not? I am not in love with Quinney. He's a rum sort of fellow. I thought you had done better for yourself."

At that moment one of the men returned. "There is no sign of him that we can see."

Belzoni frowned. "Are all the horses under guard?"

"Yes."

"Then he can't have gone anywhere. Unless he had some hidden away. But we took them by surprise. I know he's here."

"You sound as though you have done something of this sort before," I said when the man left once more.

"I thought you knew I was a man of many parts."

"But a spy!"

"I shouldn't go so far as to call it that."

"What do you call it, then?"

"Upholding the forces of law and order. It's a worthy cause, you must agree. I've been paid by the Bow Street Office a few times in my life. I know something about the business."

"Who are the others?"

"Them? Ah, well, now, Lennox is a proper Bow Street man, but the rest are just constables, signed up for the purpose."

"I suppose you will get a handsome reward if you catch him?"

"Sir Thomas has promised to stump up. Someone else might too. I shall make a good thing out of it."

"Shame on you!" said Miss Bell, unable any longer to be silent.

"Shame? For catching a man like Quinney? Men of his sort are a danger to the country."

"We're in more danger from people like yourself," Miss Bell answered hotly.

"You *are* one of them," said Belzoni. "What's your name?"

She gave it, flushed with the knowledge of her own foolishness.

"And who's he? Well, George Bell, it's a pity you let your sister rule your life. You should have put your foot down long ago." He took out a pistol and began to load it. We watched him pour the powder and at last ram the ball down the barrel. He knew we stared wide-eyed. "Oh, yes, it must be ready for use. It's a lovely weapon, this." He balanced its weight in his hand. "I know its little ways, this one. We do not aim to kill, but we can wing a bird, if necessary. You may tell your friends what a prime shot I am, Jane." He went to the door and called: "Batey! Lennox!"

Only Batey appeared, but, after instructing him to keep us under guard, Belzoni left, pistol at the ready.

When he had been gone some minutes, George Bell stirred uncomfortably. "My brother and self would like to smoke our pipes," said his sister.

"There's no law against it," said Batey. "I'm partial to a bit of baccy myself."

George cleared his throat. "You can have a bit of mine if you're so minded."

"I don't mind if I do."

"Are you a soldier?" asked Miss Bell.

"I used to be, ma'am. A trooper I was, in the 25th Dragoons. Fought in the Peninsular campaign. That's where I got to know the captain, there. They need a bit of brawn for this work, see?" He flexed his arm and smiled.

"Do you mean Mr. Belzoni?" I asked.

"The captain he always will be to me, miss. Led us back over the Galicians to Corunna, and got us all through in a piece."

George Bell shook his head and stuffed his pipe. "Terrible, terrible."

"It was, too. We'd never have come through alive if it hadn't been for him." He nodded to indicate Belzoni.

"You shouldn't be doing this," Miss Bell reprimanded Batey. "Acting against your own kind."

"Well, that's a matter of opinion, you see. They've gone and shot the prime minister, and if we don't do something, it'll be the King next. Then where would we be?"

At this moment, we heard the back door open, and Belzoni and Lennox appeared, pushing ahead of them two men, one of whom was the fat cooper. "Join your friends," said Belzoni. "There you are, Batey. You've no nose for these blackguards. They were hiding in the ditches along the lane, and they're stuck full of thorns as a hedgehog with quills. Serve 'em right. Haven't you got your pistol out, man? Don't be so trusting. I want all the weapons at half cock. We've yet to find the principal in all this. Bind their wrists. We don't want any mistakes."

"Let's begin with you," said Lennox, closing upon the cooper, whose wrists Batey was hastily tying. "What have you got to tell us, eh?" He prodded the outsize belly.

"I'm William McTavish, sir."

"William McTavish, this is," said Lennox to Belzoni. "What do you think?"

"I think William McTavish might be very helpful," said Belzoni. The cooper's face was yellow as clay and a nervous sweat beaded his nose. "I don't know what you mean."

"Oh, you will. It's very simple. Where is Matthew Quinney?" McTavish did not answer. Lennox looked at Belzoni and Belzoni very slowly pointed his pistol at the cooper, sighted along the barrel and clicked it to full cock. The poor man's flesh shook on his bones like a snail in vinegar. "I didn't see which way he went, I swear."

"Well, somebody did," said Belzoni. "What's it going to be? We can't wait all day, can we, Lennox?"

There was silence. All in a moment, Belzoni lowered his pistol and discharged it with a report that echoed like thunder around the little room. He had aimed near the cooper's feet, so close that Mr. McTavish's shoe leather was burned and the man himself hopping with pain. "Where did he hide himself?" said Belzoni.

The cooper was quite beside himself and began to blubber.

"How can we know?" The little apothecary showed himself quite courageous as he put an arm about his trembling wife, who had covered her face with her hands and was holding back tears. "He might be anywhere."

"Well, and so he might. But if he's not found, some of you are going to pay. And I shan't aim only to frighten next time," said Belzoni.

At that moment, we heard another loud report which seemed to come from the road outside the house. Belzoni leaped to his feet, while the rest of us looked at one another in horror. "Get out there, Lennox," be said. "Quick, man. If that's Cole, he won't have the wit to finish the job. Batey, keep an eye on this little covey, and for God's sake have that pistol at the ready. It has a hair trigger, mind," said he to us. "Don't startle him or you'll regret it." He followed Lennox.

Mr. McTavish was moaning with pain and fright. "May I examine my friend's injury?" requested Mr. Sefton. Batey shook his head. "It won't do, I'm afraid." But he rose and walked over to where the cooper sat nursing his foot. " 'Tis nothing anyway by the look of it."

"Let me at least unlace the shoe."

Batey was not to be convinced. He was obedient, although without the mettle of Belzoni or Lennox. I began to weep. "I should have told them. He had a horse." I buried my face in my hands.

"By God, you silly wench," groaned Mr. McTavish, "whatever prevented you?"

"Did you say he had a horse?" said Batey.

I put my face between my hands and let the tears come. "I wish I had never met him!"

"What did you say?" asked Batey again.

"Come now! Don't take on so." Miss Bell was stern.

"What is to become of me? I am alone and trusted Mr. Quinney to look after me. What shall I do?"

"Pull yourself together, girl!" Miss Bell said sharply. "Tears will do us no good."

"Did you say this fellow Quinney had a horse?" repeated Batey. I nodded. "We hobbled it in the field behind the house."

"Curse it, now what am I to do?" muttered Batey to himself.

"I don't want anything more to do with this," I said. "I wish I had never left home."

Batey considered a moment. "All right," he decided. "You'd better show how sorry you are. Go to the door and call the captain, Mr. Belzoni. Or Mr. Lennox. Tell them about the horse."

"Traitor!" hissed Miss Bell as I rose to my feet. I still had my hands tied behind me, but I saw the beginnings of an opportunity to escape. Batey stood up, his pistol pointed toward those who remained in the room. I was to go to the front door, which, if he held the parlor door open with his free hand, he could still keep in view. "I'll be obliged to shoot, if you try to deceive me," he warned. "It'll go off in a second, this will. Just you give a loud call. If you do, I promise you the captain will see you all right."

I calculated that if I moved with sufficient speed, the time it took Batey to turn and aim the pistol in a fresh direction must give me the moment I needed to escape out of the door and into the darkness. Batey could not afford to take off after me and, although the other seven men out there would hear the report and come running for certain, it must help Matthew, if only by giving the pursuers one more to hunt.

I opened the door and standing well within the sill called, with a quaver and little voice, "Mr. Belzoni!"

"He'll never hear that!" said Batey. "Louder, woman, louder!"

I stepped forward, in what I hoped was a natural way, and then took three quick steps forward and sideways into the shadows. The door began to fall shut behind me and, as it did so, the ball from Batey's pistol splintered the wood. There was the sound of running feet upon the gravel of the road, some confused shouting and the discharge of another weapon in the distance. The noise of the footsteps grew louder. Some of the company were plainly returning. Since I had come out of the front door, there was, thank heaven, no wall to negotiate, for if there had been, with my wrists tied I should have been lost. But the neat line of the Seftons' front garden, unlike the back, where there was a high wall, was separated from the lane which ran beside it only by a decorative border of piled stones, no more than twelve inches high. I stepped over it and into the lane beyond, which was sufficiently overgrown to give promise of concealment. It was also boggy and full of potholes. I picked my way as fast as I could along the line of the Seftons' back garden wall, over brambles, nettles and parsley that grew waist-high, and twisted my ankle painfully. I knew I must conceal myself.

At that moment I was surprised by a whispered greeting. Above the wall beside me, which stood about six feet high, I saw the face of the weaver, Elias Low, one of those who had contrived to escape detection. "Are they dead?" he inquired softly and at my reply muttered a heartfelt: "Thanks be to God. I thought half of them dead."

He was on the other side of the wall, standing on the top of a water butt, in which he had been crouching until the sound of the firing had drawn him out of his hiding place. He leaned down, cut the twine which bound my wrists, and then he hauled and I clambered until I stood beside him. "They will not think to look for you here," he said, having persuaded me of the sense in taking his place in the water butt. "Besides, I have had enough of standing in water. I shall make for the wood beyond." The kindly weaver ran across the garden and, with the help of an apple tree, vaulted another wall and disappeared. I lowered myself, not without distaste, into the slippery barrel which still stank of the liquor it had originally contained. I lifted the cover gently into place and crouched down to fit the barrel's height. I stood in a foot of water that covered the bottom, and my hands, with which I was obliged to support myself against the sides, encountered slime and snails. I heard the spigot drip steadily, thus lending conviction to the barrel's proper function. There had been no heavy rain for a week or the barrel would have been useless, but it was only afterward that I thought to be thankful.

I had not stayed thus for very long before the sounds of pursuit came up the lane. Who it was of the eight men of the company I could not make out, but I heard clearly enough what they said. Among some hearty curses upon the wayward cunning of females like myself and upon Batey for being so easily duped, they spoke of Matthew. He had been wounded, it appeared, but not caught. The first shot had indeed been aimed at him, and had winged him, but he was not yet taken for all their searching. The news revived my spirits. All was not lost.

When those who sought me had retreated, I climbed gingerly out of the barrel, my teeth shaking, cramp in my limbs and my twisted ankle aching. Deciding against going back into the lane, I followed Elias Low's example—although not so handily as he—climbing into a low fork of the apple tree, which was full of fruit (some of which fell to the ground with the noise of cannons, or so it seemed), then up one branch higher and on to the wall, along which I clambered for a small distance before dropping, with some awkwardness although no further damage to my ankle, into the field. I thus emerged upon the road on the other side of the apothecary's house, having all but circled it since my exit from the front door. There was no one in sight upon the road. I stepped back into the lee of the wall and considered what to do next. Since Matthew's best chance of escape lay with the horses belonging to the two men who came from Sarratt, it seemed likely that he would, injured or not, make for the Bells' cottage, which lay, as I knew, on the eastern road out of Chandler's Cross. We had passed it that very afternoon, walking in from the canal.

At that moment the door of the apothecary's house opened. Belzoni and Lennox had decided to let their prisoners go free, it appeared, but not before exacting retribution. Wrists bound, Jack Syrett was the first to emerge, and after him Lennox threw the landlord's tray and plates, so that they hit him upon the back and calves before bouncing to the ground. Syrett stumbled and then began to run, whereupon Lennox took more deliberate aim with one of the tankards. It caught the publican a stunning blow on the head, and Jack went down without a sound. Next came Sarah Bell, whom they let pass with a push and a shove, throwing her cap into the bushes and spitting in her face. Her brother fared worse. His long pipe was rudely pulled from his mouth and smashed, and then Belzoni delivered two grunting blows to his stomach, right and left, that made George double up in pain. One other scuttled past, terrified, without incident, and last came Mr. McTavish, limping. Lennox put out a hand to restrain him, while Belzoni carefully reloaded his pistol and took aim as he had done before. The poor cooper, thinking his last moment had come, fell down upon his knees, his hands clasped toward heaven. With a roar of laughter Belzoni kicked him sprawling, and McTavish crawled away, blubbering with misery. "That was an excellent pie, mistress," I heard Lennox say to Mrs. Sefton who remained within. "I say we owe you something for that pie, wouldn't you, sir?"

I could not see what passed, but I suspect Mrs. Sefton was subjected to some kind of indignity. Lennox's last action was to hold Mr. Sefton by the scruff of his neck and shake him, while Belzoni removed the apothecary's spectacles and ground them to pieces beneath his heel.

The two of them sounded in much improved spirits after these needless brutalities. They left the Seftons' house, picked up Jack Syrett, one to each arm, from where he had fallen across Mrs. Sefton's bed of yellow chrysanthemums, and dragged him across the road toward the Three Feathers saying, across the top of his insensible head: "I hope this fellow makes a good brew. I never felt more like a pot of ale in my life."

"We'll get Quinney yet, never you fear," said Belzoni. "He's not far away, not with that wound."

What I had just witnessed, together with cold and wet and fright, caused me a momentary faintness, and I was obliged to lean my head over the ditch until it passed. Then I set out for the Bells' cottage. Although I might meet up with Sarah and her brother if I kept to the road, I was too greatly frightened to do so, and pushed through the hedges that I might travel unseen on the far side of them. The likelihood of my finding Matthew seemed remote. If that band of ruffians had not contrived it, how should I? Certain nameless fears overtook me. I was attacked by loneliness, not the sort that is caused by a solitary ramble on a dark autumn night, but of a more general character. I had cast off from familiar sur-roundings and from familiar friendships. Matthew was the single connection with my old life and I did not know whether to be more terrified of finding him than of losing him.

The meadow I walked over was grassed in furrows and ridges from its former plowing and fit to turn my ankle again at every step, but I moved carefully and at least the grass was short. I stank from the water butt, and my boots and stockings were slimy and saturated. I had neither cloak nor pelisse and it grew chill. Three black-faced sheep ran from me mewing, and I startled a thrush, but otherwise all was peaceful.

I continued the length of the long meadow, busy with my own anxious thoughts, and at the end slipped through a narrow gap in the tall hedge, expecting to find myself upon the eastern road again. Instead, I found myself in a small wood. There was a well-defined path leading in what I supposed to be the direction of the road, however, and I began to follow it with no great anxiety. It was not until I heard the sound of running water that I began to think I had somehow mistaken the way.

A little shiver ran through me. If I were lost, it was in a strange place with few landmarks to guide me. I might wander all night and lose myself for good. The path led clear of the wood, to the bank of a stream, some five yards wide and swift-flowing. It was a fair-weather ford only and not for present use. I could see, however, some way downstream, the regular outline of a roof against the pale sky. I laid aside thoughts of the Bells' cottage. My ankle pained me and I did not know how much longer I could walk. The roof promised shelter and I determined to make for it. By day and in different circumstances I should never have attempted to climb through the underbrush; I would have seen the mass of briers awaiting me. But by the time I was entangled it seemed as difficult to retreat as to advance. My cotton gown was some protection, but it caught and tore with every step and my hands, arms and face were dreadfully scratched before I had gone fifty yards. In one place the brambles were so dense that I could do naught but step into the stream to go round them and thus compound my misery. How long it took me to reach the barn (for such it was) I do not know, but for certain as long as it had taken to travel the entire rest of the way. I thought of nothing by the time I reached it but warmth and sleep, and when I finally achieved the flat croft surrounding the barn, I sat down and wept a little for weariness.

When I set out toward the barn, where I proposed to sleep, however, I saw beyond it what the building itself had previously obscured: the outline of a bridge. As I drew nearer the fitful moonlight revealed a stone arch and parapet which seemed familiar. My spirits lifted as I felt suddenly sure that I had crossed this same bridge earlier that very day. The nearer I drew, the more certain I became. I had, quite unaccountably, made some kind of meandering, circular motion which had returned me to the very road I sought.

All thoughts of rest forgotten, I walked to the road, which ran a few feet above the level of the croft, and clambered up beside the bridge to reach its surface. I dislodged a few stones as I did so and looked involuntarily below me to see where they had fallen. What I saw from that angle was something to send a shiver through me. I did not descend immediately to investigate, unwilling to acknowledge what I had seen. Instead I climbed to the top and then looked down again. My eyes had not deceived me. What appeared to be the lower part of a man's body was lying half in and half out of the arch of the bridge. It was not possible at that distance to tell who it was, but you may believe the certainty that overcame me. I climbed down again, dislodging a great many more stones in my haste, and bending my head beneath the arch I tried to see his face, though it was only to confirm what I already knew by what he wore. Matthew Quinney lay there, upon his side, still and silent.

He had fallen in such a way as to fill the small sandy space that extended a short distance round the pier of the bridge. I could get close enough only to catch a half-glimpse of his profile. I should have to move him before I could judge of his condition. I cleared the stones out of the path, and turned him on to his back as gently as I could. He made no sound. Then I hauled him out from under the bridge by his legs. You cannot guess the relief with which, as I thus jolted his insensible body, I heard him groan. When I went to his head his eyes were open, but he made no sign of recognition and almost immediately closed them once more in a grimace of pain. He had sustained a heavy blow upon the temple, where there was a lump as big as a robin's egg. Above his eye, blood dribbled from a long cut, which did not, however, seem to go very deep. The worst injury was to his arm; his sleeve was soaked with blood where the ball had entered.

"Matthew?" I said. "Matthew, do you know me?"

He did not immediately answer, and I repeated his name more urgently. At last he opened his eyes again and spoke: "My arm."

Little by little, exhorting and heaving by turns, I got him first sitting then standing. He said nothing except to moan as he was obliged to move his injured arm. I could not be sure that he was sufficiently in command of his senses to know where he was or who I was, but he seemed able to follow my instructions well enough. I contrived our way up on to the road, Matthew edging up backward, inch by inch, I above him, a hand in his belt to prevent his sliding on the loose earth and stones. We achieved the road safely, if without much breath left. Then, after sitting on the parapet to gather our strength, we set off down the road, Matthew's good left arm around my shoulder and my right about his waist, in the direction of the Bells' cottage.

In the press of greater anxieties I had, thank heaven, entirely ceased to feel the pain in my ankle, but Matthew's injuries afflicted him so severely that once or twice he seemed on the point of fainting, and we had not traveled above a half mile before he collapsed against me, insensible once more. I lowered him to the ground, feeling a cold thrill of fright. Then, for want of action, I decided upon tearing my petticoat to fashion him a sling. In trying to apply it I was clumsy, but the pain I would not deliberately have caused had the merit of reviving him: he awoke with a cry of distress. We moved on once more, a little less slowly, the sling enabling Matthew to carry the weight of his injured arm more easily than before. Then, turning a sharp bend in the road, to my delight I saw, not more than a hundred yards distant, a light shining yellowly from the window of a cottage, which must, I judged, be the very one we sought.

We were not destined to reach it, however. The sound of hoofs came suddenly and rapidly toward us. I knew we must hide. The horsemen might be of no consequence at all, but there were several of them, they were traveling uncommonly fast and I had had sufficient doings with horsemen that evening to be wary. Matthew was in no fit state to appreciate the danger, but I spoke from habit. "Make haste!" I hurried him across the verge into the only available shelter, three spindly willow shrubs whose leafless branches spread out low from the ground. It proved no great effort to get Matthew lying flat. Indeed, as he lay down, I perceived that it might be beyond me this time to get him up again. Covering him, head and all, with my cloak, I turned my face down, hoping that we would thus blend into the landscape. The noise of the hoofs grew louder and as they approached, to my dismay, began to slow.

It was three of Belzoni's company who thus bore down upon us: Lennox, Batey and another, their destination plainly the same as ours. They drew up a yard or two from the Bells' cottage and held a brief, whispered discussion, after which Lennox dismounted and, leaving the others to wait with the horses, approached the cottage door. I had no doubt that his hope was, as mine had been, to find Matthew there. It seemed our slowness on the road had been our good fortune: another five minutes and we should have been exactly where Lennox wanted us, ripe for the taking. When the door opened I heard Sarah Bell's voice, its characteristic low resonance echoing into the evening air. Despite what had happened earlier, she was plainly not intimidated. "Is it you again? You have done my poor brother enough harm for one evening, I should think."

Without the courtesy of a reply, Lennox pushed his way in, and the door closed behind him. During the long time he was gone, his companions stood upon the road not far from us, conversing quietly. I caught snatches of what they said, which concerned nothing very much at all: cabbages, their pay as constables, Batey's adventures with a chambermaid, a notorious murder near this very place ten years since. "The gibbet hung a mile that way," said Batey. "She walks and calls for the lost child, they say."

Obliged to listen to such superstitious fancies, my hope of assistance frustrated by so little, I began to count numbers, as a means of quelling an unreasoning desire to rush out and announce myself. How long would Lennox take to search the cottage and be gone? Would they discover the horses, if indeed the horses were still there? At three hundred, I closed my eyes and gave up, laying my cheek against the ground, no longer interested in any of it. The cold crept into my bones and my very wits, the desire to escape being gradually overcome by the conviction that whatever I could do would not be done soon enough to save Matthew's life. Could there be anything more futile than to save him from his pursuers only to have him die as a result of his injuries and exposure to the elements?

Oppressed with these melancholy thoughts I know not how long I lay beneath the willow twigs. At some moment I was thoroughly roused by a most prodigious commotion from the back of the Bells' cottage: raised voices, blows, shouts of anger or encouragement. It sounded like nothing so much as a milling-match.

Batey and his companion, who still stood in the road, were as perplexed as I. They looked at one another longer than any men of sense would have done, until at last Batey made up his mind. Cramming his hat down over his ears, he handed the reins of the three horses to his companion, hitched up his belt and went off at a run toward the back of the cottage. This unlooked-for turn of events unsettled him who was left alone in charge of the horses, and he turned himself about apprehensively, plainly expecting to be leaped upon at every moment.

Matthew had been so quiet that I thought him asleep. Now, however, quite suddenly, he gave a great groan. It was of such volume and intensity that it startled even me, and he who watched the horses fairly jumped out of his skin. He cast his eyes around more fearfully than ever, called upon whoever it was to discover themselves, took his pistol out of his belt and pointed it at the dark, shouted for Batey, and at last, still holding the reins of the other two horses, mounted his own, presumably feeling safer in being thus prepared for flight.

Better than if he had been on cue, Matthew groaned again. It was, if anything, louder and longer than before, eerier than a screech owl's cry, and then, in hollow, lingering tones, he spoke a single name. He spoke it in some kind of delirious fever I suppose, and what the name was I could not be certain—Jack, or Jane, or Jacob, perhaps—giving the "a" such a long-drawn sighing "Aaaah" that the timorous horsekeeper entirely lost his wits. Dropping the reins of the other two horses, he turned tail and rode toward Chandler's Cross as if Beelzebub himself were after him.

As he was disappearing down the road at a gallop, Lennox came hobbling round to the front of the cottage, without his hat, his nose bloodied, utterly disheveled and holding his knee. When he saw what had happened, he yelled after the man uselessly, then, with a few hearty curses, retrieved his own mount, not without difficulty. He had just strength enough to haul himself into the saddle and then he also took off toward the hamlet, leaning forward as though in pain, but urging the beast to a gallop nonetheless.

Leaving Matthew where he lay, I ran to the back of the cottage and opened the door to find myself in the kitchen, in which, as well as brother and sister, were the Armitage brothers from Sarratt and, trussed up like a fowl in the corner, his eyes blindfolded, poor silly Dick Batey. Before I could speak a word, Miss Bell, quick as ever despite what looked like the beginnings of a black eye and some cuts upon her hands and face, raised her finger to her lips and, looking at Batey, motioned me to silence. Then she directed the Armitages to carry him outside. "Put him into the hayrick. He'll be warm and he can't cause any trouble there." Once this precaution was taken, she came to me with alacrity and put her arms about me with every appearance of affection.

The events of the last few hours had left me exhausted and full of nervous agitation. At this proof of concern I burst into tears. While John and Josiah Armitage went to fetch Matthew, with kind expressions of sympathy Miss Bell led me to the fire, beside which sat George, pale and bloodied, but still sufficiently himself to prod it solicitously on my behalf. While I warmed myself at its welcome heat, she fetched a change of clothes from the heavy oak press which stood in one corner. Clean linen, a simple serviceable gown and a warm brown woolen cloak restored my spirits amazingly. As briefly as we could, we exchanged news, she making light of her own injuries (received defending George, it seemed). The fight had been the outcome of Lennox's discovery of the Armitages, who, having tempers as short and fists as hard as Lennox himself, itched to repay him for his unkind treatment of their friends.

Everything we did, of course, we were obliged to do in the greatest haste. Lennox would be back again with Belzoni and the rest of the troop as soon as he could round them up. Matthew, who had still not come to himself, was laid upon the trundle bed. Miss Bell held up his head and, drawing from the depths of one of her capacious pockets a small silver flask, began to administer its contents. As the brandy went into him, Matthew coughed and choked and opened his eyes. "Aye, that'll bring him round," said George Bell. " 'Tis the best French that. He'll have a hard time dying with that inside him."

Indeed, although Matthew's face was still the color of porridge, and the lump upon his head turning blue and purple, he was able to eat a few spoonfuls of the excellent mutton broth which was simmering over the fire.

The brothers Armitage partook of the soup also, not without a doubt or two about our having time for it. "What about his horse?" said Josiah, meaning Batey's. "Two up on each of ours, and they'll outride us in no time."

"They would if they knew where you went," said Miss Bell, "but nobody's going to tell them. We have to get something into Matthew here or he won't survive the journey. Don't think of Batey's horse. That will make things even worse for us."

She was mixing honey, the yolk of an egg and a quartern of aqua vitae, which she poured into a small stone flagon, corked and gave to me. "It is a good Scotch remedy and will warm you through in no time. He'll be needing something, there's no doubt."

Josiah Armitage, having examined the wound in Matthew's arm, fashioned a piece of linen into a bandage, commenting: "The ball passed right through."

"Thank heaven," said Miss Bell. "Thank heaven." She looked at Matthew's features as he lay, his eyes shut, and took a deep sighing breath. "Is he not like Davey, George? Is he not the very picture of his uncle?" Her thoughts all of a sudden were many miles away, dwelling upon the past with a fondness which suggested her friendship with Matthew's uncle had been something more than political. George patted her awkwardly on the shoulder, and she turned her face into his chest in the nearest approach to tears I had yet observed. But it was momentary only. She sniffed and smiled again almost instantly. "Come, we must go, or they will have us yet."

And so we set out. Matthew and I would go to Sarratt, which was only five miles distant across the fields by a route which the brothers knew intimately, myself mounted in front of Josiah Armitage, Matthew on the big black cob belonging to his brother John, to whom he was secured by stout pieces of huckaback in case he should faint and perhaps fall.

Miss Bell and her brother were obliged to quit their cottage at the same time, to avoid the reprisals which Belzoni would undoubtedly take when he discovered he had once more been frustrated of his prey. So stalwart and brave were they in the face of this trial, indeed, so calm in making what small arrangements time allowed, that they might have been going nutting. To our inquiries, they answered merely that they had friends who would shelter them. Then George (whose legs were so long that his feet dragged upon the ground) and a few small bundles were set upon their donkey. They left in an opposite direction from us, or at least would have done. The donkey, which went by the unlikely name of Strawberry, planted her four feet square upon the ground, lowered her head and refused to move. "The parsley!" said Miss Bell immediately. "Dear heaven, if I haven't forgotten the parsley!"

It appeared that parsley was an herb the disobliging creature was wild for. Miss Bell, having plucked two large bunches, gave George one to hold in reserve and, with Strawberry's leading rein in her left hand, waved good-bye with the other as if it were a posy.

I did not think until afterward of the dreadful danger in which that evening's doings had placed the Bells and their property. When we did later learn what had happened, it proved more horrible than we could have conceived. Since the cottage was isolated, no one saw who did the damage, but its contents were utterly destroyed: its few sticks of furniture, its trundle bed and two chairs, its linen, broken, soiled, burned. Whatever proved resistant to such destruction was thrown on the dungheap. Even the great iron kettle was dented and thrown into the duckpond. The fowls had their necks wrung and the pig was speared upon a stake. The last thing of all, and the worst, was that they fired the hayrick without ever knowing Batey was in it. When at last they heard his screams, it was too late. The captain to whom Batey had been so grateful for leading him in the retreat over the Spanish mountains had saved him from one death by freezing only to bring him to another by fire.

XVI

Fortune smiled upon us in Sarratt by providing us with a means of traveling instantly to London. The great city, our original destination, was also the one place where we might be sure of losing ourselves as easily as mice in a hayfield. The Armitages' uncle, William Beddoes, a freeholder of some consequence in the village, took three wagons to the metropolis that very morning, having secured, by way of his cousin who was a corporal to the quartermaster in the 9th Regiment, a profitable contract for providing new fill for the mattresses at the barracks in Upper Albany Street. Mr. Beddoes was an accommodating man, fond of his nephews and not overfond of the law, which he had never forgiven for transporting a brother of his for the theft of two chickens when the family was starving many years before. He looked us over silently, nodded his head, and had the scene painter lifted straight into the wagon that he himself was to drive. I climbed in beside Matthew. The clean dry straw made a bed as welcome at that moment, you may believe, as the softest down and silk sheets. With more straw over us, we were well hidden and warm. I fell asleep almost at once and did not open my eyes again until the wagon set off just before dawn. Matthew was already awake, considerably restored and quite in his right mind, even though he was in pain from his arm and oppressed over the loss of his books, which he had been obliged to discard when the musket ball had hit him. He was able to recall most of what had passed since then: how, despite being wounded, he had managed to elude his pursuers, and finally found himself upon the eastern road not far from the bridge; how, fearing discovery at the approach of a large group of navigators, rough, suspicious and untrustworthy as many of those men are, he had decided to hide, and climbed over the parapet of the bridge, intending to conceal himself beside it. He remembered no more.

Despite his pale face (which atop his tall, thin figure made him appear most pitiable), the bandage supporting his arm, and the lump on his head, I was cheered. We had, at least, eluded Belzoni, as I reminded him.

"My arm," he replied. "You have forgotten that it is my right arm. We may escape Belzoni and his men, but I cannot work without the use of my arm."

I had given no thought to that particular consequence of his injury, which must affect us both. "We must manage until it is mended," I said stubbornly, mortified by my own thoughtlessness. "There is no reason to lose heart yet."

"Whatever do you think you can do?" Matthew asked, the weariness of his illness making him most uncharacteristically plaintive.

The answer to that was not easily forthcoming but I was determined to discover it. After a draft of Sarah Bell's Scotch remedy, Matthew fell asleep again and I lay and thought upon the matter. Thanks to the old-fashioned pockets tied beneath my gown, I still had safe my netted purse, grandfather's two guineas, Sophie's two, and fourteen shillings of my own. Sir Thomas had paid Matthew for his services: we were not destitute. Although there was yet no way plain by which we might support ourselves, if one step were gained, another was bound to follow and the answer might reveal itself. Who was there to help us? Stephen Turnbull was the only person with whom I could claim acquaintance in the whole of London, and I knew neither where he lived nor worked. As I considered Stephen, it lighted upon me suddenly that even if I did not know where he was to be found, Bob Sturmey, the mail coach driver, very likely would. Bob Sturmey was a man on whose good sense and kindness I felt sure I could depend; Bob Sturmey would know where he was. Moreover, I was sure I could find Bob Sturmey. Had he not, indeed (so long ago it seemed), bidden me tell

Stephen to look for him at the Cross Keys in Gracechurch Street? Resolved: we should go to the Cross Keys and hunt up the coachman. I was instantly encouraged. Where choices are few, decisions are simple.

Apart from stopping at regular intervals to water the horses, Mr. Beddoes kept his train moving at a steady pace, crossing country to Watford, and thence taking the old Roman road which leads straight into the heart of the city. He had given us the same provisions he and his drivers carried, bread and cheese tied up in a cloth, and a stone flagon of beer, and when the sun was high Matthew awoke once more, and we shared the good homely fare. It must have been October brew, for it put us both into such a deep slumber that Mr. Beddoes was obliged to shake us awake when we stopped at the barracks. It turned out that Mr. Beddoes intended, having once delivered the hay, to take tea with his widowed sister who kept a hatter's shop in Cheapside, and he was quite willing to carry us the extra distance to the Cross Keys. But Matthew would have none of it. By the time we had jolted our way to Cheapside, his spirits were so greatly improved, either at finding himself once more in London or by the operation of the beer and the Scotch remedy, that he became quite light-headed, and climbed down from the wagon with reckless enthusiasm, vowing there was no better tonic than to walk the length of a city street.

I was, you may believe, glad of his company. I should not have wished to be alone. The highway was filled with a regular concatenation of vehicles: curricles, chaises, hackney coaches, coal wagons, brewers' drays. The tumult assaulted my ears. There was no pause between the rumbling and creaking and clattering from one moment to the next; nor between the voices: low and high, they hooted, shrilled, whistled, cursed horses and called wares. I had never seen such a place, nor ever could have conceived it; and everywhere was the theater of life with a small scene playing. In the first moment we stood there, indeed, a dozy boy in a smock-frock, pulling a small handcart which carried several wooden crates full of chickens, was careless enough to catch a wheel upon a bollard, whereupon the metal rim split, the half-rotten spokes disintegrated and one of his spilled crates burst open, sending birds squawking and fluttering in all directions.

Amid such uproar, holding tight to Matthew was almost as much solace to me as it was assistance to him, for, innocent that I was, I could scarcely forbear wincing at the noise and shrinking from the jostling crowds who brushed by without so much as a glance. But, indeed, Matthew's need was greater than mine. For all his brave certainty, we had not walked above the length of a street before he was laboring from the exertion, leaning heavily upon me and pausing for breath, and by the time we reached the Cross Keys, he was pale as a sheet and altogether fagged out.

I knew we must take a room where Matthew could rest for the night and what remained of the day. There were few to be had, busy as the great coaching inn was, and the one to which we were conducted was no bigger than a box and noisy, since it was over the stables and opened on to the outside gallery which surrounded the yard. But it was warm and well-appointed, and when we had partaken of tasty soup and dumplings, hot and quickly brought, I was not disposed to find fault. Matthew fell into a doze almost instantly, and I tucked the netted purse beneath the mattress he lay upon, thinking there was no better time than the present to set out upon my search.

I took a deep breath before venturing downstairs to the yard, you may believe. I was as afraid of the metropolis as any country girl must be who has grown up knowing no more than one strange face among three score. But my fears made me hurry rather than hesitate: if I were to face this clamor and ask questions of strangers, it must be without too much thought or I should turn coward and never do it at all. I was at first unlucky. The half-dozen people to whom I spoke, beginning with the chambermaid who had seen us to the room and continuing with at least a dozen more who turned out to be strangers themselves, knew nothing of Robert Sturmey or Stephen Turnbull. Even the clerks in the coach office could not help me. But it was an inn of vast size, and I crossed the stable yard back and forth several times more, in search of ostlers, grooms, any of the horsy fraternity who might be acquainted with those I sought, while trying to shake off the attentions of the throng of pedlars who were hawking everything from pencils and pocket-knives to a tame squirrel.

As luck would have it, the arrival of a stage tumbled all the enthusiasts out in a moment and a twopenny postboy on a highland pony, making free with his time to indulge his passion, I suppose, recognized the name of Robert Sturmey. "Why, that's Bob-the-Double," said he. "Do you know him, then? I wish I did!" He directed me out of the inn yard and two doors down Gracechurch Street to the Grasshopper chophouse, which, he said, was the coachman's favorite haunt. The boy had a rosy, amiable, open countenance, and a shock of hair to match his pony's mane. I promised him a penny if he should see Bob-the-Double before I did, and tell him who was here and where we might be found. I was, I assure you, glad to have the existence of the coachman confirmed. I had begun to think that the famous Bob Sturmey did not exist in London; that he was not of the great city, but only of London-in-Mansfield after all.

The chophouse was a vastly busy place, with twenty tables, I should say, as well as boxes round the walls, and not one unoccupied. The air within steamed and smoked with the savory smell of meats roasted, meats fried, meats boiled, and the heat was so great that every door and window stood open, but even so the glowing fire where the work was done sent up enough smoke to turn six jacks before it. Ale and porter and soda water were being consumed in prodigious quantities, and no wonder. The clatter of knives, forks, pewter, saucepans, salamanders, cooks shouting instructions, waiters calling orders, was overwhelming, but having contemplated the scene for several moments through a window I plucked up courage, entered and began to search for a familiar face.

I had not long to look. There was one, indeed, but far from the friendly one I sought. Whom should I behold, at much the same moment as he beheld me, but Alexander Belzoni?

How he came there I did not consider; what he did there I had no doubt: he was come for us, for me and Matthew Quinney. What devil's pact gave him such a piece of fortune as to select, of all places in that fomenting caldron of people, the Grasshopper chophouse in Gracechurch Street, I had no time to ponder. Quick as a wink, he took his feet off the table, dropped the newspaper, knocked over the tankard which stood at his place, and came toward me. My reason deserted me. I turned as an animal will, the urge to escape the horrible Belzoni overwhelming all. Even then, had he not been obstructed, I think he would have caught me there and then, but by the time he had got round waiters and tables I had taken off. After that moment of dreadful consternation, I ran, where to I had no notion. I could not tell which way I turned as I emerged into the street: left or right, it was all one. Instinct guided my feet, not common sense. The lie of the streets, the darkening day assisted me. I ran and ran, not knowing where I went or what I passed, in a panic of fear.

Lighted shop windows, dark alleys, print shops, biscuit makers, breadmakers, great dark warehouses or manufactories, pastry-cooks, booksellers, mercers, coopers, I might have passed them all, seeing or unseeing, my bewilderment at the size and uproar of the great city mingling with my fear of Alexander Belzoni so that I ran like one possessed. And everywhere there were people I must push my way past: men carrying hods, children hawking pickles and matches, porters with chests on their backs and baskets on their heads, a gentleman or two with cane and quizzing-glass, even a boy trundling a hoop. At first, as Alexander pursued me, he shouted my name aloud, called after me, tried to set those on the street to apprehend me, but in that, thank heaven, he was unlucky. A man chasing a respectably dressed young woman, who should believe it anything but a domestic matter? No one of all we passed was sufficiently interested to give more than a curious stare before hurrying on.

I turned sharp and bent low, and paused to catch my breath in the shelter of a doorway but, just as I began to think I had lost him at last, there he was, retracing his steps like a hound upon the scent. I ran again, half-sobbing with distress, my breath catching in my chest. I sought the shadows to evade his eye and the narrowest, twisting streets where there was more chance of concealment, and still he came after me. I reached poorer streets, less busy and pebble-paved. I began to stumble, yet even now I fancied I heard his footsteps following. How far or how long I ran, I could not tell; such time increases in proportion to the intensity with which it is lived. My greatest dread was that I should run into a blind alley and find myself pent up, no escape at all, walls only, where I should be obliged at last to turn and face him. That fear eased as I came to a wider street. I paused for the merest moment to take a breath and decide upon my direction. It was, for a thoroughfare, curiously deserted. I had, I suppose, slowed my pace, and in that moment of slight relief all was lost. With a quiver of absolute terror, I felt my arms pinioned behind me.

"You didn't expect to meet me, I can see," said Alexander quietly. "But here I am, for all that, a bit too quick for you. Why do you run away from me, hey? You aren't afraid, are you?"

I did not answer but tried to shake myself free. "Oh, no," he said. "You shall not escape again. Not before we have spoken with Matthew Quinney." Looking up into his face, its handsome features twisted into the grimace of a monster, horror gave me a sudden accession of strength. I tried once more to shake myself free, was indeed half-free, when he twisted one arm up so sharply that I let out a cry and was obliged to be still. "Where is he, then? Speak up or I'll do worse, I assure you."

"I do not know."

"Of course you do."

"I look for him myself."

"Curse me if you are not a damned disobliging bitch. If you will not tell me, you shall be made to." Again he twisted my arm so that I cried out. "That's it. I'll break it if you do not speak."

"I have not seen him since Chandler's Cross."

"You expect me to believe that, do you? I know you left with him. There are some who have more sense than to lie."

"He went to the theater."

"Did he so? When are you going to stop lying to me, you cunning little vixen? Do you know how much money you lose me? A hundred guineas, that's how much. One hundred guineas I am to lose and all through you. You shan't lie to me." He tightened his hold on me. "A young female all alone in Whitechapel as dusk comes on. I'll teach her to cheat me of a hundred guineas."

A rumbling sound, which had been growing as we stood there and to which neither he nor I had paid attention, suddenly burst upon us in a thundering cannonade. Around a bend in the street some yards from where we stood, filling the thoroughfare entirely, came a great herd of stampeding cattle. There was not a drover to be seen. The mud flew up under their hoofs, and they packed so close we were in instant danger of being trampled.

The few others in the street had vanished like rabbits into their burrows. Our only hope was to make for the sole refuge immediately evident, a narrow passageway across the road. In the moment before Alexander let go my arm, without a word spoken, I knew that he considered pushing me beneath the hoofs of the oncoming mass of crazed beasts, to be pounded to death. Then, thank God, in the imperative need to save himself, he let go my arm and we both sped across the road. He was faster than I, although I had the advantage of having stood a pace in front of him. We ran almost side by side. But then, no more than five paces from safety, he tripped. In those few seconds, I achieved the refuge and he did not. Although he had not fallen, it was impossible for him to recover his balance and speed before the beasts were upon him. There was no space between them and the wall in which he could hope to save himself. I looked back as I reached the passageway, to see him reach out a hand for aid, no more than five feet from me. Then he was swept beyond reach. I could not even look out to see him for the press of beasts passing, but I heard him scream above the noise of the thundering hoofs. I covered my ears and began to sob.

"There is the wickedest thing," said a woman's voice. It belonged to an aged vendor of shellfish whose wares lay in a basket, customarily on a strap across her shoulder but, owing to the narrowness of the passage, presently at her feet. She was one of several who had also taken refuge there before me. "They does it for devilment and thievery, and nobody says nothing. I'm sorry it is your man."

I shook my head amid my tears. "It is not my man."

As soon as the cattle had passed, I ventured outside, expecting nothing but to find Alexander dead. He lay against the wall, five yards down the street, miraculously still breathing. An iron tethering ring was set into the wall above his head, and it appeared that he had grasped it to keep himself from being entirely swept under the murderous hoofs, for one of his palms was marked with a great burning weal. I could scarcely bear to look at his lower limbs. Both were twisted at unnatural angles, one of them scarcely recognizable, no leg at all but a mass of pulped flesh only. The thigh bone of the other protruded from a hideous gaping wound out of which were gushing great gouts of blood.

A crowd collected instantly, like flies to dead meat, swarming from nowhere.

"He's done for," I heard someone say.

"He must have a surgeon," I said, my sense for what was practicable quite deserting me.

"Surgeon won't do nothing."

"You'll have to walk a long way to find a surgeon!" There was a laugh.

"Here come the drovers," said another. "It's their fault."

"A surgeon was robbed here three weeks back. You'll not find one to come."

Voices at the crowd's edge began to shout accusingly at the drovers and butcher boys, some of whom had given up the chase after their rampaging charges to gape at the accident.

"You're a day after the fair. See what your beasts have done."

"There's nothing we could do. They were waiting for us."

"Twenty to ten. What could we do?"

"It happens every time."

"You never saw such a skittish bunch."

"You couldn't mind a chicken."

"Twenty to ten, I'm telling you it was."

"Twenty to ten, was it? Ninepence to a guinea it was one mad dog against the lot of you."

The attention of the crowd was diverted by the prospect of a fight between the drover, armed with a sharpened stave, and his opponent, who was twice his size and armed with a knife. No one paid further attention to Alexander.

"They does it for thievery," a voice whispered in my ear. The vendor of shellfish had come up close to me and was staring down at Alexander's poor, mutilated body. "That's a terrible mischief, that is. Did you say he was your man?"

I shook my head.

"He'll be out of this wicked world, that's certain. What was he to you?" She looked at me closely. "Better than your brother, wasn't he? What was it? A lovers' tiff?" She peered into my face more closely than ever and nodded at what she saw. "Well, it's no matter, is it? There's plenty more where that one came from. You've no cause to be alone." She nudged me and cackled, a veritable witch, and the stench of her breath in my face combined with that of her wares brought my stomach up into my throat. I leaned to the wall and vomited.

When I turned back, she was on her knees beside Alexander, rifling his pockets, altogether unmindful of the bloody mess she had to move in order to reach them. "You would not steal from him!" I cried in horror.

She looked up slyly. "What is it to you? He's nothing to you, now, is he? I see that plain. Writ in your face, that is. He don't mean nothing to you. You wouldn't begrudge a poor old woman a penny or two, would you?"

"Don't you steal from him!" I said.

"It's come to that, has it? You're as sharp as a tack, you are. I know your sort. Want it yourself, don't you? Well, you shan't have it." She heaved herself to her feet by leaning, without the least consideration or distaste, upon Belzoni's bloody remains. Then she straightened herself, wiping her hands upon her garments, and hallooed. "Dunny Arvell, are you there? It's your old friend Moley."

One of the men in the crowd turned. "Does the lady want a bit of attention, then? Glad to oblige, Moley, glad to oblige." He stepped over Alexander's body and put his arm round me. "There ain't no hardship in this at all."

"We must do something to help him. Can you not see?"

"Oh, we aren't blind, miss, never you believe it. But there ain't nothing to be done about that bit of meat and gristle, now is there, Moley? He won't even be fit for the resurrection men, he won't, so don't worry your pretty head about him."

The large man, built like a side of beef, who had been armed with the knife, came to Moley's side, she explaining to me: "There he is. That's Dunny. He's given him a whacking for your poor fancy man, haven't you, Dunny?"

"What's to do, Moley?" said he, looking at me.

Moley noted his interest and nodded at me vigorously. "Thief, she called me."

"Now that isn't kind, that isn't," said Dunny. "I take offense at that, I really do. That's downright unjust. Thief! Why, Moley is as good a dame as you'll find anywhere in Whitechapel. She's like a mother to us, isn't she?" There was laughter at this. "You can't go a-calling her names. Thief! That's a monstrous bad word, that is. I've knocked many a man down for less, haven't I, friends?"

"She's seen your mettle, Dunny," said someone.

"She might even see a bit more if she's good," said Dunny.

There was fresh laughter and he peered closely at me in the half-dark, his eyes red as a ferret's. "I don't enjoy spoiling a pretty face. Oh no, I'm a real gentleman. Better than this one any day." He pushed Alexander's limp body callously with his foot.

"Or night," some wag added.

"If he dies, surely it is not to be here?" I said desperately.

"What does it matter where he dies? He's past it. Take care of the living, that's our motto."

"She stole from him," I said.

"Did she now? Well, I never. Fancy that. Where do you come from, then? Not from round about. Too pretty-spoken. All alone, are you? What a shame! I don't like to see a fancy piece all alone. It's not right. It's a proper shame, that's what it is. You need somebody to look after you."

"You're the man for it, Dunny," someone called, and there was a shout of approval.

"If you wouldn't mind accompanying me, miss," said Dunny ironically, as I made to move away when he stepped forward to take the place of the man who still restrained me. When I struggled, for my pains he picked me up like a sack of coals and slung me over his shoulder. I beat upon his back with my hands and kicked with my feet.

"I like them with a bit of spirit," said Dunny to the appreciative crowd, but when my struggles began to annoy him he set me down, grabbed hold of my hair, twisted my head to one side and bit my neck. My cap fell off, my hair came down and I screamed as his teeth sank in.

"Sniv that, Dunny." Someone spoke. "She's a right dainty one. Don't spoil her looks."

What Dunny answered I do not know, for as he slung me once more over his shoulder I fainted.

When I awoke it was to the pungent smell of salts beneath the nose. At first in my dazed state I thought myself dreaming. I was lying on a couch and the light was dim and red and full of smoke. What I saw first was the bottle of smelling salts, the image of which I retain clearly even now. It was of silver, and the delicate tracery of vines and flowers incised upon it opened here and there to reveal, in the shape of a leaf or petal, gold underlay. Several tiny diamonds set into it caught the light and gleamed. I thought myself in Aladdin's cave. My eyes moved to the hand that held it, and then back again to the bottle, for the two seemed entirely contradictory. The old woman, the shellfish vendor, held the bottle. Moley! I thought at last, coming out of the half-daze to which the pungent odor of the salts had brought me. I drew in my breath sharply and sat up urgently to cough myself back into my right senses, only to cry out at the pain in my neck. I fell back onto the couch and then raised myself more gingerly. "She's up and kicking," Moley called out, saying to me, "I thought we'd done for you as well as him. Dunny is always a bit hasty. He's gentle as a lamb providing you don't rile him. But he has got a bit of a temper."

The motley assortment of individuals who clustered round me at Moley's call were as unkempt and ill-looking as any I had seen, but I was lying upon what seemed to be down cushions overlaid with a rich turkey-red cashmere shawl and covered with a white wool blanket which was, although dirty, bordered with exquisite embroidery. My state was not such as to make me cautious, and I looked from one to the other, trying to reconcile those who surrounded me with these rich objects. My bewilderment showed upon my face, for Moley laughed. It was not a pleasant sound, although the old witch was full of delight. "Ah! I can see what you're a-thinking!"

"And what's that, Moley, you old besom?" Dunny Arvell himself had come to look at me. He was eating a piece of chicken greedily, his mouth greasy with its juice.

"I thought you was for eating some of my oysters," said Moley. "You're usually partial to my oysters."

"Well, not today I'm not," said Dunny. "They're a bit overripe for me in my condition. They're a bit like you, Moley, you old hag: on the wrong side of the line. Don't take offense, Moley, I shouldn't like you to take offense. It used to be that your oysters would satisfy any man in London, but that was before my time."

"Get along with you," said Moley huffily. "I do all right by you, don't I, Dunny? You've no call to take against me."

"I wouldn't do that now, Moley. When have I ever done that? Look at this nice bit of dripping you've catched for me. Now that's better than any of your old oysters. That's a nice juicy bit of capon. I'm in your debt, Moley." He leaned down and put his fingers under my chin. "And how's that love bite, my pretty?"

"You'll have to look after her better than that, Dunny. That's quite deep that is."

"So it was, and it was meant to be, too." Dunny showed me his teeth, treachery and lechery together. "I've a nice set of gnashers and all my own. Kicked up quite a hailstorm with its little fists and feet, this one did."

I turned away and spoke to Moley. "Where am I?"

"Where are you? Now that would be telling!" Moley's temper was quite restored by my question. "You'll never guess, I daresay, and Dunny here, well, he might tell you, and then again he might not."

"You're thieves," I said. "All this is thieved, isn't it?"

"You're all eyes and ears," said Dunny mockingly. "You can't keep up with her, Moley." He turned my head back toward him and I grimaced with the pain to my neck. "What did I tell you?" Moley said crossly. "Put some salve on it, you great fool, before it rots, she and her pretty face all." She rose from the stool on which she had been sitting and disappeared into the dark recesses of the room. Dunny sat down on the stool Moley had vacated and looked me over with the pride of ownership he might have displayed toward the other stolen objects with which we were surrounded. He touched my hair and looked again at the bite he had inflicted. Then on a sudden he kissed me on the mouth. The rank smell of him and the greasy chops against mine, the pain which the pressure against my head gave me, brought my stomach into my mouth again. As he raised his head once more, I leaned over and retched violently onto the floor. Some coarse remarks were forthcoming about the effect of Dunny's lovemaking, and Moley, returning at that moment with a dainty blue and white china jar, scolded him. "Don't be in such a hurry, Dunny. She'll improve with keeping. Don't be in such a hurry. She'll come round. Give her time." She smeared the salve swiftly if not gently upon my neck. Unexpectedly, it almost instantly gave relief. "Come and finish your supper," she advised him and they left me blessedly in peace.

I examined my surroundings, which made, indeed, the oddest

place I had ever found myself in. It was, so far as I could tell in the darkness and being too fearful to move in case of drawing more unwelcome attention to myself, as big as a barn. Where I saw walls, the wood appeared damp, mildewed and rotten. But there were few to see. Both they and the ceiling were hung in a haphazard way with all kinds of rich materials: a tapestry, what I guessed to be the entire measure of several bolts of velvet, a number of fringed shawls, one of which, with a luminous peacock's tail brightly emblazoned on it, was suspended, like the roof of a sheik's tent, immediately above my head. Indeed, it blew in the breeze, for the barn or warehouse or whatever it was, evidently was neither sound nor draftproof beneath its lavish decoration. Handkerchiefs of silk and lawn decorated the wooden boxes which made small tables here and there, where they were not used to store the myriad of fine articles that this band of piratical ruffians had acquired. On one stood an elegant silver tea urn which, although greatly in need of a polish, was evidently in use, for it steamed gently. On another stood a delicate ormolu clock, ticking sedately, although it plainly did not register the correct hour. (Indeed, I cannot suppose any there could have read the time even if it had.) It was a strange expression of pride, this enormous space, filled to overflowing with articles of richness and beauty, neither pawned nor sold but spread about with deliberate carelessness.

I slept.

When I awoke, it was to a nightmare image of Alexander Belzoni lying on the muddy street, his limbs destroyed. The fragmented recollections stood out before my eyes, each one a live scene whose action was suddenly suspended, fixed firm, a printed, painted unbearable picture which at last, after an infinity of time, dissolved once more into movement. The noise of the hoofs drummed in my ears, and I heard Alexander's high scream. The sounds pierced me through. I may have screamed myself, for when I was fully awake I found myself sitting up trembling, hands over my ears. I shivered as I tried to live with the dreadful memory. I knew there had been a moment when Belzoni intended for me the fate that had overtaken him. All the same, I could not bear to think of him lying there, left to die. The best I could hope for was that he had perished without regaining his reason, mercifully oblivious to his terrible injuries.

The room seemed less full of movement than before, and I stood up quietly, thinking by activity to erase the horrible images from my mind. Finding myself mortally thirsty, I walked quietly toward the silver tea urn, which was still steaming gently. I was looking around for some vessel I could use as a cup when a pair of arms encircled me from behind. "Awake, are you?" Dunny whispered in my ear, and bit it, with more gentleness, thank God, than he had shown to my neck, though he made me start, as he no doubt intended. "I've been waiting. Very patient, I can be. I hope you appreciate how patient."

He offered me the use of a tin cup that he carried tied to his belt, and when I turned it over and asked if he had not something better among all his great store of treasure, he approved my impudence and found me a fluted cup of fine Limoges, painted in enamel and gold leaf, and, moreover, a saucer to go with it (although it did not match). The tea was excellent and with the drinking of it I had at least bought time.

"Is this all yours?" I gestured toward the great store of treasure and thought to flatter him. He nodded. "Why do you not sell it?"

"This is not the half we have taken. There is no need."

"But if they found it, it would condemn you."

He laughed. "Find us! They know where to find us! They wouldn't venture here by day or night. If they did—" He drew his finger across his throat and made an appropriately ugly sound.

"There are many of you, then?"

"Enough."

"Where is this place?"

"The brickyard."

He had been giving me careful scrutiny and now he fingered my dress, the plain wear given me by Miss Bell. "We have better than this." Lying back upon the couch, he called, "Sall!" and, after waiting a few moments, bawled the name again. The woman who eventually responded was much younger than Moley, not much older than I, to judge from her appearance, but a more strange, bawdy-looking harlot I had never beheld. She was dressed sumptuously in a jade-green brocade, but the elegant blue ostrich feathers which she wore upon her head were pinned quite oddly onto a lace boudoir cap that was also decorated with what appeared to be a pearl necklace. A short scarlet cape edged with ermine covered her

shoulders and, as if that were not enough, she had draped over it
a shawl of Brussels lace and a necklace of diamonds. She wore short
lilac gloves of the finest kid and her face was rouged, powdered
and even patched. I must have stared at her as at an apparition
(which, indeed, she was) for she said to me rudely, "Ain't you
never seen fine clothes?" before she demanded of Dunny, with
almost equal rudeness, what he wanted.

"Tog her out," he said. "And don't be too long about it. I've a
fancy to see you in something fine," he said to me. "And if you're
good you can keep it."

Sall flounced off and I followed, she moving so quickly that I
fell several steps behind and thus provided her with the excuse for
commanding me irritably to keep up. (In truth I could have followed her from the smell alone for she stank like a civet cat.) The
room was even larger than I had imagined, for the elegant hangings
had been so disposed as to create divisions within it, and it seemed
that we walked fully a half mile, through what was a little com-
munity entire of itself. An old country woman with two baskets
on a yoke bartered for eggs and butter; beneath an enormous chimney a huge fire blazed, heating up several iron skillets and pots,
and before it a small child sat turning a twelve-foot spit which
held upwards of five assorted meats dripping with the most enticing
odors. We passed men and women of a variety of more or less
villainous appearance. Some were busy minding their own business, some turned as we passed, sometimes silent, sometimes
chaffing.

"It'll be a cold bed tonight, Sall!"

"How would you like to visit me for a change?"

"Take no notice of them," she said to me fiercely. "You needn't
think yourself favored. He has half a dozen a week."

"And it don't make your temper any sweeter!" said one who
overheard her.

"Shut your mouth!"

We came at last to the end of the room and a door with a rusty
padlock. "I'm in charge," said Sall defiantly. "We've had one or
two who thought they were onto a good thing, but they don't last.
Washed up on the tideway, they were." She looked at me threateningly.

Within the locked room was clothing of all kinds—gowns, fans, pelisses, shawls, pantaloons, knee breeches, frilled shirts, coats, cloaks, neatly piled and folded according to kind. The room was not empty, although Sall had unlocked it: a bent, elderly man with thin, unkempt gray locks, wearing a mildewy greatcoat, was picking over the piles. "Ain't you through yet?" Sall demanded.

"Very nearly, my dear, very nearly. It takes an old man like me more time than it takes a pretty young thing like you. How much for this, now?" He held up a fur tippet.

"Get on with it," said Sall to me, and while she and the old man haggled over prices, I sorted among the piles. What should I choose for a rendezvous with such as Dunny Arvell? I supposed that Sall represented something of his taste, if taste it could be called, but I certainly had no wish to encourage his appetite for me. On the other hand, I thought him well able to take offense at any deliberate attempt to make myself plain. I selected in the end a gown of spotted jaconet. Sall directed me with no less irritation than before to remove the clothes I wore and, when I proved slow in obeying, herself pulled off my chemise and slip with unseemly pleasure. She then teased me by holding the jaconet out of reach and making me stand shivering, stark naked, before the lascivious eyes of the two of them. "What do you think to it, Mr. Gostard? Dunny's latest article. Would it suit you, do you think?"

"Very nice, Sall, my dear, very nice indeed." Mr. Gostard, permission thus granted, approached and pawed me, chuckling delightedly. "Delectable, my dear, but a bit fragile for Dunny, I think, don't you?" The old fawner knew what he was about. "Not quite enough meat here, I should say." He pinched my bottom. I would have pushed him away but Sall prevented me, at which he, becoming more animated, cupped his horny hands, enclosed in prickly wooly mittens, round my breasts. "But here, now that's very good indeed, that's very presentable." He was so short that his head was well below my chin, and what convenience this allowed him in taking liberties with me you may imagine. Sall laughed delightedly. "Go to it, you old goat!" At such an invitation he immediately began untying his breeches, but by the time he had fumbled his way out of them and his stockings were round his ankles, she had tired of the game.

"Are you mad, you old lecher? *He*"ll know in a minute." Old Gostard, denied his pleasure, mumbled over into a corner and began upon the piles of clothes once more. Sall meanwhile threw aside the gown I had selected, and in somewhat improved humor provided me with one of transparent yellow gauze and began to help me into it. "Don't you wear nothing underneath. He don't like it and it would only get spoiled." Before she pulled the gown over my head she ran her hands over my body lightly several times with relish. "He won't like that either," admonished the old man who was watching from his corner.

"What would you know about what he likes?" snapped Sall, her black and surly looks returned. But she let me alone. The gauze, as I lacked both chemise and slip, left me thoroughly indecent and once we had left the small room, which she carefully locked, I was obliged to travel all the way back through the warehouse with her making every effort to draw attention to my appearance. My face was on fire for shame.

Dunny lay where we had left him, now raised upon several large cushions and smoking a hookah. He looked me over appraisingly, his eyes half-shut, before he said, "That's very nice, that is. I like that. I can see you know how to please. Come here." He ran a hand over me so far as he could do so without moving. "Was our Sall kind to you? She can be a bit of a tartar, can our Sall. Were you kind, Sall?" Sall tossed her head. "I said, were you kind, Sall?" Sall still declining to answer, Dunny, all appearance of somnolence gone, dropped the mouthpiece of the hookah, sprang from the couch with a bound, seized her round the waist and squeezed her to him until it seemed her bones might crack. "Mercy, Dunny," she cried at last. "Mercy! I didn't do nothing, I swear."

Dunny set her down and, grinning, turned to me. "Was she kind?"

I swallowed hard and nodded. "Very kind," I choked out.

"There's a real lady for you, Sall," said Dunny. "If she knows, she won't say. Aren't you grateful, Sall? I'll lay she's kinder to you than you were to her. Did she make you stand bare naked and let that old familiar of hers lay his fingers on you. Did she?"

I said nothing, but Dunny read it in my face. "She lets him have a go at her too, if she feels like it, don't you, Sall? Do you think I don't know? We all know Sall. You broke the rules, didn't you? She's a nasty habit as to rules, our Sall. Mustn't go messing about with the goods ahead of Dunny. Nobody does that. That's a prime rule of this establishment. But you did, didn't you?" He sat down again. Sall began to move away but he stopped her. "I haven't finished yet." He began to fondle me and pursued his game with fervor, the jealousy on her countenance only increasing his desire. "What shall we do with her?" he said to me as he began to pull at the yellow gown. "She's not to be trusted."

Sall watched him with black dislike. "I know," he said. "I've just the thing. We'll pay her in her own coin." He leaned back against the cushions once more. "Take off *her* clothes." I looked at him uncomprehendingly. "Haven't you ever taken clothes off before?" He laughed. I did not move and he pushed me with his foot. "Get on with it."

Sall's mood had once again changed. This was a game with which she was not unfamiliar. By the time I had got as far as unlacing her jade-green gown, she had become positively animated, and writhed like a snake in my grasp. She wore nothing beneath and grasping my hands she rubbed them over her, kissing me. When she was completely disrobed, she clung to me and moved her body up and down in rhythm against mine, uttering puppyish whimpers of delight. When she knelt at my feet, Dunny left his couch, from whence he had been observing the activity with increasing interest, and began himself to participate.

What else took place it would not be proper for me to relate. There was no carnal pleasure in which Sall was not practiced, and what she did, she or he obliged me to imitate, my evident sensations of disgust merely driving her to degrade me further. Dunny's lust was increased by Sall's lascivious abandon. As he saw her take petty vengeance upon me with the imposition of some unnatural act, he pretended punishment by making her watch while he mounted me, the two of them thus urging each other to climaxes of sensual delight.

When at last, exhausted by her activity, Sall fell asleep, I was still tied to her at wrist and foot by two braided cords of silk. Dunny then took up the hookah again and blew the smoke into my face, insisting that I inhale it. Whether the purpose of this was to make me dozy I do not know, but if it was, it did not succeed. Indeed, after a little more amorous play in which Dunny confided his appreciation of me in ways I could well have done without, he also fell asleep.

I lay upon the couch in dry-eyed misery, Sall snoring beside me, my mind bent upon escape. I willed myself to think of it, indeed, such thought of action being the sole means of relieving disgust, loathing and despair. It was all I could do to lie quiet and move slow, so eagerly did I wish to jump and shout and cry aloud to exorcize uncleanness. I turned my nails into my palms that the sharp pain might spur me into reason. Then I waited.

Patience was indeed the key. I waited until I knew by his heavy breathing that Dunny also slept soundly, and then I began with my free hand slowly to untie the cords, making as little disturbance as I could and pausing after each movement. This achieved, I took another lengthy time, as much as I could well bear, in getting myself off the couch and to my feet. The chiefest difficulty now facing me was clothes: I had none. Even the lemon-colored gauze gown was now ripped and useless. But if I could contrive to dress myself decently, there was, so far as I could tell, little else to hinder my escape. It was likely, indeed, that Dunny had no great desire to insure my remaining once he had made use of me as he wished. He lay upon his back beneath a parti-colored quilt and Sall was stretched out full naked upon her belly across the foot of the bed. Indeed, she began to stir as she became chilly and I was obliged to cover her in case she should awake before I had achieved my object, for it was her jealous temper I most feared.

I tied around myself the large turkey-red cashmere shawl which now lay on the floor, retrieved the key from Sall's scattered clothing and made my way as inconspicuously as I could to the far room where the clothes were stored. The huge fire burned low, and most of the meats had been eaten. Some men and women with tankards in their hands still sat at tables beneath which not a few more were snoring. Several looked up at my passing but no one remarked upon it.

To my relief, old Gostard was nowhere to be seen, and I searched quickly through the clothes, lighting upon a brown cambric muslin, a spencer of kerseymere and a merino cloak. I dressed quickly, some practical instinct leading me to wrap the red cashmere shawl around me beneath the cloak, pulled the hood over my head and crept out. I had no idea which way was escape, and I was still anxious lest anyone should stop me but, as I looked fearfully toward some noise in a corner, I saw the old woman who had been trading butter and cheese lifting herself painfully from the floor and dusting herself down, in a state of intoxication so far as I could judge, from which she had been rudely awoken by the accidental discharge of her water. She was unsteady on her pins, grateful for my help and in no fit state to inquire the reason for it. Indeed, if it had not been for my reminder she would have left yoke and baskets behind, so befuddled was she. But she retained enough sense to know the way out.

It appeared that I was in a regular fortification. It was, as Dunny had said, a brickyard, but so altered as to make it the perfect abode for a large congress of thieves. The building was evidently a former warehouse, windowless but with the remains of lifts and pulleys to doors in each of its three storys, of which we were on the first, for to reach the ground floor we were obliged to descend a set of stairs. With peepholes and slits roughly chipped through the walls and a regular watch, the ground floor was plainly designed for defense. Rifles and muskets were scattered and stacked around the walls in disorder as careless as that upstairs. Five or six men were posted as sentries, and two stout oaken doors, defended by a great iron bar, were the sole means of egress. My heart beat rapidly. If I were to be stopped, this was the place. But although the man who opened the small portal within one of the large doors peered closely, he said nothing; from which I devised that Dunny's careless impudence as to his safety was shared by many.

When we got outside, I understood that they had some reason to trust their defenses, for the warehouse was surrounded by a large open space of refuse-scattered mud, with a pool of stagnant water and only one or two tumbledown sheds to obstruct the view of a sturdy wall, which appeared to enclose the whole. The space was lighted generously by flares, and it would have been impossible for any large force to have crept in unnoticed, even supposing they could have surmounted the prime obstacle of the wall, which appeared to be in excellent repair. There was only one way out: a door in the wall of similar strength to that in the warehouse. The guard of this exit proved a trifle less willing to let me depart, but I had by this time so won my way into the good graces of the old dame that she spoke for me as though I had been a friend of long standing. Her words were, at any rate, sufficient to allay his suspicions. I was free.

We began to make our way down the muddy lane on which the brickyard fronted, the old dame leaning upon me and chattering garrulously about heaven knows what; her breath reeked stalely and I was not listening. Although I had walked out of the brickyard without let or hindrance, I still feared pursuit, with reason, as it turned out. We were no more than ten yards from the door—still in the lee of the wall, indeed—when I caught the sound of commotion within: shouts, calls, doors opening, feet running. With, I fear, little consideration for the old dame, whom I left hiccuping in astonishment against the wall, yoke and baskets on the ground, I fled. The wall was long and it seemed an eternity before I reached the end and was able to turn the corner along another side of it, glancing back as I did so to see, beyond the old dame (slid down into the mud and like to remain there till morning), a medley of assorted ruffians issuing from the door. I legged it down the road, hoping that they would not perceive the direction I had taken, and thankful for my dark cloak. How many were after me? How far would they pursue me? How long could I run this time? Where might I hide? They knew the warren of alleys and dwellings and I did not; moreover they had the benefit of a lantern.

For all my fear, I had not far to run before the sounds of pursuit ceased. Was it perhaps not me they sought? It was more likely that they tired of the chase, careless in this as in other respects. A fine sleet fell and had no doubt dampened what little enthusiasm they possessed. It also reminded me that I had in my fright become more alone than ever. I had lost even the old dame's company, not to speak of her nose for leading me out of the wretched maze of streets in which I now wandered. I was alone in one of the most squalid districts of London, without a penny in my pocket nor the least notion of which direction would lead me to safety.

I know that the wretchedness of my condition was as nothing compared with some; I know also that there is something worse than the horrible unreality of suddenness with which these things had come upon me, and that is the endless circle of misery and degradation to which so many are subject. That circle brings despair to numb the sense and halt the habitual ingenuity of the mind toward improvement; it provokes submission and acceptance. I cannot speak with complete authority of such things, thank heaven, yet the shadow of those horrors brushed me close that night. Only two days since and I had been walking along the towpath on the canal with Matthew, declaiming Juliet. In the little space between I seemed to have crossed and recrossed the boundaries between heaven and hell. I knew well enough the stories of young females who were lost forever in London, and I saw quite well how I might make one of them.

I continued to walk as though with purpose, preferring not to look more like a cony to be catched by a night fox than I already did, and more frightened of those I met abroad at such a time and in such a place than I was of being alone. The further I went, the worse became the streets. Narrow, dark and noisome they were, thick with mud and the stench of overflowing cesspools and refuse rotting in kennels. The houses leaned toward one another across the streets, what little sky was left obscured by mopsticks on which the poorest rags and tatters were hung out to dry. Narrow passages led into dark, high courts whose entrances gave forth stagnant air as I passed. All was decay. Plaster had fallen from the walls of the houses to reveal the lath; no window but was broken; no fence but missing half its palings; no step that was not about to crumble. A few furtive figures clung to the shadows like rats, and bundles of rags lay in doorways and stirred at my approach.

At last, in an open space where piles of rubble and dust suggested that one of the crumbling houses had but just collapsed, I sat down upon a plank lying atop a heap of rubbish that made a rude seat, and some kind of oblivion overtook me. Perhaps I wept a little. I do not know. I am sure I did not sleep. My past life paraded before me in scenes more substantial to my sense than the derelict ugliness of the place in which I actually sat. I watched my grandfather's hands as they grafted a scion, his skillful, stubby fingers with their battered nails, slitting, inserting, binding with oiled cloth and twine. I did not see his face. With a juddering interruption, a shuddering brutal ferocity, I saw Alexander Belzoni, his limbs grotesquely trampled, a mess of blood and bone and flesh, lying in the dung and mud. I saw Sophie smiling at me in her neat blue cambric gown, mixing vermilion and butter, and suddenly it was not Sophie at all but Sall, three-quarters naked, her features so thickly coated they resembled a puppet's, and her black painted eyes and the patch on her cheek close to my face. Then the face changed into that of Martha Mary, who clutched my shoulder most painfully tight and screamed at my father's back as he retreated into the Park. Again, with violent suddenness, came the image of Belzoni, lying there, horribly mangled to death. Then his face changed into Matthew's, and Matthew lay dead. Now Belzoni caught me, or was it Dunny Arvell? I was a prisoner and there was no escape.

Who shall say what part these experiences may have played in improving my ability to portray scenes of tragic misery or terror? The imprint they left upon my mind, still most vivid, the manner in which they seemed to interconnect with other aspects of my life, until that past itself could be viewed as in a new and unexpected dimension, most certainly affected me profoundly. Can the experiences of life alter the portrayal of them upon the stage? It is something I have often heard debated. Insofar as the actress herself is changed, surely it is reasonable to suppose that so personal a matter as the assuming of a character is affected also. One must discover the wellsprings of emotion which animate this fictional personage, so that one may reproduce them, not with exactness but with a feeling and delivery that have power to move. The callow girl I was when I left Mansfield had dipped into the shadowy depths of other unsuspected lives in a way that few experience and survive. I should be less than true to my own later musings if I did not admit it possible that my professional self had some benefit from those savage occurrences.

When I finally came to myself, it was with no consciousness of how much time had passed. It might have been one minute or twenty, an hour, so far had I been from the real world in that curious dreaming fit, or whatever it was, that overtook me. I found myself the object of the curious gaze of four little waifs, of whose approach I had been altogether unaware, wide-eyed, starving things, on the streets when they should have been asleep, stolen up like cats and, like cats, not unwilling to jump if a prey presented itself. When I stood up, straightened myself, sniffed and sighed, they made off as noiselessly as they had come, and I began to walk again, wary in case they were gone to fetch others. I walked and walked, in circles for all that I knew, until the coming of dawn, when more respectable persons were abroad; then I approached a likely-looking female and requested her to lead me to Gracechurch Street, offering her the red cashmere shawl as payment for her services. Thus I once more arrived at the archway of the great coaching inn where I had left Matthew the previous afternoon.

XVII

It was a curious circle I had completed, so small in circumference, so short in time, so large in incident, so lasting in impression. I walked again beneath the archway into the yard at the Cross Keys and so much the same it was and myself so different that I was obliged to stop to recover myself, if that self I had been ever could be recovered. I had left Matthew dozing. It was probable that he did so still, had done nothing since.

If I could have chosen to be standing on the little steps in the conservatory at Mansfield, or walking along its upper corridor to Sophie's room, or standing on the swell of land looking down toward Sotherton, I might anticipate an encounter with someone dear to me, who with a gesture, a look, a single acknowledgment, would instantly unite me with my former self, but here I was a stranger. I stood, unsteady with a sort of faintness, as I felt almost palpably a split and severance within. I did not know who I was, and for a moment I was no one.

The most trifling event served to reattach me to the world and to myself. The postboy, whom I had yesterday encountered on his highland pony, and who must, I suppose, have been son to one of the establishment, came running across the cobbles biting into a large, juicy, red-skinned apple. "You owe me a penny," he called out cheerfully. I smiled in reply without the least notion what he meant. The boy stared. "Are you hungry?" he said finally. "You are gone very pale." I shook my head. He held out the apple. "You may have this. I can get another. They are just come in from Kent."

I savored the crispness of that apple, and the juice ran down my chin. It was of the earth, it was wholesome, sweet and restorative. If an apple was, indeed, the innocent instrument of Eve's being put out of Paradise, then I am sure, in recompense, she later found no greater pleasure than in the eating of them when she and Adam were obliged to make do with the blessings of this world.

The postboy watched me eat. "I saw Bob-the-Double," he said. "I saw him. How do you like that? He said he had a friend who would be exceedingly glad to have the message. He's going to let me ride on the box with him. I don't need the penny."

"I was hungry, after all." I spoke at last. "That's the second good turn you've done me. You shall have the penny later."

The boy ran off, pleased to see me recover, and I sat on a form in the courtyard and finished the apple, core, pips and all (which is not my habit). The merino cloak was handsome, and the brown cambric muslin pretty, as well as serviceable and ladylike. So be it. I looked around me to remember which set of stairs I must climb to reach the room in which I had left Matthew, and went to find him, longing, in a sudden rush, to see his face and hear him speak.

Whom should I find sitting with him but Stephen Turnbull? To open the door and discover not one but two friends within affected me deeply. Tears started to my eyes when I embraced Stephen and then, somewhat to his surprise, Matthew, who sat up in bed with a nightcap on (got from where I could not think), the lump on his head as red and blue as ever, but the color of his face much returned, and a plate beside him on the coverlet with indications that he had made a hearty breakfast. He had slept soundly, he assured me, until an hour since, and was quite jovial, having no more notion of what had happened to me than that I had gone out early without disturbing him. He did not even notice my change of clothes.

Stephen had awoken him when he had come hunting me up on receipt of the message delivered by Bob Sturmey, and the pair of them were but just becoming acquainted and all the better pleased to see me. I had no wish instantly to begin upon an account of my night's travail. I was happy to be once more in familiar and convivial company, to answer Stephen's urgent inquiries about Sophie and listen to his account of what had happened to him since he had quit Mansfield.

The undercoachman had been prized loose from Mansfield Park with no greater ease than an oyster from its shell but, having now discovered independence, he flourished, in high twig, as I could not help but notice, in a green coat and buckskin breeches. As Sophie had surmised, the greater sphere of the metropolis had rapidly provided a wider appreciation of his talents than Mansfield and its environs could ever do and, in something less than the two months since his arrival, he had made friends in all sorts of places, from St. James's to St. Giles's. Indeed, amazingly for one who had seemed so attached to his rural existence, he had so adapted himself to London that you would have sworn he had been born and bred to city life.

Stephen gave much of the credit for his instant success to Bob Sturmey, Bob-the-Double, who had proved his first and best friend in London. Sturmey's nickname was twofold derived. Not only did he go all the way to Northampton instead of making an exchange halfway with another driver (such a practice enabling both to sleep in their own beds); Bob kept two beds, two houses and two wives. Whenever he was questioned about this duplication, he said he could not do without either of his women. Indeed, in so large a man such an appetite seemed not unreasonable. Each wife knew of the other, and was quite comfortable with the arrangement, the one in London, who had no children, sending packages of useful articles and pages of advice to her in Northampton with five.

Bob Sturmey's London wife's brother had been the means of setting Stephen on his way in the great metropolis. He, Caleb Colley by name, was a sharp dealer and in the way of becoming a wealthy man as a coachmaster. His ground was London to Folkestone and, as is customary, he horsed his own coaches on the first stage out and the last stage in. By a fortunate coincidence, at about the time of Stephen's arrival in London, Colley proposed to increase the size of his stable from twelve horses to twenty. When he heard his brother-in-law, Bob, whose skill as a whip-in-hand gave him some authority in the matter, speak in such glowing terms of Stephen Turnbull's ability as a judge of horseflesh, he suggested that Stephen accompany him to Tattersall's and provide him with a second opinion on the purchase. Caleb Colley was a knowledgeable man himself and knew another when he saw one. The enlargement of his business requiring just such a reliable assistant, Stephen was engaged on the spot, and soon treated more like partner than servant, Caleb being an affable man who had himself risen from stableboy. Colley's foresight in enlarging his stable (even though he had to sign a few bills to do it) may be judged by his present establishment of three hundred horses; some of his more cautious competitors lost their business because they did not take similar steps to improve the speed and reliability of their service.

As a consequence of Colley's patronage, Stephen was in and out of Tattersall's every day of the week and, in that horsy company, quickly recognized by dukes and dandies, honorables and dishonorables, jockeys, legs and ring men, once or twice as Tom Bertram's right-hand man whom they had encountered in the past, but mostly for his own singular knack of understanding the best and worst of any horse. He could tell to a hairbreadth what animal was well fitted for performance between the shafts in a four-horse team. It is no great talent to choose a wheeler, for, strength being the first requisite, a wheeler must be sound, but Stephen was unmatched in the choosing of a leader, where strength is not as important as spirit and stamina. Bob Sturmey told with great satisfaction how, on that very first occasion, Stephen justified his friend's high recommendation. At Stephen's word, Caleb Colley purchased for ten pounds a horse considered unsound and vicious, and found himself possessed of the best leader he had ever had. Stephen had already been wooed with offers of similar employment by other horse fanciers, but he said quietly that he had had enough of "gentlemen," by which I knew him to refer to Tom Bertram. He had, in any case, no taste for further change, nor need of it either: he was often consulted and scarcely ever made less than a couple of guineas for the giving of an opinion.

We must have spent an hour in such talk, Stephen, something to my relief (and wonder, recalling his former uncommunicativeness), having so much to tell of his own doings that there was no great space for ours. We related something of our unfortunate encounter with the King's men, and Stephen examined Matthew's arm, in the mending of which, once the wound had closed, he was sure he could assist. He persuaded us to accompany him to the Sturmeys', with whom he presently lodged, and who would, he assured us with a most complete conviction, welcome us gladly. His confidence would have quite overruled any doubts, had I wished to voice them, but I did not: such a prospect of refuge never appeared more desirable.

If anything, Stephen had underrated the warmth of our welcome. Mrs. "London" Sturmey (she was called by her fond husband "Mrs. L." and, most frequently, "Ellie," her counterpart in Northampton being referred to as "Enna") was a warmhearted, generous soul, whose maternal instincts, she being childless, were directed toward all those waifs and strays who came within her ken. However rudely healthy such a one might appear, he was pale and wan by her reckoning, and needed feeding-up at her ample table. The only daughter of a wax chandler of some substance, Ellie had recently inherited upon his death the commodious house in which she and Bob now dwelled, together with a property or two in Wapping and Rotherhithe, from which she received rents which materially increased the comforts of the Sturmey households in both Northampton and London. She made pies as large as cartwheels for the five children she had never met. Bob regularly joked that it was in hopes of a taste of those pies, whose smell so frequently pervaded the coach, that so many passengers chose to ride with him instead of the other driver who shared with him the two sides of the ground from London to Northampton.

Ellie Sturmey's reaction to Matthew Quinney you may devise. By nature thin as a wafer and injured to boot, he was soon in fair danger of being suffocated with kindness. Ellie would not hear of him staying for less than a month at the least. The later discovery that he was an artist further recommended him. She had been brought up with some pretensions to accomplishments, in recognition of which a piano still stood in her parlor gathering dust, and she was much in awe of any who could achieve what for all her dancing, drawing and music masters (the wax chandler doted on his daughter) she could not.

Her generous hospitality enabled Matthew to take full advantage of Stephen's skill in the manipulation of bones and healing. What was good for horses was even better for human beings, as Mr. Wilcox had been wont to say. With massage and application of his liniment, Stephen effected continual improvement, especially in restoring the flexibility of Matthew's fingers, which was, in view of his profession, of prime concern. Stephen's uncanny ability to ease pain and stiffness with a few gentle strokes amazed the scene painter's rational mind. While his arm mended, he spent long hours practicing drawing with his left hand and trying to work out some explanation of Stephen's gift. He concluded that it was a power latent within every individual, which should be developed and used to benefit all. Despite many questions, however, Stephen could say only that he felt it through his fingers. Matthew said to me, idly attempting to draw arms, hands, legs and feet—as if by the depiction of those useful extremities he could fathom the matter—that he supposed Stephen considered he might lose his skill by thinking too much upon it. He became quite heated, indeed (though not in Stephen's presence), about the distrust of learning and prevalence of superstition from which such an attitude might arise, but I have often wondered if Stephen's instinct were not right, and there is a delicate balance, of an almost antithetical nature, between thought and feeling, which we would do well not to overlook in our placing of reason above all.

As his recovery progressed, Matthew drew several sketches of Ellie, which she and Bob much admired. So enthusiastic was Ellie, indeed, that she was all for him going up instantly to Northampton and performing the same service for Enna and her five little ones. I thought privately that Matthew had not caught a good likeness; such portraiture was not for him. Indeed, wild to get back to his own sort of painting, he further won Ellie's heart by covering a wall of her boudoir with a painted scene. Such light, bright colors, such greens and blues and yellows he used, that he brought a rustic spring into wintry London. I could not but note with admiration how different this scene was from that which he had drawn for *Lovers' Vows*, with all the careful detail necessary to please in a continuing and close acquaintance. Some painters came through our village lately, and I engaged them to provide such wall scenes for some of our tenants, who were much pleased with the effect. I myself was, I confess, somewhat disappointed in the execution, which lacked the fire and animation of that scene of Matthew's for whose remembrance I had employed them.

Ellie Sturmey made a friend of me instantly, and she it was in whom I first confided the horrors of the brickyard. Her china-blue eyes widened with thrilled and sympathetic curiosity. She drew out every horrid detail of my adventures (from which I omitted Alexander Belzoni), especially avid for those concerning Dunny Arvell and Sall, which she contrived to hear at least once a day for a week. Curiously enough, I benefited from the frequent relating of the episode to Ellie, for whom it had, despite her genuine sympathy, no greater reality than the Ratcliffe Highway murders or any other of those scenes of horror from which her own daily existence was comfortably distant: it began to acquire for me some tincture of the unreality it had for her. I became almost as desirable a guest as Matthew. Indeed, had I not objected (although when I did she was instantly persuaded that such a thing would, indeed, offend against propriety), she would have summoned her friends for a game of whist that they might share her indignation at my tingling tale.

Bob's absence every other night left her in want of a companion, and I fitted the part admirably, rendering her small services with which she was delighted out of all proportion. I dressed her hair, ran errands, accompanied her down Piccadilly to wonder at the elegance of the shops, and to Wapping and Rotherhithe when she went for the first time to inspect the dwellings for which she was receiving rents. This was an outing of a different sort, for the places were dark and full of the stench of decay, the tenants of the lowest sort. I shuddered at the memory of the brickyard. It was not what Ellie had expected. She vowed she would never go there again, and had us carried to Don Saltero's, which served the best custard buns in London, to raise our spirits.

It was the most agreeable thing to be the object of her interest, for she took benevolent pleasure in gratifying a country girl's desire to view the curiosities of the metropolis. I saw a balloon put up from Green Park, wondered at Barker's Panorama and Miss Linwood's Gallery of Needlework, viewed Westminster Abbey and the former residence of Jonathan Wild. As to what we should do when the weather improved, there was no end to it: we were to go up the river and see the Tudor palace at Hampton Court; we should visit Finch's Grotto Garden and Vauxhall and climb the winding stair of the Monument.

Ellie, in the first flush of indignant rage at my misfortune, tried to persuade me to lay a complaint at the Bow Street magistrates' office against Dunny Arvell and his thieves, but this I refused to do, pleading a dislike of the unpleasantness and notoriety which must follow such an action, and a conviction that the Brickyard Gang were as impregnable in their fortress as Dunny had intimated. I was also anxious that nothing should connect me with Alexander's death, nor any accidental revelation endanger Matthew, although I kept these considerations to myself.

One morning Ellie was reading aloud from the paper an account of the apprehension of a man for wantonly wounding a young woman in the head with a cutlass. The offender had been sent for his punishment to the treadmill at Coldbath Fields, and the magistrate had expressed a desire that all persons who had lately been robbed or molested by members of the Brickyard Gang, of whom he suspected this desperado to be one, would resort to the prison in order to view him.

By the time Ellie had finished reading, she was all for an expedition to the house of correction. In the end I capitulated. There would undoubtedly be numbers of people who would go to gape out of idle curiosity, and I should be inconspicuous in the crowd. This was not Ellie's view, however. She insisted that I be well wrapped about the face, in case the villain recognized me (as though he might break down the bars), and that we needed protection, for which, Matthew declining the honor, she prevailed upon Stephen Turnbull.

People of all degrees had been drawn to Coldbath Fields by the prospect of a spectacle and the notoriety of the gang, but since we had arrived by coach we took precedence over many, and we were obliged to wait not above a half-hour to view the prisoner. I had thought we should file past a cell and spy through a peephole, but the treadmill was in a large room, and accommodated many prisoners, among whom ours stood in the end position where he might most easily be seen. Thus twenty or so visitors at a time viewed him—and, indeed, the others upon the wheel—as one might gape at objects in a freak show. The man proved to be as large and fierce as a bear, black, piratical and saturnine, with a striped stocking cap such as navigators wear. He stared at the crowd without shame, climbing the steps which slowly revolved the cruelly heavy drum as though he were climbing the shrouds, steadily and tirelessly, endlessly moving, endlessly in the same place, endlessly achieving nothing.

I did not care to contemplate the sight for long. Ellie, digging me in the ribs with her elbow and raising her eyebrows questioningly, was disappointed when I shook my head; I was quite certain I had never seen the prisoner before.

One jackass shied an egg. It was poorly aimed and broke on the frame, giving forth a nauseating stench. Quick as a wink, the bear spat, with much greater precision than his tormentor, whom he hit squarely in the face. This earned him a prod from the soldier who stood by with a bayonet, as well as a mixture of cheers and jeers from the crowd, who took this as the signal to pelt him with whatever they had. Under such fire the bear lost his regularity of step, and the piece of wood designed to discourage idleness hit him hard on the crown, to the further delight of the spectators. At this a young woman who stood at the front, barefoot and ill-clad, with a bandage tied around her head, attempted to remonstrate with the tormentors. They were not inclined to heed her and one or two of the missiles intended for him found their mark on her. She lost her balance and fell to the ground at about the moment that whispers went around the crowd: " 'Tis her!"

"That's her he wounded!"

"Whatever does she here?"

"See where her head is bandaged!"

" 'Tis the poor body herself, to be sure."

"The more you beat them the better they be!"

Nothing more was thrown and the interest in the young woman served to draw the crowd's attention away from the prisoner, who said not a word although his eyes gleamed with a sort of maniacal light. With no further prospect of excitement and the stench of the egg for discouragement, the spectators, including ourselves, began to make their way toward the door. We were almost out of it when I noticed that Stephen Turnbull was no longer beside us. He stood like a post where we had left him, his gaze riveted upon the young woman, who had raised herself painfully to her feet and now spoke to the soldier who guarded the prisoner. When I laid a hand upon his arm, he turned to me as if awakening from a dream. "It is Kitty," he said slowly.

"Kitty?"

"You told me Kitty was come to London. That's her. It is Kitty."

Kitty Huckle, if indeed that poor unfortunate female was she, carried a small cloth bundle, and seemed to be entreating permission to give its contents to him on the treadmill. When Stephen grasped her arm, she turned with a little cry of apprehension. A multitude of emotions chased across her face: fear, doubt, recognition, followed by disbelief, and then, at the last, a sort of guilty horror. She did not speak, but drew in her breath with a rattling sound and gave a great start, so clumsy in her amazement that her bundle fell to the floor, where the greater part of its contents were spilled. At that she did softly shriek, kneeling down instantly and scrabbling in the dirt in an attempt to save the scattered meats. At the sight either of her distress or the waste of food the prisoner turned more bear than ever, uttering a string of imprecations and contriving by some means to exert such force upon even that mammoth instrument of torture that he set the whole hideous contraption rattling against the stone flags with a noise that might have emanated from the mouth of hell. Dawdlers in the crowd turned in their tracks, and some pushed back eagerly into the room. The soldier's attention was now given to his charge, although the pricks of the bayonet seemed to have little effect upon the man's rage.

"Give him money," I whispered to Ellie, indicating the soldier, while I bent down to help the woman in gathering up the half-eaten, moldy victuals.

Ellie's shilling produced the desired effect and, at a signal from his companion, the soldier at the door held back the entry of the next group. Then the bayonet was put to gentler purpose as a wedge to prevent the punitive operation of the wood block, while the prisoner, who had by now ceased his rattling, rapidly and ravenously ate the mess which we had contrived to save from the bundle. Unexpectedly, he nodded his thanks, but his only words were to the woman, threat and affection mixed. "You'll not fail me? You've found some fine friends, but you'll not forget me, shall you? I shan't forget you."

Ellie was all agog: a tragic story such as Kitty's was the very thing to excite her sympathy and she took it as a matter of course that the destitute female should accompany us home in the carriage. Certainly no one could have been more in need of her kind ministrations. Kitty was in desperate straits, all but starving and the wound upon her head reopened where a rotten potato thrown by the crowd had hit her. Little was left of the handsome features that had once attached the affections of both Stephen Turnbull and his master. She was tall and long-necked, but wasted, thin and racked with coughs. Only in her eyes was her former beauty discernible. Violet-blue as harebells, they were the more striking for being set in such a gaunt and sunken countenance.

In the art of making a body comfortable, no one could outdo Ellie Sturmey, and she and I and the two maids went at it with a will. Some broth laced with brandy put heart enough into Kitty to survive the necessities of cleaning, disrobing and bathing, though truly her body linen was nothing but rags. We were obliged to burn her pitiful clothes instantly, and the coach had to be smoked out, washed and sprinkled with pine needles. Kitty had not been much bitten, and for this we did not know whether to be thankful or sorrowful, since small vermin are reputed to leave a dying body in peace. Although it went unspoken between us, both Ellie and I thought her far gone in a consumption. Once she was warmly dressed in a flannel nightgown and put to rest upon a feather mattress with a stone water bottle at her feet, however, there was an improvement in her appearance despite her poor injured brow, and the hectic flush that suffuses the cheeks at certain times of exertion during the latter stages of the disease tinged her churchyard skin with a delicate beauty.

The gash she had sustained from the cutlass crossed from temple to ear. When we had cut the hair from around the wound and washed it, Stephen stitched it. Kitty did not scream: she bit upon the leather, sighed and fainted, but the salve he then skillfully applied eased the pain, so that when she once more came to her right senses she instantly felt the benefit, although to effect any improvement in her general condition was beyond even him.

Stephen was in a curious state of abstraction, reverting, it seemed, to the silent, sober self best known to me. He took his place in a chair at the foot of Kitty's bed, and gazed at her in a reverie, as if he could scarcely believe in her existence. Seeing him so, I could not but think of Sophie. How was it to be between them? The fond inquiries he had made after her, the affectionate letter he had written at my urging and (being no penman) with my help; his apology for the long period of silence; his conviction that he should be able to take the lease on a pretty house and make her his wife in the new year, where was all this to be now? He had loved Kitty dearly once, and I knew the steadfastness of his nature. He later moved his chair so that he sat at her side, and held her hand. All through that first night and for three thereafter, he insisted upon watching her, leaving her side only to attend to the most urgent of his appointments.

Little by little, her story was told. Despite his attack upon her with the cutlass, it appeared that Kitty had pleaded for her quondam protector, as a consequence of which the magistrate had imposed a lighter sentence. The ruffian's session in the treadmill had come about as the result of his own intractable behavior while under detention. How she had come to take up with such a brutish fellow in the first place, let alone plead for him after he had wounded her, was a matter of wonder, to be understood only as the conclusion of the ever-worsening series of events which had begun with her departure from Mansfield Park. It was not until she falteringly told Stephen of having borne Tom Bertram's child, however, that that good man was aware of it. Stephen was curiously innocent in matters of the flesh. He had not known, never once suspected, that Tom Bertram, whom he had served so faithfully, had done him such a wrong. The blood rose like a tide into his face and then receded. He got up and walked around the room, staring unseeingly at the fire and pulling the curtain aside to look without purpose into the drear and rainy street. "So it all begins with him!" He spoke in his customary quiet tones, but Kitty began to weep softly and, not wishing further to discompose her, Stephen left the room, to return an hour later, apparently quite restored.

The allowance Mrs. Norris had promised had ceased abruptly when Kitty's child was three months old, and Mrs. Baillie, the farmer's wife, kindly disposed toward Kitty and her pretty infant, had offered her a post as servant, which, Baillie having a lascivious eye and his wife a jealous though hitherto unsuspecting one, Kitty had refused. Leaving her child where she knew she would be well cared for, the mother chose to try her luck in London, where she had hopes of obtaining employment through her father's second cousin who was a milliner.

What took place after Kitty's arrival in London was a familiar tale of deception and fraud practiced upon an innocent female who thinks to find the rainbow's end in the great city. I shivered to hear it. Was I not one of those very women myself? I, who had been guilty of the selfsame folly, could not bring myself to condemn her. As in a game of hazard, the odds may be calculated and yet the dice fall against you. They had fallen against Kitty. I, by contrast, as I now see plain, won all stakes. How can I not think so, remembering the singular irony of fortune by which, when Kitty found herself on that first day all alone in the great metropolis, she was engaged in conversation by a woman of genteel appearance who, under pretense of concern for her welfare, enticed her to a house in Covent Garden (that very location whose theater, named after it, saw the making of my own success) and there, by various bribes, ruses and threats persuaded her into a life of vice?

I tell myself that in her place I should have run away, and why did not she? Yet how should anyone who has not suffered such desolation and despair answer for her? She did not, and at the last she could not, being under the influence of a villainous man called Morton, who first used her himself and then sent her out to be used by others, exacting from her three guineas a week for her board and lodging and threatening to strip her of her clothes and turn her into the street if she did not meet the payment.

After some months of this miserable existence, two sailors visited the house (which was no more than a common brothel), and then claimed that they had been robbed of more than thirty guineas by the women with whom they had lain. After a fierce argument with Morton, who was a better pugilist than they had allowed, they were driven out, but later returned with a number of their messmates to take revenge, breaking every window in the house, taking hatchets to the furniture until it was no better than sticks, ripping down hangings, breaking china and befouling the carpets in an orgy of destruction. A large crowd gathered to encourage them and share in the plunder, and after some hours the proceedings had all the appearance of a riot. As a final gesture, the perpetrators piled a great heap of goods from the house in the street and set light to it, dancing round it in drunken triumph. The huge bonfire and the customary foolhardy fire-eating and running at the crowds with burning brands began to threaten the nearby buildings so dangerously that the parish engines were summoned, but they never arrived, and it was only by good fortune that the whole district was not burned to the ground.

The odious Morton was thus justly ruined at a stroke, but the poor women of the house, of whom Kitty made one, were also the objects of the rioters' dislike and not a few of them were stripped and subjected to bestial indignities; one indeed was tied naked to a post and set in the midst of the bonfire, whence she was finally rescued only as the flames licked at her. He of the treadmill had joined the crowd for the purposes of plunder and, although he was undoubtedly prompted by nothing more than a selfish desire to have Kitty for himself, she perceived him as the instrument of her deliverance from a similar fate. Ever since that occasion she had dwelled with him, partly out of fear but also out of gratitude. It seemed to us all a curious and unnecessary sort of obligation, for he was coarse and brutal, especially when, as happened not infrequently, he was drunk. The evidence of regular beatings was to be seen all over Kitty's poor, wasted body. The cutlass with which he had inflicted the wound she now bore was, it appeared, a memento of the mutiny of Vellore, his own weapon to which he was strangely attached and with which he had often before threatened her though never used. He had, it seemed, served as a soldier in India; indeed, Kitty insisted that it was the delusions which came upon him as a result of those experiences which made him ill-treat her. Kitty's own attachment to such a man seemed to me no less a delusion, a remnant of more elevated feelings, to which she clung in the face of worse alternatives. It was a sad measure of how far she had fallen.

XVIII

My encounter with Alexander Belzoni, his death and what followed was a fiery memory burned into me. At night I dreamed of him (as I still do) with his terrible wounds and his torn limbs, waking up with my heart palpitating, wanting to run but locked into immobility, thinking I had screamed out loud but not certain, lying down again in the silence, wide-awake but unable to escape from the hideous Belzoni, whose body turned into a fearsome, writhing, red-hot snake which bound its coils around me until it was my own limbs which contorted and broke and bled.

When I first gave Matthew a full account of what had happened that evening, it took him by surprise. He listened in silence, and when I had finished he shook his head, saying at last: "If I had known. If I had only known such things awaited you . . ."

"How were you to know? I do not regret leaving Mansfield. I never shall. I am here, whole, to prove it."

He laid his hand upon mine. "I shall not forget that you saved my life. You have done more in a month to assist our cause than most of those who have professed faith in it for ten years. And then that this should happen!" He paused. "Belzoni was a spy, a deceiver, a man of violence. He brought his end upon himself." He paused again. "As to what followed—I scarcely know what to say—you did bravely, Jane, that is sure. You withstood it all. You did more than bravely, by heaven."

Matthew never questioned the detail of that night's doings again, as he did not tell me directly that I should separate myself from his political activities, although I understood him to wish it. To tell the truth, I was not unhappy that it should be so. Although what he fought for seemed to me eminently just, there was no great part for a female to play, even had I desired one. I admired Miss Bell. She played a man's part, certainly, but I did not envy it, seeing how she and her brother had been all but deprived of their livelihood by attending an innocent meeting. For the moment I wanted no more participation and Matthew was plainly of the same mind. He spoke to me of his activities only when pressed, although I was aware that, on a number of occasions when Ellie and I were absent on our excursions, he would slip away. I knew him to be in communication with a committee of like-minded people in Westminster, who had been active in the last election, and whose prime mover was a master tailor. The news which most gratified him (and which he volunteered) was that the formation of the Hampden Club, the association of gentry and nobility sympathetic to the aims of working men, in which Matthew saw the greatest hope of change, was now certain. I remained anxious in case he put himself into danger, but he assured me that the possibility of his being apprehended was greatly reduced. The force Sir Thomas Bertram had sent after him was left in disarray by the loss of Alexander Belzoni, and in any case London was Matthew's own ground, where the courts, alleys and bystreets were as well known to him as his own ten toes, and where he could rely upon some influence in high places to protect him from arrest.

It was on that cheerful occasion that he reminded me with a smile that I was not in London merely to gape at the sights. I must look steadfastly to the future and, since he anticipated returning to scene painting as soon as ever his wrist was well mended, attend to the preparations for my theatrical career which he had begun and then been obliged so abruptly to discontinue. I welcomed the prospect.

As luck would have it, Ellie was wild for the theater. We visited Drury Lane and that most sociable of all the theaters, the Little Theatre in the Haymarket, as well as the King's Theatre, where I was first introduced to Italian opera. It was in Ellie's company that I first saw the great new theater at Covent Garden. We entered through the majestic portico, stopping to admire the frieze over which everyone exclaimed, and took our place in the pit (the prime place to view the play, for all its other disadvantages), from whence I could admire to the full the theater's size and splendor. Its walls towered high as a cathedral's, through three levels of boxes to a circular ceiling painted to represent a cupola. Slender, reeded gilt columns and gray panels painted with wreaths of honeysuckle and gold were its chiefest and most beautiful decoration. I lost my heart on the instant. Even now, when I am aware that its horseshoe shape prevents an actress from readily establishing a desirable rapport with the audience, when I freely admit the superiority of the Paris theaters in this respect, there is still no place in which I would rather play.

When I witnessed for the first time the lavish spectacles upon the Covent Garden stage, the talents of those on the boards, which so greatly excelled anything I had previously imagined, the prospect of myself making one of the performers seemed, though quite impossible, more infinitely desirable than ever. At my suggestion, Ellie and I read all sorts of plays together, by which I acquainted myself with many parts and even made a start at learning them. The activity quite delighted my kind hostess, although I did not confide in her the high nature of my ambitions, being a little ashamed to do so. She had no talent herself for delivering lines, nor any facility in remembering them, but she generously praised my talent and made her husband sit and applaud our performances. Poor Bob was thus obliged to endure not only our modern melodrama and tragedy but also Shakespeare, when he really liked nothing but farce. I treasure the later occasion on which he thought it proper to give me the benefit of his true and considered reflections upon the theater: a nobby place, but too much talking and too little action. Shakespeare was overlong for a certainty, though *Hamlet* would be a fine play if it were but reduced to the ghost scene, the funeral and the duel. Bob's general conclusion, which he strongly advised me to convey to the manager, was that more fighting should be introduced into every piece.

There is a particular smell to the back rooms of a theater. I remarked upon it the first time Matthew introduced me to those at Covent Garden, and I shall never forget it. It observes no national boundaries, for it is the same in Paris as in London. It is the smell of home, as unmistakable and redolent of pleasurable associations as new-baked bread. Compounded of size, gum, turpentine, powder, sawdust and oil, it is by no means so wholesome, but just as apt to set going the juices of every performer.

When Matthew led me through the mass of rooms, some lighted and busy, some rising in cavernous darkness to unseen spaces, full of pulleys, ropes, cranks and sleeping energy, I was enthralled. Superadded to the performances I had witnessed with Ellie, it was all I needed to persuade me to commit myself to the theater. From that instant I resolved to live my life in such a place, to be part of it howsoever I might. You may feel doubtful of so much resolution in the heart of one whose recent experience should have made her wary. For who should have anticipated anything but disappointment if not disaster? What chance is there of comfort, let alone success, in a theatrical life? The fingerpost announcing "Fame, five miles" announces on its othermost side "Want, three miles." Yet I know of few who work in the theater that have not a similar infatuation. It is not a profession for the fainthearted, nor for those who weigh their life carefully upon the probabilities. But then, the rational has little place in a theater; it is constructed upon illusion and extravagance. I wanted, beyond everything, to act; to be behind the drop before it rises to reveal the audience, that instant which is ginger in the mouth no matter how experienced the performer. I was filled, in short, with a wild excitement.

My enthusiasm was a little dampened, to be sure, when the best work that Matthew could find me turned out to be as a seamstress with the wardrobe keeper. But the room where the costumes were made was large and well lighted, with patent oil lamps burning brightly to offset the darkness of the afternoon, and a mixture of men and women cutting and stitching around several large tables and clacking cheerfully. I took my place at once, set to with a will and after a few days found myself very content, for the work was congenial and, once I had learned a few tricks of the trade, easily within my capacity. The best of it was that I was well placed should any supernumeraries be required, for the Garden preferred to use supers whose abilities they knew rather than choosing from the gapers on the street as a traveling company is often obliged to do. Even for the largest scenes we never called above half our supers from outside. I do commend this practice, since, no matter how excellent the principal performers may be, many effects can be ruined by a super who walks downstage left when he should have moved downstage right, or trips over the drapery as he moves around the deathbed, through want of talent, experience or practice.

The manager had a regular company of types he could draw on when needed, a number of whom were employed about the theater and thus could be ready at a moment's notice. Some, like myself, hoped some day to shine in a different spot; others had a particular appearance that suited them for certain parts. One elderly carpenter had a gnarled countenance that must have done credit to Tiresias and, although he was so afflicted with rheumatics that at times he could scarcely stir the size, he was always pressed into service in the front rank of the crowd, where a nod from Ben Croft, as sage counselor to king or emperor, was the stamp of approval on a point. For all his appearance of serene wisdom, I rarely heard Ben speak a word either onstage or off. He worked, ate and slept in the theater, looked after the cats and never went out but to fetch a quart of ale for the company.

As the Christmas season approached there was more than usual need of supers for the pantomimes and extravaganzas, where crowds in great numbers and bright costumes are *de rigueur*. Matthew and my pretty face commended me to the manager, and I had my chance to go upon the stage, one among a score of others, but not summarily dismissed, like some, whose awkward gait and inelegant treading of the boards were certain to call down laughter and worse from those in the gods.

I loved it, even though the piece was a most frightful harlequinade. We were all for Harlequin that year, Drury Lane and ourselves, but Drury Lane had the best of it, I confess. Grimaldi was not there to clown for us, and a lamentable young man from Bristol with a sheaf of undeserved recommendations played the lead. He could somersault decently but dance not at all, and his nose was a door knocker. But the piece proved suitably entertaining for the juvenile visitors during their school vacations and ran for several nights. There was plenty of glitter under the lights, massed crowds and spectacular effects to make up for other inadequacies, and the spectators were not more than usually noisy, though Harlequin attracted orange peel and nutshells like a magnet. His poor Columbine, who suffered by close association, was even less fortunate, being the recipient of a rotten tomato which, since she insisted it was meant for him, caused a dreadful row.

I came on three times, once as a starry nymph in a spangled skirt and twice as an Indian princess, in which role I had to stand in the front row and make a tolerable curtsy. I should like to be able to say that my talent so demonstrated itself then and there that my future was assured, but it was not so. Chance took a hand, as ever, and my second part had nought to do with my first.

Once the Christmas season was past, a melodrama was mounted with a small cast of tried performers. It was a new play and had nothing much to recommend it, being in the usual run of popular successes, with a heroine who is brought to the brink of ruin by a series of unfortunate and improbable circumstances, and a hero who is under such misapprehensions about his beloved that anywhere but on stage he would be taken for a regular ninny. The sets were Matthew's largest commission since he had recovered from his accident, however, and his invention, perhaps for being so long pent up, was never better. The climax of the play occurred in a scene on the bank of a river, the representation of which was wildly applauded at every performance, quite justly, for it was the best thing in the piece. The water came through a tumble of rocks on one side into a tank that lay out of sight before the backdrop in imitation of a river. The scene, lighted as for dusk, with a pale sky and a sliver of moon, was ethereal and ghostly. Into this river, at the height of her distress, the heroine precipitated herself, and was rescued, dripping, as she sank for the last time, by the hero, who finally acknowledged the injustice of his suspicions. It was a splendid moment, to which the audience quite breathlessly attended. Miss Leadbetter, who played the heroine, survived this dipping for three days, but then, as was not altogether surprising in the depths of winter, took cold. She was plucky, and determined to brave the nightly dousing despite her fevers, but it was bound to aggravate her condition and, quite suddenly, after four more performances, she lost her voice.

The manager was in a regular taking and, when Matthew suggested that I might replace her, prepared to consider what in other circumstances he might have dismissed out of hand. I saved him money, of course, but I have no doubt that my chance was owed to Matthew's good offices, for, as the one to whom the play's success was principally due, his opinion carried some weight. Once he had heard me read, the manager agreed to try me out, the cancellation of one night's performance giving me a day to learn the part. I could not read my way through, of course, although if I had been well known I might have done. Not that that is a practice of which I approve. The lines may sound well enough out of a book—although if they are not known by heart, how can they be felt?—but nothing breaks the illusion so much as a book in the actor's hand. In any case, most of those who must stoop to it are old, infirm or too fond of the bottle. I should not like to have to make such demands upon the patience of an audience and, thank heaven, I have never yet had to. My facility in learning lines is no small advantage; it was the first thing the manager found to praise in me. He decided that I should be presented as an actress newly arrived from the provinces, which he located at a suitable distance from London. I recall the handbill exactly: "The exquisite Miss Hartwell, never before seen upon the London stage, fresh from her numerous successes in Carlisle, has graciously consented, at short notice, to take the place of Miss Leadbetter, who is unfortunately indisposed."

Had I failed, I suppose I should have plummeted to oblivion with much the same celerity as I had been granted a chance at fame, but I was an overnight success, and I and the play, whose run was quickly extended, became the rage of London. No doubt it was less my acting than the way in which the damp muslin clung to my form as John Sangster, who played the hero, lifted me out of the tank; we certainly perfected a very graceful attitude which could be appreciated from every seat in the theater. I was not so heavy as Miss Leadbetter, to begin with, and he could hold the pose longer. I lay back in his arms, apparently lifeless, with (the *Repository* reported) "an air of tragic beauty." The pathos of my drooping hand was said to be masterly, and a plaster cast of it decorated the windows of a number of shops and coffeehouses. Lately I can boast of having, like Mr. Garrick, a statuette modeled after me, which may be purchased either in Bow china or plain Staffordshire. That pose became so popular that any number of ladies of fashion wished to try it; some of them even represented the scene with me present, the muslin wetter or dryer as their modesty dictated, and the latest beau got in to perform John Sangster's role. One such performance was the direct cause of a duel, or so I heard. I always complimented these genteel efforts, but it impressed upon me the instinctive and unlearned aspect of my achievement, for none of them could do it half so well. I trust you will forgive this vanity; it is more in the nature of a reflection upon my art. All the lessons and experience in the world are no substitute for an original talent, however much they may add to its luster. In that respect I take no credit for my success, only bless the good fortune that bestowed it on me. I was also fortunate in having a stronger constitution than Miss Leadbetter, who did not altogether recover her voice for three months, whereas I did not even take a chill. For that I am no doubt indebted to my grandfather's insistence upon a regular icy dousing under the pump in the kitchen yard at Sotherton.

What followed upon my success in *Seraphina's Reward* was an alteration in my circumstances so great as to be nothing less than a transformation, so sudden that I hardly knew how to manage it. Everyone was agog to meet me, and forty invitations to balls and routs and assemblies lay on my table at once, so that I was obliged to refuse more than half of them. And everywhere I went people turned to stare and crowded in upon me once I was announced, as though I belonged to a freak show. The manager, knowing the value to his theater of my being seen in public places and the best society, encouraged me to accept as many invitations as I well could, taking upon himself the nice decisions as to whether I should attend Lord A.'s assembly, or whether the acceptance of Sir B.'s offer of a carriage would be compromising. Matthew said there had been nothing like it since Master Betty, although that was the lesser half of a compliment; by the time I met him the precocious child who had once set the theatrical world afire was a gangling, knock-kneed, ill-made calf with no more gift for acting than a turnip and even less manners. I trust I have proved myself deserving of a less temporary regard.

I have often thought of those in my profession who, with ability equal to mine, have struggled long and achieved no recognition, or only such as was unworthy of their talents. I had a natural aptitude for acting without which my spectacular rise would not have been possible, but my skill in the histrionic art was unproven, unpolished and, in that piece at least, not greatly in demand. Chance played the chiefest part. Nevertheless, I take credit to myself for what came after, for there are plenty of comets in the heavens, and only those with something more than handsomeness to recommend them stay to shine.

The manager intended that I should play some pretty, youthful parts in well-known comedies, and later, if these proved successful, try me in Shakespeare. That would put me to the test and I welcomed it. The technical business of the stage I learned quickly, especially how to match my movements to those of the actors about me so as not to hinder them while producing the best effect I could in my own part. I have never played in a company which is entirely free of sour comment about those who will steal the best spots, but I am not aware of offending in that respect myself. Very early on, the manager commended me for my neat movements upon the stage. Everyone behaves differently, of course. Some well-known persons are notorious for inflicting painful ordeals upon members of the company against whom they have a grievance by changing their moves by a yard in every performance. You would think such behavior likely to damage their own reputations, but some will go to excessive lengths to vent a petty spite. For my own part, I believe in careful rehearsal down to the last detail. That is the only way to achieve consistency. When we are on tour I make sure that the supers are put through their paces at least six times and I have never regretted the hours thus spent.

I think there never was, even in those early days, a moment when I did not feel the stage to be entirely my home. Some exclaim with alarm and disapproval over the falsity of a play, its shadowy imitation of life, the exhibition of passion it demands. I see it quite otherwise. I never cease to wonder at the power of a play to move an audience to laughter or tears with its enactment of carefree high spirits or those moments when man achieves his highest grandeur and nobility. I thrilled to it then as I do now.

The first success I truly savored, feeling that it owed something to my developing talent as an actress rather than to my reputation as a beauty, was Sir Harry Wildair in *The Constant Couple* (that very play contained in the book Matthew gave me, which I eventually retrieved, along with Sophie's yellow carpetbag, from the apothecary in Chandler's Cross). The manager, having measured my ability, calculated that it would be best to set me up as a natural successor to Peg Woffington, and selected the part accordingly. I was flattered in the comparison, although no doubt his choice was as carefully designed to intrigue the public as it was to make the best of me, for I made a dashing young beau in tight breeches and a silk shirt, and the outfit pleased more gentlemen than my maidenly gowns. Since that time I have always been primarily a comedy actress, so strongly do these early parts impress themselves upon the minds of both managers and public. I have also donned breeches, as Macheath as well as Viola, Imogen and Rosalind. My own pet role is that of Miss Hardcastle in *She Stoops to Conquer*. I have played the tragic roles, but never to such acclaim. I do not accept, however, that playing tragedy requires more skill than playing comedy. Mrs. Siddons, it is well known, could not make comedy at all. As Rosalind she could bring herself to be neither girl nor boy, and insisted upon wearing hussar boots with a gardener's apron and petticoat behind. She looked a perfect fright. Nobody would exclaim, of course, since it was she.

I saw her in tragedy, and while I admire, as all must, the statuesque beauty and majestic stillness which set off the intensity of her declamation, I could not conceive how they would suit comedy. I may certainly claim a larger success for my own Rosalind, though I did not share Mrs. S.'s prudishness, and made myself up into a pretty, dandified young rustic, with a spotted red silk neckerchief to set off my dark hair. My voice is lighter than Mrs. S.'s, but I am more nimble and active upon the stage, especially in these latter days when she has run so much to fat. She is unexcelled as Lady Macbeth, but as Rosalind or Viola I would take my chances against her.

I think I should have liked Peg Woffington. Old Ben Croft, who sleeps with the theater cats and has been at the Garden longer than anyone can remember, knew her, and the stories he told encourage me to think we should have been friends. She was never the grand lady. On the few occasions Mrs. S. spoke to me, it was from a great height. I trembled before her, of course, and felt the intensity of those blue orbs, which drew the gaze as the evening star in the night sky, leaving all others insignificant by comparison, but I could not imagine liking her.

XIX

S oon after the opening of *The Constant Couple* I received an invitation to a party being given by a certain Mrs. Fraser. This was a further sign that I had arrived. Mrs. Fraser's husband was something in the city and extremely wealthy, although without title (much was made of Mrs. Fraser's sister being married to Lord Stornaway), and Mrs. Fraser had made a reputation for herself with her parties by being somewhat daring in her choice of guests, this night by inviting me. It was decided that I should accept, and I did so happily, although had I known who was to be present I might have stayed away.

Such gatherings are not the most cozy way of passing an evening, and nowadays I avoid them whenever possible, but at that time I was new to high life and it was a matter of wonder to me, the attendant discomforts quite outweighed by the splendor of the occasion and the opportunity of mingling with the *beau monde*. At a party in Mansfield or Sotherton there would have been cards, music and conversation; here there was nothing but the urgency of being seen. Indeed, there was scarcely room for anything else, the crush was so great. Even to alight required a delay of nearly half an hour while the long lines of carriages took turns in depositing the guests. As for the heat, it would have tried the constitution of a porter.

We were received at the door of the principal apartments by the Frasers, Mrs. F. being a lady of large confidence and bosom, taper waist and more diamonds than fingers for them. As my name was announced there was a stir in the room, and I was grateful for my new gown, in the making of which my dressmaker had excelled herself. It was of blush-colored gauze over white satin, cut low and ornamented with seed pearls and moss roses. With it I wore matching satin slippers, white kid gloves and a plume of ostrich feathers attached to a circlet of pearls upon my hair. I was confident enough in my appearance to respond to the turning of heads with a combination of graciousness and reserve which I still adopt as best suited to the diversity of opinion regarding the propriety of my profession.

Sir Driffield Eliot, who was escorting me, had introduced me to the gentlemen who came buzzing round, and was elbowing his way through the crowd into the second room, when, without benefit of a moment to compose myself, I suddenly found myself face to face with Maria and Julia Bertram.

I do not know who was the more shocked. My carefully acquired confidence departed, and they were equally disconcerted. Julia was first to speak, without any great presence of mind: she merely pronounced my name, in a manner that revealed her amazement and our former relationship.

"Hartwell!"

Maria, more collected, said nothing at all.

Sir Driffield held my elbow and was close enough but not quick enough to catch the drift. He supposed us friends. "I see you know one another. What a happy chance, Mrs. Rushworth, Miss Bertram. Have you had the pleasure of seeing Miss Hartwell in *The Constant Couple?*"

"We are but lately arrived from Brighton," replied Maria coldly.

"Then let me recommend it to you. Miss Hartwell is the toast of the season. Lord Ravenshaw has seen her performance six times."

"I cannot believe it," said Julia.

Sir Driffield blinked. "Oh, I can assure you it is so. Lord Ravenshaw is a devotee. So are we all." He smiled gallantly at me.

"You must exclude us, I fear," said Maria.

"My dear Mrs. Rushworth! How can you say so! Lord Ravenshaw's knowledge of the theater is unsurpassed. He makes a point of seeing everything. He makes notes on the performances. I never applaud until I see him begin. You would be most unwise to disagree with him."

"I daresay I should not dream of doing so except in this one aspect: it seems he cannot distinguish between an actress and a maidservant."

"You must excuse our surprise," Julia said. "Hartwell was until recently so differently employed that we are quite astonished."

"Ah!" said Sir Driffield. "What a quiz you are, Miss Bertram!" He wagged his finger playfully. "Miss Hartwell is not the first to move successfully from the cutting table to the boards."

I spoke at last. "I have had great good fortune."

"You shall not be so modest. Genius will out! That is my conviction. Genius will out! Mrs. Rushworth, Miss Bertram, you shall be obliged to admit it when you have seen Miss Hartwell as Sir Harry Wildair."

"We can speak of her competence in sewing," said Maria, "but our appreciation of her stage performance shall remain incomplete."

"Do not dream of it! You will miss the performance of the decade! It is oversubscribed, of course, but you shall make use of my box. I shall be only too delighted to escort you myself."

"I fear that will be quite impossible," answered Maria, foiled at last by Sir Driffield's obtuseness.

"When we saw Hartwell in a play," said Julia, "she had only three lines to speak."

"Ah!" said Sir Driffield, turning to me. "That must have been in Carlisle, when you were just beginning to spread your wings."

"It was in Northamptonshire," observed Maria acidly, "just before she ran off. What was the reason, sister? I forget whether she had covered the drawing room carpet with soot or put grease spots on the linen."

"It was', I answered, "because the man with whom you were infatuated preferred me."

Sir Driffield began at last to recognize what he had stumbled upon. He might have rescued the situation by making a hasty departure, but between awkwardness and curiosity he remained rooted to the spot. So did several others, whose conversations were dull enough to be arrested by the liveliness of ours.

"I think you might still be brought up before a magistrate for breaking contract," said Maria. "I must make sure of speaking to my father on your behalf so as to protect you from such humiliation."

"It is remarkable how you have prospered. But you always were of superior talent. I said so more than once, did not I?" Julia addressed her sister.

"I do not recall it," replied Maria. "But then I do not customarily pay much heed to housemaids."

"Perhaps if you did," I said, "they would not catch you at the goat's jig in the grass on a hot day." There was a titter in the surrounding company and Maria drew herself up.

"I should expect nothing better than such vulgarities from you. You are well suited to the stage. It is no occupation for a lady."

"You had no doubt of its propriety when you played in *Lovers' Vows*."

"That was quite different."

"Your father did not think so."

"Maria has changed her mind since then," observed Julia, whose recollections of being overlooked in the Mansfield Park theatricals inclined her to sympathize with me. "She is married now and no longer participates in plays."

"I beg your pardon. Of course. I had forgotten. No sacrifice could be too great for the pleasure of becoming Mrs. Rushworth."

There was a brief pause in which it was plain that the elegant company near enough to overhear what we said was hanging upon our every word. Sir Driffield, at last asserting himself in an effort to regain the usual tedium of conversation, inquired after the health of the remainder of the Bertram family, and the ensuing civilities were sufficiently dull to remove us from the center of attention.

"My younger brother is here, Sir Driffield," said Maria. "You may find him in the company of Miss Crawford, if you care to. They are impossibly in love and will be closeted in some dark corner blind to all else for the evening." She turned to me. "Speaking of Miss Crawford, you will be rejoiced to know that her brother, Mr. Crawford, Mr. Henry Crawford, is to be present."

I cannot say that I had not anticipated such an encounter; I had lived many times through it, imagining how he should like me as a star rising in the theatrical firmament instead of a lady's maid. Now the moment was come I could not prevent a shiver of excitement, nor hide it from Maria, whose sentiments concerning Mr. Henry Crawford had something in common with mine. A shadow passed over her face as she noted the effect upon me of her news. With studied carelessness she added: "Mr. Crawford, you must know, is presently paying his addresses to my cousin, Miss Price."

"Fanny Price?" I could not disguise my amazement.

Maria was gratified. "Is not that the oddest thing in creation? I see you are surprised."

"Have I met Miss Price?" asked Sir Driffield of no one in particular. "Why have I not met Miss Price?"

"Are you sure she will have him?" I asked.

Both sisters laughed. "Fanny? Not have him! Why, she had better have him, if she does not wish to be an old maid," said Julia.

Sir Driffield attempted ineffectually to enter the lists once more: "Let us hope not. Let us hope that no young lady shall ever be condemned to such a fate!"

"Refuse him! Fanny refuse Mr. Crawford!" said Maria. "How droll! Of course she will not refuse him. You need not think to find hope for yourself there."

"None of us has him," reflected Julia, not without some small satisfaction. She had been least favored and had lost Henry soonest.

"That is true," said Maria, looking at me. "None of us has him, not even the brilliant Miss Hartwell who is presently dazzling society."

"Does Mr. Crawford know of your success?" asked Julia curiously.

"If he does I am not aware of it," I answered shortly, unwilling to reveal how much I hoped that he did.

"Well," said Maria, looking toward Sir Driffield, who had been engaged in conversation by another acquaintance, "there are enough shatterbrains in the metropolis for one to fall prey to your attractions. I advise you to turn your success to good account. It cannot last."

"I shall heed your advice. In the choice of a marriage partner and an advantageous connection, there can be no one better qualified to give it than the new Mrs. Rushworth."

Maria took fire at that. "If it had not been for you," she said, keeping her voice low, "he would have married me. If it had not been for your evil influence, he would have spoken to my father, he would have proposed."

"I really rather doubt it, sister," said Julia.

Maria ignored her. "He shall not put me out of countenance. He may do as he pleases. I shall not be made miserable by him, though I daresay he expects it."

"May I greet the new Mrs. Rushworth with my warm felicitations?" The voice belonged to the very him of whom we spoke. In the press of people, Henry Crawford had approached us unnoticed. He took Maria's hand with no less bold, flirtatious warmth than ever. "I trust your husband is in good health. Is he here? Ah me, he does not grow careless of his lovely wife already, I hope." Henry greeted Julia, and then turned in my direction. When he recognized me there was a momentary pause while he collected himself. Henry had never come closer to being disconcerted.

As for me, I had determined to forget him many times. It had, I assured myself, cost him no pains to forget me. But when I came face to face with him, in all the neat elegance of his person, clad in dove-gray velvet with a white silk stock and a gold pin, trim, dark-eyed and quick, I was overcome at once with the recollection of times past, with dread and delight. My heart most noticeably jumped, even though it did not quite leave me.

He spoke at last. "What shall I say? Do I see what I think I see? Ja—Miss Hartwell, is it you indeed?"

"Can there be any doubt?" said Maria, the currents that passed between Henry and myself prickling her into irritation.

"I knew of your success, of course," said Henry. "Now I see it must be great indeed."

Sir Driffield, comparatively alert by this time, felt called upon to deliver once again his little speech about Sir Harry Wildair. By the time he had finished, taking my hand and laying it upon his arm with an assumption of familiarity which I regretted, Henry was altogether in possession of himself. "What a pleasant circumstance to arise out of our little playacting at Mansfield," he said. "Who could have guessed it?"

"You might have," said Maria. "You were in a position to know more than any of us, as I understand it."

Henry laughed pleasantly. "So were we all, Mrs. Rushworth."

"You shall not deny your intimacy," said Maria icily.

"I think others can lay claim to greater," Henry answered. "That scene painter—what was his name? You went to London in his company, did you not, Miss Hartwell?"

"Yes, indeed!" Julia interrupted. "What did you have to do with him? He was no scene painter at all, but a revolutionist. Only imagine! That we should have had such a one in the house!" She shuddered. "How very glad I am that *I* did not take part in that play!"

"They never got Quinney yet," said Maria, "and my father spent near three hundred pounds of his own money too. I trust you are parted from him, Hartwell, or you may still be taken up as an accomplice. But perhaps it is he to whom you owe your present success."

"If I do, I shall not regret it," I answered. "Matthew Quinney is a man of principle and courage, as well as a talented painter."

Sir Driffield roused himself once more. "Miss Hartwell need be obliged to no one for her success, I assure you. Genius will out! Do you not agree, Mr. Crawford? Genius will out!"

"Did you hear what happened?" said Julia to me.

"Principle and courage!" said Maria. "What should you know of principle and courage!"

"More than you, I have no doubt," I replied hotly.

"Belzoni was horribly injured, all but killed," said Julia. "And all because of Quinney!"

My heart near stopped, and Maria noted it. "There," she said triumphantly. "We have caught you out, have we not? She is guilty of something in this matter, mark my words. You may think yourself in luck just now, *Miss* Hartwell, but your misdeeds shall catch you up. Genius will out indeed!" She moved away disdainfully. "Come along, sister. We must not waste time. There are people of consequence to whom we must pay our respects." Her departure was marred by the fact that Henry Crawford remained, and also by Julia, who followed her sister dutifully but turned to call: "I do think I shall see the play. I declare I shall come if I can."

Henry for the first time allowed his eyes to rest upon me. "You are quite ravishing, Miss Hartwell."

"Ain't she, though?" said Sir Driffield approvingly. He was vastly diverted by the incident, and full of admiration at the way I had comported myself. "By Jove, Miss Hartwell! You showed 'em a thing or two! They didn't bolt with you."

"I offer my congratulations," said Henry. "I remind you that I recognized your talent long ago. I shall not for a moment hold it

257

against you that your success is built upon my disappointment."

"How can that be?"

"You refused to accompany me to Bath with such a high-minded determination that my respect was quite won. Next thing I hear you are run off to London with the scene painter." He spoke lightly, but was angry for all that.

"I had no choice. Tom told his sisters. I had no choice but to leave."

"Nor to become Quinney's mistress, I suppose."

"I say, Crawford!" Sir Driffield interrupted. "That's going a bit far!"

"You are quite mistaken."

"I only wish, for his own safety and the comfort of those around him, that Quinney would attend to the theater and leave politics aside. His representation of a prison cell on the stage is infinitely to be preferred to a ward in Newgate."

"You are taken in by the false stories like everyone else."

"Forgive me if I choose to think it is *you* who have been taken in."

"He is no revolutionist," I said. "He is for justice through reform. All the rest is trumped-up fakery."

"He has certainly made a disciple of you," said Henry. "I thought you to be more rational."

"Let us find some refreshment, Miss Hartwell," Sir Driffield suggested. The conversation had lost him. "It is devilish warm in here, don't you know?"

"If you could persuade that lackey over there to move his tray in this direction," said Henry, "we should be eternally obliged to you."

Sir Driffield somewhat unhappily battled his way across the room toward the footman in knee breeches and a white satin coat who contrived against probability to balance a tray of cream ices above his head.

"Where did you find him?" said Henry disdainfully. "I am scarcely flattered to find myself jilted for a radical scene painter, but that fop is beyond belief."

"I might say the same of your own latest affair."

"What do you mean?"

"I have heard about Fanny Price."

"What of it?"

"Whatever possessed you to take up with that little mouse?"

He looked a trifle discomfited. "I was bored."

"Bored!"

"At first I was bored, but then—" He paused.

"Then what?" I prompted him. "I hope I am to hear convincing reasons for your conquest of Fanny's heart. I think *you* heartless for attempting it."

"Fanny is a sweet creature and worth two of her cousins. She has suffered much from their inconsiderate ways. It is a pleasure to bring her out a little, to let her know her own merit, to accord her the attention she should receive as a cousin, the sort of attention of which she has always been so unkindly deprived."

"And a flirtation with Mr. Crawford is a desirable part of every young woman's education?"

"What of it? It need not concern you. You have greater matters to occupy your time. You are to be the new actress of the day. I merely hope for your sake that it is the decade rather than the day."

"You suppose that I shall fail."

"Not I. But you stake all on a doubtful profession. The natives are fickle. You had best nail your aristocratic admirer to a set of banns. Marriage to a wealthy idiot is many an actress's salvation."

"As marriage to a mouse shall be yours."

"You do Fanny great injustice."

"By no means. She is a sweet creature, entirely fit to pander to a man's vanity by clinging to him like ivy, though for little else. Do not frighten her with revelations of your past, I beg. The oak to which she clings must have grown straight and true all its life."

"She will take me in hand. There is a particular appeal to a reformed character."

"Be sure that you are well and truly reformed, then. Even so, I should not acquaint her with your previous indiscretions. She would die of shock."

"I do believe you are jealous. You could not speak of her with such contempt if you were not."

"Fanny Price is insipid. She never has a thought of her own that could not be bullied out of her. She will break under the strain of any but the most quiet, well-ordered, rural life. How could she possibly please you? How could you possibly agree for more than two minutes together?"

"I should not expect you to understand that. But she *does* please me. And I have no doubt of pleasing her. You have described in her precisely those qualities I most admire. She is the very one to make me happy."

"You deceive yourself. She would be as unhappy with you as you with her. But do not let *me* prevent you. Run away to her with all speed and seal your fate."

"I am convinced that I might seek far and not find a more suitable wife."

"How little you know yourself that you could think so!"

"How well *you* presume to know me!"

"You cannot do without the flattery of every woman's affection."

"You may be sure that I shall do without yours."

At such a moment, Sir Driffield chose to return, out of temper because one of the ices he carried had spilled down his white waistcoat and spotted his blue velvet coat. I was sufficiently angry with Henry to flatter the silly man into humor again, and Henry, with most impeccably polite ill manners, declined the cream ice and departed almost instantly. I saw later that he sought out Maria Rushworth once again. She, vain as ever, peacocked about, fluttering her fan like a wren's tail as she basked in his attentions. Neither was unwilling that I witness their reconciliation, as I knew full well.

I was grateful for the presence of Sir Driffield, with whom I shamelessly played, out of pique, a similar game. He was a kind-hearted sort of simpleton. Matthew had many times expounded upon the evils of hereditary aristocracy, gentility without ability, like a pudding without fat, but for my own part I think the weakness nothing more than inadequacy of upbringing and occupation. Poor Sir Driffield, like the others, had never enough to do. He had no vocation but hunting and shooting, and a sensibility so untutored that he could never see aught in the scenery but fox and duck. What else is to be expected from an existence so altogether lacking the lasting pleasures that come from the performance of useful work well done? Even the best gifts of character and temper rust without use. A few gentlemen contrive to find a worthy occupation and become sensible, but the rest merely vegetate. Sir Driffield was one of a long line of admirers who would willingly have given me their protection (and their name), but in all the number there was not more than a brace whom I cared two pins for. He did at last achieve his ambition by marrying an actress, but she has led him a terrible dance and he has all but drunk up his inheritance.

I viewed with alarm the rumors and gossip which must surround me after Mrs. Fraser's party. What should the manager of Covent Garden think of such a scandal after the pains he had taken to put it about that I was an actress from Carlisle and bestow upon me some much-needed respectability? I lay awake all night anticipating the disgrace of an immediate dismissal, quite needlessly as it turned out. Now that I had proved my talent, the gossip merely improved attendance at the theater: there can be no objection to having a housemaid (Maria's unkind half-truth stuck) on the boards if she increases the profits. The theater is in any case a democratical place. I was refused entrée to some of the good houses, of course, but that would have been so in any case. The audiences were very lively in their comments, and it was a little provoking at first to be constantly referred to as a housemaid when I had been several degrees higher, but then, the greater the gap the more the leap is relished. One wag called out for "Miss Abigail" soon after and it has been my affectionate nickname ever since, especially in London. I have come to be rather fond of it. They do say it is because of me that the name has lost some of the opprobrium attaching to it of "female servant" and is no longer in disfavor.

XX

It was in the aftermath of Mrs. Fraser's party that Sophie Boucher arrived in Queen Street. Stephen had confided in me nothing of his feelings toward Sophie after Kitty had been found, but he had requested no more assistance in writing letters, from which I concluded he had sent none. It was thus nearly four months since Sophie had heard from him, and how she must feel, daily hoping for a letter in which lay all the promise for her future, and daily disappointed, I could not bear to think. Once I had seen Maria, however, and knew that the Rushworths were in London, I determined to see Sophie, hesitating only in trying to decide how best it would be to raise the matter with Stephen so that I might bring them together.

In the event, Sophie forestalled me by seeking me out at the Sturmeys', where, despite my rising fortunes, Ellie had prevailed upon me to remain. I was content to be ruled by her, having no great desire to set up in lodgings for myself and knowing also that she would receive inordinate pleasure from referring to her friend the well-known actress, and presenting me to the ladies of the whist table, which, for the present at least, I thought I could well bear. The only other request was that I provide a copy of an engraving that had been made of my head and shoulders, suitably inscribed, to be sent to Enna and the little ones in Northampton, which, with the addition of a prettily wrought silver frame, I did willingly.

Ellie was most reluctant to part with any member of her flock, although it was, despite her remonstrances, reduced by one, for as soon as his arm was mended Matthew took a room in a court off Charing Cross Road, where he lived in contented solitude up two flights of stairs, being quite unconcerned with domestic comfort, and preferring to come and go privately. His sole addition to the stool, table and bed, which were the only comforts of the room aside from its being next the chimney (and uncomfortably over-heated on the single occasion that I visited it), was the painting of a scene upon the wall, and that not for beauty but to elaborate an idea for Jupiter descending in a thunderbolt in *Cymbeline* (in which I was, for the first time, to play Imogen).

Since Kitty Huckle was still under Ellie's care, and thus Stephen Turnbull more often than not in Queen Street, Ellie had plenty on whom to lavish her kind and capable attentions. It seemed that Sophie, indeed, would take Matthew's place, for she arrived with bag and baggage, having quit Maria's service for good. The tantrums thrown by the new Mrs. Rushworth, whose discontents even the delights of Brighton were unable to alleviate, had proved too much for Sophie's stoic temper. The marriage was as disastrous as Sophie had anticipated. "He is quite incompetent! On the wedding night he drink one bottle of port, then another, then another. Then he snore all night! He keep *me* awake, even me, and there is a wall between us! *She* stay awake for nothing! *Quelle bêtise!* On the wedding night, not to sleep because the husband snore! It is worse than to sleep. He does his duty since, but what a comedy!"

There was, however, a more immediate cause of her departure. In the wake of the accommodation between Maria and Henry, made to spite me at Mrs. Fraser's party, the affair between them had resumed hotter than ever. James Rushworth, old Whinny Prinny, was gone off to push his mother's wheelchair in Bath, and there was nothing to prevent Maria from indulging her passion to the full. In less than a week she was openly parading her infatuation, which, so far as Sophie knew, Henry reciprocated. Nothing was more certain than the most prodigious scandal. Sophie had had enough. Whether or not Stephen was still her lover, she knew me her friend and, having the rumor of my rapid advancement confirmed by Maria, she had determined to leave, wishing no part of the misery consequent upon the behavior of a mistress for whom she had never entertained either affection or respect, and confident of finding a temporary home with me.

Sophie knew it most likely that in encountering me she must also encounter Stephen, and anticipated the meeting with a mixture of dread and delight. What she did not know of, and what at once aroused her warm compassion and dealt a bitter blow to her hopes, was the discovery of Kitty Huckle. She had been unaware of Kitty's deliverance, and instantly read in that omission, in the letters she had not received from Stephen, in my own reticence, the certain loss of her own prospect of marriage. So much of this was understood during the first ten minutes of our being reunited, although, as you may devise, there was nothing that did not need many further hours' elaboration.

In the early morning after Sophie's arrival, we sat with Kitty in the neat sickroom, with its bowl of vinegar and bunches of aromatic herbs, chatting pleasantly, Kitty pleased to see a face from the past which, despite the woes it held, she now regarded most fondly, and exerting herself to discover all those hundred and one trifling details by which Mansfield Park and its inhabitants might once more become vivid to her.

Upon this quiet but cheerful little company Stephen entered, carrying the jug of milk which, whatever else went done or undone, he regularly fetched every morning fresh from the cowhouse for Kitty to drink. He took in the scene at a glance, his eyes going first to Kitty and resting at last on Sophie. Then he set down the jug and, most uncharacteristically, spilled some of its contents. Sophie, knowing herself the cause of his confusion, hurried to wipe up the milk. Neither he nor she spoke more than the obligatory words of greeting, but the color rose in Stephen's face, and Sophie quite forgot the end of the anecdote she had been relating, which concerned Mrs. Norris's taking a pair of shears purposely to cut the strings of little Dick Jackson's kite.

I made nothing very much of this scene. The sudden awkwardness consequent upon Stephen's arrival was no more than what is inevitable upon any face-to-face encounter with a former lover whom one has, if not treated ill, caused to suffer. Kitty, however, viewed it simply and differently.

Her consumption, as we had feared, was not to be cured. Soon after her arrival in Queen Street, she had spoken of her desire to see her mother, and Bob Sturmey, who had delivered Mrs. Huckle to the abode of her cousin, a watchmaker in Clerkenwell, went thither to find her, only to return with the news that she had died soon after her arrival. The watchmaker was a disagreeable man, who had taken exception to paying for Mrs. Huckle's funeral, she being quite without means, and was chiefly concerned to demand reimbursement. It seemed she had died of complications from the blow she had received from Octavian, although her cousin insisted that it was also the result of a broken heart caused by her daughter's desertion. Needless to say, we did not pass on this unkind opinion, but Kitty was much cast down by her mother's death, and did, indeed, blame herself. She wept bitterly, and from that moment seemed to resign herself to death, never ceasing to regret the fate which had seen fit to have mother and daughter, whose dearest desire was to see one another, separated all unwittingly by no more than a few miles. Kitty also spoke often of her daughter, little Betsey, but when Stephen offered to go to Ely to fetch the child, she grew exceedingly agitated and implored him not to think of such a thing. Some superstitious belief that the child would be infected with her mother's folly and wickedness, as she perceived them, operated upon her; Betsey must stay away in order to grow up more wise and fortunate. It seemed a terrible penance to exact upon herself, but Kitty was adamant in nothing but this.

Then she saw Sophie after so long an interval, trim, neat and kind, with all the recollections of Mansfield to endear her. Without any apparent understanding that Sophie and Stephen had been anything more to each other than common acquaintances, she decided upon a match between them. Kitty knew that Stephen had once loved her; indeed, she regretted that she had not been sensible enough to love him in return. In encouraging him to marry Sophie, she saw a means of providing him with a wife, and her own child with loving parents. What happy instinct gave her this thought I do not know, but such a satisfactory completion could scarcely have been hoped for. Kitty wished for that which would give Sophie more pleasure than anything in the world, and Stephen, who, by some curious operation of his conscience, regarded the peculiarly horrible circumstances in which Kitty had been found as the result of a failure of affection on his part, was in his own mind forgiven, and in those of others rewarded for his constancy and affection. Kitty's last request, made most earnestly to them both two days before she quietly died, was that they should undertake the upbringing of her child, little Betsey.

The fulfillment of Kitty's wish in this respect was no hardship. Stephen went immediately into the country, to Willishall, where Betsey was lodged, with the purpose of bringing her back to town with him. Then, the banns being duly read, St. Ann's Church in Macclesfield Street would be the place of Sophie and Stephen's marrying, as it had been the place of Kitty's burying.

To our consternation, however, instead of the return of Stephen and Betsey, as we had confidently expected, a letter arrived, in which Stephen informed us that the child was no longer at Willishall. On a whim of seeing his natural child for himself, Tom Bertram had recently visited the farmer, been captivated by Betsey's infant charms and her exceeding close likeness to himself, and carried her off.

XXI

This was as wild and unexpected a deed as Tom had ever done, and more wanton and thoughtless. What madness had overtaken him? It was impossible that he sincerely wished to provide for the child. Sir Thomas might have desired to do so, but it was unthinkable that Tom, whose concern was ever to circumvent his father's wrath, should now confront it for the sake of an infant in whom he had never before taken the least interest. That no unselfish principle operated on him was plain: he had been bound for the races at Newmarket and had not changed his intention, quite heedless of the unfitness of such a place for the child who now traveled with him. Stephen's fierce resolve to recover Betsey, whom he now considered his own, was evident in the brief note we had received. He intended to set out instantly for Newmarket in pursuit of Tom Bertram.

Here was a hobble indeed! This was not the first time Tom's monstrous behavior had occasioned Stephen anguish. What should happen if Tom refused to give up the child? Smarting under the remembrance of past injuries, his slow temper roused to fury by this last unkindest deed, what might not Stephen be driven to? What might not happen between them, master and servant, man and man? I foresaw calamity. I did not express these misgivings, however. Sophie's hopes, so new-risen and so high, being thus disappointed, cast her into an unaccustomed lowness of spirits, and

267

I did not want to increase her despondency. She had formerly, as I well knew, reconciled herself cheerfully to spinsterhood and a life as waiting maid she did not greatly relish. Now the prospect of a comfortable independence, but just secured by the promise of union with a man whom she loved and respected, appeared threatened by Tom's abduction of Betsey, by re-establishment of the connection with the Bertrams (which she desired most heartily to put behind her). She could not and would not believe that all might yet be saved. Tom Bertram was an evil spirit, like his sister, blighting her hopes. This was a Sophie I had never seen, and yet, remembering the vicissitudes of her childhood, I understood how she might, having schooled herself to expect little, be brought to a sort of extremity of despair.

I was not so doubtful of myself in these matters as I might once have been, and I was determined that my dearest friend's happiness, so nearly achieved and so well deserved, should not be destroyed by Tom Bertram's callous selfishness. And, indeed, that he should not blight the life of the child, that same child of whose existence he had been so supremely careless when he originally heard of it. As is my habit, I acted first and thought afterward, but that is not always folly in someone like myself, who has only to think upon a thing in order to perceive fifty different ways out of it, all with some merit and no clear way to choice. By virtue of my present high connections, it needed only one or two inquiries to discover what Stephen did not know: the company Tom Bertram kept and where he was to be found. I was obliged instantly to act upon this intelligence if it were to prove any advantage.

I took the stage from White Horse Yard in Piccadilly. The coach was excessively crowded, but the journey was uneventful, and when I reached Newmarket I took a chaise over the last seventeen miles to Glassbury Park, where Tom stayed with the sons of Lord Eversfield. What manner of place Glassbury Park was, the night and the weather, as black and threatening as the circumstance which brought me, did not allow me to discover, and the house itself displayed only two lighted windows. The fellow who opened the door swiftly enough was no servant; indeed, he swore, mildly and without anger, when he saw me, and called loudly for one; evidently I was not the company he had been expecting. He said not a word more, but climbed the stairs, hauling himself hand over hand along the banisters, drunk as an owl, I following after. He bethought himself to tell me that Glassbury Park was no place for such as I, and warned me off the dining room, to which it appeared he himself was going. As I was already aware, Lord Eversfield himself was permanently confined to bed and the care of a surgeon in London. From my few questions and the fellow's half-witted replies, I understood that the house was never much occupied, except during the racing season, when Lord Eversfield's three sons took up residence. At other times they were off madcapping around the country in pursuit of those pleasures which, so rumor went, had produced such dire results in their father. And this was the house to which Tom had seen fit to bring his child.

The large dining room, stuffy with heat and the exhalation of wine, was occupied by a fraternity of bucks and blades. It was impossible to see whether Tom Bertram made one of them: the candles were burned down to the sockets and many had gone out. The company was in similar condition to him who had opened the door. Several had their heads upon the table, fast asleep; others lay back in their chairs snoring with their mouths open. One at least was on the floor, so far as I could tell from the boots which protruded from beneath the table, a long, narrow, old-fashioned table on which stood a mess of bottles, some upright, some toppled, most empty. Four or five fine gentlemen were racing maggots out of nutshells and betting on the outcome, while others sang a tuneless and ragged chorus to some unrecognizable ballad. When he who warbled the verse in falsetto declared he was put off by the snoring, one wag conveyed a pickled walnut into the open mouth of the greatest offender, thus bringing him rudely to his senses, convulsing the singers and putting an end to the song. A small monkey in a red jacket moved about the table, helping itself to titbits and broken morsels of food. There was also an assortment of dogs, one of which, barking as I entered, set the others on to it. I felt the touch of soft fur against my hand, and looking down perceived Tom's great Newfoundland, Juno, flagging her tail, near invisible in the half-light, a sure sign that he whom I sought was present.

My entrance at first had less effect upon men than dogs, but gradually as I began to move around the room in search of Tom Bertram, they took note.

"I say, is that what I think it is?"

"Who's that?"

"Curse me, if that ain't a female."

"A what?"

"You shouldn't be in here, my dear, if you know what's good for you."

"Perhaps that's why she came."

"A glass of port wine for our visitor!"

As I reached the huge mantelpiece beneath which the remains of a large fire smoldered, more ashes than wood, I caught sight of Tom and he, after a pause to peer in the dim light, recognized me. "Blast me if it ain't—! The devil take it! What ill wind blows you in?" The company made general inquiry as to who I was. "This is a regular interloping female," he said loudly, "not the sort we like at all."

The company was inclined to quiz him. "Speak for yourself."

"She looks like my sort."

"She *looks* all right," continued Tom ponderously, "but a pretty figure's not everything."

"It's enough for me," called someone.

"She has a pretty figure," said Tom. "She has. Never let it be said that I did not give credit where it's due. She has a pretty figure, but she's proud and treacherous. You wouldn't like her at all."

"Who is she?"

"Who is she?" repeated Tom. "Why—"

Impatient with Tom's befuddled answers, I spoke first. "My name is Jane Hartwell."

This liberty roused Tom, and he stood up, somewhat unsteadily.

"What did I tell you? What did I tell you? She's monstrous haughty for a serving maid."

"She's got spirit."

"I like spirit."

"I should like to speak with you," I said to Tom.

"She wants to speak."

"Let her speak if she wants to."

"I like 'em better when they hold their tongues."

"We know what *you* like, Farrar."

This passed for wit and there was some clapping and table-thumping in approval. "Who are you?" someone called.

"Who is she?" Tom said. "I've been trying to tell you. This is your waiting maid gone for an actress, that's who. Ran off to London."

"Don't care for that."

"Some of 'em won't be told."

"I should like to speak with you," I said again to Tom. "It is a matter of consequence or I should never have come."

"Who is she?"

"I'm only waiting the chance to present her. Gentlemen, this is Jane Hartwell. Jane Hartwell, lately my sister's maid, also a viper in the bosom, and now an actress. This is an actress."

"Jane Hartwell?" I heard someone say. "Lombard Street to china orange, I do believe it is! Damn me, if it isn't Miss Abigail."

"Who's she?"

"The actress, muttonhead. Why didn't you tell us, Bertram? We didn't know it was Miss Abigail."

"What do you mean?" said Tom. "This is Jane Hartwell."

"Miss Hartwell, I'll say it is. Raise your glasses, gentlemen. We must toast Miss Abigail."

The suggestion provoked more questions. "Miss Abigail?"

"Who's she?"

"What's so particular about her?"

The explanations were repetitive but good-natured; the company was disposed to view me favorably.

"I've come on purpose to see you, Tom."

"I am honored, deeply honored." Supporting himself with one hand against the table he made an exaggerated bow.

"I should like to speak with you privately."

"That's a chance," someone called. "Will you take ten pounds for it, Bertram?"

"She's no good, Farrar," said Tom. "I've told you that. She's a viper."

"I come to you for your own good," I said.

"D'ye hear that? The infernal trouble she's caused . . . For my own good! That's rich!"

"Will you not listen?" I begged.

"Whatever you have to say can be said in front of my friends. These are all my most particular friends. Anything may be said in front of them." Tom gestured with wild benevolence, caught his hand on the chair back and thus knocked the glass out of his hand. A chorus of support mingled with the sound of it breaking.

"It is about Stephen," I said finally.

"Stephen?"

"Stephen Turnbull."

"Ah, you mean Turnbull. Well then, you have gone to a great deal of trouble for nothing. He's already here." He bellowed. "Are you still there, Turnbull?"

"He's here? So quickly?"

"Of course he's here. Bygones are bygones. I'm generous. Where are you, Turnbull?"

A voice replied steadily and with complete sobriety from the shadows. I went to Stephen's side. "Thank God I have arrived in time."

"Why are you come?"

"I was anxious, Sophie was anxious."

"I am only come to fetch the child."

"Does he know it yet?"

"He has another bottle to go before he'll be drunk enough."

"I beg you to be careful. If there is trouble between you, you would be the sufferer by it."

"He has deceived me too many times."

"What do you have to say to one another?" cried Tom. "Let us hear it. We are all friends here."

This sentiment was applauded. "Share the beauty around a bit."

"Give us a speech, Miss Abigail, do."

"A speech, let's have a speech."

"A scene. We ought to have a scene."

More table-thumping ensued. It would be difficult to refuse the request if I lingered.

"If the child is here," I whispered to Stephen, "let us go and find her."

"Stealing away with her, do you mean?"

"But Kitty—"

"I'm going to tell him, first."

"Think of Sophie," I urged. "Think how much you have to lose. Sophie is quite distraught. Everything is in a regular train. All we have to do is to find the child. Once you have her, what does it matter?"

Stephen began to be persuaded, but, when at last he rose from his seat and we began to move round the table toward the door, our departure drew unwelcome attention.

"Where are you going?"

"She can't be much of an actress if she won't give us a scene."

"That's not sporting, Miss Abigail."

"It was a civil request," said Tom. "The gentlemen wish to hear you spout. You shall not be allowed to decline."

"I fear I must."

"I fear you shall not."

"We are leaving," said Stephen.

"Not before the little actress has shown her paces. She owes us that."

"We are leaving."

"What have you to do with this?"

"They do not really want to listen," said Stephen quietly.

"Are you to be the judge of what a gentleman wants?"

"They are drunk. What difference can it make to them?"

Perceiving Stephen's temper rise, I spoke: "I shall be quite happy to do as they ask."

"Are you accusing my friends of drunkenness?" Tom bridled.

Stephen shrugged his shoulders.

"It is of no consequence," I said. "I shall perform willingly."

"Indeed, it is of consequence," said Tom. "It is not a servant's place to say when a gentleman is drunk."

"I have carried you out from under the table on more occasions than I can count."

"And been well paid for it."

"Paid! You borrowed off me more than you ever paid!"

"I've treated you like a friend, that's what I've done. Never treat a servant as a friend." Tom turned to advise the company.

"I am not a servant."

"Beg pardon," said Tom ironically. "I forgot. Not a servant. Of course. But it don't give you the right to address gentlemen as equals."

"I should prefer not to address you at all."

273

There was some hissing at this. "D'ye hear that?" said Tom. "That's what you get for treating 'em like friends. Killed my best horse, he did."

"That's a lie." A slow flush crept up Stephen's face.

"I gave—" Tom stopped short and fixed his eyes on Stephen. "What did you say?"

Again I tried to intervene. "It was nothing."

"You killed Octavian yourself," said Stephen, "you and your stubborn notions. And that's not all you've destroyed."

"What do you mean?"

"You brought Kitty Huckle to her death. If it wasn't for you, she would be alive now. She's dead, and it is your fault."

"You dare say that to me!"

"It's the truth."

The company was affronted. "Throw him out!"

"Thrash him!"

"Don't just stand there, Bertram!"

"Shame!"

"I'll dust his jacket if you won't."

"I know your tricks," said Tom. "It's a fight you want. But I don't go in for milling-matches with servants."

"You haven't the courage," said Stephen scornfully. "You know you'd get the worst of it."

"By God, you go too far!"

Stephen controlled his anger. "It's not a fight I want, it's my daughter."

"What?"

"My daughter. Kitty Huckle wished that Betsey be brought up as my daughter."

"*Your* daughter? Well, there's a thing!" Unexpectedly Tom began to laugh. "Betsey will never be your daughter. Have you looked at her? It's plain enough in her face whose daughter she is. Why she's as like me as she can stare! She's not yours, she's mine."

Tom's laughter was the final provocation. Stephen brought up his right fist and landed it on Tom's jaw with a mighty thwack that drove his head up so hard you would swear to hear bone upon bone. Tom, who in other circumstances might have foreseen the blow and dodged it, was slow with drink. He fell back against the table with blood running from his mouth. At this, several of his companions threw back their chairs and prepared to go to his defense.

"What the devil!"

"Shall I deal with him, Bertram?"

Tom raised his hand and shook his head to stop them.

Then, wiping the blood from his mouth with his other hand, he heaved himself upright and lunged toward Stephen, who stood quietly, his arms pinioned. But as Tom approached he bent and twisted so that his captors seemed to have no more hold on him than on a greased pig. Tom's blundering assault caught him only on the shoulder and threw Tom himself off balance. Then Stephen delivered one ferocious punch to Tom's belly. It was enough. Tom went down like a sack of coals, hitting the table as he fell, and while he lay still, groaning, Stephen walked to the door. I followed him, the rest of the company too befuddled to do more than call for brandy and crowd round Tom where he lay.

In the hall Stephen glanced round at me. We had to find the child quickly. I shut the door of the dining room quietly but, as he set foot on the staircase which led to an upper floor, I motioned him to stop. I stood a moment, listening, and heard the faint sound of a child whimpering not far off. The corridor in which we stood went both ways, but candles lit it in only one direction, and with a well-executed instinct for speed, without speaking, Stephen and I began to open the doors of the rooms alternately. Behind the fourth door, within a small closet or dressing room where firelight flickered, a maidservant paced with a child in her arms. I held out my arms. "Betsey!"

The maid, deceived by my assumption of authority, allowed me to take the child from her. "She's been fretting a while," she said, evidently pleased that someone had come to relieve her. The child was indeed fretful, and the change from the arms of one stranger to another merely increased her whimperings. She was about two years old, a flaxen-haired, rosy-cheeked cherub, even when her face was screwed up with tears. She began to wriggle in my arms miserably. Tired and unhappy, far from all places and people she knew, it was scarcely to be wondered at.

"Fetch a blanket," said Stephen, coming over to me and taking

Betsey with exceeding gentleness. "We must be on our way. I shall need something to secure her to me."

"Take the post-chaise. It waits."

He shook his head. In the few minutes it took me to collect her few necessaries, Betsey had leaned her head against Stephen's shoulder and ceased complaint. I had been aware of Stephen's extraordinary power with dumb animals, yet I think even now of that magical stilling of peevish temper in the child as some kind action of fate, of God, of her poor, dead mother, in watching over the little mite's future and insuring her something better than being made into the plaything of her natural father. Nothing was more convincing proof of Stephen's right to be parent than Betsey's instant ease with him. It surprised even the maid into comment, but Stephen merely nuzzled the pale hair which lay upon his shoulder and said: "She is my daughter."

The maid was puzzled but biddable, and we made our way down the back stairs to the kitchen and through it to the yard and then the stables. All this was done without haste and without hindrance, myself curiously certain, after witnessing that small miracle, that all would be well.

The two of them were mounted and ready to go in no time. The cold nip in the night air had awoken Betsey, but she remained quiet, sitting in the saddle in front of Stephen and secured to him with a piece of linen, her bright eyes and cheeks peeping out from above the warm blanket in which she was muffled like a cushion. She had no fear.

"Kitty wished it," was all Stephen said.

"I know."

He touched his heels to the horse's sides and cantered off into the darkness.

Thinking I might invent a ruse to prevent Tom taking off in full cry after Stephen and Betsey, I did not immediately leave in the post-chaise, which still awaited me, but returned instead to the kitchen, where I found one of Tom's friends. "Get me a towel," he said to the maid, she who had been with Betsey (there was no sign of any other servant). "I'm going out to the pump." He returned with a wet head which he scrubbed vigorously. "I am going to fetch a surgeon. We cannot revive him."

This was unlooked-for. I knew that Stephen had hit Tom hard, but I had not considered the possibility of his injuries being severe.

It appeared the nearest surgeon to be had was in Newmarket. "Oh, lord," said Tom's friend to himself. "What is it about this evening? Everyone is gone mad." I offered my assistance. "I don't think there's much to be done. We've tried a hundred and one patent remedies. He's on a couch in the library, pale as ashes."

A number of men, considerably sobered by the accident, were clustered round the couch, although whatever notions they had for restoring Tom were evidently exhausted, for by this time they did nothing. Indeed, relieved to see myself and the maid appear, some of them departed. Tom was waxen, breathing shallowly and with a slow pulse. He was motionless. I sent the maid for hot water and salts.

"If he dies, it will be murder."

"He hit his head when he fell."

"It was the servant's fault."

"What happened to that fellow, Miss Abigail?" one asked me curiously. "You saw the going of him, did you not?"

"He is gone," was all I answered.

"Run off, I shouldn't wonder. He won't get far," said another.

"Didn't someone stop him?"

"Why didn't you stop him yourself?"

"What's behind it all, Miss Abigail?"

"It is a long, sad story."

"You couldn't have a more agreeable fellow than Tom Bertram. That servant of his is a regular bad one."

"The blame is not all his," I observed shortly.

"He'll have a deal to answer for, all the same."

"What about the child?"

I said nothing.

"Deuced odd, bringing a child to a race party, but she's a fetching little thing."

"Where is the child?" The question was repeated. The pause in which I again said nothing set the addlepates a-thinking. "She hasn't gone with—By George, she hasn't, has she?"

"Where is she?" they demanded of the maid. "She was with you, wasn't she?"

The maid was defensive. "It's nothing to do with me. He said

277

he was her father. You said he was, miss, I'm sure." She looked at me.

As they began to realize what had happened there were murmurs of outrage and disbelief and I was regarded with dawning suspicion. "Bertram's not going to like that. Better get after him now if he's got the child with him. We can't let poor old Bertram down."

"We'll catch up with him at Newmarket. The question will be whether he's turned north or south."

"He won't go far at this time of night with a child unless he's a fool."

"It's clear where your sympathies lie, Miss Abigail," said one of those remaining after two took off in pursuit of Stephen. "I thought Bertram was quizzing you, but I see I should have taken him seriously. You are no friend to him."

I stayed merely until the apothecary arrived (the surgeon being unavailable). By this time it was dawn, and when I left an hour later Tom showed no sign of recovery. Afterward, rumor had it that his health was permanently damaged by his being left at that time entirely to the care of servants. I do not believe it. There was only the one that I saw, to begin with. Any number of Tom's particular friends were still present at Glassbury Park when I departed, and it was reasonable to suppose that they would either care for him themselves or make proper provision. No doubt when he lay for so long without regaining his right senses they drifted away to their trifling occupations; I cannot suppose that steadfastness and good sense were their strongest virtues. But of course it is always convenient to blame the servants. The two of Tom's friends who rode after Stephen never caught him, you may be sure. He had Betsey safe in Queen Street while they were still riding in circles round Newmarket. I am sorry that there should have been some apprehension for Tom's lungs, but since he is now, I hear, quite recovered, I find myself more concerned with the misapprehension as to how the whole accident came about. I most certainly acquit myself of neglect. Tom Bertram brought his trouble upon himself.

XXII

I did not immediately pay heed to the sedan chair, although it is not so common a form of transport as once it was. They are conspicuous among the crowd of other conveyances outside a theater, but there is often a brace or two belonging to eccentric elderly ladies and gouty gentlemen who, clinging to the ways of their youth, consider the comfort of a sedan chair in short journeys about town superior even to that of a well-sprung carriage. This particular chair was of undistinguished appearance, its leather battered and its windows scratched, but it had once had some pretensions to gentility, as could be seen from the designs beaten into the leather and the carved carrying poles. The same could not be said of the chairmen, who looked like ruffians even though they were not ill-dressed. One with a pock face and a bulbous nose was never without a bottle in his hand that I could see; the other was of a striking height, with a belly like a bag pudding but immensely strong: when he lifted that chair he set off as though it weighed no more than a yoke of empty milk pails.

The first time I took more than a passing interest in the vehicle was when this giant of a chairman addressed me. I thought it mere devilment, for it was not unusual for me to be so accosted, but I looked at the chair with greater attention since I thought it likely he had been set on to it by his master. I noted then that the curtains were drawn, but I knew someone was within, for I saw the curtains twitch. I took it for granted that its occupant was some shy admirer who did not choose to be seen in a carriage with a crest on it.

I came out one evening later than usual, to a street more than commonly empty of traffic, and there stood the elderly sedan chair with, as I supposed, its no less elderly occupant. This time, however, Fatty came over to me and with unaccustomed formality bowed and then gestured that I should approach the chair. I saw no harm in thus gratifying the desire of an admirer for a closer look at the object of his infatuation, and moved across to the corner where the chair stood in shadow at one end of the great portico which ornaments the front of the theater. Fatty opened the door. A figure within, whose shape and features I was unable to distinguish, greeted me by name and then called for light. At once Fatty lit the old-fashioned torch which sat in its holder upon the back of the chair and held it so that the light shone upon my face. It was a little strange, but I had no premonition of fear and let the occupant look his fill.

"Now bring it here," the voice from within commanded, and Fatty lowered the torch so that it lighted the interior. There, his lower limbs buried in coverings, his upper supported by cushions, was the maimed body of Alexander Belzoni. Weasel-faced and shrunken he was, no more than a shadow of the man I had known. He read the horror in my face and leaned toward me with a swiftness and strength that belied his shriveled appearance. I, startled and afraid, would have drawn back but that his henchman intentionally crowded me from behind. Belzoni's hand clamped on my wrist like a vise.

"You're frightened, are you? Don't be frightened, Jane Hartwell; don't run away again. You've risen in the world, and I've fallen, but you haven't forgotten me, have you? Still the pretty Jane, I see, but now Miss Abigail in powder and lace. How fine you are!" He twitched my cloak with his other hand and drew his cold fingers down my face, slowly turning the long nails in so that I felt their sharpness. "How do you like me? An admirer come back from the dead. You never thought to see me again, I'll warrant. Ran off and left me to die in the gutter." I said nothing, but shivered involuntarily. "You do not like to look on your handiwork, eh? That's hard. I am come to this by your fault. But I am not altogether ruined. Almost but not quite." He twisted my wrist so sharply that I almost cried out. "See? That's what the weights do for me. Every day I spend an hour lifting weights, don't I, Issy? No, I'm not quite helpless. And what I can't do, Issy does for me. I saved his life in the Spanish mountains; now he saves mine. Isn't that right, Issy?" The big chairman laughed, enclosing the back of my neck with his free hand and squeezing, then pressing my head forward until I thought my neck would break. "Why, I've been looking forward to this moment for a long time, planning for it, you might say, thinking about how pleased you would be to know I was still alive. You are pleased, aren't you?"

"What do you want with me?" I said faintly at last.

He brought his face close to mine and I saw the veins standing out upon his head, such was the quiet passion with which he spoke. "Want with you? What should I want with you? Why, I'll have the life back you took from me in a crack, or I'll take something from you in exchange. That's fair, isn't it?" He leaned back again, cat baiting mouse. "No, no, you will think I threaten you if I say so. But you wouldn't be afraid, would you, Jane? Not a bold hussy like you. What do I want with you? Only a little conversation in memory of old times. The chance of making the money I am owed."

"What do you mean?"

"Such a little innocent! Or is it, I wonder? We have so much to talk about, you and I. That scene painter of yours, now, where is he? And that jumped-up undercoachman who nearly did for Tom Bertram? Tell me, where are they? That's all I want to know. Where are they?"

I shook my head. "Is that a refusal, Miss Abigail? I do hope that it isn't a refusal." I shook my head again. "Well, I shan't tease you any longer, and then you'll have to tell me, won't you? Let's talk about your friend the coachman, Turnbull, that cock on a dungheap. Sir Thomas would be very glad to know what has happened to him, I assure you."

"Why?"

"Do you ask why? You were there, and ask why? To prosecute him, that's why, for assault and battery, as well as the theft of a horse. He may be hung for that."

"Does Sir Thomas know how it came about?"

"He knows enough to be very angry."

"Does he know that the fight was over a child, Tom's illegitimate child? Sir Thomas's own granddaughter I speak of, who was born while he and his son were in the West Indies?"

"What?" Belzoni was taken by surprise.

"Tom had taken the child. The dead mother's wish was that Stephen should bring her up as his own. There is a paper, signed. Tom would not give her up."

"What is this to me?"

"Sir Thomas would not wish to lay a charge. Think of the scandal."

Belzoni paused. "It was small beer. The real matter of it is Quinney. Let us consider Quinney. Matthew Quinney. If you remember his name. If you don't, I refer you to the latest handbill from this very theater on which it is writ large just below yours. But he's a ghost, that man. There's his name in letters a foot high and he himself not to be found any easier than a needle in a haystack. Matthew Quinney, where is he?"

"He has friends in the city. If you would catch him, you may get caught yourself."

"Ah, now, I know all about his friends. A more unhealthy collection of friends I never heard of. They want to watch out for themselves. You can't frighten me with his friends. No, I want to know where he lives. I want to know where Matthew Quinney lives, and I want to know now. If you don't tell me, your pretty face shall be spoiled by Issy here, and Miss Abigail shall disappear from the handbills no matter what happens to her protector."

Alexander let go my wrist and leaning back felt among the cushions, withdrawing from them a small-bladed dagger with a cruelly sharp edge. "See this?" He turned it in his hand and then, with a vicious swiftness for which I was unprepared, jerked his body forward again and raised the dagger as though to plunge it in my breast. As I pushed backward against Issy with a cry, Alexander flicked his wrist, so that the weapon pointed at him and it seemed as if he showed me the hilt. "A pretty thing, is it not? All the way from China via Samarkand. Do you see the golden dragon?" Issy pushed my head forward and down so that I was obliged to regard the knife closely, the eyes of the dragon, each one a tiny gem, one ruby and one emerald, sparkling in the light of the torch. "Note how it coils around the handle. An exquisite thing; one of my favorite curios. I keep it finely honed." Alexander's soft voice threatened. "I never thought to use it, but now—" With another sudden movement, he spun the blade dexterously so that its needle point touched my face, and he drew it down my cheek, scratching me from eye to chin. I closed my eyes. "Where is he, Miss Abigail? Where is he? You shan't deprive me of Quinney this time."

"Stephen has money," I said wildly.

"It's not just money, I want, my dear, though if you think a humble coachman can match what your scene painter's worth, you don't know what's going on."

"What will you do to him?"

"Me? I shall do nothing. It's what the magistrates will do. But don't let that concern you. It will be nothing terrible. A week or two in the hulks and then a few years across the sea. Many fare worse. They'll not be too hard on him."

"Why do you wish him harm?"

Alexander leaned forward and whispered with a cold rage into my face. "Can you look at me and ask? You and he together, look what you have done!"

He controlled himself once more. "If I catch him, it will make my fortune. Sir Thomas Bertram is not the only one who will pay handsomely to be rid of such a troublemaker."

"How can you be sure of that?"

He laughed. "I have made it my business to find out. I have the word of two dozen gentlemen at the least. How many, do you suppose, want to see sedition stamped out? How many, do you suppose, would like to see the Westminster Committee destroyed? Quinney's connections with that bunch of revolutionists will bring them all down like a house of cards, and the gentlemen who are so misguided as to sympathize with them will be thoroughly discredited."

"I know nothing of this."

"What need have you to know? All that I require is to know where Quinney may be found. These cursed leveling theatricals hedge and cavil and play dumb; I can't waste my time with them.

But you—now *you*; it would be a pleasure to damage you. A sweet, pretty, heartless miss who would leave a friend to die—"

"They were thieves and ruffians! I was carried off against my will!"

"Against your will!" He clicked his tongue. "There's no need to plead innocence. Whatever you have done shall be as if it never were—providing you tell me where he is. All will be forgotten and forgiven. Isn't that so, Issy?" When I still did not answer he became more ominously quiet. "I shall not wait forever. If you hesitate much longer no audience in England will ever pay to look at you again. You shall be marked as you marked me."

The needle point of the knife was two inches from my face, and I had reached the end of what little invention I had. "Hopwood Court, Charing Cross Road," I whispered.

At his master's nod, Issy pushed me roughly out of the way and with his companion lifted the chair and loped off into the night. I put my handkerchief to my cheek and looked at the blood upon it. The scratch stung, but not near as much as my shame. I had saved my pretty face at the probable expense of Matthew's life. In the various adventures I had, willing or unwilling, been caught up in, I considered myself to have behaved creditably. Now I felt that they were nothing but the result of quick wit and good fortune. In this genuine trial of courage, I had failed wretchedly.

I ran back into the theater, hoping to find Matthew still there, although I was certain he was not: I had been late myself and knew the theater to be altogether empty. Yet I explored every corner in a futile attempt to prevent the consequences of my cowardly action, running hither and thither where I could, trying to still the beating of my heart, telling myself that they would not, surely not, murder Matthew as he lay sleeping in that room whose location I had revealed. The theater was in its strange-looking, silent character, a body with no soul, its racks of pasteboard and canvas towering at the side of the stage, its shadowy recesses, vaulting heights and receding depths, unpeopled and unlighted, its vast amphitheater shrouded in holland covers. Empty and dead. I sat down upon a costume basket and burst into noisy tears, which brought me at last to the attention of the one who never did leave the theater, Ben Croft. I heard the soft, felt shuffle of his feet before he arrived with a candle and as many cats and kittens as the man from St. Ives. In him, from whom the theater and its inhabitants had no secrets, I confided what had passed.

I had never seen him betray the least sign of anxiety, whatever cross accidents or disasters occurred, and he did not now. He nodded sagely. "Quinney's a one," he said. "But he likes it, you know." I was familiar with his oracular statements. I waited. "That poor cripple's been round here a few times. I've spoken to him myself. Matthew knew."

It was something which, in my anxiety, I had not taken into account. Of course Matthew knew. Had I not known myself, after Mrs. Fraser's party where Julia Bertram had accidentally informed me, that Belzoni was still alive? I had told Matthew then, in some agitation, but he had passed off the news as of so little consequence that I had all but forgotten it myself.

"They may still get him," I said, but doubtfully.

Ben merely shook his head, with that wise certainty which made him so invaluable in his cameo parts on stage.

XXIII

By this time, I had taken the lease of a small but pretty house a little fashionably further west than the Sturmeys', with a picturesque vine to recommend it. It had yet to be white-washed and scrubbed and furnished, but Belzoni had contrived to frighten me so thoroughly that I proposed to move in before the preparations were complete, especially when it seemed, from lack of report, that Ben Croft had been right, and Matthew had once again eluded his pursuer.

Ellie Sturmey, however, with characteristic generosity, and a most complete refusal to be frightened, insisted that I was best off to remain with them, in the proof of which she purchased a patent iron locking device of immense dimensions, better suited to the Tower of London, and had it affixed to the street door. Had I not discouraged her, indeed, she would have set a mantrap in the small square at the back that her house shared with others around it. Bob Sturmey, for his part, instructed the servants to admit no one to the house until they were absolutely assured of his identity. I did, indeed, feel much safer in Queen Street than I ever should have done on my own.

I was awoken one night by a most insistent knocking. What the time was I could only guess, but it was still dark. My thoughts flew instantly to Belzoni, and I was fully alert in a moment. I raised myself in the bed and listened. Because of the uncommon lateness of the hour, I could hear that Bob himself went to the door. It seemed that whoever it was came for me. I threw on a wrapper and raised the window. A woman stepped into view and looked up in response to my call. By the light of the lantern which hung beside the door (and which, as another precaution, Bob Sturmey kept burning all night long) I recognized her instantly, for she wore no bonnet and nothing but a thin muslin gown and silk shawl hastily flung around her shoulders, although she carried, most unaccountably, a small dog, which commenced to yap. It was Julia Bertram. A hackney cab stood near by, the horses steaming even though the night was mild. She had been in a hurry to get here.

When Ellie's great patent lock had been undone and Julia entered, it was plain that she was in great distress. Her face was unpowdered and her hair hung round her face in disarray; she had had no time to make any toilette. She tried to regain her composure when she saw me, however, and set her little white dog on the floor, where it was restrained by a collar made of plaited ribbon and a silver chain. She saw me looking at it. "This is Fifine. Mr. Yates gave her to me," she explained. "I am not to be parted from her. Is she not the most angelic thing?" She could not contain herself and burst into tears. "You must wonder to see me here. I never thought to have come. But that is a fault in me. There is no reason why I should not."

This was an argument with herself I could well do without. "If you come with good will, you are welcome. What brings you?"

"I am come to ask your help." She sniffed and hesitated. "That may seem ungenerous, but you know I always liked you. I saw the play. Indeed I did, despite my sister. She would not. She was furious with me for going. But I went, all the same, myself and Mr. Yates. I am married now, you know, to him, to Mr. Yates. That is why I am here." She picked up the dog and fondled it.

"Mr. Yates?" I was mystified.

For some reason my incomprehension quite discomposed her and she began to cry once more. I rang for some brandy.

In a little while she continued. "You heard about my sister and Henry Crawford?" She watched me as she pronounced his name, but I merely nodded. "It has been a horrible disgrace beyond anything. And even now that they have run away together, he still

287

will not marry her. Mr. Yates and I eloped, but that was nothing."
A few more tears escaped her, and she buried her face in the fur
of the dog, which began to wriggle. "I could not bear to return to
Mansfield. It is the dullest place in the universe. I do believe my
father would have locked me up after what Maria did. She has no
thought for anyone but herself. She is so hasty. So we went to
Gretna Green, you know. It was quite an adventure. Some of my
friends quite envied me. Sir Thomas was horribly angry, but he
came round, and now Mr. Yates is almost one of the family, don't
you know." She paused. "That is why I am come. I am so afraid
everything will be spoiled!" She burst into tears once more, put
down Fifine and gulped the brandy. I replenished the glass and lent
her my handkerchief. She blew her nose. "They are to have a duel."
She looked for my reaction, and when there was none repeated,
"They are to have a duel. With pistols." I nodded. It was not
uncommon, after all. "I thought you cared for him," she said.

"Cared for him?"

"Don't you?"

"Care for whom?"

"Mr. Crawford."

"Mr. Crawford?" My heart leaped in my bosom like a fresh-
caught fish in a creel. "Do you mean that Mr. *Crawford* is to fight
a duel?"

"That is why I am come."

"With Mr. Yates?"

She looked at me in bewilderment. "Mr. Yates? No, no. With
Mr. *Rushworth*. Mr. Yates is to be his second. It is the worst possible
disaster in the world. Mr. Yates encouraged him to challenge Mr.
Crawford. I knew nothing of it until tonight. He told me this very
night. Even then I should not have heard of it but that I happened
to be awake when he stumbled in and I saw the case."

"The case?"

The dog began to pull on its chain. "Fifine! Come here, Fifine!
The case of pistols. Mr. Yates is all for it. He says Mr. Crawford
has behaved abominably. But if my father hears of it! If he hears
that my husband has encouraged Mr. Rushworth to challenge Mr.
Crawford to a duel, it will be all up with us. And we are but just
now reconciled! What shall I do?"

"You have defied Sir Thomas once already," I said gently.

"Oh, that was different. What shall we do without my father's help? The tailor and the chandler were arguing with the cook even today. I swear it is all Maria's fault." She picked up the dog again and kissed it distractedly.

"What do you suppose I can do?" I asked, when Julia had ceased to sigh over Maria's thoughtlessness, Mr. Yates's indigence and her father's severity.

"Why, you can stop it, if you will. Henry always wanted you. Even Maria knows that although she never will admit it. It is only because you were cold to him at Mrs. Fraser's party that he took up again with her. She would not listen to me, of course. She has never listened to me. Nor to anyone else, for that matter. *I* could see how it was. She would not leave him, though we all urged her to. I tried my best to persuade her, but I was already married to Mr. Yates by then and she thought me only saying it to make up to my father. She never believes good of me if she can help it. Mr. Crawford will not marry her. She was sure that once she was free he would marry her. Of course he will not. Everybody knows he will not. She is totally disgraced. She is beginning to hate him. He hates her already, I do believe." I still did not quite understand what my role in all this was to be. "Mr. Crawford will listen to you. If you speak to him . . . Otherwise they will kill each other, I know it, and no one will have any peace again."

I was as anxious for Henry as Julia could wish, but I could not forbear saying: "I think it is Mr. Rushworth who will be in danger. I know him of old, you will remember. He is as clumsy as an ox. It is he who puts himself in danger."

"Oh, no. It is not as you think. He has bought the very best dueling pistols, so Mr. Yates says. They come from Mr. Manton, you know. Mr. Yates advised him. He is very well informed about such things. If Mr. Rushworth holds steady he cannot fail to shoot straight, not even he."

At this little vanity I almost lost my temper. "The seconds are supposed to reconcile the parties, yet here is your husband spurring · Mr. Rushworth into it! Next you will tell me he had him practicing at a gallery! What a silly, dangerous business! We should summon the Bow Street officials. They would be certain of preventing it."

"You would not!" Julia was ready to weep afresh, and the little dog licked her face in sympathy.

"It is the best means of preventing the duel from taking place."

"But there is no time. They fight this morning. And it would be all over town, the very thing of all I most dread."

A thin mist lay over the ground as we drove around Hyde Park beneath the lightening sky. Deer were grazing near the margins of the walks, as they customarily did, so tame that even the rattling of the post-chaise did not frighten them away more than a few steps. It was a clear sky that promised a beautiful day, a low, pale radiance upon the horizon, the harbinger of sunrise. In the distance I caught sight of the still surface of the Serpentine river and a cluster of swans. If Fifine had not barked horribly all the while, and our journey been so urgent, it would have made a pleasant outing at a time of day when no one in fashionable London (excepting always those who must fight duels) is ever stirring.

Since the choice was Henry's as to place, Julia did not know where the meeting was to be held, and in the attempt to locate it, her anxiety mounted. "Will it not be the Ring? It must be the Ring, must it not?" But no activity was to be seen in the Ring, and the driver, who might have been expected to know the other likely spots for such an encounter, was fresh from the country. "Suppose one of them objected to the ground and they are gone elsewhere?" Julia was distraught. She brightened, however, when a carriage overtook us at speed, its driver cursing our slowness. She convinced herself that she recognized it, and as a consequence we took off after it, bouncing in the cab like chaff under a flail, the sole advantage being that Fifine had not breath enough to bark. When, a mile or two down the road, the carriage stopped, we pulled in behind. The gentleman who had descended from it was looking around in some perplexity, and approached us with an expression of relief which vanished when he saw who it was. He turned out to be one of the surgeons called upon to attend the duel, but he was late. As he proved to himself once more by consulting his large gold repeater, the hour appointed was now past by two minutes at the least. This was undoubtedly the place which, according to Mr. Rushworth, had been named by Mr. Crawford, but, since none of the participants was visible, he was led to suppose (this with some irritation) that the meeting took place elsewhere. His distrust of the proceedings was increased by the irregularity of two ladies chasing in search of the duelers, although he agreed, somewhat unwillingly, that we should follow his carriage as before, warning that he intended to try but one more place, and one only, before he went back home to bed.

We had almost reached Kensington Gardens when he leaped down and made toward a large and handsome stand of elm, beech and willow some two hundred yards from the road. There was only the single figure of a man that we could espy, but since the surgeon carried his case of instruments and went at a run, it seemed he thought he had found the meeting place. We descended and followed him as best we could across the long, dewy grass.

A clearing lay within the stand of trees, a most retired place and altogether invisible to the casual observer, since even the entry curved so as to disguise itself. Six or seven men stood in the enclosed flat space of greensward. Some of them looked up and welcomed the surgeon, with whom they were evidently familiar, but, when they saw Julia pulling Fifine on her silver chain, the animal's sodden fur giving it a distinctly ferretlike appearance, and myself following after, like the draggled tail of a kite, they were taken aback.

"Who's that you've brought with you?" I heard one of them inquire disapprovingly.

" 'Tis none of mine," the surgeon replied shortly. "Ask Yates."

Mr. Yates was holding a case of pistols for the inspection of Henry Crawford, but at this he looked up and was evidently mortified by what he saw. His face creased into a frown and he exclaimed testily: "What the deuce! My wife! Why are you come! This is no place for a lady, don't you know? It's a fine thing for a new wife to embarrass her husband. What are you thinking of?" He paused. "Two of you! Who's that? Who the devil have you brought with you?" Mr. Yates at that moment looked like nothing so much as a skinned mouse.

"Do you not remember the country girl in *Lovers' Vows*?" Henry broke in, although he had not acknowledged me and still did not. "This is she. The actress. Miss Jane Hartwell, as she is now."

One of the gentlemen immediately introduced himself to me.

"Charles Maddox of Stoke," he said. "Do you remember the rats? I nearly got to act with you in *Lovers' Vows* until Tom Bertram's brother decided to take on the part. What a chance I missed!"

Mr. Rushworth, who, despite his leading role in the scene, was destined as ever to be upstaged, called out petulantly: "Yates, I say, Yates! You might help me with this coat."

Julia, having released her pet from its leash, sought his attention. "Mr. Rushworth!"

He would much have preferred not to answer. "I see you, Mrs. Yates, and I see Jane Hartwell with you, but I cannot think either of you should be here. This is a gentlemen's affair."

"Do be guided by common sense, Mr. Rushworth. What would your mother say if she knew of this?"

"Sometimes even the fondest son must put aside a mother's claim."

"What would she do if anything should happen to you? It would break her heart. She reposes her dearest hopes in you."

"I beg you not to play upon my feelings, Mrs. Yates. I have suffered in these past months. Indeed, you cannot imagine how I have suffered. Your sister has behaved exceeding ill. I should not have believed the lies and deception she has practiced."

"But what you propose doing now is against the law," I said.

"I know it. Indeed, I know it, and it grieves me, but under such circumstances I am obliged to do my duty. My honor is at stake."

"The law of which you speak is broken every day of the week, and most say there should be no such law," said Henry.

"Surely that does not justify you breaking it?"

"This is no time for debate," said Mr. Yates impatiently. "We must load the pistols, Maddox. Come." Maddox having shown Henry's case of pistols to Mr. Rushworth, the two seconds began to measure the powder.

"We have delayed enough," Henry agreed. "This shall be settled once and for all, Rushworth."

"Do not say so!" said Julia, thinking the worst. "Surely all this may yet be settled amicably. Only think what amusement we all used to have together. Can you have forgotten it? Can we not all be as we were then?"

"I always envied you the play," called out Charles Maddox cheerfully. "That must have been a cracking good spree."

"It is my recollection," said Mr. Rushworth ponderously, "that the play began it."

Julia's reply was arrested by the appearance on the other side of the glade of another female figure. She drew in her breath. "Maria! Surely that cannot be Maria? It is. Dear heaven, it is! I do believe that is my sister. Maria! Oh dear, oh dear! What shall become of us now? Fifine! Oh, Fifine!" She ran across to the dog, which had puddled on Mr. Rushworth's coat, although he, thank heaven, had not noted it.

Maria half walked, half ran across the intervening space, consumed with such anxiety that she had called, "Henry! Wait!" before she comprehended the size and constituents of the company. She stopped running and collected herself. When she spoke it was quietly, but under the stress of much feeling. "What do you do, Mr. Yates?"

"Is it not obvious, ma'am? We prepare for a duel. This is become like a drawing room, I declare. Shall you take a lesson in loading a pistol?"

"I hope that barrel is quite dry," said Mr. Rushworth nervously. "There is a very heavy dew this morning."

"Trust me," said Mr. Yates cheerfully, as he rammed the ball into the barrel. "I never had a misfire but twice."

"Mr. Crawford, do not persist in this venture, I beg you," said Maria. She paused, but Henry made no reply. "It is all a misunderstanding."

"If it is a misunderstanding, then it is not mine," said Henry. "I did not offer the challenge."

I spoke. "Then you may be more honored for your generosity in refusing it."

Maria looked at me angrily. "I wonder at your impertinence, Hartwell. This matter cannot concern you. I do not know why you should be here. We can do without your interference."

Henry, ignoring Maria's outburst, replied to me. "On the contrary, I should be dishonored everywhere. Whatever the law says, in this respect it is altogether disregarded. I should be laughed at as a fool, if not a coward."

"How come you here?" Maria demanded of me.

"I asked her," Julia hastily answered. "It is at my request that she is come."

"Then you are the completest fool."

"She may prevent what your folly has brought upon us." Julia was spurred by her sister's contempt.

At this Mr. Rushworth entered the lists. "I hope you notice, ma'am—I cannot defile the name of Rushworth by addressing you as my wife—I hope you notice that even your sister admits you have behaved ill."

Maria rounded on him. "You think it very fine to participate in a duel, I suppose. The aggrieved husband will fight a duel to regain his honor. You, fight a duel! It is the most ridiculous thing in the universe!"

"What a harpy!" said Mr. Yates. "If you ask me, Rushworth, you may be glad she has run off."

Maria heard him. "You were not asked! You parade your worthless opinions by virtue of being married to my sister for five minutes. It was you who encouraged my husband to challenge Mr. Crawford, I know it. Why should you poke your nose into everything?"

"I might ask the same of you," replied Mr. Yates.

"It is a gentleman's obligation to settle an affair of honor with a duel," said Mr. Rushworth. "Yates and I think as one in this." Mr. Yates nodded with vigorous encouragement as he wrapped the ball to load the second pistol.

"Think!" Maria replied. "When did you ever think for yourself? When you do, you may consider that someone in a duel gets shot and that it may be you. Do you wish to end up lying in your own blood in the grass with your arm shot off?"

"Dear, oh dear!" said Julia and burst into tears. Fifine began to utter short, sharp barks of distress.

"Rushworth's pistols are loaded," said Mr. Yates. "Are Crawford's done yet, Maddox?"

Mr. Rushworth began to look a little green and Mr. Yates threw an arm around his shoulder to provide physical and moral support. "You shall see that the husband you malign does not lack valor," he asserted dramatically. Mr. Rushworth took heart and stood straight.

"How can you do this?" Julia appealed to her husband. "What will my father say? One or both will be injured and our disgrace will be complete. My father will never speak to us again."

"Then we shall be two outcast daughters," said Maria spitefully.

"You may care nothing for that, but I do," said Julia.

"How considerate you are of my father all of a sudden! His feelings did not concern you much when you took off for Gretna Green. But then, if you make up to my father, he will assist your husband to a competency."

"If we do not get on with the business at hand," said Henry, "we shall be exchanging shots at noon. I have no wish to be had up for a breach of the peace. What distance do you choose, Rushworth?"

"Do not do it!" said Maria.

"I shall do it," said Henry. "I shall do as I please, and you shall go home."

"You shall not insult me so," said Maria, catching hold of his arm.

He shook off her hand. "You mistake the situation. It is you who insult all of us. Fishwives speak softer. You have the very devil of a tongue. As I know to my cost."

Maria's face went white. "You think because I have sacrificed everything for you—everything!—everything! you have the right to treat me as you please. Well, I say you shall not. I am not a piece of furniture to be so used."

"It might be an advantage if you were," he replied with a terrible calm.

"We must decide upon the terms of firing," said Mr. Yates. "I suggest a signal, Maddox. Do you agree? Shall I raise my hand?"

"Save your disagreement," said Julia imploringly to her sister. "Mr. Crawford, my sister is only concerned for your safety. If you will shake hands with Mr. Rushworth, all will be well."

Mr. Yates remonstrated. "You speak of things you know nothing of, Julia. Mr. Rushworth has suffered unimaginable pangs. A reconciliation is out of the question."

"You and your husband had best learn to agree before you endeavor to persuade me," said Henry. "I did not offer the challenge."

"The paces," said Mr. Yates. "Rushworth, did you not say twenty paces?"

Julia turned to me beseechingly. "Miss Hartwell! I cannot bear it! Will you not support me?"

Maria was outraged. "Hartwell! Why must she be part of this? It is no business of hers. She has been the ruination of all our hopes. She is at the bottom of my brother's illness. She incited my maid to leave me! What possessed you to bring her? We have enough trouble here without your importing more."

"If you had not come, my dear Maria," said Henry, "I rather think there would have been no trouble at all."

"If I had not come! Oh, if I had not come, you could make sheep's eyes at your little actress without hindrance. You could have flirted to your heart's content."

"You are altogether impossible. I cannot speak to you."

"It is come to that, is it? But a few weeks ago and I might have the moon for asking. I have been totally deceived. You lied to me and betrayed me."

"It seems your wife is coming to her senses at last," said Mr. Yates to Mr. Rushworth.

"I am afraid it is too late," Mr. Rushworth replied. "You have forfeited the right to be my wife; you have forfeited the life you would have enjoyed as Mrs. Rushworth. It is too late for regret. You can never be wife to me again."

Maria laughed most unseemly loud. "Wife to you! I had rather be dead!"

"I never lied," said Henry. "It was you who persuaded me to take you away. You used more wiles to win me than I to win you. I have not betrayed you."

"You would betray me if you could. Do you think I do not perceive your desires? Do you think I do not know what passed between you and her?"

"No more than has passed between the two of you," I spoke up.

"Your rudeness to Miss Hartwell is intolerable," said Henry.

"*Miss* Hartwell! You shall never find me dignifying her as *Miss*."

"Mrs. Siddons was a strolling player once," I said. "You may not choose to admit it, but it is possible to earn a respectable title through an honorable profession."

"Honorable! I assure you that none thinks so but those in it. You! You dare compare yourself to Mrs. Siddons! I have heard how you dress up in man's attire to encourage the attentions of the gentlemen!"

"Whether or not I have earned respect, it is certain you have none. You have lost whatever you once possessed."

"I shall not stay here to be insulted."

"Then leave by all means," said Henry. "It would be the greatest favor to us all."

"I do believe we come to it at last," said Mr. Yates. "Thank heaven. Twenty paces it is, then, and I shall raise my right hand, so. Are you both clear as to that?" Since no one listened, he addressed the other second. "Maddox, is that clear?" But Maddox had by this time given up all pretense of preparation.

Maria was cut to the quick by Henry's indifference. She spoke low. "I came here to prevent you from this duel. You have not addressed to me a single word of affection or regard. Is this the way to use me? Is this the thanks I am to get for my devotion?" Henry did not reply. "You prefer not to speak to me. Now I am to bear that."

"You bring it on yourself," said Henry wearily at last. "Go home. I must finish this business. Go home. There is no place for you here."

"There is no place for any female," said John Yates. "Tell them all to go, if you please, including my wife."

"We shall not leave until we have stopped this folly," said Julia.

"We only wish to prevent bloodshed," I said.

"Go home, Miss Hartwell," said Henry gently. "What misplaced duty brought you here I do not know, but I am caught in a net of my own weaving and must do what is required."

Still determined upon pursuing the duel at all costs, Mr. Yates bent down and picked up one of the pistols from the case. "We are all ready," he said again.

"Listen how he speaks to her!" said Maria bitterly.

"Spare me your jealousy, in this at least."

"Jealous? I am not jealous. How should I be jealous of an ill-bred, whoring miss such as she?"

Henry moved toward her threateningly. "Go! Go! Or I shall be obliged to leave you at last! You will drive me mad!"

What Maria saw in his face, indifference goaded almost to hatred, made her turn away, misery, rage and despair terrifying in her countenance. Close to her was Mr. Yates, who held ready the dueling pistol he had now fully cocked, in expectation of the event he was so foolishly bent upon. With a swift and unexpected motion, she turned and seized it from him. "If I cannot have him, then you shall not." And so saying she discharged the pistol at me. There was a loud report, and I fell to the ground.

XXIV

What shall I say of what followed? A great deal of it was to be expected, and some of it was not. I was fortunate enough to escape serious injury: the ball passed sufficiently close to make a superficial wound upon my left temple, but otherwise left me unhurt. The wound bled copiously, however, and since it also rendered me temporarily insensible, my condition at first gave rise to considerable anxiety. The services of the two surgeons were immediately called upon, and I was carried to the Yates's lodging where, after the application of sal volatile, I came to myself.

Who was that self? Who is she now? The leather inlay of my writing desk before which I sat when first I began upon this tale, before which I sit now, shines darker where my hands and arms have rubbed it. It is not so smooth as it was: some scratches and indentations mark its surface, although I do not find them ugly. The walnut has a patina from beeswax and use that makes it more pleasing to me than ever it was new. Its familiarity endears every blemish. Much written upon, you may say, as in the course of a natural life is true of every one of us, myself probably more than most.

All things are ruled by nature's scheme, the cycle which celebrates both sameness and change operating even upon those events in human lives in which it is not immediately apparent. The tranquil landscape outside my window has marked the passing of a season and more since I began to write. The grass is greener now than it was in those hot days when we celebrated Waterloo; the female infant named for the victory died of a putrid fever only a month after she was christened, poor babe. I have had a border dug in front of the smooth darkness of the yew hedge that shall show primroses and daffodils in the spring. The elm trees I see upon the horizon, where the park sweeps down to the lake and then upward again, stand out leafless against the sky, the rooks' nests visible among their branches. The coats of the grazing sheep are longer, and many of them are gravid with lambs that shall increase the flock when January comes. Do they feel joy at the kick of new life within them, I wonder, as I do when I feel it within me? God willing, I shall be safely delivered in the spring, and then shall be such a celebration that will put even Waterloo in the shade, so my dear husband says. He has ordered fireworks, Roman candles, gold and silver rain and petards by the dozen, and the October brewing overflowed the cellar by ten barrels (which stand most inconveniently in the dairy). He is as proud as chanticleer, and I love him for it.

Much has, indeed, changed in the two years since I opened my eyes after the duel to see Henry Crawford's face looking into mine, love and concern mixed with relief and pleasure as he perceived my recovery. How shall I describe my sensations? The recollection of our former attachment, which had persisted despite the petty vanities and irritations with which chance and the faults of our own dispositions had tried it, overcame me most powerfully. The glance I returned Henry was the mirror of the feelings I read in him. How should it have been otherwise? Such a momentous event, more uncommon in real life than in the theater, to be sure, brings about those fervent reconciliations and declarations of passion which we are accustomed to see depicted upon the stage. During the week when, due to my injury, I was obliged to be absent from the theater, Henry scarcely left my side. With a flattering, fiery ardor, he desired above all things that I should become his wife.

He had, as I knew, begun to hate Maria, but, recognizing his own willful caprice in pursuing her, was beginning to think he must marry her at last. Any such obligation was removed entirely by her behavior; no part that he had played in encouraging her affections could excuse her in attempting murder. For that is, of course, what it was, although it takes a certain determination to write the word. Maria Bertram attempted murder. Such a word belongs only upon the placards and in the newspapers. Curiously enough, that is where it remains when I consider what she did to me. I have no difficulty in forgiving Maria for that criminal attempt: she had given up all for love, selfishly, vainly, in mad folly, but with a single-mindedness which I could admire. Directed toward some better end, who knows what she might not have achieved? It is the small irritations of her everyday imperious disposition, which Sophie and I had known so well as servants, which are harder to forgive. I cannot find it in my heart to pity her exile in Bruges, where she now dwells with her aunt. For Mrs. Norris joined her favorite niece at last, thus proving herself possessed of a sort of unselfish affection, I suppose, although it was not because she perceived the truth and loved despite it, but that she made everything out to be other than it was. From what I heard, she was filled with indignation and resentment at the way in which Maria was treated by the family. Like to like; for her niece, despite the enormity of her offenses, still thinks herself wronged, to judge from the bitterness of the occasional letter which, although forbidden, is sometimes sent. How she and Mrs. Norris should agree for more than two minutes together in a small apartment in a foreign country, Mrs. Norris having no French, it is impossible to conceive. No one could invent for them a worse torture. I cannot doubt that Maria regrets even that booby of a former husband; for, of course, James Rushworth has by now divested himself of her for good. He is not remarried yet, but is undoubtedly fool enough to try. I think it were better he do it before his pate is altogether bald; his handsome strawy hair blows away like dandelion seeds, I hear, despite daily application of bears' grease.

I did not discover until almost a year later, in a letter which reached me from America, exactly what had happened to Matthew, although I knew that he had not been arrested. He wrote from Virginia, having spent some time in New York, where he had been the scenic artist for several productions at the Park Theatre. He had visited the grave of his uncle, David Archbold, who was buried in Concord, Massachusetts, spoke in glowing terms of the progress of the Republic and made no mention of returning. The affair with Belzoni had undoubtedly faded in his memory, for he left the recounting of it until the end, where he wrote at right angles across paper that was already full, and thus made his words horribly slow to decipher. Being aware of the renewed pursuit, he had taken steps to know as much of Belzoni as Belzoni knew of him. The pockfaced, bulbous-nosed second chairman was, in fact, a friend to Matthew, not Belzoni, and only half as drunk as he looked. Belzoni, acting upon my information, had gone to Hopwood Court, Charing Cross Road and there surprised the scene painter but, when he tried to arrest him, the second chairman showed his true colors. A regular milling-match ensued, but at the last Belzoni was obliged to make an ignominious retreat, carried home on Issy's back without even the sedan chair, which was appropriated before morning by some enterprising thief who had ventured out of St. Giles's.

As a result of this incident, which may have shaken Matthew more than he cared to remember, after consulting with his political friends, he had determined to leave the country. He had done nothing to offend against any just principle, and although he had broken the law, it was not generally difficult to avoid the penalty, but Belzoni was so determined against him, and had so lobbied opinion, that for Matthew to continue to flaunt his name on playbills and pursue his political activities became increasingly foolhardy. Having always had a fancy to see America, once he had made up his mind he was outward bound on a vessel from Liverpool within the week.

Matthew has not, however, altogether disappeared from my life. He returned from America this past spring, in high twig and very prosperous, suggesting that he could arrange an engagement for me in New York at my convenience, and getting on wonderfully well with my husband. To my astonishment, he told me he had bought a small estate in Virginia. For a man who casts his net wide, has friends everywhere and, espousing causes rather than people, never seemed to wish to settle, it seemed the most unlikely thing. The New World has plainly done much for him.

I have seen nothing more of that terrible man Belzoni, except in my dreams, from which I think he never will be banished. But I had a most strange premonition this past summer when we were in the metropolis for a few days: I saw advertised at Richardson's booth in Bartholomew Fair, a singular performance: a cripple with terrible deformities who was said to play the violin and sing like an angel. I did not go to view him for fear of what I might find. Perhaps, if the act is there again next year, I may persuade Ellie Sturmey to go in my place; it is the very sort of expedition she most adores. It was through her agency that I learned the fate of Dunny Arvell. That brickfield and warehouse which were his head-quarters was a derelict place which had got into Chancery. He and his gang had bid defiance to any number of constables, but at last a stout gentleman of some substance, a dealer in tea and coffee, who had been robbed and assaulted by them, swore to the identity of four of his assailants, one of whom was hanged and the rest transported for life. A young woman who also gave evidence at the trial was murdered in revenge, and it was upon that deed that Dunny himself was hung. Whether the young woman was Sall or not I have no means of knowing, but that Dunny was hung there can be no doubt. An old woman who said she was his mother displayed his body in a coffin with a glass plate in the lid and kept it on show for two months, charging a penny a look. Ellie went (and tried unsuccessfully to prevail upon me to accompany her), and was certain the old woman was Moley, because, making one good business out of another, she was hawking shellfish to those who lined up.

I have nothing to do with the Bertrams, you may believe. I might catch sight of them at an assembly or a rout but that they never attend such things, living an excessively retired life since the ca-lamitous events I have described. The only one to whom I nod in an occasional encounter is Julia, but although she would dearly love to boast of closer acquaintance, I have no wish to encourage it. Of course I hear about the rest of the family, although more in the early days than now. One friend or another in the servants' hall at Mansfield Park sent a brief letter, or a scandalous titbit via Bob Sturmey. The Bertams were shaken as Vesuvius by the eruptions within the family, amid which Julia's anxiety about her father's attitude toward Mr. Yates's part in promoting the duel was as nothing. (Although I often wonder whether Sir Thomas ever un-derstood that Mr. Yates's obstinate stupidity was entirely respon-

sible for providing Maria access to a fully cocked pistol.) Whatever
the reason, Sir Thomas made nothing very much of Mr. Yates's
part in the affair; as he has made nothing very much of Mr. Yates
since, and does not seem likely to. Mr. Yates is not a gentleman
of whom very much is to be expected, and rather resentful, I believe, of the way in which life has disappointed him of its most
interesting incidents, such as parts in plays and duels. He and his
wife have the lease on a house in Soho Square, no distance from
Queen Street, and I understand there are always creditors at the
door. They have not yet been obliged to flee to Boulogne, however,
even if they sometimes keep within doors and take the air only on
Sundays. That is a common enough predicament, after all. Sir
Thomas attends to the most pressing creditors. The butcher, baker,
farrier, coachmaker, chandler, dressmaker, etc., bear the brunt of
the rest. For, of course, the Yateses live in high style. I believe one
tailor has been quite ruined. I find Mr. Yates's "Honorable" most
singularly undeserved.

I must not omit to record Fanny Price's fortunes, which rose as
her cousins' fell. She netted her cousin Edmund, the clergyman, in
the end, for he, after his one disastrous foray into passion with
Henry's sister, was exactly in the mood to settle for comfort over
concupiscence, and who better to provide it than Fanny? Fanny
could, and does, I would be certain, listen to him preach the same
sermon three times together, that which would provoke in others
a bad headache banishing hers completely. She suffers from them
no longer, and, as further proof of her improved health, ten months
after the marriage gave birth as easily as a cow drops a calf. The
most pleasant outcome of that circumstance was that Amelia Ellis,
she who always suffered most from Mrs. Norris's ill temper, went
to Fanny as nursemaid, a position for which she is admirably suited.
I am glad that Fanny values her. Indeed, when Fanny and Edmund
came to town, Amelia was allowed to attend a performance of *The
Stranger*, in which I played the erring wife. I do not truly think she
understood much, but she wept a good deal, whether at the play
or my transformation to actress it would be hard to say. Fanny
herself did not attend.

Tom Bertram recovered from his illness (for so it was always
referred to), and with his health came the courage to confess the

story of Kitty Huckle and the child to his father. Perhaps he was even a little repentant, for he made sure that blame for his accident was not all laid at Stephen's door. Sir Thomas, who had set Belzoni on to Stephen at the word of one of those many friends at Glassbury Park before his son had recovered sufficiently to prevent it, was heartily sorry that he had done so, and sought to make amends. He had always perceived the undercoachman as a man of sense and superior talent, and made a point of visiting him and his wife when he was in the metropolis. When he saw the neat, pretty house and Sophie so becoming in her new role, he admitted himself at fault in consenting to believe ill of Stephen in the first place. It was quite understandable, in the light of the other troubles which simultaneously weighed upon Sir Thomas, of course, but is it not a prime example of how the ties of family and class instinctively take precedence over reason? And how, indeed, the master always assumes the worst of his servant?

Sir Thomas naturally supposed Sophie and Stephen eager to be relieved of Betsey's care, but when he discovered that they wanted nothing better than to bring her up as their own, he was pleased to agree. (Indeed, had either he or Tom been tempted otherwise, Stephen was ready to produce a legal document signed by Kitty, which established beyond doubt their right to the child.) Stephen refused Sir Thomas's offer to contribute to Betsey's upbringing, although he finally agreed that Sir Thomas should settle a sum upon her in the event of her marriage. What he and Sophie did insist upon was that none of the Bertrams should ever attempt to see the child, desiring above all (though it is scarcely to be expected that Sir Thomas should perceive it) to be rid of the Bertrams, stick, stock and stone. To this Sir Thomas, not without a little reluctance, assented. My own opinion is that this little grandchild of Sir Thomas's, as winning, sweet and pretty as he could have wished any such to be, for all that she was born the other side of the blanket, will grow up to outshine any of her cousins who may bear the Bertram name. She will also grow up no less a lady, if, as I do not doubt, money makes the difference. For Sophie and Stephen thrive amazingly, their one disappointment in a union that seems otherwise so blessed being that they have as yet no other children. Stephen has set up for himself as saddler and harness-maker, round the corner from Tattersall's. It is, of course, merely a sort of extension of his interests. He had some ideas for small improvements in the matters of saddles, cruppers and suchlike, all of which were eminently sensible, and since he had already many patrons who sought his advice on other equine matters, the business has every reason to flourish, especially since Sophie proves herself such an excellent businesswoman, exceedingly able in all the practical aspects of buying skins and fleece, hiring work-fellows, keeping accounts, the hundred and one necessary activities upon which a successful enterprise depends. She thus enables her husband to pursue the other skills for which he becomes ever more renowned, and which in turn increase the business. When we made a pleasant excursion to the heights of Highgate and Hampstead village, principally to exclaim over the comforts of Sophie's first carriage, she whispered to me that when the old king dies it is rumored Turnbull and Company shall become Saddlers and Harness-makers to His Majesty.

My own career has prospered similarly. I did not, after the duel, retire from the stage, although that was what Henry most strongly desired. He urged it upon me eloquently, arguing that our marriage must be contrived with the utmost circumspection because of the prodigious scandals in which we were aleady involved, and that for me to return to the stage would make secrecy impossible. I could not deny his reasoning: the well-known actress who had barely escaped death, the gentleman who had but just run off with the new Mrs. Rushworth, *married*? It would, indeed, inflame the public. Henry's notion was that we should disappear to the quiet of Everingham, escape the placard boys who already hawked the *Public and Private Life of Miss Abigail*, forget the gossip of the unkind world and take refuge in our own, learning the joys of being all in all to one another.

I laughed at his charming enthusiasm and loved him more than a little. I had but just arrived upon the stage; it was scarcely a half-year since I had first appeared upon the boards as an Indian princess; I had the promise of ten prime parts, all of which I longed to try; a singing master from Italy had given me my first lesson, and pronounced me teachable; my grandfather, in the company of Mrs. Whitaker, was about to make the journey to London to see me perform. There was, in addition, the pleasure to be looked for in the furnishing of my little house, for which I had designed in my head a most pleasing small salon—had, indeed, already visited the Western Exchange in Bond Street with Ellie Sturmey to select velvet for the sofa. I expected to be able to receive visitors in unobtrusive elegance, perhaps even (there was talk of it) a regal one. Was I prepared to relinquish all these things for the pleasure of being married to Henry? Did I love him more than the sum of all that I should be obliged to forgo as his wife? I sighed a little at the thought of times past, but there was never any doubt: I would not do it.

After a week's absence, then, when the wound upon my head was beginning to heal, I returned to the stage. I was, you may believe, more eminently interesting to the public than I had ever been, though for a reason I had not anticipated. Those who had seen Maria fire the pistol held their tongues, but news of the duel got out, as these things will, in somewhat strange distortion: she and I it was who were supposed to have fought it. Nothing could have better fed the public's appetite for novelty. Attendance at the theater increased, and the manager requested me to wear the band I wore to protect the wound longer than was absolutely necessary, so satisfactory was the long sigh that went up from the spectators when they first beheld it. (The scar fortunately extends for the most part into my hair.)

It was one of the performances of this play which my grandfather and Mrs. Whitaker attended. My grandfather had never visited the metropolis, nor was he acquainted with the theater. The noise and soot of the former were not to his taste, but the vastness of Covent Garden awed and delighted him, and so did the play, *The Students of Salamanca*, a comedy of no great quality, but full of incident and bustle. They were both immoderately proud. I took them afterward to see the gaslights outside Carlton House, and then to the oyster shop opposite Drury Lane Theatre, where we dined excellently on salmon, shrimps, bread and butter and ginger beer, while they gaped at the flamboyant beaux and belles and the oddities of fashion paraded before them. My grandfather pronounced the excursion a right good do, bang up to the mark, one he would remember all his life. Sadly that was not long, for he died quite suddenly of an apoplexy last summer, recovering his senses only enough to exclaim to Mrs. Whitaker that it was all the fault of the heat. He had a most decided distrust of the heat, strange in an otherwise so rational man. Not a day passes but I think of him.

The scandal of the duel fought by two women faded, as these things must, and fresher stories satisfied the public appetite for drama. Henry bore with his disappointment at my refusal to retire, and instead attended my every performance for several weeks. Then he disappeared for the shooting season, to reappear equally persuasive and certain that I must retire, if not now then later. During this time proposals came daily in every guise, even from Everingham: a paper heart cut as delicately as lace and decorated with a frill whose pattern repeated "Marry me" all round its edge; a myna bird that said in most elegantly deep tones "I love you"; a red silk rose in whose center was a dewdrop diamond upon a gold pin inscribed with both our names. And there were verses by the dozen, which spoke of well hearts and ill hearts, and water in all its forms of wells and fords and flowings together. ("Craw" he had more difficulty with.) The best rhyme he set to a tune with which I was serenaded by a charming light tenor, accompanied in unlikely combination by a fiddle, tambourine and triangle. Ellie Stumey delighted in it all, you may believe, and was very much in favor of Henry's suit. Even I could not help but enjoy the ingenuities of Henry's wooing, in which he contrived to beg and plead with lively, teasing elegance. To be pale and wan, to repine, was not his way.

He did love me. Of that I have no doubt. But he is a man who loves many women and is loved by many in return. I did not see how it should in the end be different for me. Youth has its instinct in these matters, and I knew that I required a deeper-running constancy. Perhaps my knowledge of his past influenced me in that judgment; perhaps because I never altogether, not quite, or at least not long, lost my heart to him. I do most certainly cry shame upon those who cinsure his behavior during the events I have described. They judge too narrowly, mistaking hot-blooded appetite for cold-blooded vanity. Young men who are considered exemplary in restraining their passions have generally little passion to restrain; if they behave decorously it is only because they are not greatly tempted to do otherwise; not at all the sort of gentlemen whom most young women would choose to marry. I am at one with Sophie in this. Only look at Mr. Rushworth.

Henry's assiduous attentions continued until I moved out of Queen Street (giving to Ellie the myna bird, since she so much admired it. It has now quite a vocabulary of sayings and is one of the curiosities of the neighborhood). I invited him to inspect my new house with no little pleasure. Its exterior was unassuming, but it had a half-moon fanlight over the door, and within the hall a pretty staircase curved upward to the drawing room I had so carefully furnished. A chandelier with a fountain of crystal teardrops hung from the center of the ceiling, and the windows were decorated with loops and drapes of fringed rose-colored velvet (the same as that of the sofa). I had some handsome chairs covered in striped satin, and a crimson rug. I had as yet but one print, a pretty engraving of Mrs. Jordan, and nothing in the niches on either side of the fireplace except a dainty camellia in a basket, although for the mantelpiece of the elegant marble surround I had found a quaint birdcage clock. Henry gracefully praised my taste, and took tea with every appearance of enjoyment, but afterward, when I reflected upon his visit, I thought him a trifle subdued. The house spoke to him, perhaps, of an independence in me which he regretted. It was a more definite statement than ever words could make that I did not intend to retire to Everingham yet.

The next time he called, quite by chance, he found himself in the company of the Duke of Oadby and Lord Grandison, with neither of whom he was well acquainted. He conducted himself with his customary engaging manners, and was invited by the Duke, whose estate was said to be the best fox-hunting country in the Shires, to visit him. He did not, however, take too well to Lord Grandison, for by this time Lord Grandison had taken to me, and I, no doubt by paying such close attention to the book Lord G. had brought me, an illustrated description, written and engraved by himself, of the rare plants he had collected, showed myself beginning to take to him. The following evening Henry did not come to the play, even though it was *As You Like It*, which he had always sworn he loved me in better than anything.

The last time I saw Henry Crawford was during this last winter, at the great frost fair on the Thames, when it froze over between London Bridge and Blackfriars, and the whole population turned out to enjoy the spectacle, a fair on the ice, hot loaves, roasted meat, piemen and Punch and Judy shows. I was overlooking the scene from the stairs beside the new bridge, when I was hailed by a gentleman so well wrapped up in scarves and hat that I did not instantly recognize him. "How does the world wag with you, Miss Abigail?" said he, as he came across the ice to greet me, and then, of course, I knew it was Henry, wearing a girl on each arm, all three of them eating hot roast potatoes. He was delighted to introduce me as "the great actress" (winking at me as he did so). His companions were twins, alike as two peas, dairymaids at Everingham (or so Henry said) to whom he was showing the sights of London. They were lovely cherry-cheeked wenches with soft country speech, wild for their black-haired gentleman, as was plain even as they burned their mouths and fingers, dropped the potatoes and contrived to brush against him as he bent to retrieve them. Then Lord G. arrived with some gilt gingerbread and two pair of skates and Henry raised his hat and disappeared. I fancy Everingham continues fruitful and well-tended even though its master remains unmarried.

When first I began this account, I had only just retired from the theater, having achieved, if I may say so without presumption, a considerable measure of success. Following our marriage, Lord Grandison accompanied me to Paris, where I performed to great acclaim. Now there is Matthew's invitation to cross the Atlantic and play in America. Who knows? My husband does not insist upon my permanent retirement. Indeed, he hopes to see more of the world in pursuit of his botanical interests, which have already taken him to many strange lands, with accounts of which he sometimes entertains me. I myself at the moment settle to rural delights with increasing content. But we do not disagree. How I should have lighted upon the single member of the nobility so sensible, discerning and good-natured as to be truly worth loving is a question I daily tease my husband with, his reply being that I saw my chance to increase the number, as I shall only fully understand when I behold the superior talents of that member of it whom I presently carry within. Whatever the future holds, nothing shall make us stir for a twelvemonth or so, until our prodigy has made its entrance into the world and contrived to stand upon two legs. Then come what will, come what may. Nothing is impossible to a willing heart.